Happy Valley

Books by Lin Stepp

Novels:
The Foster Girls
Tell Me About Orchard Hollow
For Six Good Reasons
Delia's Place
Second Hand Rose
Down by the River
Makin' Miracles
Saving Laurel Springs
Welcome Back
Daddy's Girl
Lost Inheritance
The Interlude
Happy Valley

The Edisto Trilogy:
Claire at Edisto
Return to Edisto

Christmas Novella:
A Smoky Mountain Gift
In *When the Snow Falls*

Regional Guidebooks
Co-Authored with J.L. Stepp:
The Afternoon Hiker
Discovering Tennessee State Parks

Happy Valley

A MOUNTAIN HOME NOVEL

LIN STEPP

MOUNTAIN HILL PRESS

Happy Valley
Copyright © 2020 by Lin Stepp
Published by Mountain Hill Press
Email contact: steppcom@aol.com

This is a work of fiction. Although numerous elements of historical and geographic accuracy are utilized in this and other novels in the Smoky Mountain series, many other specific environs, place names, characters, and incidents are the product of the author's imagination or used fictitiously.

Scripture used in this book, whether quoted or paraphrased by the characters, is taken from the King James Version of the Bible.

Cover design: Katherine E. Stepp
Interior design: J. L. Stepp, Mountain Hill Press
Editor: Brittany Dowdle
Cover photo and map design: Lin M. Stepp

Library of Congress Cataloging-in-Publication Data

Stepp, Lin
Happy Valley: A Mountain Home novel / Lin Stepp
        p. cm – (The Smoky Mountain series)
ISBN: 978-1-7343883-0-5
First Mountain Hill Press Trade Paperback Printing: April 2020

eISBN: 978-1-7343883-1-2
First Mountain Hill Press Electronic Edition: April 2020

1. Women—Southern States—Fiction   2. Mountain life—Great Smoky Mountains Region (NC and TN)—Fiction.   3. Contemporary Romance—Inspirational—Fiction. I. Title

Library of Congress Control Number: 2020900732

This book is dedicated to Joan Elliott Phillips of Happy Valley who helped and encouraged me in so many ways with this book. Her generosity, kindness, and friendship will be long remembered.

ACKNOWLEDGMENTS

Each day I have so much to be grateful for
And so many to be grateful to.

Thanks to the Lord for loving me and helping me to use my talents to His honor and glory.

Special thanks to all the new friends my husband J.L. and I made in Happy Valley, TN, while working on this book. Joan Phillips graciously invited us to Homecoming at Happy Valley Missionary Baptist Church where we were warmly welcomed by all the church including Pastor Beecher Whitehead and his wife Janette, Velda Jean Blevins, Deliliah Whitehead, and many others too numerous to mention. We are so grateful for their kindness.

Gratitude and appreciation to those who work to make my books the best they can be:

    ___ Brittany Dowdle, editor
    ___ Elizabeth S. James, editorial advisor
    ___ J.L. Stepp, production design and proofing
    ___ Katherine Stepp, cover design and graphics
    ___ Jim Palmer, final proofeditor

And continuing gratitude to all my wonderful fans for loving and reading my books.

If you keep reading and loving my books
I'll keep writing them!

MAP for
HAPPY VALLEY

CHILHOWEE MOUNTAIN

Morton BLUFF

FOOTHILLS PARKWAY

DADE's Mtn Home

old Cabin

CLAIBORNE FARM

Boone Cemetery

HAPPY VALLEY Missionary Bapt Church

Community CENTER

Red Top Chilhowee Primitive Bapt Church

HAPPY VALLEY RD

BUTLER's

BELL BRANCH RD

WALKER FARM

Mill Creek

HAPPY

Sawmill Ridge

Huckleberry Branch

Bell Branch

ABRAMS RIDGE

JOHNSON'S HOME

Huckleberry GAP

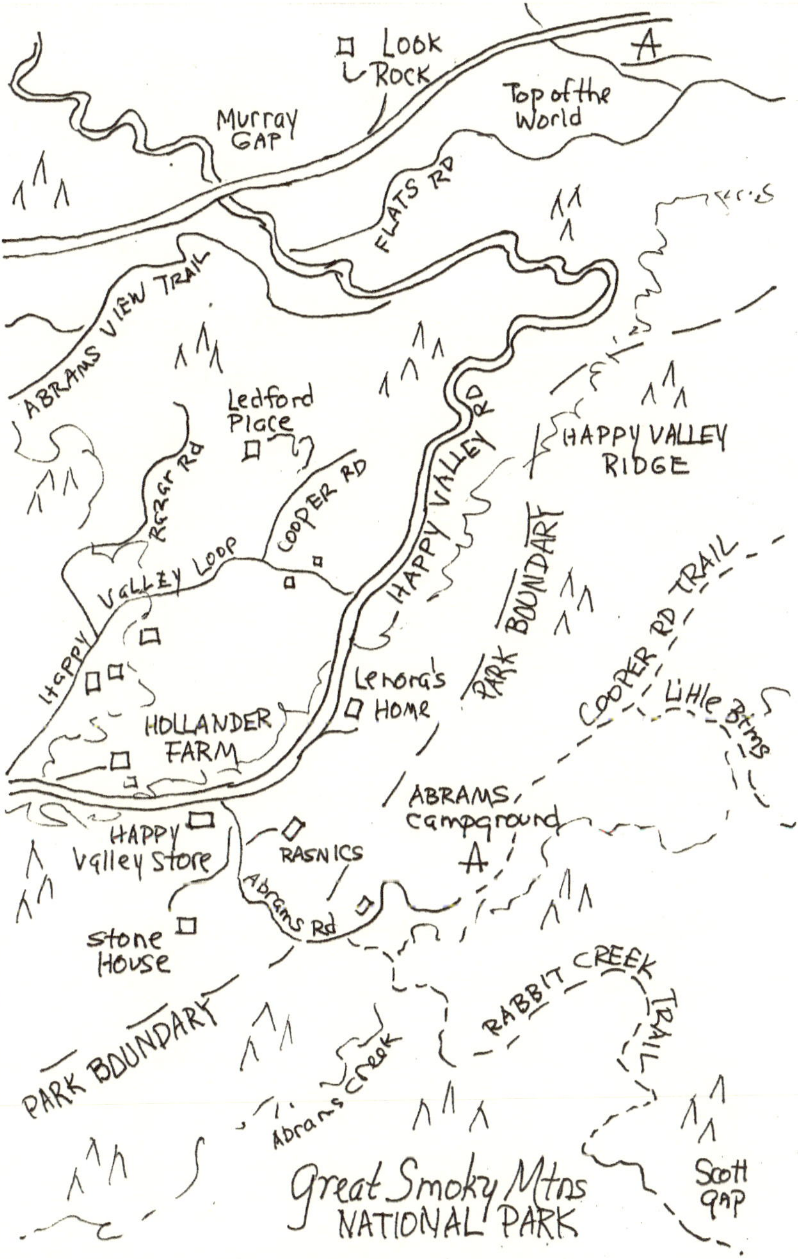
Look Rock
Murray GAP
Top of the World
FLATS RD
ABRAMS VIEW TRAIL
Ledford Place
Razor Rd
COOPER RD
HAPPY VALLEY RD
HAPPY VALLEY RIDGE
HAPPY VALLEY LOOP
PARK BOUNDARY
COOPER RD TRAIL
Lenora's Home
HOLLANDER FARM
Little Btms
ABRAMS campground
HAPPY Valley Store
RASNICS
Abrams Rd
Stone House
RABBIT CREEK TRAIL
PARK BOUNDARY
Abrams Creek
Scott gap
Great Smoky Mtns
NATIONAL PARK

CHAPTER 1

Someone was following him. His heartbeat kicked up, and he felt a thin sweat break across his brow. Walker could see the black van still behind him. It had followed him for the last several miles. Revving his cycle, he turned off on the side road ahead, glancing into his rear view mirror as he did, only to see the van drive by him. He'd been wrong. Again.

It was time to get past this—long past time.

He slowed on the narrow country road and then gunned his motorcycle into a rough gravel driveway. Roaring to a stop, Walker switched off the motor and dropped his feet to the ground. He pushed the cycle over to prop it against the gate of the rural property, trying not to glance back to see if the van had returned. But he could only hear the quiet of the country now.

Walking around to shake off the tension, he let the sounds of the birds, the hum of insects in the field, and the sun overhead calm him. He hated these moments. It was time for a change, and he was headed in that direction. He'd be danged if he'd let one flashback spook him again.

Walker glanced at his watch. Twenty minutes early with time to spare. Making his way back to the gate, he pulled out his cell phone, leaned against the gatepost, and punched in a familiar number.

His sister, Victoria, answered on the first ring. "Hi, is anything wrong? You never call during the week."

"Everything's fine, Vee. Are you busy with a client?"

"No. I'm in the home office today." He heard her rustling papers.

"Emma and Kaycie picked up one of those stomach bugs going around. Chandler is covering the main office with Mrs. Burke."

"Burke the battle-ax." He smiled.

"Don't knock Mrs. Burke. She keeps our lives—and our business at Pendleton Interiors—on a neat and clockwork schedule."

Walker began to relax hearing her voice. "How are the twins? Very sick?"

"No, and both better today, watching movies. They'll be fine and running around by tomorrow." She paused. "What about you? Are you sure everything is all right there?"

"I'm sure." He hesitated. "I'm looking at a piece of property and a house."

She caught her breath. "I'm stunned. What brought this on? You've been on the road for two years."

"I'm tired of traveling." He felt the words deep into his bones as he spoke them.

"Who could blame you?" Her voice softened. "Why don't you come look at property in Virginia near me, Chandler, and the girls or near Aunt Jessie?"

"I don't think I should do that."

She sighed. "It's been two years. Surely any danger is past."

He didn't answer, not wanting to argue with her.

"Maybe you could go back to Colorado now, near Stewart and the family there," she added.

"No." Nothing more needed to be said.

"Stubborn as ever." Her voice broke off. "Where are you, anyway? The last time you phoned, you were camping on the North Carolina side of the Smoky Mountains near Bryson City."

"I'm on the Tennessee side of the mountains now, camping at Abrams Creek Campground, not far from Townsend and Maryville." He glanced toward the two-lane road that wound up the hill to the property gate. "I was out walking with Marsh yesterday and saw a place I liked in a valley below the trail. I'm waiting for the realtor to come meet me now so I can see more of it."

"What's the house like?"

"Big old stone house tucked under a mountain ridgeline, within walking distance of the campground and the Smokies boundary. The property lies between the Smoky Mountains and the Chilhowee Mountains in a pretty little place called Happy Valley…"

She interrupted. "Walker, you don't need to hide yourself out in some remote valley in the Smoky Mountains if you're ready to settle down."

"I like it here."

"You've been on the road too long, by yourself too long," she argued.

"That was my point, Vee, to get away."

Her voice grew cross. "Well, this is the first I've heard about you having a sudden desire to settle down again."

He searched for words. "I didn't realize I wanted to until I saw this place. There are some things I really like about it. It feels right. It sort of called to me."

She was silent for a few minutes. "Oh well, if you're feeling ready to settle down finally, I don't want to discourage you from that—no matter where the place is. What can I do to help?"

Walker grinned. "If I buy the place, I'll need a good decorator. Pendleton Interiors came to mind. I wondered what your schedule is like this fall? You know that I let everything go when I left Colorado. All I have is what's in the Sportsmobile. Not much." He took a breath. "I'd prefer not to do business with anyone here, so I was hoping you could help."

He heard her flipping through her calendar book. "I can make some time in my schedule if you buy the place. I could even fly down and bring the girls if you make a decision before they go back to school, get a sense of what is needed, take measurements and photos. What shape is the house in? How big is it?"

"Let me look at it first. I'll call you and let you know if I like it, if I decide to buy it." He saw a vehicle heading up the road, a car this time and not a van as before. "I think I see the realtor coming. I need to go."

Hanging up and tucking his cell phone in his back pocket, Walker watched a sleek silver car pull into the rutted gravel drive off Abrams Creek Road. A tall black man, good-looking and dressed in a sharp business suit and tie, waved and flashed Walker a grin as he climbed out of the car.

"Cameron Johnson," he offered, walking over to shake Walker's hand. "You must be Walker Logan. Nice to meet you."

"Good to meet you, too." Walker glanced over the man's shoulder to see a teenage boy still sitting in the car.

Cameron sighed. "That's my brother, Quillen. He just turned sixteen this summer. His old truck broke down and I had to pick him up after his work shift. I meant to run him down the valley to our place before I came to meet you, but my last appointment ran over and I didn't want you to wait."

"You live here in Happy Valley?" Walker asked.

"Yeah, at the lake end of the valley, to the west. It's why I often get the area listings from the agency. I know the valley better than most." He paused. "You sure you want to see this property? As I told you, it's been empty for five years. Although the house is structurally sound, the home and grounds haven't been kept up well and it's remote here."

The man glanced toward his feet with distaste, where a nasty mud puddle from last night's rain sprawled across the driveway. "The drive is rutted out, overgrown, and not paved. I have other properties in much better shape I could take you to see—a nice vacation cabin tucked under a hillside, a log home with a large tract of land, and a new construction house on the top of Chilhowee Mountain." His eyes brightened speaking of the latter. "Everything is spotless in that house and the views across the Smoky Mountains are stunning."

"Thank you, but I think I'd like to see this property first."

Cameron's eyes traveled up the driveway choked with rocks, weeds, and mud puddles. "We may have to walk in," he said with resignation.

"I don't mind a walk." Walker's eyes shifted to the boy in the car. "Maybe Quillen would like to walk with us."

The boy's eyes lit up, and Cameron nodded at him. "Sure. Come on if you want, Quill," he offered as the boy spilled out of the car, obviously pleased at the invitation.

Although not as tall as his brother, the resemblance between the young men was strong, except Quillen wore baggy khaki slacks and a navy shirt with a hardware store emblem on it versus a sharp suit.

Walker studied the teenager with a smile. There was something fresh and appealing about the kid he liked right away. An easy manner. Honest eyes. He liked the older brother, too. Traveling as much as he had helped a person learn to size people up on a quick glance.

Turning back to his motorcycle, Walker leaned over and locked it to the fence post beside the property gate.

"That's a cool motorcycle," the boy said, walking closer to examine it.

"It's a Ural two-wheel drive I picked up in Washington. It's Russian made. It can go anywhere."

"You from Washington?" Quillen asked while Cameron fished in his pocket for keys to open the metal gate across the driveway.

"No, but I am originally from out west. I've been traveling the United States for the last two years."

"No kidding?" Quillen's eyes widened. "Do you write travel articles or something?"

"No. I came into a little money and thought I'd see the USA while still young."

"Wow, I'll bet you've had some great adventures." Quillen grinned. "Have you been in all fifty states?"

"Yes, and it *was* an interesting adventure but I'm thinking of getting off the road now."

Cameron rolled his eyes at these words. "And you decided on Happy Valley after traveling like that?"

Walker noted the sarcasm. "You got something against the valley?"

"No." Cameron shook his head. "I told you I live here with my family—my mom, dad, Quillen, my three sisters—Vanna,

Sally, Della Sue—and Della Sue's little girl, Jaida. We live in a big farmhouse about a mile from Chilhowee Lake and we have a houseful."

"Having family is a blessing."

Cameron glanced at him. "You married? Have family around here?"

"No family in the area. Just visiting and camping at Abrams Creek Campground down the road."

"You a married man?"

"No."

Cameron paused, as if hoping for more information, his glance flicking over Walker's ratty jeans, faded T-shirt, and well-worn boots. He cleared his throat. "You know, even though this place is run-down, Mr. Logan, it is a large house and a big property." He glanced toward a high ridge in the distance ahead of them. "The land runs all the way to that ridge behind the house, over it and down to the park boundary near Abrams Creek. To the front, the property extends all the way to Happy Valley Road. You can see the road through those trees." He gestured toward a cluster of trees below a rolling field. "We're standing on the east boundary of the property at Abrams Creek Road; the west boundary lies at the top of that hillside." He pointed toward a forested ridge.

"I read the property acreage in the specs. And the price," Walker offered, hoping to move the conversation along.

"Okay." Cameron nodded, leading the way up the drive at last and giving up on quizzing Walker for any more personal information.

As they walked, skirting their way around rocks and puddles, Walker noted the road needed extensive repair, every section rutted from rain and erosion.

"The locals call this place Old Stone House," Cameron said, initiating conversation again. "I don't show it often."

Quillen stomped through a big mud puddle without concern. "Lots of folks say the house is too fancy-schmancy for this valley. That's mainly why it hasn't sold...." His voice dropped off as Cameron frowned at him. "Sorry," he murmured.

Walker pulled his ball cap down to hide a smirk.

"It's not that the house isn't a great place with a lot of potential," Cameron amended. "It's just different from most of the real estate in the valley. A corporate executive, Lawrence Creswell, built it about twenty years ago as a vacation retreat, but he never visited much after the first few years. The home and property were well maintained, though, until he died. Now his widow Evelyn is selling out. It's not the sort of place for a woman on her own, too big and too remote."

When Walker didn't answer, Cameron walked on in silence, picking his way around yet another mud puddle. He paused as they turned a corner in the road, the house coming into view. "Pretty setting, isn't it? You can see the Chilhowee Mountain range and some great views across Happy Valley from the front porch."

Walker studied the house more closely now—the place he'd spotted several days ago from a ridge trail high above while walking with his dog, Marsh. Built of handlaid limestone rock, the house sprawled across the top of the hill on an open green ledge of land. It had a rustic appearance, with a weathered gray slate roof, inviting porches, and three gabled windows across the upper story.

"Way cool. I've never seen this place up close." Quillen shaded his eyes from the sun. "Even though it's empty and looks neglected, it feels kind of like a good place, doesn't it?"

"Yeah, it does feel like a good place," Walker agreed, letting his eyes roll over the big rock house set amid lush shade trees, hedgerows, and beautiful landscaping, the latter now choked with brush and weeds.

Cameron pulled out a sheet of paper to study it. "Besides the house and an adjoining garage and carport, you'll find a small barn and a long shed behind the house where you could keep yard and farm equipment. On the lower property is a second barn—a big gray one." He pointed toward it, set to one side of a long field that rolled gently downhill toward Happy Valley Road. "This was once an active farm according to my notes. The original farmhouse burned a long time ago, but the Creswells built their house on the foundations of the old homesite for the mountain views."

Quillen pointed a finger toward a broad expanse of mountain ranges. "You can see all the way to Look Rock Tower on Chilhowee Mountain from here."

Walker located the outline of the high tower in the distance. "I've climbed the trail to that tower."

"Me, too," Quillen said, sending Walker another of his happy grins.

The three walked on, heading toward the house's front door, painted a deep crimson in colorful contrast to the house's gray stone and white trim. Two red brick chimneys added the only other spots of color, except for the myriad collection of unkempt flowers in purples, reds, and yellows crowded among the weeds around the front porch steps.

"Well, let's check the place out," Cameron said, pulling out his keys to open the door.

The house was larger than Walker imagined, seeing it only from his ridgetop view yesterday, with a total of over three thousand square feet. Cobwebs, dust, and a general feeling of neglect prevailed in every room they walked through. A living room lay to one side of the main entry hall and a dining area to the other, with a doorway leading back to a large sunny kitchen with a windowed breakfast nook looking out to the backyard.

Walker could visualize enjoying breakfast and coffee there, gazing across the yard and up to the mountain ridges beyond. An old bird feeder hung from a big maple branch and a stone birdbath stood amid an overgrown flower bed.

To the back of the downstairs of the house sprawled a big family room with a vaulted ceiling, plus a master bedroom and bath. Doors led from both rooms to a long screened porch, offering wooded views all around.

"Man, this porch is great." Quillen peeked out to admire it.

Walker agreed, and despite the fact that the screens needed replacing, he could imagine the porch as a favorite spot on summer evenings.

They tromped upstairs next, where Quillen stopped to hang over the balcony rail to look down on the family room below. "This is a really big house. What's upstairs, Cam?"

Cameron glanced at his spec sheet again. "Three bedrooms, each with walk-in closets, two baths, and lots of storage under the cape cod eaves."

They wandered through each bedroom, pushing aside spiderwebs and leaving footprints in the dust on the hardwood floors. As they walked out of the last bedroom, Quillen pointed to a door at the end of the hallway. "Where does that door lead?"

Cameron led the way down the hall to push the door open as he answered. "To a recreation room over the garage."

"Super." Quillen's eyes moved around the big room. "A guy could put a pool table in here, leather sofas, a big TV, and turn this into a great man cave."

Walker bit back another smile at the boy's enthusiasm.

"It could make a good office, too," Cameron added. "Separate from the activity of the main house."

Walker nodded, liking that practical idea more.

"As you see, this is a big home for a single man," Cameron repeated as they headed down the stairs and out onto the front porch.

"Yes, it is." Walker agreed.

"It's filthy, too. I'm sorry about that." Cameron wrinkled his nose, glancing down at the layer of dust on his shoes. "I even saw rat droppings in several places. I really need to get in touch with Evelyn Creswell about cleaning this place up." He pulled a sheet of paper from behind the specs he'd been studying. "Why don't I take you to see a couple of the other listings we talked about, Mr. Logan? I have time. Again, I regret the problems with this place." He glanced toward Walker as he started down the front steps, waiting for an answer.

Lost in his own thoughts, Walker didn't reply at first. His eyes moved down the long expanse of green field rolling gradually downhill from the house to the main road. He smiled. "I'm going to build a store right there on the corner of Happy Valley Road and Abrams Creek Road where the land levels out." He pointed to the spot.

"A *store*?" Cameron turned stunned eyes to his.

"What kind of store?" Quillen asked, less shocked than his brother.

"An old-fashioned general store where you can pick up basic groceries, camping needs, firewood, ice, and local crafts."

"No kidding?" Quillen's eyes looked down the hillside as if trying to imagine it. "We don't have a store of any kind here in Happy Valley."

"I noticed that when I needed a few things at the campground," Walker said. "I had to drive all the way into Maryville to pick up ice and a few basics. Took me nearly thirty minutes to get to the nearest store and thirty more driving back to the campground again."

Cameron cleared his throat. "Uh. We've had a few stores around the area, Mr. Logan. None could make a go of it; they all closed."

Walker leaned against a post on the porch. "I know that. I actually looked at the boarded-up store across from the church. It wasn't big enough for what I have in mind. I stopped to check out the abandoned store on the highway in Tallassee, too—a pretty brick structure with big picture windows. Too bad it closed."

"The Tallassee General Store used to be a thriving business in its day—even had a post office beside it," Cameron said.

"Well, it's falling down and neglected now," Quillen put in. "I heard folks say they really miss that store. Mama is always wishing for a store near the valley for times when she runs out of something. It's a long drive into town to get milk or a can of soup."

"That's my point." Walker smiled at the boy.

Quillen leaned forward, his eyes brightening. "Hey, do you think I could work at your store?" he asked, almost bouncing in place at the idea. "I've been working at a hardware store this summer. I can run a cash register, put out stock; I'm good with customers, even the difficult ones. I could work for you after school and on weekends. It wouldn't be so far for me to drive to get to work. I have to drive all the way into Maryville now."

"Quillen." Cameron sent him a cross look. "The man's only looking at the house today, tossing out ideas. He isn't advertising for employees. Besides, there's nothing on that lot on Happy Valley Road now except for weeds." He paused. "My guess is that after Mr. Logan looks into the feasibility of a store from a business perspective, he'll realize that building any kind of store in Happy Valley will hardly turn a profit."

Walker turned to look at Cameron. "You might be surprised at how well the right kind of store would do here. I'm sure other folks in the valley, like your mother, people at the Top of the World Community, or families camping down the road at Abrams Creek Campground might like having a general store here in Happy Valley, especially a picturesque one. That's exactly the kind of store I intend to build, too."

Cameron scowled. "You'd need a lot of money for that," he replied with some annoyance, obviously not picking up on Walker's vision.

"I *have* a lot of money." Walker shrugged, looking across the fields toward the main road again. "And Quillen, as soon as I get the sale on this place finalized, I'm going to need a good worker to help me clean up this property and to work in the store later when I get it finished. You any good with a hammer and tools?"

The boy's face lit up like a Christmas tree. "Yes, sir, and so is my dad. He could work for you, too. He's retired and has extra time on his hands now."

Cameron turned to study Walker again. "Do you really want to buy this place, Mr. Logan?"

"Yes, I do." Walker answered with surety.

Cameron glanced around in surprise, a little stunned at the idea; then he shrugged and grinned. "Well, okay. I figure you know what you want, so I'll start getting the paperwork ready for you in the morning." He put a hand on his brother's shoulder. "And since Quillen is going to work for you, maybe you'd like to come over to the house tonight to meet the family and have dinner. My mom always cooks plenty with so many of us. One more won't make a difference. I'm sure everyone would enjoy hearing about your travels and getting to know you."

"Will you come?" Quillen asked, his eyes shining. "We don't live in a fancy place like this, that's for sure, but my mama is an awesome cook. Everyone says so. If you haven't had a good homemade meal in a long time, you'll really like her cooking."

"That sounds great," Walker said and he really meant it. He couldn't remember the last time he'd sat in on a big family dinner— or the last time someone invited him to dinner at a real home.

Their talk turned congenial then. Cameron checked with his folks about the dinner invitation, gave Walker directions to their house, and then set an appointment time with him for the next day to begin paperwork on the home and property. When Cameron and Quillen started toward their car, Walker slowed his pace. "I think I'd like to walk around a little more before heading on back to the campground."

"Sure," Cameron said. "We'll see you down at our place at six. You text me if you can't follow the directions I gave you."

After they left, Walker circuited the old house again, looking at it from all angles, and then strolled behind it, passing a barn and shed, a patio under the trees with a battered metal bench, a stone table and chairs covered with mold and leaves. Several pathways led appealingly in different directions behind the house, and Walker began to explore, feeling again that sense of rightness about this place in Happy Valley.

Doesn't every place deserve to have a store? Walker thought. *And who knows better about stores than me?* In his mind, he knew exactly what type of old country store he would build on the road below his home. A vision of it came to him while standing on the porch earlier. He could see it as clear as day even now—weathered gray wood, like the colors in the stone house, with a rustic appearance, a big front porch, a winding drive curling up to it, and a big parking lot by that grove of shade trees.

He'd visited many old general stores while traveling the back roads around the United States these last years, and he knew the type of store that drew and charmed him—the kind that drew tourists and travelers, too.

A sound caught his attention, and Walker paused on the pathway. *Was that singing he heard?* Walking closer to the sound, he realized it was a mix of talk and song, the voice a lilting, girlish one.

Turning a corner in the path, he saw the girl—more a young woman than a girl—straddled perilously on the limb of an old apple tree, stretching to get apples almost out of her reach on a long branch. She had thick dark hair, almost black, tousled and wavy, that she kept pushing back behind one ear to keep it out of her face. He couldn't see her face well, but she wore a long colorful skirt, a poor choice for tree climbing, and the skirt kept snagging on one of the branches, causing her to fuss at it.

Intent on her task, she didn't see him. Tucking an apple into a colorful embroidered tote bag hanging around her neck, she muttered to herself. "If I can shinny out a little more, I can get those last two apples on the branch." She began inching her way out on the long limb, singing the words of an old folk tune as she did, but Walker heard a small cracking sound as the limb began to resist her weight.

Sprinting forward on impulse, he reached out just in time to catch the girl as the limb broke from the tree, tumbling her toward the ground.

"Ooof." Walker caught her, but tripped and stumbled backward to the ground under her weight, the girl falling across him in a sprawl, the bag of fruit spilling, apples rolling in every direction.

She lay against him for a minute, stunned, and then pushed up to look down at him with lovely, wide, chocolate-brown eyes. "Wherever did you come from?" she asked.

He grinned at her, enjoying the warm feel of her along his body. "It seems to me like your response ought to be: Thanks for catching me."

She looked around then, glancing up toward the cracked limb

above. "Well, you did save me a tumble," she said, wriggling away from him.

Walker pushed himself off the ground, stood, and helped her to her feet. Although she'd looked small in the tree, she was about his height. Her black, curly hair drifted around her face in disarray, and she had a fresh outdoor appearance with pink lips and cheeks and a rich olive skin. Walker especially liked the pixie smile that lit her face and crinkled the corners of her eyes.

She leaned over to pull up the hem of her skirt to examine it, giving Walker a quick look at her legs, pretty legs. He let his eyes travel over her shapely figure, enjoying what he saw there, too.

"Shoot, I've torn my skirt." She frowned at it. "And I dropped all my apples." She began picking them up off the ground as she spoke, and Walker bent to help her.

"Just stuff them in this bag." She picked up the colorful pouch bag that had fallen from her shoulder.

"These apples look a little green," Walker said, studying one.

"They're supposed to be green. They're Pippins—Newton Pippins." She smiled at him. "They're an old apple variety and a great keeper. Crisp, a little tart, with a nice aroma." She held an apple toward his nose, and he caught its fresh, spicy scent.

"They make great cider and are good for cooking in pies, cakes, and breads. Great in jams and preserves, too. Thomas Jefferson grew them at Monticello." She bit into an apple, savoring it, before passing it to him to sample. "I come to pick these every year—in late August and early September. No one lives here, so they'd go to waste otherwise. My Gramma Newell counts on them for her cider, her baking, and her jams." She pointed around her. "There are a lot of old fruit trees on the back of this property, all planted in the late 1800s, when this was a working farm."

Walker munched on the apple, enjoying it—and enjoying the chatter of this bright, sunny girl, friendly and obviously warm-hearted. He liked easy, natural people, comfortable with themselves and their world. He'd seen too much phoniness and deception for his liking in the past.

She turned to study him. "By the way, who are you?" she asked. "Are you camping down at Abrams Campground?"

"Yes, I'm camping at Abrams," he replied, answering her last question. "But I've been traveling a lot these last years."

"Well, you picked a beautiful time of year to visit our valley and the Smoky Mountains. The fall colors haven't started yet, but the air is crisp with that sweet hint of autumn hovering close at hand, especially in the early mornings."

He nodded, liking the lyrical poetry of her words. "Do you live here?" he asked her.

"Yes, for right now. I'm living over at my grandparents' farm across the road." She gestured. "I grew up in the valley."

She tucked her colorful patchwork bag across one shoulder, slipping her feet into a pair of old tennis shoes she'd left at the base of the tree. "I'd better get back before Gramma begins to worry," she said. "Feel free to pick some apples for yourself to take back to the campground." She walked toward him as she spoke. "Thanks again for catching me when I fell, too." She leaned up to kiss him impulsively, surprising him.

As her lips touched his, tasting of sweet apples, Walker pulled her closer to kiss her more fully. She was simply irresistible, and he doubted she even realized it.

"Ahhh," he heard her sigh, leaning into him.

He deepened the kiss, enjoying the taste of her and the feel of her against him. Like the big stone house behind them, she felt sweet and right.

The girl pulled back after a minute, studying him. "Too bad you're traveling on," she said, giving him another of her impish smiles before starting off through the yard.

He watched her go, walking away with a smooth, swinging, natural gait, her colorful skirt swishing around her legs.

As if sensing him watching her, she turned back to wave at him, sending him a last bright smile.

"Very sweet," Walker said. He thought this day a great one already, but it certainly had only gotten better. He set off down the worn path now, leading back to his motorcycle, whistling and looking forward to his life to come.

CHAPTER 2

A year later, as Juliette settled into her usual place at the kitchen table of the Hollander farmhouse for breakfast, her grandmother said, "You think those Pippin apples might be ripe enough to pick yet?"

"I don't know," Juliette answered, reaching to serve herself scrambled eggs and bacon from the old blue platter on the table. "You know I just got here last night." She'd been away all spring and summer, teaching quilting classes at the John C. Campbell Folk School in Brasstown, North Carolina, and working part-time at her friend Sharon Bard's craft store, The Full Moon, in nearby Murphy.

Her grandfather cleared his throat, reminding her to pass the platter of eggs and bacon his way.

She studied him as she did. "You look better, Grandpa," she said, but couldn't help noticing he was thinner since his heart attack, his short beard whiter than Juliette remembered.

"I'm fine. You didn't need to come home because I had a little spell with my heart." He snapped out the words, making her wince, but his face softened as he caught her eyes. "But I'm glad you're back again, Julie-girl."

"Me, too," her older brother, George, put in. He'd stopped in for breakfast this morning before heading out to the fields to work. It was a common occurrence for him to drop by for breakfast when his wife, Laura, worked the early shift at the hospital in Maryville. "I don't know why you can't simply settle down here in the valley and stay."

Juliette sighed at his words. She split her days all too often between her life in North Carolina and her life here in Happy Valley. Her grandparents, who'd raised her since her mother died, were both older now, and it didn't seem right not to help out when she could. Especially when one of them fell ill. Juliette had driven home this weekend after completing her last class at the Folk School, the soonest she could get away after her grandpa's hospitalization. Her friend Sharon understood, of course, and had already hired one of her crafty friends in the area eager to fill in Juliette's hours at the shop.

"I'll stay for the fall and winter until I'm sure Grandpa is better," she told Sharon before she left. "But I'll come back for the spring."

Juliette had traveled to Happy Valley last summer, also, when her grandmother caught pneumonia, and stayed until early fall helping out. Sometimes she felt like a yo-yo.

"You may not be able to sneak over and get those Pippin apples anymore now that the Creswell place has sold," George said as he passed her a basket full of hot biscuits Gramma Newell just pulled from the oven.

"I didn't know the place finally sold." She glanced at George in surprise.

"You *did* know but you simply forgot." Her grandmother sat down at the table, handing her a glass of juice as she did so. "I wrote you about it last fall, remember? Actually, the place sold right before you left, if you'll think back. You ought to remember everyone talking about it at the time."

Juliette searched her memory. "I do remember the talk now. No one seemed sure who bought the place. A man with a family, I think you said."

"Well, everyone thought so at first since a woman and two girls stayed at the old house for a while. But then they left."

Grandpa leaned toward her. "The woman comes back now and again by herself but she never stays. Everybody thinks that's real curious, her comin' and a-goin' like that…"

George interrupted. "Here's the big news, though, since you left," he said, buttering another biscuit. "The man who bought the place has built a store right on the corner of Happy Valley Road where Abrams Creek Road turns to wind down to the campground. It's a big old gray country store. We've all watched it being built from the ground up since last fall. I hear he's about ready to open. Even put up a sign: Happy Valley Store."

"Didn't you see the place as you drove in?" Grandpa asked.

"No." She shook her head. "I turned off on the farm road before that intersection and it was dark when I arrived."

"Well, everybody thinks the man is a little bit crazy building a big store like that here in this rural valley." Gramma shook her finger. "He must have a lot of money, too, because he paid a bundle to fix up that old rock house on the hillside that's sat empty so long. He did hire some local folks to help him with the work, like Eldon Johnson and his boy Quillen, but he hired outsiders to do most of the labor on the house and store. Workers came and went all fall, winter, and spring over there."

George crossed his arms. "Gramma, the man could hardly find local people in Happy Valley with the skills to build a store that big."

"Well, I think he's plumb crazy." Grandpa scowled. "And my guess is that store won't even last the year."

"I agree," said a voice from the kitchen doorway. Dade Claiborne pushed open the screened door to let himself in from the back porch. "Hi, Juliette. I heard you were home." He winked at her as he took off his battered white cowboy hat and hung it on a peg by the door.

"Nice to see you, Dade," she said, wishing she really meant it. Dade's family lived farther down the valley on a farm as big as the Hollander place, and he'd been sweet on her for quite a few years. Not that she'd done anything to encourage him. Not much, anyway. But Dade was used to getting what he wanted, and he was persistent in his suit.

"Pull up a chair," George said, smiling. "I know Juliette is tickled you came by."

She pasted on a congenial grin. It made life more difficult that George and her grandparents really liked Dade and pointedly pushed her in his direction. Gramma hustled around, bringing coffee and hot biscuits to him now. Her special attentions reminded Juliette how fond she was of him.

"How's the car business?" Grandpa asked.

"Business is good," Dade said as he loaded the plate Gramma gave him with breakfast food.

It was hard these days to make a living from farming alone, as everyone knew, so Dade's father, R. D., had started Claiborne's Auto about thirty years ago. He'd successfully built a large, lucrative dealership before he died a few years back. Dade, who loved the car business, inherited it, while his younger brother, Ronnie, inherited the Claiborne farm in Happy Valley.

Dade winked at Juliette again. "I've got my property cleared on the mountain and my house up there partly done now. I'll take you up there to see it soon. Pretty place with great views. Everything modern and new."

She forced another polite smile.

"There's some fine big homes coming up along that high ridge on the mountain," Grandpa put in. "Don't know why that new rich man didn't buy one of them big places instead of wasting his time fixing up Old Stone House and building himself a fancy store that's sure to go bust."

"He may have a lot of money now, but he's sure to take a fall with the investments he's made." Dade grinned at Juliette. "These days having work outside the valley to supplement your life is smart. I'm sure it's a help to George that his wife, Laura, is a nurse over at the hospital. Gives them a steady income when farming takes a turn."

"Our farm still does well," Grandpa defended. "Your family's place does, too. Your mama, Onalee, says Ronnie has the gift for farming. He's made some fine improvements around the place."

"Yeah, but they struggle." Dade frowned. "I had to give Ronnie a truck when his old one gave out recently. I was glad, too, that I could help you with a loan last year when you needed it, George."

George's face reddened. "It was good of you to offer to help, Dade. I'll be getting it paid back by this time next year, like we agreed."

Great, Juliette thought. George had let Dade loan him money. Knowing Dade like she did, Dade wouldn't be discreet about the debt, and he'd expect something in return for his generosity. That's the way he was.

She glanced down at her plate as the men talked. Ten to one, George would put even more pressure on her now to marry Dade Claiborne. He'd grown up with Dade and Ronnie, and he'd made it clear to Juliette for years that he thought she should marry Dade.

It wasn't that Dade wasn't good-looking or personable. He could charm the birds out of the trees when he wanted to. She could remember a few weak moments when she'd softened under that charm.

"Well, we all think it's real fine you've done so well with your daddy's business since he passed," Gramma said, getting up to pour Dade more coffee and patting his back fondly. "I know your mama is real glad Ronnie and his wife are staying on at the farm to run it with her, but she's proud of you, too, taking over your daddy's dealership like you did."

Before the breakfast hour had passed, Dade talked Juliette into a dinner date later in the week. He'd been so nice, and cagey, in the way he asked her out, making it awkward for her to graciously decline his offer in front of her family. Juliette knew, however, she needed to tell him, when they were alone next, that she wasn't interested in taking their friendship to another level. She wanted to stay at the farm to help until her grandpa got better, but dreaded having to fight off Dade's advances—especially if they escalated.

After breakfast, Juliette insisted that her grandmother sit down to rest while she cleaned up. "Let me help, Gramma. I know you're worn out from all the caregiving Grandpa has needed."

"It's good to see him up and better, though. I was right scared through it all that I might lose him."

Juliette turned from the sink to look at her grandmother,

noticing the new worry lines on her forehead above her glasses. It seemed her short hair was whiter, too. She hated seeing both of her grandparents getting older.

"What are the doctors saying?"

"That the old man needs to rest more. The heart attack was a minor one. They told us some big name for the kind of attack he had. Laura will remember it."

"I'll talk to her," Juliette said. "I want to be sure we do the best things to help Grandpa heal and strengthen like he should."

"He's gone out to the fields with George this morning. They're cutting and baling hay on the farm, and Grandpa thinks he needs to be out there keeping an eye on it all." She glanced toward the doorway. "George will try to see that he doesn't overdo though, and Laura says he has to come in and rest midday."

"It's always a trial to make that man rest," Juliette said, turning back to the sink again.

"Well, I'm glad you're here to help me fuss at him some." She smiled. "He takes it better from you than me."

Juliette finished the dishes and came to sit beside her grandmother, who was working on one of her quilts.

"What's the quilt you're working on?" she asked.

"It's one of them handkerchief quilts." She held up a piece. "You take old handkerchief pieces and cut them into the shapes of doll dresses and then use some of the remaining fabric to create a matching sunbonnet. It makes a pretty quilt and a nice heirloom piece for those who collected or saved old handkerchiefs over the years. I'm working on the needlework around the handkerchief skirts right now and putting some little buttons on the bodices of each of the dresses."

Juliette studied the large white quilt draped over her grandmother's lap with its rows of handkerchief dolls. "It's really pretty, Gramma."

"A nice compliment coming from you." Gramma laid a hand on Juliette's cheek, a sweet familiar gesture. "You do fine work yourself."

"Quilting and sewing has always been the one special thing we hold in common." Juliette picked up a skein of embroidery floss to turn it in her hand. "As a little girl, I felt so out of place when I first came here from Italy, so far away, my mother gone. Then one morning I came down and found you sewing in the kitchen. Sewing was something I knew and understood, something I'd done with my mother. Finding I could do it with you, and carry on the skills I knew, helped me to begin to heal."

"You carried a gift even then for handling a needle, choosing the right colors and materials, artfully arranging everything. Your mother's people were artisans and tailors. You came by those gifts honest."

Juliette smiled at her grandmother. "I'd say I got some of those gifts from your side of the family, too. Look at all the beautiful things you make." She ran her hand over the quilt.

Her gramma changed the subject. "I hate it that you had to let your job go to come help us out again," she said, an anxious line forming across her forehead.

"Don't worry about that," Juliette told her. "Sharon knows I'll come back, and I don't have more classes scheduled at the school until next spring. For now, I have my quilt business online and some festivals lined up around the area to attend this fall. I might even look for a part-time job. You know that I'm of little use around the farm, but I will help with the house, run errands for you, and drive you and Grandpa to the doctors when he needs to go. I can take you into town to get groceries, too."

"Will you go see if you can pick me some apples, too?" Her grandmother grinned over the words. "Maybe those new owners wouldn't mind for you to pick some if they don't freeze or can."

Juliette stood. "I'll go over and check things out. I could use a walk this morning anyway." She leaned over to give her gramma a kiss on the cheek. "I'll check out the new store building while I'm there, too—see what it looks like. It might be nice to have a store nearby. We'll be able to get milk or eggs when we run out without driving all the way into town."

"Me and Onalee were just saying the same thing the other day."

A short time later Juliette skirted across the fields of Hollander farm, following a familiar pathway to the log bridge over Bell Branch. Beyond the bridge, the path climbed a short hill to reach Happy Valley Road. The well-worn farm trail came out right across from the intersection with Abrams Creek Road that wound downhill to the Abrams Creek Campground. She and George had used this route since they were kids as a shortcut to hiking trails in the Smoky Mountains and to their favorite swimming hole in Abrams Creek.

As she reached the main road, she stopped, stunned, at the sight before her. A huge country store of weathered gray wood stood across the street on the corner, where only an overgrown field and a scattering of brush and trees stood before.

"Wow. Isn't that something?" she said as she started across the road to get a closer look.

Although Juliette knew the store only recently built, the weathered, settled look of it suggested it had stood on the site for many long years. Limestone rock formed the building's foundation, and a long, broad porch spanned the front of the store. Juliette could see colorful rockers and furniture along the porch, and lush flowered plants hung from the rafters and spilled from pots around the steps. The doors and trim were painted a cheerful, cherry red, reminding her of the front door at Old Stone House on the hillside not far above the store.

Walking up the paved sidewalk and onto the porch, Juliette could see a screened porch full of tables and chairs, all the tables covered in red-checked cloths. Evidently the owner planned to have a small café in addition to the main store. This was certainly a bigger place than Grandpa and George suggested.

Even more curious now, Juliette walked along the porch, peeping into the windows. Inside she could see a rustic interior with beamed ceilings and wood floors, the shelves already packed with store goods and products. Everything inside was built to look like the store had been a staple of the community for fifty years or more, and Juliette knew it took money and intelligence to create a look like that.

"You can come in if you want," a voice said from the doorway nearby, making her jump at the sound. "I'm not open yet but I don't mind if you want to look around for a minute."

Turning at the sound, Juliette glanced toward the doorway to see a tall dark-haired man standing there, holding the screened door ajar for her. As her eyes moved to his face, she knew her mouth dropped open and she actually gasped.

A slow grin spread across his face. "You're the girl who fell out of my apple tree."

"And you stayed and actually bought the house and property?" she asked, shocked to see him again. She hadn't forgotten the day he caught her after she fell out of the tree when the limb broke. Or the kiss that followed.

"Yes. I bought the house and I built the store this last year," he said, standing aside to let her pass into the building. "I plan to open soon. Maybe I'll catch some of the late summer campers coming for a final vacation and, hopefully, more tourists in the fall, visiting to see autumn color or camping a last time before the winter comes."

Making an effort to calm her emotions and collect herself after the surprise of running into this man again, Juliette walked around the store, studying the vintage lighting fixtures hanging from the ceiling overhead, looking at the weathered wood floors and the old shelving lining the walls and marching in neat rows up and down the aisles. Canned goods and groceries filled the shelves, along with jars of jelly, soaps, handcrafts, handmade baskets, toys, and stacks of colorful note cards. Against the wall, she could see hardware supplies, bundled kindling, camping needs, flashlights, pots and pans, and in the middle of the store a cluster of old wooden barrels full of penny candy. Hats of different types hung on pegs from the store beams as did whisk brooms and American flags, and here and there around the store sat rocking chairs and a few old benches to rest on.

"You have everything here," she said, amazed. "I can hardly

believe it. Even an old-time soda fountain." She walked toward it in delight.

He grinned with pleasure at her remarks.

"Wherever did you find an old counter like this?" she asked, studying the vintage counter with its red vinyl stools and a mirrored wall behind it. "Even the signs on the walls are fifties classics." She pointed to worn metal retro cola and milkshake signs on the store wall.

"My sister is a decorator up north. She has a broad range of contacts for vintage items like I wanted." He perched on one of the counter stools. "A guy in Gatlinburg, Cooper Garrison, specializes in building log homes and buildings. He caught the vision for what I wanted here and made the store happen for me."

"It's unbelievable." She sat down on one of the soda fountain stools, continuing to look around.

"Do you think I'm crazy, like everyone else, to build a store like this?" he asked.

"No, how could I think that when I've already fallen in love with the place." She leaned toward him with a smile. "Will you hire me to work here part-time, let me help you get the place started and going? I'd really love that. I needed to come back to the valley for a season because my grandpa suffered a minor heart attack. When in North Carolina, I work retail in a crafts store called The Full Moon in Murphy near the Blue Ridge Mountains. Sharon, the store's owner, will give me a good reference. I also teach quilting nearby at the John C. Campbell Folk School in Brasstown."

"I've stayed in that area in my travels."

"I seem to remember you said you'd traveled a lot."

"All over the United States for two years."

She looked around in surprise. "Then out of the blue you decided to settle in Happy Valley and build a store?"

"Yes, that's about it."

She shrugged. "So what about the job? You'll need help. You can't run this place all by yourself." Juliette pressed her advantage. "And it would be good for you to have someone from the valley working for you. You're an outsider, but I grew up here. I know everyone and I know all about everyone. That's helpful when you're new in a small place like this."

He studied her, weighing her words. "I've got a boy from the valley working for me already, Quillen Johnson. You know him?"

"Sure." She felt a sudden letdown. "He's a great kid."

"He's still in high school, though. With school starting, he can only work after school and on weekends. Can you work days?"

She sat forward, excited again. "Yes. I can arrange to work any hours you need. I can start right now helping you get the place ready to open. I have a good artistic sense."

"Hmmm. Maybe we can work something out." He pivoted on the stool, studying her.

"I'm Juliette Hollander," she said, extending her hand to him. "I live across the road at Hollander Farm. I'm sure you've seen the arched sign at the entry off the main road as you've driven by."

He nodded. "Do you need to get permission from your family to work for me?"

She knew her mouth dropped open. "Whatever for? I'm twenty-eight years old. I've lived away at college and been on my own, working, for a long time now."

Juliette heard a low chuckle roll out of him. "Most everyone around here thinks I'm crazy. I thought your family might think so, too, and object."

She crossed her arms. "Whatever I do is my own business, Mr….." Her voice drifted away as she realized she didn't know his name yet.

"Walker Logan," he said. "And Walker will be fine. No need for the 'Mister.'" He got up and walked around behind the counter. "I'll need you to fill out some forms so I can put you on the payroll."

She grinned. "You won't be sorry you hired me."

"We'll call the first weeks a trial and see how things go."

Juliette watched him pull open a file drawer under the counter below the antique brass cash register. He pulled out a few papers and selected a pen from a tin cup on the counter, passing the papers and pen to her.

She filled out the paperwork at the counter while he checked messages on a smartphone.

Seeing she was finished, he put the phone away and then glanced over her papers briefly before filing them away.

"Juliette, you'll notice I purposely placed the register here at the end of the counter so when you're working you can see anyone who comes in—or anyone who goes out—of the front door." He gestured. "You can also see who goes into the café and you can see up and down most all the store aisles from the register. That's important when you're working the store by yourself." He pointed to a spot under the counter. "This red button is a security button, in case there should be a serious problem and you need the police. The silver button beside it will simply make a heck of a lot of noise. It sounds official and scares people off—sometimes a good thing with a troublemaker." He laughed and Juliette loved the sound of it.

She listened to more instructions, clear and well articulated, as he explained how he'd set up the store and how it operated.

"This isn't your first store," she said after a time, certain her words were true as she spoke them.

"No, it isn't." He didn't add more, although she waited.

"People often come to small out-of-the-way places like this because they're running from something," she said at last.

"Yes, that's often true." His hazel eyes met hers. "And when that's the case I expect they wouldn't like a lot of probing questions asked. You can understand that, can't you?"

"Yes." She offered him a small smile.

Uh-oh, she thought. *He has secrets, and he wants to keep them.* She'd honor that desire, at least for now. She wanted the job, and she wanted to work in this fabulous store and to get to know this man better, too. Admittedly, running into him again—as much as anything else—prompted her to ask for the job. She'd thought of him, and remembered that day in the orchard over a year ago, far more than she cared to acknowledge to anyone. The soft memory of that time had interrupted many a night's sleep and stolen into her thoughts. That didn't happen often to Juliette, and she needed to understand why that memory had stayed with her for so long, working its way into the fabric of her being.

CHAPTER 3

Walker wasn't sure he'd done the right thing hiring Juliette Hollander to work in the store with him. He felt confident, even without checking her references, she could handle the work in a small rural store—or that he could train her as he was training Quillen—but he wasn't sure he could handle being around her so closely. He was very attracted to her. He'd thought about her many times since he bought his home on the hill and began work on the store, looked for her in the orchard and around the valley. But he'd never seen her again. Until today.

"Can you cook?" he asked her, leaning against the counter across from her.

Her eyebrows lifted and she made a face. "Did you hire me hoping I could cook for the café?"

"A little work behind the counter is a part of the job."

She glanced around the area, wary now. "What did you have in mind?"

"I put in the café to help generate income for the store. In the mornings, I plan to keep coffee, juice, doughnuts, and sweet rolls on hand. Nothing fancy. At lunch, there will always be hot dogs. I'll make chili and slaw for them every morning—an old family recipe for both—and with the soda fountain atmosphere, I want to offer homemade milkshakes, coke floats, ice cream cones, sundaes, and banana splits." He walked over to the refrigerator, got out a carton of ice cream and spooned out several scoops into a tall glass. He then added a small splash of vanilla fountain syrup and popped the glass under a drink dispenser to run fizzy carbonated cola into it. Sticking a long spoon into the float, he handed it to her. "It isn't a hard job to make a few items at the counter, even while keeping an eye on the register."

"Is that coke float mine?" She batted her eyes at him.

"If you want it." He watched her dig in, spoon out a bite, and then close her eyes in pleasure.

"Ummm ... I love the touch of vanilla."

"I keep cherry-flavored syrup, too, to make cherry-cola floats. Just a touch of cherry or vanilla, plus the carbonated cola, gives a float that old-fashioned taste you can't get at home. To fancy it up further, you can squirt whipped cream on top and add a maraschino cherry."

He leaned on the counter, watching her while she enjoyed the float. She wore a fitted pink T-shirt and a jeans skirt with some sort of rosebud embroidery sewn lavishly around the pockets of it. She'd tied back her hair today, but it was curling out of the tie she'd wrapped around it. He remembered that long, thick, curly hair.

She glanced up at him, smiling.

He smiled back at her. "Do you think people in the valley will come in for ice cream treats or a hot dog at lunch once in a while when they don't want to cook?"

"Yes, in a heartbeat." She licked her spoon. "And especially if your chili and slaw are as good as your floats."

"Both are my granddaddy's recipes from an old store we owned. People put us on their travel routes for granddad's chili-slaw dogs."

"Hmmm. You know, you could serve other foods to expand the café idea if you wanted to," she said between bites.

"I could. We'll see. But this is a store first. If you start to expand food offerings too much, you need additional help, and you get food waste every day. Ice cream and hot dog products only need to be popped into the refrigerator or freezer every night, and the cleanup is minimal."

"That's true." She studied the counter and the shelves behind him, each lined with classic soda glasses in different sizes. "You seem to have everything you need here—a mixer for the shakes, glasses, a soda dispenser, one of those go-around things to keep hot dogs warm, and a stove top to heat the chili."

He glanced behind him. "That go-around thing for the hot dogs is called a roller grill. It can cook hot dogs in under ten minutes and keep them turning while warming buns in the drawer underneath at the same time."

"Very efficient."

"I plan to keep the chili warm in that Crock-Pot versus keeping the stove on all day, too." He pointed.

"Good idea." She dipped her spoon into her float again.

He propped an elbow on the counter near her. "I'll try to be here during the lunch hour to help you, or I'll get some extra help if we need it, but your day might be busier during the midday hours, working the café while ringing up store sales."

"Folks can wait a minute to get some items rung up while I put a few scoops of ice cream in a cone for someone."

He smiled. "That's the way I see it. This isn't intended to be a fast-paced establishment."

She considered what he'd told her. "So when I work I'll need to help a little with the café, ring up sales, straighten the store, put out stock in quiet moments, and clean and sweep in the mornings and evenings. Is that about it?"

"Pretty much."

"I'm in then." She tipped up her glass to drink out the last of the cola.

"Good. Let me show you around."

He walked her around the store, explaining its arrangement, pointing out the refrigeration unit along the back wall, discussing the products he carried. Stopping by the candy barrels near the register, he said, "I put these barrels near the register so we could keep a watch on them. Pieces of loose candy have a way of dropping into pockets."

She laughed, a rich melodic sound he liked.

He walked by the register to push open the door to the café.

"The only door to the porch and café is from inside the store. The tablecloths are oilcloth, easy to wipe off and keep clean, the décor simple. On pretty days, all the windows can be pulled open to let in the breezes through the screens. People like that when the weather's pretty. In the back of the room are two small restrooms." He gestured.

"I imagine you didn't create an outside door into the café area because you didn't want people letting themselves into the dining area or using the restrooms when the store was closed."

He nodded.

"That was smart. Bathroom and dining areas can get nasty if they're too accessible to the public from outside." She wrinkled her nose. "I know because I've stopped at some like that while traveling." She glanced at him. "I guess you've seen that, too, traveling all over the US." She paused, tracing her hand over one of the red-checked tablecloths. "Maybe you'll tell me about that someday."

"Maybe." He knew she hoped for more information with her comment and felt disappointed when he didn't offer it.

After a minute she gave him a saucy smile. "Well, maybe someday I'll tell you about growing up in Southern Italy, too."

Ignoring her baiting, he turned to let his eyes slide over her. "Southern Italy," he repeated. "I can see the Italian looks now that I think about it—black hair, dark eyes, olive skin tone—although I know it's a stereotype to expect that. Was your father or mother Italian?"

"My mother." She turned to walk back into the store. "We all have our own little private stories to tell, Walker."

He followed her, grinning at her candor. Juliette obviously wanted to know more about his past. He needed to decide what he wanted to tell her and when.

"Do you speak Italian?" he asked, interested in this aspect of her background.

"*Solo un po*—just a little," she answered. "I only remember bits and pieces from my early years growing up in Italy, from occasional visits, and from keeping up with my Italian relatives. In truth, *il mio italiano è orribile.*"

"Your Italian is horrible," he translated, guessing what her last expression meant.

"It is. Do you speak any other languages?"

"No, only English," he answered. "I've never traveled abroad and in high school I took Latin."

She smiled. "You'd have to step back in time to find someone to converse with in Latin. But I've heard studying Latin is a help to learning other languages."

"I've heard that, too." Returning to the store, he headed toward the back door, continuing the store tour. "In this alcove is the employees' bathroom. I keep it locked, as I do the storage room behind the refrigerated area and the back door." He unlocked the door and pushed it open. "This porch room is for employees only. We want all store customers coming in or out of the front door or café door near the register, where we can see them."

She looked around the long, broad porch spanning the entire back of the store with interest.

"My sister put a scattering of wicker furniture, a table and chairs and some decorative items out here to create a quiet break area," Walker explained. "It can be heated in winter, too."

"I like this room. It has nice views across the fields from the windows." She turned to head back into the store. "Where's your office?"

"It's up at my house on the hill, but I keep a laptop under the register so I can check emails, place orders, or work when it's not busy. You can bring one of your own and do the same if it's a slow day."

"I'd probably want to sit in that rocker by the front door and quilt instead." She turned to smile at him again. "I'm a quilter."

"As a hobby?"

"As a profession. I'm an artisan quilter. I create quilts and unique quilted items and sell them through my business site online, at The Full Moon store in Murphy, at the school where I teach, and through a variety of specialty store outlets. I also travel to festivals to demonstrate my art and sell it." She looked around. "I could put a quilt rack in the store and sell some quilts here if you wouldn't mind. There might be a market, and I'd give you a percent, of course."

He hesitated, not sure what to say.

She reached into her skirt pocket to pull out a business card. "You can look at my website sometime and see some of my work, decide if you think it fits the store look. I think it would."

"I'll do that."

Juliette glanced around. "You carry some really nice crafts in the store, many handmade. Who are your suppliers?"

He walked over to sit down on one of the soda fountain stools again. "I had some old contacts from the past I drew on and this fall, while the store was being built, I visited stores around the area to see what they carried, to get ideas for other products."

"I know that ploy. You note the company name of any item you like, google the company and check out their product line later to see what you might want to order." She grinned. "Sharon and I do the same thing looking for new ideas for the craft store in Murphy."

"As I mentioned, I'm fortunate, too, that my sister is a decorator. She's good at scoping out contacts, finding products to fit a certain look."

"Where does your sister live?" Juliette asked, perching on the stool beside him. "Is she the one everyone saw this fall visiting with the little girls?" Her eyes dropped to his ring finger on the counter. "I guess I assumed you weren't married but maybe I was wrong. Was that your wife?"

He felt himself scowling over her questions. "I'm not married, nor have I ever been," he answered, trying not to let his annoyance seep out. "My *sister*, however, is married. She and her husband own a decorating firm in another state and have twin girls. She came down last summer to help me decorate the house and to help with plans for the store. She brought the girls with her on one trip. Our parents are both dead and, as you guessed earlier from my retail knowledge, I owned another store before I started traveling and moved here."

"The family store you talked about?"

He inclined his head slightly.

"Do you still own it? Is it still in the family?"

"You ask a lot of questions." He tapped his fingers on the counter, a little annoyed at the direction of their conversation.

She shrugged. "Only the general sorts of questions people ask each other when they are getting acquainted. I simply wondered if it was still in the family, since you talked about your granddad's recipes and all."

"My cousin runs the store now. It gives me comfort that it's still in the family, and the store does still have the family name." He could have bitten off his tongue for adding that last bit.

"So the store is called Logan's?"

"Enough questions." He got up. "Do you think I've told you all you need to know about the job and the store?"

"Sure. *Non c'è problema*—no problem." She put her chin in her hand and gave him another sunny smile. "When do you want me to start?"

He pulled out his phone and scrolled to a calendar. "I want to open this Saturday. It would probably help if you could come in and work a day or two this week to get comfortable with the layout of the store, to try your hand at making a few of the café items, and to meet Quillen and his dad, Eldon Johnson. Both work for me part-time as needed. Quillen is a little young to carry full responsibility in the store by himself. His dad plans to cover some of the store shifts with him when I can't. On busy weekends, several of us may need to work."

"There might be a few fall weekends when I can't work. I scheduled several festivals where I'll demonstrate quilting and sell my quilts and products."

"We can work around that."

She nodded, glancing over his shoulder to the phone's calendar.

"Why don't I come in Tuesday and Thursday this week and then plan to work most of the day Saturday with Quillen and you for the opening. It will be a busy day. Everybody in the valley will drop by. You'll need all the help you can get then."

"That sounds good. I may get Eldon to help Saturday, too."

"You'll need him." She slid off the stool and shook out her skirt. "Well, I am tickled about getting this job. I told my grandmother only this morning I thought I'd get a part-time job while I'm home. Won't she be surprised when I tell her I already found one?"

Walker stood up to see her out.

"Speaking of Gramma ..." She stopped and put a hand over her mouth. "I promised her I'd check to see if I could get some of those Pippin apples for her from behind your house on the hill if they're ripe. Do you think it would be okay if I checked? If you'll let me pick some apples for her, I promise I'll bring you one of her apple pies and a jar or two of her homemade apple jelly after she cans. It's the best."

"Sure." He smiled. "I'll walk with you and we'll check on the apples."

"I know the way. You don't need to go with me."

"I need to take Marsh out for a walk, anyway. He's my dog."

"Okay then." She started toward the door.

"Besides, I see you're wearing another of those skirts. I wouldn't want you climbing out on a limb, tearing your skirt, and getting hurt again."

She wrinkled her nose at him. "You had to remind me of that, didn't you? I don't usually fall out of trees, you know. I grew up at the farm and climbed trees all the time."

"I thought you said you grew up in Italy." He turned to lock the door as they left.

"A little of both," she answered, starting down the steps after him. "My mother died when I was ten and I came to stay with my gramma and grandpa at Hollander Farm then. Daddy was in the military and not stationed where I could live with him at the time."

"But you stayed on here?"

"Yes. It was thought better for me than traveling around with Daddy."

"Tell me about that," he said as they started up a path through the field toward the house.

"I can tell you it's hard to be a newcomer in a small tightly knit community like Happy Valley. You'll see. You're an outsider and everyone else is connected or related in some way." She laughed. "I was different, too, being partly Italian. Many of the families in this area are descendants of the original settlers to Happy Valley, Cades Cove, or the Richwoods. Most are white by origin, which is true of many areas around the Smoky Mountains. It's not a very ethnically diverse area."

"Being partly Italian doesn't usually cause discrimination," he said.

"No. *Non solitamente*—not usually." She frowned. "But in my case it did. My father, Wyatt, had first been married to a valley girl, Patsy Rhea, who died shortly after my brother George was born. My daddy had chosen the military versus the farm, not a popular decision with my grandparents or the Rheas. After Patsy died, Daddy sensibly brought little George from Hawaii—where he'd been stationed—to Gramma and Grandpa's farm to live. Daddy came to see George whenever he could but he was soon sent abroad to a field hospital in a combat zone and then to Italy. He met my mother while stationed in Italy and remarried. That was the beginning of the trouble. The Rheas never quite forgave Daddy for marrying again."

Walker considered this. "Did your father marry too quickly after his wife's death?"

She shook her head. "No. It had been nine years but Daddy always said it was love at first sight—*amore a prima vista*." She paused, smiling over the words her parents had used so often. "I was born the following year, so my brother George is ten years older than me. After my mother died, Daddy brought me back to the valley to my grandparents as he had George. It's hard for a career military man to raise a small child alone."

Walker scratched his head. "I guess I'm still not seeing why this was a problem."

She kicked at a stone in the pathway. "That's because you haven't met Patsy Rhea's mother, Hettie Rhea. Patsy was Hettie and Stanley Rhea's only daughter. Hettie felt Daddy should never have married again and she resented me from the first moment she saw me because I was the product of that second union."

His mouth dropped open. "How could that be your fault?"

"I don't know. I've never figured it out, and it was hard enough coming to live here in America after my mother died without Hettie Myers Rhea and her husband Stanley all but hating me and treating me like I had the plague. Hettie forever stirred up trouble for me of one kind or another, too."

"Are you imagining any of this?"

"No, I wish I were. Wait until you meet Hettie Rhea. You'll see. She's a hard, strong-willed woman and not one to let go of any grudge, no matter how absurd. I heard that whenever Daddy came back to America with my mother, before she died, to stay at the farm and spend time with George, that Hettie Rhea refused to even acknowledge my parents if she ran into them. As George's other grandmother, she so poisoned George about my mother, too, that Mama was never able to build a strong and positive relationship with him. For a time, it caused real problems between George and me, too, when I first came, but we moved past it."

Walker thought about this as they walked on. "I'm sorry about that for you, Juliette. People can surely disappoint you."

"Yes, that's the truth." She stopped, her mouth dropping open. "Oh, look at your house," she said, changing the subject. "I haven't seen it since you renovated. It looks wonderful. *Bellissimo*! Not neglected and sad anymore." She put a hand to her heart. "You've done so much with it since last year. I am really impressed. I don't ever remember seeing the yard so nicely kept."

"Thanks, but I can't take too much credit. I had a lot of good help."

Walker could hear Marsh barking now as they drew closer to the house. "You walk on around to the orchard. I'll come find you after I get Marsh. I think I saw fruit on several of the trees."

"Okay. Can you bring me a strong bag or a little box to put some apples in? I originally planned to only look today but not pick."

"Sure."

A short time later, he came to find her in the orchard. Marsh barked at her and pulled at the leash until he spoke to him to sit.

"That's a beautiful, big dog." Juliette walked toward him slowly, putting a hand down for him to sniff. "What kind of dog is it?"

"He's a Chesapeake Bay retriever. I found him tangled in an old rope in a marshy spot on my travels, just a young gangly pup—skinny, lost, looking pretty sorrowful. There's no telling how he got back in that marsh. No collar. No chip. I camped around the area for a couple of weeks and tried to locate his owners. Put up signs. Checked with the vet I took him to and the area shelter. Marsh and I bonded while I was looking, so he traveled on with me."

"So Marsh traveled all over the United States with you." She scratched the dog's head and then squatted to pet him more, talking to him as she did.

Walker watched them together. "Marsh likes you. He doesn't like everyone."

"He's a handsome dog, looks strong, and his red-brown coat feels thick. I've read Chesapeake retrievers are fine hunting and water dogs. Loyal and protective, too. I'd say Marsh was a good companion for you."

"He has been. I hadn't planned on getting a dog for the trip. Thought it might complicate things. But fate had other ideas, I guess."

"Or the Lord did. I like to think He orchestrates good things for us." She looked up at him. "Do you believe in God?"

"Sure, raised in the faith." Seeing her eyes studying him led Walker to add, "Seeing all the beauty around our country gave me a greater appreciation for God, too."

"He's the original creator. I know what you mean." She smiled and got up, reaching out to take the bag he carried. "Nice canvas bag."

"It was a sample from one of the companies I buy from." He glanced up at the tree beside her. "Are the apples ready to pick?"

"Some are—enough for me to fill part of a sack for Gramma. She'll be pleased."

"There seem to be several fruit trees here. I found peaches on that old gnarled tree earlier this summer." He pointed toward it. "And I picked one of those yellow pears the other day but it didn't taste very good."

She giggled. "If you pick pears when still yellowish green, you need to let them ripen for several days before you eat them."

"Ahhh. I'll need to do some reading up about fruit trees." He leaned down to unclip Marsh's leash, deciding to let the dog sniff and run around the area while he helped Juliette with the apples.

"Did you know there are two pear trees in this old orchard? You always need two to pollinate to have fruit." She blushed slightly over the words. "There's also a peach tree, a persimmon tree, and three kinds of apple trees." She picked up a green apple from the ground. "The Pippin, like this, is an early-season apple; the Jonathan apple tree over there will fruit later in September, and the Arkansas Black apples on the tree near the old rock wall ripen in late October. My gramma told me farmers often planned their apple trees to have different varieties fruiting at different seasons."

She picked some Pippin apples from the lower branches while she talked, tucking them into the canvas bag. "Gramma Newell used to come here to pick fruit and bring me with her. I always loved all the wisdom she taught me about growing things, even though I don't have much of a green thumb or much of a love for working the farm. I'm a bit of a disappointment to my farming family."

"It sounds like you have other gifts if you quilt professionally."

"I do, but most women in the valley that quilt also work on the farm. They bake, freeze, can, and they love all aspects of working with the crops, caring for the animals, and growing things in the garden." She shrugged. "I'd rather climb up in a tree and read a good book or sit underneath it in the shade and design a quilt."

"Well, today, I think you should let me climb up in the tree if you need apples from higher up."

She turned to grin at him. "You think I might fall again?"

"You might, but even if you didn't, I don't want you to snag another of your pretty skirts."

"Tell you what." She looked up at the tree above her. "If you'll let me climb up on your shoulders, I can reach that branch heavy with fruit and get all the apples I'll need for Gramma."

"Okay, that would work." He looked around. "Climb on that old bench first; then you should be able to get on my shoulders if I squat down."

"Are you sure you can hold me?"

"I can hold you."

A few minutes later, Juliette had climbed neatly up on his shoulders and Walker held her legs steady while she reached to get the apples she wanted. "Just a few more," she told him, handing down two apples for him to put in the canvas bag she'd draped around his shoulder.

Enjoying the feel of his hands on her legs and looking up to watch her progress, he didn't see Marsh racing toward him until the big retriever jumped up to put his paws on Walker's chest, upsetting his balance so he and Juliette tumbled to the ground.

"Are you all right?" he asked Juliette as soon as he could catch his breath. She'd fortunately landed sprawled across him instead of falling backward and hitting her head.

"Yes, how about you?"

"Fine." He rubbed his arm. "That dang dog," he added, watching Marsh run off again, totally oblivious to the trouble he'd caused.

Juliette pushed herself up to look down at him. "This scene feels all too familiar." She giggled. "I think we first met this way." She scrambled to her feet, reaching down to offer him a hand this time.

He stood, brushing the grass and leaves off his clothes, and then winced and put a hand to the back of his head. "Ouch."

"Let me look at your head," she said, moving closer to put her fingers in his hair, checking for injury. "There's a bump where you hit the ground when you fell, but no blood. It might be a little sore tomorrow, but I think it's okay. Does it hurt?"

"Only a little. It's no big deal."

Coming around to face him again, she touched his cheek. "You've scraped your cheek, too." She traced her finger over it, the scent of her filling his senses.

"You can kiss it and make it better," he said, wrapping her in his arms and kissing her before she had time to answer, wanting to see if the kiss today would be as good as the one he remembered.

Giving a little sigh, she settled into his arms and kissed him back. "Ahhh, *molto dolce*—very sweet," she said at last, pulling back to smile at him. "That old memory had almost faded. Now I'll have a new one to savor."

He smiled at her. "I probably shouldn't have done that. You're my employee now. It's inappropriate."

"Well, we'll only kiss in the apple orchard and not in the store." She touched his cheek again. "I do like the way you kiss, Mr. Logan."

"Consider it a job perk," he said, kissing her again until Marsh came bounding up to nuzzle his head between them.

"Marsh is not so sure about sharing you," Juliette said, laughing and reaching down to hug the big dog curling around their legs. "He's had you to himself for a long time."

"He has." Walker glanced at his watch. "I hate to say this, but I really need to walk Marsh and put him in the house again before I head back down the hill. I have a delivery coming to the store at noon, so I'm in a time crunch today. Why don't you come with me and I'll fix you a hot dog at the store afterward."

She brushed off her skirt. "No, I need to get back to the farm. Gramma will be putting lunch on and I need to help her with it. She'll worry if I'm not back soon." She put a soft hand to his face. "You wash that scrape and put some medicine on it."

He nodded, picking up the canvas bag full of apples to hand to her. "Tell your Gramma Newell I'll be looking forward to that apple pie."

"I will." She dropped her eyes. "About that kiss ..." She hesitated.

He lifted her chin. "That kiss was even better than the one last year and that's saying a lot. I've thought about that day often, and about you, ever since."

Her eyes grew large. "You did?"

"I did, and I'd given up on ever seeing you again until you walked in the store today."

She bit her lip. "I doubted I'd ever see you again, either, since you said you were traveling and camping at Abrams."

He leaned down to kiss her lightly again. "Well, life has a way of giving us some sweet unexpected surprises sometimes, doesn't it?"

She blushed. "Yes, it does."

Marsh came running back to nudge his leg. "I'd better walk the dog and then get back to the store."

She nodded and started back down the pathway toward the road. "I'll see you Tuesday," she said, waving at him and reminding him of yet another memory he'd saved from before.

"*Arrivederci*," he said back softly, knowing only he would hear it.

CHAPTER 4

Juliette cut open another cardboard box of candy and then dumped it in the candy barrel in front of her.

"We sold a lot of these Sugar Daddy candy suckers this weekend," she said to Walker, who sat perched nearby on a stool behind the counter, working on his laptop.

He glanced up. "Those and more. We completely sold out of a lot of our store inventory and back stock. I'm placing orders now."

"Isn't that great? *Congratulazion!* The store had a fantastic grand opening on Saturday. I'm so happy for you about that."

"Well, I'm grateful you suggested asking Quillen and his dad, Eldon, to work with us that day. We needed the extra help. The store was packed all day. Quillen helped direct cars outside when the parking lot started jamming up and Eldon pitched in like a pro to help behind the soda counter."

Juliette opened a box of Necco Wafers to refill another of the candy barrels. Walker had dividers in the tops of each barrel so four different types of old-fashioned candies could be displayed.

"I like Eldon," she said as she arranged the candy. "This was the first time I've really gotten to know him. In fact, I met a lot of people who live in the valley and around the area at the opening on Saturday. I like meeting new people. Don't you?"

Walker frowned. "I liked seeing a big turnout."

She giggled. "I saw you frown before you replied. Everybody hit you up with a lot of questions, didn't they?"

"I don't see why people think it's their right to poke into your private life and to know everything about you just because you run the local store."

Juliette shrugged. "It's the Valley way and the way it is in most small communities. Only a little over five hundred people live here in Happy Valley, versus nearly two hundred thousand in Knoxville nearby. People take care of each other here. They know each other better than in larger urban areas. Isn't that one of the things that attracted you to the valley?"

"No. I just thought they needed a store here, and I liked the area and the house I bought."

She shook her head. "Well, if you weren't such a man of mystery, people would quit probing into your life. You have too many secrets."

"If I do, they're my secrets to keep."

Juliette added Tootsie Rolls to a final bin and then reached down to pick up the boxes piled beside her. "I've finished restocking the candy bins. I'll take these boxes to the trash outside and then start stocking the snack shelves. All those chips, peanuts, and candy bars went out the door quickly, too."

"You can add your empty boxes to the pile already on the back porch. I'll get Quillen to flatten them and put them in the trash later." He glanced at the clock. "School is out. Quillen should be here anytime."

"If that old truck of his doesn't break down again." Juliette laughed, heading toward the porch. "Bless his heart. That truck is a wreck, but I'm sure it's hard to afford much else at sixteen."

"He's saving up. I told him I'd match whatever he saved."

She raised her eyebrows as she stopped by the back door. "That's very generous."

"It's how my father taught us to save money."

"Yes, but you're not Quillen's father."

"No." He looked at her across the top of his computer. "But Quillen caught my vision for the store and he asked to work for me the first day I looked at the property. He's worked for me for over a year now, given up many weekends to help me clear brush, pull weeds, plant grass, clean out old sheds, paint, and later work with the building crew as needed on the store. When I take a trip, he stays at my house, walks Marsh, and watches out for things. He's been an invaluable help to me. I could afford to buy him a good used truck, but it wouldn't mean as much."

"I didn't know all that about Quillen, but I can see he admires you—and he obviously loves Marsh." She glanced toward the big dog, curled up in his bed by the back door.

"Marsh is crazy about Quillen." Walker's eyes moved to the sleeping dog, too. "Quillen plays with him, tosses balls and sticks for him, and takes him to swim. Marsh really loves the water. It's best not to ask him if he wants to go to the c-r-e-e-k." He spelled the word.

Juliette smiled. "Marsh is smart and you've trained him well."

"You have to train a large, high-energy dog like Marsh well or you could have a real problem on your hands." He stroked his chin in a gesture familiar to Juliette. "I was living in a Sportsmobile on the road the last two years with limited space in it. We were on the move, staying in new places all the time, meeting new people. I had to have a dog I could control and Marsh needed to show good manners, to not act aggressive or cause difficulties, in the places we stayed."

"He's doing great in the store," Juliette said, dumping the pile of boxes on the porch and then heading back into the store to perch on a stool by the soda counter. "He patrols, picks up trash and carries it to the trash can, lets the little kids pet on him, and it's rare that he ever acts even a little bit aggressive toward anyone."

"He's getting there. We're training in a new locale—both at the house and here in the store." Marsh lifted his head, seeming to know Walker was talking about him. "I want Marsh to be a reliable store dog as well as a good house pet so I don't need to leave him at the house alone every day. Dogs are pack animals; they really like companionship."

"I noticed you were teaching Quillen to work with Marsh." Juliette leaned over to pet the big dog as she headed back into the store.

"Yes. Quillen was letting Marsh call the shots with him and get out of hand. Quillen didn't seem to realize how important it is for a dog to respect you and your rules. You need to teach a dog to obey commands—to lie down, to sit, to walk at your side, to not jump on people or interact aggressively with other dogs."

The door swung open and two dark-haired boys tromped in noisily.

"Hi, Walker," they said almost simultaneously.

"Hey, guys. Where's your dad?"

"Not far behind us. We were biking and Dad's locking our bikes on the rack in front of the store. He said we could stop by to see you on our way home."

A tall dark-haired man with a long angular face came into the store then—greeting Walker with obvious affection, before glancing toward Juliette.

Walker's eyes followed his. "Jonas, have you and the boys met Juliette Hollander?"

"No, we haven't," the man answered.

"She works for me in the store part-time and lives across the road with her grandparents right now." He paused. "Juliette, this is Jonas Rasnic and his twin boys, Brevan and Bryan. They live on the property across the road from my place."

She stopped to think. "In the big rustic log home on the hill? Grandpa said someone bought it last year."

"Yes." Walker nodded. "Jonas moved to the valley a few months before I did. He's an artist. Maybe you've seen his work."

"Jonas Rasnic." She repeated the name, trying to place it. "I think I have. Big oils, mostly landscapes, rich colors, bold strokes?"

The man's mouth quirked in a smile. "Sounds like you've seen my work."

"I've seen it in a few galleries in north Georgia. I think you did a workshop one summer at the John C. Campbell Folk School, too."

"I did." He gave her a curious look.

She smiled. "I teach quilting there."

"You're a quilter, then?"

"Yes."

"My wife, Kimmie, would love to meet you. She's a fabric designer, and she hasn't made many friends in the valley since we came."

"It's hard to make friends quickly in a small, tight-knit community like Happy Valley," Juliette said, not adding that the Rasnics, like Walker, didn't fit the common mold of most of the residents in the area. The sprawling log home above Abrams Creek Road they'd bought came with a high sticker price as had Walker's house. "You tell your wife to stop by the store one day."

"I'll do that." Jonas glanced around. "The store looks great, Walker. Sorry we didn't get by for the open house. We spent the weekend in Atlanta at Kimmie's parents."

"Dad, can we get an ice cream cone?" one of the boys asked.

"Sure, if Walker doesn't mind making you one."

"Not at all. Study the board and name your flavor, boys," he said, closing his laptop.

"They'll both want chocolate," Jonas said. "But only one scoop each. It isn't long until Kimmie will be starting dinner."

Walker moved around the counter to scoop out chocolate ice cream for the boys and then began visiting with Jonas, the two catching up on their lives, while the boys enjoyed their ice cream cones.

Juliette busied herself getting boxes of snack items from the storage room and putting them on the shelves. The store had been busier at lunchtime earlier in the day but had quieted down this afternoon. Like the crafts store in Murphy where she worked, the Happy Valley Store had its busy times and its downtimes.

Several more customers—locals and tourists—came in while Walker visited with Jonas and the boys. Already behind the counter, Walker rang up their sales.

One of the men, buying a bag of ice and groceries to take to the campground, said, "It's great to have this store here now. We're camping at Abrams and I had to drive all the way into Maryville to pick up ice and groceries when we came last year." He glanced at the board behind the soda fountain. "I really like your soda fountain, too. We'll drive up for lunch tomorrow and bring our wives. They'll love this place with all the crafts you stock. Both always want to pick up some locally made items to take back to Indiana."

The two men left, followed by several locals who dropped in for milk, juice, and a few grocery items. Then Jonas and the boys left, leaving the store quiet again.

"It looks like you've made a friend in Jonas Rasnic," Juliette said.

"I met Jonas and the boys hiking on the Cooper Road Trail one day. We walked along together and got acquainted. The Rasnics were the first family to invite me over for dinner and to reach out a hand of friendship to me, after the Johnsons. It's convenient, too, that they live right across the street from my place. Jonas and I often hike and fish together now. I like him and I like Kimmie and the boys, too." He turned hazel eyes her way. "I think you'd like Kimmie. She's artistically inclined like you and well-known for her fabric designs. You'd have a lot in common."

"I gather they're from Atlanta."

"Kimmie is. Her parents own a couple of restaurants downtown. One in Buckhead. Jonas grew up traveling more than Kimmie, but he spent his teenage and college years in northern Georgia near Ellijay. His dad is a state park ranger and works at Amicalola Falls State Park. You probably know where the park is. It's not too far from Murphy."

"I've been there and the big waterfall is gorgeous."

Walker cleaned up the work counter as he talked. "Jonas is a big outdoor enthusiast. He and Kimmie came looking for a mountain home in the area and fell in love with the log house on the hill."

"I can see why. The views from the house are beautiful."

"The house came with two great areas to use for studios, too. It's probably why they fell for the place as soon as they saw it. Both of them work from home and Kimmie homeschools the boys."

"That explains why they were out biking this time of day on a

Monday."

The front door pushed open to let Quillen in.

"Hey, you guys," he said, flashing them both a big grin.

Marsh perked up at his voice, giving out a soft series of roo-roo sounds, typical of Chesapeakes.

"Hey, Marsh. Come give me a hello." Quillen squatted down, and the big dog bounded across the store to greet him, nuzzling Quillen and talking to him in doggy sounds.

"Quillen, do you want a hot dog for a snack?" Walker asked him. "I have some left over from lunch, still turning on the rack."

"Yeah, but I'm going to walk Marsh first." He slipped behind the counter to get the dog's leash. "I need to practice getting him to walk beside me like he's supposed to instead of bolting ahead and trying to jerk my arm out of its socket. He's a big guy."

Walker smiled. "Remember the commands I taught you." He reached under the counter to give Quillen a handful of dog treats from a jar. "Put these in your pocket and reward him when he does it right. Walk him up the loop trail through the field, around the house and back down again. I'll watch from the back. See how he's doing."

"Okay." Quillen leashed the dog and headed out the door.

Walker moved toward the back door, nearer the snack shelves where Juliette worked, so he could look out the window to see the boy and dog head up through the field.

Juliette came to peek over his shoulder. "He's doing good," she said, watching the big dog prance alongside Quillen.

"He is." He turned to look down at her with a soft smile. "So are you."

"You mean in the store?" She knew her breathing escalated with him so close now.

"Good in every way." He leaned down to kiss her.

"We aren't supposed to do this in the store," she whispered against his mouth.

"Rules are made to be broken." He kissed her again, making her mind spin, before he stopped suddenly to step behind a shelf as they heard footsteps on the porch.

Dade Claiborne sauntered in the front door, pulling off his white cowboy hat as he did. "Hey, sugar," he called to Juliette, walking toward her. "Your gramma said I'd find you here. I still can't believe you decided to work in this place." He looked around. "Nice setup. Too bad the guy decided to build it in Happy Valley. It's bound to go belly-up." He stopped, seeming to suddenly notice Walker.

"Dade Claiborne, this is Walker Logan." Juliette introduced the two. "Walker owns the store."

"Sorry, didn't see you behind that shelf before." Dade winked at Juliette. "Juliette here grabbed all my attention."

Walker sent her a questioning look.

She rolled her eyes.

"This is quite a place you've built," Dade continued, looking around. "Nice décor. Good look, just a bad location. I hope you're not offended I said so. You're not from around here, of course, so you wouldn't know much about business in this area. I've lived here all my life so I've got the edge on you. I own Claiborne's Auto over on the Airport Motor Mile on the highway heading into Knoxville. We get a lot of traffic in that location."

He wandered around picking up things and dropping them carelessly back into place as he talked. "Whose old wreck of a truck is that outside?"

"Quillen Johnson's," Walker answered, moving to look out the back window again.

"Is he that black kid that lives down the valley? I heard you hired him to work part-time for you, like Juliette." He moved closer to Juliette now. "Sugar, you know you don't really need to work over here at all. You came back from North Carolina to help your gramma. She's canning some late sweet corn today and I imagine she could really use your help. George's wife, Laura, is at the house giving her a hand, but you know that's a big job."

Juliette winced. Dade and her family frequently threw out these comments to try to make her guilty she wasn't drawn to farm work.

"You may not care for canning much," Dade said, as if reading her mind. "But your gramma's not getting any younger." He glanced around. "I'd say this Walker guy could get someone else to work here part-time, and if you need a little spending money I'll be glad to give you some since you and I are sort of promised." He raised his voice on those last words, glancing toward Walker as he moved closer to Juliette.

She crossed her arms in annoyance, frowning.

Dade winked at her and then leaned forward to try to kiss her cheek.

She pushed him back. "No, Dade."

"Aw, sugar," he started to protest, sliding an arm around her waist, but then heard a low growl.

Turning, they all saw Quillen come through the front door with Marsh, and the big dog was pulling on his leash and straining toward Dade, growling low in his throat.

"You'd better mind that dog, boy," Dade called out, pointing at Quillen. "If he takes a bite out of me, I'll file a lawsuit you won't be happy to see."

"Sit, Marsh," Walker said in a firm voice, moving toward the dog to take the leash from Quillen.

As Marsh sat and stopped growling, Walker added, "This is my dog, Mr. Claiborne, and he evidently thought you were threatening Juliette in some way. He's usually very friendly."

Dade backed a step away from Juliette now, still not comfortable with the dog, who watched him with unfriendly eyes. "A public store is no place for a big dog like this." He glared at Marsh. "He might hurt someone. You need to keep him chained up."

"Marsh is a great dog," Quillen burst out in defense. "I've never seen him act aggressive toward anyone before today and I've been around him for a year now. It was because you were pushing yourself on Juliette that he got upset. He heard Juliette say 'no' and it didn't look like you were backing off the way you should."

"You'd better be careful how you talk to me, boy," Dade said, moving toward Quillen and fisting his hand. "Haven't you been taught to respect your elders?"

A low growl began again in Marsh's throat as Dade drew closer to the boy.

Walker cleared his throat. "Mr. Claiborne, unless you came in the store to buy something, I think it might be good if you moved on now. Both Quillen and Juliette are my employees. I don't care to see either of them bullied."

"Bullied?" Dade's face grew red. "You don't know who I am around here, do you, Mr. Logan? But I'd suggest you find out. Mine is one of the most respected families in this valley and it will pay you to remember that. You'd better see to it that the next time I come in here that dog isn't here either. I could make a complaint to the sheriff about it, you know."

"Oh, for heaven's sake, Dade." Juliette frowned at him in irritation. "Marsh is a great dog. He just hasn't liked your actions today, but you shouldn't let it put your back up like this."

She walked over to take his arm. "I'm going to walk you out of here before you cause any more trouble. This is where I work and these are my friends. You had no reason to waltz in here being rude and threatening and it seems you've forgotten our talk on Friday night already...." Her voice trailed away as she led him out the door.

CHAPTER 5

"**W**ho was that?" Walker asked Quillen as Juliette pushed the front door closed behind her.

"That was rich boy Dade Claiborne," Quillen answered, squatting down to pet the dog. "I'm sorry I didn't control Marsh better."

"It's not your fault. Marsh sensed trouble, saw Dade move in on Juliette, and he reacted. Chesapeake Bay retrievers are very protective and they *will* respond aggressively if they feel threatened or think someone they love is being threatened."

Quillen hugged the dog again. "You wanted to protect Juliette. Didn't you, Marsh?"

The dog growled softly and looked toward the door.

"He's still worried about her," Quillen said.

Walker nodded. "Does that man have some claim on Juliette?"

"I don't know." Quillen shrugged. "He acted like he did, but it didn't seem like Juliette agreed."

Walker frowned. "Tell me about the Claibornes."

"They're an old valley family that owns a big farm down Happy Valley Road about a mile past the church. My sister Della Sue said they have ancestors dating back to some of the earliest settlers." He shrugged. "She's interested in stuff like that. Dade's father's name was R. D. Claiborne, a good man and enterprising. He started a little auto dealership that grew into a big one. It really helped his family financially. He built up the farm, put a lot of money away. I heard that Dade always loved working at the dealership with his dad while his younger brother, Ronnie, liked working at the farm."

Walker put Marsh's leash away while Quillen talked and then filled the dog's bowl by the back door with water.

"When R. D. died some years ago he left the dealership to Dade and the farm to Ronnie," Quillen continued. "R. D.'s wife, Onalee, still lives on the farm with Ronnie and his wife, Dottie. They have two little kids now. I can't remember their names, but Dade isn't married yet. I heard he's been sweet on Juliette for a long time but that she's never said yes to any of his proposals."

"You heard exactly right," Juliette said, coming back into the room. "Dade seems to find taking no for an answer difficult, however. He's always gotten pretty much what he wants."

"And he wants you," Walker said, catching her eye.

She crossed her arms and sat down on one of the stools at the counter. "It's complicated. We've been friends for a long time, even dated a little in the past. I see that for what it is but Dade keeps trying to see things differently."

"Sounds like a problem," Walker said.

Quillen moved behind the counter to find the hot dogs Walker had saved for him. "My brother, Cameron, says guys can't be just friends with girls, that a guy always has something else on his mind."

Walker laughed. "That sounds like one of Cameron's observations. I think he has a couple of girls on the string right now."

"Three. My sister Stella says he's a real ladies' man." Quillen spooned chili from the Crock-Pot to slather it over his hot dogs.

"Well, I believe a man and a woman can be friends," Walker said.

"Me too," Quillen said, sitting down at the counter to eat. He changed the subject. "Hey, there are two weird guys hanging out behind the parking lot. Have you seen them? They keep eyeing the store and ducking behind the trees whenever anyone drives by or looks their way. I saw them when I came in from school earlier and again when I came back from walking Marsh."

Walker felt himself stiffen, a thread of anxiety sliding up his spine.

"What did they look like?" Juliette asked. "Were they both tall skinny guys with short ratty beards? Wearing camouflage clothes or rolled-up blue jeans with beat-up boots? And was one of them wearing a scruffy brown fedora hat?"

"Yeah, how'd you know that?" Quillen looked surprised.

Walker walked over to the window to look out toward the parking lot, paying little attention to their conversation. "Maybe I'd better call the sheriff," he said. "I keep a gun in the safe, too, if we need it."

"Were you not listening to me?" Juliette said with impatience. "It's probably those crazy Ledford brothers." She started toward the door, moving past him. "I'll go talk to them."

"No." Walker grabbed her arm. "It might be dangerous."

She stopped to look at him. "Whatever is the matter with you? This isn't an attempted robbery we're talking about—just two goofy brothers who live here in the valley." She pulled her arm away from Walker, heading toward the door again. "Getting all upset or calling the sheriff won't help. I'll go see if I can get them to come in the store to meet you, but don't expect too much right away with Vernon and Harley. They're survivalists. Do you know what that is?"

Quillen laughed. "Yeah, crazy guys who always think someone is out to get them, to infiltrate the valley or something. I've heard about those Ledford brothers. They live in an old ramshackle house at the end of a dirt road on the mountain. Cameron said not to ever walk up there because they might shoot at me."

"He's probably right. They're very territorial." Juliette opened the door. "So if I get Vernon and Harley to come in here, you two stay calm and act nice. They can be a little jumpy, and they're definitely weird."

"I'll go with you." Walker moved forward.

"No." She pushed him back. "They don't know you yet. And you being an outsider, they probably think you're one of *them*."

"*Them*?"

"The term *them* doesn't have a definitive answer with the Ledford brothers. I doubt you'd get a decent explanation if you tried." She headed out the door, calling to the brothers as she did.

"You think she'll be all right?" Walker said, watching her head across the porch toward the parking lot.

"Yeah," Quillen said, finishing off his hot dogs and guzzling down the last of a can of cola. "Dad says they're kooky, but probably not dangerous except to strangers."

A short time later Juliette returned with two tall mountain boys behind her. One glowered, looking around him uneasily, while the other grinned somewhat sheepishly, peeking in the windows as he came across the porch.

Juliette pushed the two men in the door ahead of her. "I told Harley and Vernon they'd stopped by at just the right time, that we were giving away free hot dogs this afternoon as a Monday special." She sent Quillen a significant look and pointed at the last two hot dogs still turning on the rack.

"Yeah, I'll fix them right now," he said, catching on quickly. "Our Valley Dogs with chili and slaw are great. Do you guys want both chili and slaw with your hot dogs?"

The men nodded, shuffling their feet and looking around uneasily. The taller man in the brown fedora focused on Walker then, letting his eyes slide over him suspiciously. "You the owner of this place?" he asked.

"Yes. Walker Logan." He walked toward the man and held out his hand.

When the man didn't respond or introduce himself, Juliette answered for him. "This is Harley Ledford." She prodded him forward. "Harley, it's okay to shake Walker's hand. You be nice."

With some hesitancy Harley offered his hand and then quickly withdrew it.

Juliette pushed the other man forward. "This is Harley's younger brother, Vernon."

Walker reached out his hand again.

"Howdy," the man said, grinning a little foolishly as he shook Walker's hand a little too fast.

"Hot dogs are ready," Quillen said, putting two plates on the counter. "You guys want a couple of cokes with that?"

"Sure." Harley glanced at him as he sat down on a stool at the counter, and then he turned to speak to Walker. "I heard you had interracial types working in here, Italians and African Americans."

Walker watched Quillen's eyes widen.

Juliette snorted. "Don't take offense," she said to Quillen. "I grew up here and I'm still suspicious in Harley's mind because I have an Italian heritage."

"You can't be too careful," Harley said.

"Yeah, you have to watch about outsiders," Vernon said, dropping his voice. "You never know about people."

Quillen passed a telling look to Walker. "I think I'll take Marsh out for a walk again," he said. The big dog was watching the two men somewhat warily, picking up on their unease and peculiarity.

"Good idea," Walker said. "You can take him out the back way."

Juliette settled down on the stool beside Harley while Walker moved around behind the counter. He filled two glasses with cola for the men and snagged them each a bag of chips when he saw Vernon eyeing them wistfully.

"You've been gone a while," Harley said to Juliette. "But I noticed you'd come back."

"Grandpa had a little heart attack so I thought I'd come home for a time to help him and Gramma on the farm."

"Are you helping by settin' up in the mimosa tree drawin' pictures?"

Juliette laughed, raising her eyes to Walker's. "You can tell these two have known me for a long time."

"She used to draw purty pictures for me." Vernon grinned.

Juliette crossed her leg. "Harley and Vernon live up on Ledford Mountain at the end of the Cooper Road behind our farm. They've lived there for as long as I can remember."

Harley scowled at her. "You ought not to tell folks where we live." He glanced at Walker and lowered his voice. "Especially outsiders."

She patted Harley on the back. "I doubt Walker will want to come up to visit. Neither your father nor either of you have ever been ones for hospitality. Besides, you've got that place of yours barricaded around like a fort. Some of those visible guns sticking out of the holes of your house would scare most people off before they knocked."

"Daddy's been gone five year," Vernon said.

"I remember," Juliette said.

Walker saw Harley watching him. "Where are your people from?" he asked.

Juliette answered before he could. "Walker has been traveling around the US before he settled down here."

Harley's eyes widened further.

Seeing Harley's unease, Walker added, "My family are from out west, but I liked it here and decided to make it my home."

As Juliette got up and walked across the store to pick out two candy bars for the boys, Walker leaned over to Harley and said softly so she couldn't hear, "I needed a safe place to live away from them."

Vernon's eyes grew wide. "They after you?"

Walker nodded, putting a cautionary finger to his lips and glancing toward Juliette.

"We'll keep a watch," Harley said.

Walker leaned toward him again. "Especially keep a watch for a black van with out-of-state plates."

Vernon glanced around. "The kind with them tinted windows."

"Just that kind. You know what they're like," Walker added, keeping his voice low.

"We'll watch," said Harley again. "We know everything that goes on in this valley."

Juliette came back to perch on the stool beside him, passing two candy bars across to Harley. "Well, if you know so much," she said, catching only his last few words, "how come the two of you haven't figured out who's been doing all the thieving around here?"

Harley scowled at her while he handed one of the candy bars to Vernon.

She turned to Walker. "A rash of petty thefts have been going on around the valley for about a year now. Grandpa and George were talking about it at breakfast today. The thieves seem to know when people are gone to work or away on a weekend trip, so they know exactly when to hit."

"I haven't heard about that," Walker said.

"That's because you're an outsider," Harley told him. "Ain't nobody going to tell you much. There was talk it might have been you doing the thieving. It started about the time you moved here."

"That's ridiculous," Juliette sputtered. "A man who could afford to build a store like this, and buy Old Stone House and renovate it, would hardly need to steal bikes, motorcycles, cars, and electronics."

"Some folks get rich stealin'," Vernon added. "But it be wrong."

"It's probably *them* stirring up trouble around the valley." Harley gave Walker a significant look. "You might want to lock up your place and get some ammunition. For protection."

"I doubt Walker is going to stockpile weapons because of random thefts going on around the valley." Juliette looked at Walker. "But it might be wise to lock up the store and house securely. The losses might not hurt you as much as they do some of the people in the valley who don't have much, but no one likes to see their things stolen."

"Who do the police think is behind all this?" Walker asked.

Juliette shrugged. "They don't have a clue, and small thefts so far from town don't get as much attention as crime in more populated areas."

"That's why we're trying to look into it ourselves," Vernon said, leaning forward with an excited gleam in his eyes.

"Well, you two be careful skulking around everywhere," Juliette warned. "I've heard a lot of folks saying you brothers might be doing the thieving. You certainly know the valley well enough."

Vernon sat up straight, looking horrified. "We don't steal. No Ledfords steal. It's not our way."

"I know that." She reached out to pat his arm. "But a lot of folks don't, and people are getting anxious and upset about all these thefts and starting to watch their homes and property more carefully. You keep in mind that many of them have guns, too."

"You think they'd shoot at us?" Harley asked.

"They might without stopping to think," Juliette said. "Grandpa was warning George and Laura's kids Kirsten and Robert to be more careful about going exploring and cutting through people's private property. Folks are really on edge right now."

The door opened, letting in a group of tourists with obvious New Jersey accents.

"Them folks are from *away*," Vernon hissed. "You can tell by how they talk. We gotta go now. You'uns be careful."

The brothers stood up and edged toward the door.

Walker followed them. "Remember to keep a watch," he reminded them quietly. "Stop in and talk to me every now and then, too."

Harley nodded, opening the door to glance around carefully before he walked outside.

Vernon looked back with longing at the counter before following Harley out the door. "When we come by to talk, do you think we might get more hot dogs?" he asked.

"Sure, anytime you come in to report," Walker said, biting back a smile as he closed the door behind them.

An hour later after the tourists and an influx of late afternoon shoppers had finished their buying, and after Quillen and Marsh had returned, Juliette commented, "Walker, you actually got on rather well with the Ledford brothers."

"Better than with Dade Claiborne." Walker gave her a pointed look.

She wrinkled her nose. "Dade can be difficult."

"Did you go out with him Friday night?" Walker asked. "I heard you mention something about seeing him when you hauled him out of the store."

Her face flushed. "I got trapped into it by the family. They're fond of Dade and …" Juliette's voice trailed off.

"They'd like to see you make a match with him?" Walker finished.

She twitched uncomfortably. "The two families have been friends for a long time. It would be considered a good alliance."

"I see."

She leaned toward him. "No, you *don't* see. My family is interested in Dade, but I am not interested in Dade. I keep trying to make that perfectly clear to my family, as well as to Dade, but they are not listening to me." She crossed her arms in annoyance. "I went out with Dade on Friday to make it clear to him once again that I did not want our relationship to progress to the next level. Or to progress further than being friends and neighbors at all."

"I didn't get the impression he got that message."

Quillen jumped into the conversation. "Dade acted like he thought you and him were an item, Juliette. Maybe going out with him wasn't such a good idea. Cameron says if a girl says she'll go out with a guy, it means she likes him."

Walker smirked. "I think I've heard that, too."

"Oh, you two." She reached under the counter to get her purse. "I'm going home now and leaving you to your fun. Gramma will be needing help with dinner."

"Especially after being so worn out from doing all the corn by herself." Walker couldn't help teasing her.

Surprising him, she walked over and grabbed up a handful of his shirt. "Don't you start that with me, Walker Logan. I get quite enough of those kinds of comments from my family. And I'd like to add that Laura volunteered to come and help Gramma put up corn today because she so enjoys doing it. Laura has f-a-r-m all through her genetics. I don't." She said the last two words slowly and emphatically.

"Sorry." Walker apologized. "See you tomorrow?"

"Yes, and make a note on your calendar for next Tuesday that I promised to go to my friend Amy's to help with her little girl Rose's birthday party. I'll be in at about one that day. Can you handle lunch on your own?"

"Sure."

"You can call my dad to help if it gets busy," Quillen added.

"I'm sure I'll be fine."

After she left, Quillen said, "She seemed right upset about Dade, didn't she?"

"Yeah, I got that memo."

Quillen changed the subject. "Do you think those guys, Harley and Vernon, are going to cause us any trouble?"

"No," Walker answered. "But try to stay on their good side if they come in the store. Give them free hot dogs if no one's around. Guys like that are good to know. They can watch your back."

"Why would you need guys like that to watch your back?" Quillen scratched his head. "Those survivalist types are a little crazy, thinking people are out to get them."

Walker busied himself at the counter, not wishing to get into this subject too much with Quillen. "Well, it's better having the Ledford brothers on our side than thinking we're suspects and out to get them."

"I suppose that's a point." Quillen began to walk around straightening stock on the shelves of the store. "The person I guess we need to worry about more is that Dade Claiborne guy. Are you going to keep Marsh away from the store because of him?"

"No." Walker frowned. "This is my store. Dade Claiborne doesn't have any say here."

"He sure thinks he does." Quillen snorted. "He has a nice family, but I don't think much of him, I can tell you. I didn't like the way he acted around Juliette, either."

Walker frowned. "Another good reason to keep Marsh in the store."

Quillen got a broom out of the closet and started sweeping up while the store was empty. "Did you know that Dade Claiborne is building a great big house on top of the mountain behind the valley? Cameron showed it to me one day when he was checking listings up there."

He paused to lean on his broom. "Dade's father sold off part of the family's property to one of those developers who's building fancy homes with mountain views up there. Cameron said it was land they couldn't farm and with the new development starting, it made good sense to sell it. Cameron told me Dade asked his father if he could keep a piece of the land at the end of the subdivision so he could build a house of his own up there someday. Now that his dad's gone, he's building it—a huge fancy place. Cameron showed it to me. Dade must be making a lot of money with the car business to afford that big a house, plus the expensive car he drives and all the money he spends left and right."

"Not all good businessmen are nice people," Walker said.

"Yeah, I know that," Quillen said, and then changed the subject. "I've almost got enough money saved up for a new truck now. Will you go with me and Dad to help us find a good used one?"

"Sure, and remember our deal. Whatever you save, I'll double."

"Dad said you didn't need to do that."

"I know. I want to do it. You've been a good help to me this year." He looked across the counter at the boy. "Money isn't a problem for me, Quillen. Giving you money to help with a truck would be like you giving me ten dollars because you wanted to. It's not a big deal for me."

Quillen considered that. "Okay, but I don't want to buy my truck from Dade Claiborne's business."

Walker laughed. "You can be sure we won't."

CHAPTER 6

Juliette smiled to see the colorful balloons tied on the mailbox when she pulled up to the Butlers' farmhouse off Happy Valley Road the following Tuesday. It was an older two-storied house, painted a soft blue with red trim, where Juliette had spent many happy hours. She felt glad she'd been able to get off work today for Rose's fourth birthday party. Rose was her godchild, and little Rose's mother, Amy Boone Butler, had been Juliette's best friend since the first year she came to Happy Valley.

Juliette could hear the excited voices and laughter of the children as she parked her car and walked around to the backyard of the farmhouse. With the weather sunny and fair, the party was being held outside on a large open patio under the shady arms of a giant maple.

"Hi, Juliette." Amy Butler waved a greeting from a spot by two picnic tables pushed together and decorated in colorful party attire.

Juliette walked over to give Amy a hug and put her gift for Rose on the table amid a tumbled pile of other gifts in gaily wrapped boxes and gift bags.

"Where's the birthday girl?" Juliette glanced around. Usually Rose, and little Adam, Amy's son, ran to greet her the minute she arrived.

"Mother is entertaining all the children with Pin the Tail on the Donkey on the side of the barn." She pointed.

"Wow. I'm impressed." Juliette laughed. "How did your mom get out of her college classes to come to Rose's party?"

"She got a colleague to cover her early class, but she has to leave soon to drive back to Maryville for her Appalachian culture class." She gestured toward an outdoor chair. "Sit down for a minute and talk. Mother has captured the kids' attention for now, but at their age it won't last long."

Juliette dropped into the chair beside Amy. "Rose has a built-in birthday party group with your daycare kids." Her eyes scanned the group of small children. "How many do you keep now?"

"Mostly the same ones I had last year when you were here. I keep Seth and Barbara Jean's children—Viola, four and a half; the twins, Patrick and Paxton, three; and the baby Evalee, who's one." She pointed out the children as she named them. "I also still keep Travis and Joanne's two, Carleen, three, and Minnie, one and a half." She smiled. "Look how much Minnie has grown since you were here last. She's the one jumping up and down in the playpen with Evalee, watching the other kids and wishing she was big enough to play."

"You didn't have Evalee last year."

"No. Barbara Jean's mama kept her at first, but when Evalee started pulling up and crawling around, her mother couldn't keep up with her anymore. She has back trouble."

Juliette frowned. "Amy, you know that means you have eight children here now, counting Rose and Adam. Didn't you tell me the state regulations say you can only keep seven maximum in your home?"

"I know, I know." She made a face. "Mother has been after me ever since I took Evalee, but Barbara Jean couldn't find anyone else, and you know she and Seth can't afford those fancy daycares in town." She heaved a sigh. "There are several other families who have been asking me to keep their children, too. There really aren't any daycare centers nearby except for mine."

Juliette smiled at her sweet-faced friend. "And everybody knows you're wonderful with the kids and that you've fixed up that big playroom off the back of your house and have all this great outdoor area most city daycares don't."

"Well, that playroom in the house seems smaller every day as the kids keep growing, Juliette. What worries me, too, is that next year Rose and Viola will go to kindergarten. Somebody will need to take them to school and pick them up. I'm not sure how I'm going to manage that." She paused. "If I could use the community center, keep more kids, and start an after-school program that would be so nice. With a bigger place like that and more children, I could afford to hire extra help. There are several rooms in that building and a big play yard in back. It would be a good location."

"It sure would, and the building sits mostly empty. Have you talked to anyone about it? Surely the community would love to see the building used and especially for something as needed as a daycare center."

Amy wrinkled her nose. "Have you looked inside that community center lately—really looked closely—or walked around outside? It's in bad shape. It would never pass inspection for a place to keep kids."

"That's too bad," Juliette said. "Now that I think about it, I guess the building is getting pretty run-down. Would it take a lot to fix it up?"

Amy sighed. "A lot more than Keith and I have."

"Well, until you get a situation worked out, you need to talk to Barbara Jean and tell her she's going to have to find someone else to keep Evalee. Amy, you don't want to risk losing your license."

"I know, but the extra money for keeping Evalee really helps right now. Keith lost another job."

"Oh, Amy, I'm sorry. He liked that job, too. What happened?"

"They told him they needed to cut back, but Keith knows it was really because of his leg. He fell twice in the last two weeks, once with an armload of boxes, too. Some items got broken that were valuable. Keith offered to pay for them, but ..." Her voice drifted off.

"Maybe the store really did need to cut back."

Amy gave her a look. "No, and Keith's taking it really hard this time. He feels so diminished as an amputee, and about the time he gets his confidence up and starts feeling good about himself again, something happens to take him down."

"Is he depressed?" Juliette asked, remembering some of the early dark days Keith went through as he came to terms with losing most of his leg after a bomb explosion in Iraq.

"Not that he would talk about, but I can tell it upsets him."

"Where is he today?"

"He and Grandpa are out at the south end of the farm, plowing up the big field there, since the harvest is finished. They're adding fertilizer to restore nutrients to the soil, too, before they get ready to plant again." A little smile crossed her face. "Grandpa is keeping Keith busy around the farm so he won't get into a funk."

"I'd say Keith's grandfather can use the help at his age, too." Juliette crossed her legs. "The farm will be Keith's one day. He needs to learn every aspect of it while he can. You know he loves the farm, too. Isn't it enough for Keith with his problems?"

"It could be, but it's expensive to keep a farm. You know that. And we're still paying off bills for things not covered by the VA." She made a face. "Keith hates it that I have to run the daycare here at our home."

"Why?" Juliette turned to her in surprise. "Surely Keith doesn't think you should be the little wife sitting at home and not working?"

Amy made a face at her. "No. Keith simply doesn't want to feel dependent. He also hates the fact that I had to start the daycare while our own children are still so small and that I work so hard with it."

"Have you minded so much?" Juliette asked. "You always used to love to babysit, even when I never liked it, and you said you wanted to teach kindergarten or manage a nursery school one day."

"Yes, I did, but that dream didn't involve starting—and running—a daycare center around all of Keith's rehab and recovery with two small children of my own. If you remember, I started this daycare when Rose was a toddler and I hardly had a month's break after birthing Adam before I was back at it again." She shook her head. "Juliette, chasing after a group of preschool kids every day doesn't leave much time for anything else. After the kids are picked up, I still have my children to take care of, plus dinner to fix for everyone, and the laundry and cleaning to do in the house. Sometimes I envy you all your single freedom."

Juliette put a hand over hers. "It might make you feel better for me to tell you that sometimes I envy you with your wonderful husband and two gorgeous children."

Amy squeezed her hand. "I guess I'm simply feeling down today about Keith's job. He's done so well recovering after getting injured, facing the shock of losing his leg, and having to leave the military. I hate for him to experience another disappointment, even a little one."

"Keith has good administrative and leadership skills. He would be a good help in running a larger daycare center if you could find a place. Would he feel better about your business if the two of you shared it?"

Amy glanced at her in surprise. "You know, he probably would, and Keith would be good working with the older children. He could drive the school runs, as well, if we owned a van. In fact, Keith has often talked about how the community center would be a good place for scouts or youth programs, as well. He's always worked with kids, even when in high school."

"I remember that."

"Oh, well." She shrugged. "It's all pipe dreams now. All those dreams cost money we don't have and aren't likely to have anytime soon. Life is what it is."

The children's game broke up, and Amy's mother Lenora directed the little group toward the outdoor center of swings, slide, seesaw, and several other play structures before heading their way.

"Hey, you sweet thing," she said to Juliette, leaning over to kiss her on the cheek and then sitting down in the chair beside her. "I heard you were back. You haven't been to see me yet."

"Mama, you know Juliette just started working at the new store," Amy reminded her.

Lenora waved a hand. "Yes, and I've been meaning to get by there.

But I attended a conference the weekend that the store opened and I've been playing catch-up ever since." Her eyes moved to the group of children laughing and enjoying the playground. "Whew! Keeping all those little ones on task sure was a challenge."

"It looked like you were doing all right." Juliette grinned. "They're the perfect age to enjoy playing Pin the Tail on the Donkey."

The three women chatted for a few minutes until Lenora glanced at her watch. "I'm glad I could get out of the office this morning to come for an hour or two on Rose's special day—and I enjoyed seeing you, Juliette—but, regretfully, I need to head back to campus now. I can't be late for my class."

"Thanks for coming, Mama," Amy said, rising as her mother did to give her a hug. "Rose loves the little playhouse you bought her. Thanks so much for that." She pointed toward the colorful structure on the play lawn. "Look how much fun she, Viola, and Carleen are already having, playing in it right now."

Lenora patted Amy's cheek. "I still remember how you and Juliette loved the old playhouse behind our home when you were small. It brings back fond memories for me to see the girls playing in their little house and having such a good time."

"I'll text you some pictures of the party later, Mama."

"You do that." Lenora picked up her purse from the table and rooted around in it for her keys. "Keep your spirits up about Keith, too," she said to Amy. "He'll be okay, and he does have the farm. Remember that. Much of the strength of his identity is bound up in this farm. And it was smart of Raylan Butler to get Keith right back out in the field today working and to not let him brood about losing that job."

"Thanks for the money, too, Mama," Amy said quietly.

"It's nothing, but don't tell Keith about it. That's why I brought cash. Tell him it's birthday money for Rose if you need to mention it; go buy Rose some new clothes or something so Keith won't get in a snit about it." She draped her bag over her shoulder. "He can be so proud, you know."

"I know." She walked with her mother to her car, and Juliette watched the two fair, blond women with fondness. Lenora had lost her husband, and Amy's father, when Amy was only a toddler, and raised Amy alone while working full-time at the college. With Lenora's home so near the Hollander farm, Gramma kept Amy many days after school, and Juliette played at Amy's as well, spending the night on weekends and learning many life lessons from Lenora's wisdom and strong ambition. Juliette had admired Amy's mother, and Lenora encouraged her to follow her own dreams, to work hard for what she wanted, and to be proud of who she was, of her own talents and gifts.

Looking back to a time in the past, Juliette recalled Lenora saying, "You're more like me than my own daughter."

"How's that?" she'd asked, taken aback at the words.

"You have a strong drive and ambition. You're restless, and need to find a way to utilize all that creativity and those ideas bubbling in you."

"Amy has dreams," Juliette had defended.

"Of course she does." Lenora had smiled at her. "But they are quieter ones. Amy wants to love and be loved, to marry and raise a family, and she would be content to live right here in the valley all her life. My guess is she'll do it with Keith Butler."

Juliette had been surprised Lenora realized how much in love Amy and Keith were at that time.

"I'm not blind, Juliette. They've dated since starting high school, and Amy has known Keith all her life. I've watched their relationship grow. It's obvious the two are in love."

Remembering several late-night conversations with Amy, Juliette had told Lenora, "Amy's afraid you'll be disappointed in her if she marries Keith and doesn't go on to college."

"I'll be sure to let her know it's her happiness I'm most interested in. There will be time enough for more education if she wants it later." Lenora had smiled then. "I know Keith is going straight into the military after all that high school JROTC. Amy will want to follow as soon as she can. She'll grow and mature as she travels and there will be colleges in the places where Keith will be stationed."

Her thoughts drifting back to the present, Juliette looked across the lawn to watch Amy hug her mother goodbye. Lenora had never pushed Amy to be something she was not.

Amy headed back to join Juliette then. "If you'll watch these kids for a few minutes, I'll go inside, change Minnie and Evalee, and then bring out lunch and all the birthday fixings for the party. Would you mind?" She grinned at Juliette, seeming happier than before—her usual sunshiny nature popping back into place. "If a riot breaks out, you call me."

"I'll be fine," Juliette said, waving her toward the house. "I'm going to walk over to see Rose's new playhouse while you're gone."

An hour or two later, the party over, Juliette opened the door to the Happy Valley Store to let herself in. "I'm only a few minutes late," she called out to Walker, spotting him behind the counter.

"I'm docking your pay," he teased. "How was the birthday party?"

"Crazy and fun, like you'd expect with eight children under five."

"Did you get lunch?"

"Sure. Cute little sandwiches, fruit cups, celery sticks with pimento cheese in them, birthday cake and ice cream. I can't complain." She grinned at him. "It was a nice break from hot dogs."

"I think most of the lunch crowd is gone," he said. "Come talk to me while I clean up behind the counter."

"I can do that and you can sit down and rest."

"No need. It hasn't been busy." He began putting clean glasses back on the shelves while she walked over to perch on one of the soda stools.

"Tell me about your friend," he said. "You told me you've known her since childhood."

"You'll meet her soon, I'm sure. Amy is a lovely, fragile-looking blonde, but she's much tougher than she looks." Juliette propped her elbows on the counter. "I've watched her go through far too many sorrows."

"What kinds of sorrows?"

"Her father was tragically killed when she was a toddler—hit by a tree that fell after being struck by lightning. Can you believe it?" Juliette made an effort to smooth back a swatch of wavy hair escaping the clip she'd tried to contain it with today. "Amy and I both lost a parent young and we knew we liked each other the first day we met. It's like that sometimes, you know."

He sent her a smile over his shoulder. "Yes. Sometimes you do know right away. So you've been friends all these years?"

"Best friends since we were ten years old." She studied his back while he worked cleaning up from lunch. "Did you have a best friend as a boy?"

"Sure. Two best friends—my cousin, Stewart, and our friend Burton. We all three lived on the same street, went to the same school, played together, loved all the same things. A happy threesome all through school."

"Are you still friends?"

"We are." He said the words in a clipped tone, not adding more, and then changed the subject. "Why did you say your friend has known sorrows? You must have meant more than losing her father so young."

"I did." She pulled a straw from the dispenser to play with while she talked. "Amy married her high school sweetheart, a valley boy named Keith Butler, right after graduation. I know you've seen the Butler farm where Keith grew up with his parents and grandfather. It's that big blue farmhouse down on Happy Valley Road past the church on the left. Pretty place."

"I've noticed it."

"Well, Keith is a super nice man, always has been. He lost his parents in an auto accident while in high school. His grandmother died not long afterward. Then Keith lost most of his leg in the war."

"In Iraq?"

"Yes, from one of those mines that blew up, a tragic thing. Several others were injured and some died. I know Keith was lucky, but sometimes I guess he doesn't feel that way. He's faced a lot of difficulties with his leg, recovery, rehab, and all. Job discrimination has been the worst lately."

He turned to give her a questioning look.

"Keith just lost another job he liked. Amy was upset about it today. It makes things difficult for them financially—and emotionally hard for Keith. Amy told me Keith often feels bad about her being the primary breadwinner of their family with her daycare center."

"Maybe Keith will find something else soon. Many employers are very supportive of amputees and those injured in the military."

"So I've heard, but Keith's experiences haven't been very positive." Juliette sighed. "I wish I was rich."

"Why?" Walker snorted. "Having money has its problems, too."

She raised her chin. "Well, I'd like to try it. Look what you've been able to do because you had money. You built this dream store you envisioned and watched it come to life."

"What would you build?" he asked, turning to wipe the counter and shifting the subject slightly.

"Perhaps my own little house if I decided to stay here. I never can figure out where I belong." She shook her head. "But what I'd really like is to have money to help some of the people in the valley. There are a lot of poor people in Happy Valley, Walker. Many struggle although they seldom complain. Most are good, wonderful people, and I'd like to make some of their lives easier and make some of their dreams come true."

"Like what?"

"Today, Amy wished the community center wasn't in such disrepair so she could use it for an enlarged daycare center and start an after-school program there. I suggested Keith could help her with that, drive the kids to the center after school, work with the older children's activities, and do the administrative tasks. He's good at that kind of thing; he has a degree in business."

"And?"

She put her hands on her hips. "And the Butlers don't have the money to fix up that community center, nor does the community. It looks simply awful! I stopped by to look at it more closely on my way back to the store today. I knew it was getting run-down, but I didn't realize how much it had deteriorated. It's sad to see. It was once the grade school in this valley, you know, so it's actually ideal in layout for a daycare center and it's centrally located. It has a nice backyard play area, if a little overgrown now, plus ample yard space in front. I can imagine a basketball court and envision civic groups or scout groups using the center, too."

"I looked at that building when thinking about a store. It has a good business location. There's room for expansion. With a new roof, paint, repairs, and some added space it would be a great place for community meetings and for a daycare center, like you said."

"It's hard for the families in this area to afford the childcare centers in town and they have to drive so far to get to them, too."

"Would Amy's husband Keith be willing to oversee the center if the place got fixed up? Or is that only a pipe dream of yours and Amy's?"

She considered this. "I think Keith would like the idea. He's always loved the valley and its people. He's very capable—won leadership awards in high school and in the military. He won't brag about it, but he got top honors in JROTC in high school. He was always a school leader and a sweet guy, too, unlike Dade." She wrinkled her nose.

"I gather that despite being a valley boy and making some money, Dade isn't rushing in to help folks around the area."

No." She frowned. "Not unless there's something in it for him."

The two got busy in the store with customers, but a little later in a lull, Walker came over to lean against a counter where Juliette was making a new arrangement of craft items.

"What else would you do if you had a lot of money?" he asked.

She continued working as she answered. "You heard Mackie Phillips talking in here earlier. There's been another of those thefts in the valley. They hit several of the Walker family homes this weekend while they were in Gatlinburg for a family wedding and staying overnight." She stopped from her task to make a face. "Now how did they know those families would be gone at the same time and that all their homes sat near each other on family land? They hit all four homes. Took computers, televisions, tools, and farm equipment. They even took Pearline and Earline's new truck and they needed that truck."

"Pearline and Earline?" Walker raised an eyebrow at the rhyming names.

"Twins—Eldridge and Ada Blanche Walker's two unmarried daughters," Juliette explained. "A lot of Walker women never marry. Earline and Pearl—Pearline usually just goes by Pearl— act as the valley animal rescue team. They take in strays, ferals, hurt animals, and then help to find homes for them. See, there's another good work I'd fund if I had money. Earline and Pearl do all that work on their own for no remuneration and all for such a worthwhile cause."

She lifted her eyes to his. "The thieves stole their truck they use to put their traps in and to transport their animals in. It will cause a real hardship for them. They also stole their computer, and the sisters advertised a lot of their animals through a blog and their Facebook page. It's so mean for thieves to take things from people who have so little and who do such good work."

"Don't all the Walkers live across the ridge from the store along Bell Branch Road?"

"Yes, and you know that's a very remote, little-traveled road. Who would be back in that area to know the Walkers would all be gone? It's creepy to think someone in our valley is watching everything and everybody so closely to know things like that."

"I agree. What did the police say?"

"Very little that comforted anyone." She opened another cardboard box to add more Smoky Mountain note cards to the display. "The sheriff's office sends a different police officer over here every time from Maryville. They all keep saying they're working on it, that it must be an inside job, probably kids who live nearby needing drug money or something. But so far they haven't found a single suspect. To be quite frank, no one in the valley thinks the police department is working very hard to resolve the thefts."

Marsh woofed softly several times from the back corner of the store, where he'd been napping.

Walker glanced at the clock and grinned. "Marsh always knows when it's time for Quillen to come."

"He's smart—*intelligente*—and Quillen always takes Marsh for a long walk. He looks forward to that."

"It's good for both of them." Walker reached down to pat the big dog as he came over to bump against his leg.

Juliette petted him, too. "You know, I haven't seen Marsh act defensive or aggressive with a single person who's come in the store except for Dade Claiborne. He's even gotten used to Vernon and Harley slinking around the place and acting weird like they do."

Walker laughed. "I thought Vernon and Harley would freak out the other day when those helicopters came flying over the valley."

She grinned. "That's why we haven't seen them at the store since. They're probably holed up for a while, feeling threatened."

"Funny guys," he said.

Juliette closed up the cardboard box and re-taped it. "Since Quillen will be here in a minute, I'm going to put these boxes in the storage room and head home. I have some business orders I need to pack for the mail, and I want to work on a quilt that's a special order."

"Sure, go ahead. The store's not busy."

As she came back from putting the boxes away, Walker said, "By the way, I ordered a quilt rack after looking at your business website. It should be here later this week. You can put some of your quilts on it—maybe beside the front door near the bench. You can display some of your handmade purses and aprons on a rack beside it, too. There's a wooden coatrack in the storage room you can use. I'll buy the merchandise outright like I do from my other crafters."

Her mouth dropped open in surprise. She'd forgotten that she'd asked Walker about selling her quilts the day he hired her. "*Molte grazie*—thank you very much."

"It's my pleasure. You do good work. Pick the quilts and items you think will work best for the store."

"I will. I have several I think will be a good fit."

He nodded. "You'll know best how to arrange everything."

She headed over to get her purse from under the counter and then looked up to see him standing near the end of the counter watching her. "What?" she asked, trying to read his expression.

He rubbed his neck. "We're both off tomorrow. I thought I might go hiking. You know the area better than I do." His voice dropped. "I thought you might like to go with me."

She smiled at him. "How long has it been since you asked a girl out on a date, Walker?"

He grinned. "Quite a while. I'm rusty."

"Well, it sounds fun." She draped her purse over her shoulder. "What time do you want to leave?"

"Maybe about ten if that's good for you. I need to walk down to the store, let Eldon in, talk to him for a few minutes. Then I can meet you wherever you suggest. At my house? Or at yours?"

"I'll come to your place." Juliette wasn't quite ready for her grandparents to have a go at Walker yet, and she didn't plan to let them know she was spending a day with him outside of work either. "Where are we going to hike?"

"I thought you might have an idea."

She stopped to think. "Ever hiked to Abrams Falls?"

"No, but I've heard of it."

"You can reach it from the campground on this side of the mountain, but I think it's a prettier walk to hike to the falls from the Cades Cove side. Besides, I need to make a stop in Townsend at a craft shop on the way to drop off a few quilts if you wouldn't mind. How does that sound?"

"It sounds good. We can pick up some sandwiches for lunch in Townsend. I can toss them in my backpack with two bottles of water."

"All right—*va bene*. I'll bring a waist pack, too, and pack a few things in it I need." She walked closer to him as she headed out from behind the counter. "Did you think I'd say no?"

He put an arm out to block her. "I wasn't sure."

Juliette grinned up at him. "Well, I could hardly say no to a guy who saved me more than once when I fell out of his apple tree."

"There is that."

They stared at each other for a few moments and then Walker leaned over to brush his lips over hers. "You need to go home before I take this any further," he said in a husky tone. "Quillen may walk in any second."

She moved past him just as the door swung open and Quillen burst in, carrying a pile of books. "Man, I've got so much homework tonight." He groaned. "I think every one of my teachers ganged up and all decided to give tests tomorrow."

Juliette laughed, and after talking with Quillen for a minute, she waved at Walker and let herself out the door.

Well, well, she thought. *I have a date with the boss.*

CHAPTER 7

A muffled woof from Marsh alerted Walker to Juliette's arrival at his house the next morning. She'd come early.

He headed toward the front door, Marsh ahead of him barking loudly until he heard Juliette's voice.

"Sit, Marsh." Walker spoke to the dog as he opened the door.

"*Buongiorno*—good morning." Juliette shoved a foil-wrapped tin pie pan into Walker's hands as she let herself in and then dropped to pet Marsh inside the doorway. "Good dog," she said, hugging him in greeting. "You're such a good dog to sit so nicely and not bark or jump on me."

Walker glanced at the pie pan in his hand. "What's this?"

"Gramma Newell's homemade cinnamon rolls. She was pulling them out of the oven as I left, so I wrapped some up for us. Got any coffee made?"

"Yeah." The smell of the rolls wafted into the air as he led Juliette back toward the kitchen.

He retrieved a couple of mugs and two plates from the cabinet, and then pulled a handful of silver from the drawer. He handed Juliette the plates and silver, gesturing toward the table while he poured coffee into the mugs.

"If I remember correctly, you like a big splash of milk and a little sweetener in your coffee." He glanced toward her, where she was putting the plates and silverware on the table. "You'll find sweetener in that small canister with the flag on it by the napkins."

"I was just noticing all the Americana in the room while I set the table." She stopped to look around. "Stars and stripes in the table runner, American flag canisters on the kitchen counter, red and blue dinnerware. Very patriotic."

He shrugged, bringing their coffee over to the table and sitting down. "I'm a patriotic guy, and I was born on the fourth of July. Turned thirty this summer." He grinned at her. "My sister decided to have a little fun when she decorated the house, knowing I liked red and blue."

Juliette sat down, reaching for a packet of sweetener for her coffee. "I like your patriotic décor, especially since my favorite color is red."

"I've noticed you wear a lot of red."

She gave him one of her pixie smiles. "Well, I was born on Valentine's Day. Red fits the holiday."

"Nothing like having a holiday birthday." He reached for the pan of cinnamon rolls.

"Gramma makes these rolls from scratch," Juliette said, putting a warm roll on her own plate after he snagged two for himself.

He tried one. "Ummm. These won't last long."

They ate, and drank coffee for a moment, before Juliette said, "This is the first time I've been in your house. It's nice, which in Italian is *la vostra casa è bella.*"

He loved the way she tucked those little Italian phrases into her conversation now and again. "The house may look nice now, but you should have seen it when I bought it." Walker told her. "Quillen, his dad, Eldon, and I worked for weeks cleaning the house and the yard before a work crew could even consider coming in to begin painting and doing needed repairs. Eldon and Quillen are both good handymen, too."

"I thought Eldon was a minister at a church in Alcoa."

"He used to be. He stepped down as full-time pastor last year but still works part-time as assistant to the new minister. He's really invested in that church; he helped to start and grow it."

"I knew the family didn't go to one of the churches in the valley."

Walker grinned. "From the church visits I've made, I think they might be the only Black family in any service if they did."

She frowned. "That doesn't mean they wouldn't be graciously welcome."

"I'm sure that's true, but both the churches in the valley are Baptist and that's not Eldon's family faith either."

She raised her eyes in question.

"They go to a full gospel type of church. It's lively. It will make you tap your feet and clap your hands."

"You've visited?"

"Once when Eldon's daughters were singing. They wanted me to visit to hear little Jaida sing a solo with the three of them."

"She's cute. I've seen her in the store." Juliette looked out the window toward the birds again. "I guess you've visited a lot of churches in your travels."

He nodded. He'd often felt the need for faith and reached out for it. The last few years had not been easy ones.

"Did you enjoy Eldon's church?"

"Are you curious about it?" he asked. "I find people are often curious about faiths not their own and yet they're often reluctant, or fearful, to visit other Christian denominations different from theirs."

"You may have a point, but I've lived in several different places and visited other churches, too."

"Eldon asked me after the service if I'd enjoyed myself and I told him I really did." Walker smiled. "He laughed, gave me a hug, and said, 'You only need a touch from Jesus to have a good time.' That's an old Smith Wigglesworth quote."

"Wigglesworth was a British evangelist in the early 1900s, wasn't he?"

"Yes, and a good one, too." Walker reached for another sweet roll. "I hope you didn't mean to save any of these."

"No, they never last more than a day at our house. Help yourself."

She sipped at her coffee, looking out the bay window. "You must love eating breakfast here every day watching the birds." She gestured toward the old birdbath and an array of feeders hung from the trees with others clustered on posts around the outdoor patio.

"I do."

"Did your sister incorporate Americana in other areas of the house?"

"Yes, she did. She called it a theme, said having bits and pieces of it throughout the house would unify the home with using similar colors." He ran a hand through his hair. "I told her I'd go along with the idea as long as she kept it subtle. My sister can get carried away sometimes with her decorating themes."

Juliette laughed. "I believe the theme of Gramma and Grandpa's house is 'old attic.' It's full of old furniture, family photos, collectibles, Gramma's quilts and needlework, and Grandpa's farm magazines and seed catalogs. But it's comfortable—*confortevole*."

"That's a good feeling. I asked Vee to try to make this house and the store look like they'd been around for a long time. I'm not into the sleek, modern minimalist look so popular today."

"Me neither. As an artisan and quilter, I guess you'd expect that of me."

She smiled at him. "Will you give me a short tour before we head out for the trail?"

"Sure. I guess I didn't realize you hadn't been here before."

She blinked her eyes at him flirtatiously. "You haven't invited me before."

"Message received." He polished off another bite of cinnamon roll, licking his lips around the sweet icing oozing out of it. Then he glanced across at her. "You haven't invited me to your place yet, either."

She looked away. "My grandparents know I'm working for you, and you've met them a few times when they dropped by the store." She hesitated. "I haven't told them we're friendly outside of work."

"Meaning you haven't told them the boss kissed you under the apple tree and snagged a few kisses in the store?"

"No."

"Are you worried about my reputation of being a crazy outsider that's still circulating? Vernon and Harley say folks still predict my store won't last the year. Some even placed bets on it."

"Well, I think they're wrong in that. Everyone loves the store and it's growing in popularity. Besides, I have a feeling you could weather a couple of bad years if you needed to even if it didn't do well."

He smiled, liking the thought she believed in him.

She sighed. "Gramma and Grandpa are old-school, Walker. If I invited you over, they'd immediately begin sizing you up and watching us to see if anything was going on. It wouldn't take either of them very long to pick up on ..." Her voice trailed away.

"On the fact that we're friendly?" He grinned.

"Yes." She didn't meet his eyes.

"And you're not ready to go there yet?"

"No, and not because of what you think. It's simply difficult with my family to keep my life to myself. They often try too hard to direct my decisions and they always think they know what is best for me."

"Most parents and grandparents are like that, Juliette. Even sisters. Mine wanted me to move near her rather than here to Happy Valley."

"Why didn't you?"

"I didn't think that would be wise," he said, knowing his voice had taken on an edge.

She shook her head. "So many secrets. See, that would be another problem with my grandparents. They'd ask a million questions and expect answers. Not getting them would make them suspicious that you harbored a dark past and are someone I shouldn't get involved with."

He met her eyes. "Maybe I do harbor a dark past."

"Perhaps so, but I doubt you'll cut my throat on the hiking trail today." She stood to take her dishes to the sink. "And I'm holding you to that promise to give me a quick tour of the house before we go. I'm not letting you out of that."

He took her through the house, walked the dog, and then put

Marsh in the big double garage for the day.

"Did I see a metal tub of kitty litter in the corner of your garage?" she asked with surprise as they settled into Walker's dark blue Jeep.

"Yes." He chuckled. "When I found Marsh as a pup, we were traveling all over in my Sportsmobile. You've seen the Sportsmobile parked out back in the shed. It's like a big oversized van with pullouts and I had to figure out someplace for Marsh to go to the bathroom without dealing with paper messes or puddles in such close quarters. Vee sent me an article about litter training small dogs, so I gave it a try. It worked when Marsh was a pup and even though Marsh is a big dog now, he'll still use litter when I have to leave him. However, I needed bigger and bigger containers over time and that old metal tub I found in the shed is perfect. Most people don't think you can train dogs like that, but you can. They're smart."

"Marsh is smart." She glanced back at the garage. "Will he be okay while we're gone?"

"Sure. He has the whole garage area, food, water, and a dog bed and toys." Walker looked in the rearview mirror as he backed out of the driveway. "When Quillen comes in from school he'll check on him and take him out for a walk. Marsh will be fine. He knows the drill."

"I remember you saying that traveling as much as you did, Marsh had to be well trained."

"Either that or become a major problem."

Juliette looked around, sniffing the air. "Is this a brand-new car? It has that new-car smell."

He nodded. "Yes, it is. I only owned the Sportsmobile and a motorcycle when I came to Happy Valley. I decided I needed a car now, too."

"You certainly picked a nice one. This is a Jeep Grand Cherokee."

"I wanted something that could pull mountain roads and get me out of the valley when it snows."

"I'd say this one will certainly do it."

He glanced over at her. "What do you drive?"

"A little red Honda, showing some age, but still a good car." She ran her hand over the Jeep's leather upholstery and grinned at him. "I made colorful quilted slipcovers for my car seats. I don't imagine you'd like a set?"

He laughed. "No, I don't think so."

As they headed out of the valley, she leaned back and closed her eyes.

"What are you thinking about?" he asked.

"I'm still remembering how nice your house is. Please tell your sister she did a wonderful job decorating. She wove that little thread of Americana all through the house in the pillows and rich rag rugs mixed with that wonderful brown and red leather furniture. I loved the old portraits of presidents scattered here and there, the weathered maps framed in your study, that red star-studded afghan draped over the old rocker, and the flags tucked in unexpected spots around the house. That old Revolutionary flag framed in the dining area was a beauty."

"It has some sort of history," he said. "Vee gave me some papers about it. I have them filed away somewhere."

"Vee is your sister?" she asked, catching the name he'd dropped.

"Yes." He didn't add more.

She waited a minute and then continued. "I like the guest bedrooms she created upstairs, too." She tucked a wisp of hair behind her ear that the wind had blown astray. "I assume the cute room with the wrought iron twin beds, red and blue quilts, and all the books and games was designed for your nieces when they come to visit."

"They all might come for Christmas, my Aunt Jessie, too."

"That would be nice for you."

"Maybe. If we can work it out and depending on a lot of other things. We'll see." He changed gears to start the Jeep up the steep road out of the valley. "What's the name of the store you want to stop at on the way through Townsend?"

"It's called The Apple Barn. It sits right beside the Hart Gallery, an art gallery, and The Lemon Tree, a lunch and sweet shop owned by two sisters. We can get some sandwiches for our hike there after I drop my quilts off with Raynelle Oliver at The Apple Barn." She laughed. "*Please* don't come in with me. Raynelle will talk your ear off and ask you a million questions. If I tell her I have someone waiting on me, it might help me get out of the store quicker."

"Okay. Maybe I'll pop into The Lemon Tree and get our sandwiches while you deliver your quilts."

"Good idea. The club sandwiches the sisters make are great. They will taste wonderful about the time we get to the falls." She put a hand out the window like a child, enjoying the breeze on it. "Remember to get some lemon cookies, too. Goodness knows we've had enough sweets and calories for the whole day this morning with those sweet rolls, but by the time we hike to the falls, I'm sure we'll welcome more."

She entertained him as they drove on with light chatter and local yarns. As they neared Townsend, she told him stories about the people who lived there she'd met through festivals and events in the area. She was a natural storyteller, and Walker was well entertained. The small businesses and scenic spots along the way came to life through her tales.

When they stopped at The Apple Barn, Walker popped over to The Lemon Tree to get their sandwiches and cookies and snagged two bags of corn chips, too.

Back on the road again, they soon passed the National Park sign and headed into the Great Smoky Mountains. The road wound along the tumbling Little River, the waters dotted with colorful tubers this warm August afternoon, all enjoying a float down the stream in the sunshine.

He pointed to them. "That looks like fun."

"It is. We should come and tube one day. Maybe the Rasnics would like to come with us and bring their boys. It's fun to link several tubes together and talk while you float down the river."

He cleared his throat. "By the way, Kimmie and Jonas invited us to dinner at their home this Saturday night. I forgot to ask if you wanted to go. Kimmie really wants to get to know you better."

"I'd like that. We hit it off the few times she stopped by the store. It's great to have someone to talk about art with. I'm looking forward to seeing her studio and some of her design work."

"You'll get to see Jonas's studio, too. Knowing him, he'll be working on some giant canvas stretching nearly to the ceiling."

"He really does striking work. I admire it."

"Yes, I'm thinking about getting one of those mountain trails paintings of his for the long wall in the upper hallway, so it will look like you're walking right into the woods as you approach it."

She turned toward him, her mouth dropping open. "You can afford one of Jonas Rasnic's paintings? *Incredibile!*"

"Maybe he'll give me a discount." Walker shrugged, avoiding a direct answer.

Juliette snorted. "Well, if you have money like that to spend, I have a great patriotic crazy quilt you might like. It would look wonderful across the end of your bed."

"Bring it by the store for me to see one day." He sent her a challenging look. "Maybe I'll like it."

"I'll do that." She looked away with a flush of embarrassment creeping up her neck.

He slowed for the intersection at the Wye, a popular swimming hole, and then turned right on Laurel Creek Road toward Cades Cove.

"Settlers once lived all through this area," Juliette said, collected again now. "If you've hiked much around here, you've noticed remnants of their old farms, rock walls, cleared fields, and farm roads. In Cades Cove in the spring, there are tons of daffodils planted by early families who lived in that mountain valley. It's a beautiful sight to see in March."

"I drove over and explored many of the old cabins, churches, and cemeteries preserved by the park around the cove. I visited the Cable Mill Historic Area, too."

"Our trailhead is only about a half mile before the historic area. The trail to Abrams Falls is a well-known and popular one. We won't have it to ourselves, even on a weekday. Hopefully the traffic on the loop road around the cove will move along today. During summer and fall weekends, it can be a bear, but now that schools are back in, the traffic shouldn't be as bad." She pointed out the window to a rustic sign by the road. "See that trail sign? There are hiking trails like that scattered all along the Laurel Creek Road we're on now and throughout the Cades Cove area. If you like to hike, there are always trails to explore here."

"Do you hike often?"

"I used to with George, Amy, or my school friends when younger, but I haven't hiked much in the last years. I don't think it's safe to hike alone and I haven't really had anyone to hike with."

Walker thought about the last years when his own company, or that of Marsh, was all he had to enjoy on the road—sometimes for days on end. It was novel for him, too, to share a day on the trail with someone.

Glancing into the rearview mirror, he saw a black van pull out from a parking spot along the road to move in behind him. The windshield was tinted, and the van seemed to ride much too close to his bumper. Walker gripped the steering wheel as the van drew nearer. Then it pulled out suddenly to pass his Jeep, roaring by and turning off on a side road ahead. He released a long breath.

"What's wrong?" Juliette asked. "I asked you a question and you didn't answer. Then I saw you gripping the steering wheel and glancing in the rearview mirror every three seconds."

"Everything's fine." He made an effort to smile at her.

She didn't reply, looking out the window. And she stayed quiet for a time as they drove on, not the norm for Juliette.

"You thought someone was following you," she finally said.

He didn't answer.

"Your past life is certainly your own, but I'd like you to be honest and answer me this: Are you wanted by the law for a crime of some kind? Have you done something illegal you're running from?"

He glanced at her in surprise before answering. "No."

"Good. Well, at least I can comfort myself with that," she said, her tone slightly sarcastic. "Is someone after you for some other reason?"

"Probably not anymore." He decided to be honest. "But there was a time that wasn't so."

"Do you want to talk about it?"

"No," he answered. "I'm trying to leave that time behind. But I want you to know I've done nothing illegal or wrong, and I've never hurt anyone or threatened anyone. There was simply a situation in my life that brought too much spotlight to me and mine, and we became threatened."

"That's why you began to travel," she said quietly.

He nodded, starting to relax again now as the sounds of the stream and the fresh smells of the mountain air drifted into the car.

She reached over to put a hand on his leg. "Someday you'll talk to me about this when it's time."

Walker sighed—glad she wasn't going to quiz him further. He liked Juliette. Actually, he liked her a lot, but he wasn't ready to change their relationship to a deeper one yet or to trust her with his secrets.

"Look, there's a deer in the woods over there by the road." She pointed, her face lighting up. "We may see more in the Cove as we drive to the trailhead. Or maybe even a bear." She laughed. "However, if we see a bear, you can expect every car ahead of us to slow down to a crawl or simply stop in the middle of the road while the tourists gawk or take pictures."

He watched the deer bound off into the woods. "That's a white-tailed deer," he said, glad for the change of subject. "They're the most common deer in the eastern US but out west you also see mule deer. I saw moose and elk on my travels, too. They're in the same species family."

Their talk turned back to nature then and to lighter subjects, for which Walker was grateful. He hadn't let anyone grow close to him for a long time, anyone who hadn't known him from before. Considering what happened the year before he left Colorado and hit the road, he still wasn't eager to reveal himself to anyone too freely. Even Juliette.

CHAPTER 8

Juliette pointed out late flowers blooming on the roadsides and chattered with Walker about mundane things as they made their way into the Cove to the trailhead to Abrams Falls. It was obvious Walker had a past he wasn't comfortable talking about, but he'd begun to reveal little bits of his past here and there as they spent more time together.

Today she learned he and his family had been threatened in the past because of a situation in his life that spotlighted him. He claimed he'd done nothing illegal, never hurt or wronged anyone, and she believed him. She wished he trusted her more. Had he become famous so that paparazzi pursued him? His wealth had to come from somewhere, and he mentioned before he hadn't always been rich. He really freaked out today, too, when he thought that black van was following them, and he admitted it brought back memories of being pursued.

She turned to study him. He seemed like such a normal guy in every way, in appearance, talk, and actions, and not one to harbor deep secrets.

"What are you thinking?" he asked, catching her eyes on him.

"I was thinking what a nice guy you are—*bravo ragazzo.*"

"Always a line a man wants to hear."

She giggled. "Are you fishing for compliments? I could come up with a few."

"No, I only wondered what caused that deep and thoughtful look you were giving me."

"You're a man with a lot of mysteries."

"Mostly my life has been very ordinary, Juliette." He slowed the Jeep to cross a wooden bridge. "I grew up in a small town where my family had always lived. My father ran a general store downtown that my grandfather and great-grandfather owned before. I started working in the store as a kid and always thought I'd work there all my life." He paused. "My mother died when my sister and I were small. My dad's sister—Aunt Jessie—came to live with us and stayed until Vee went off to college. I worked with my dad in the store, attended college in my hometown, went to the church where my uncle pastored, played a little baseball, hiked and fished with my cousin Stewart and my friend Burton, the threesome I told you about before. My life was a plain and simple one."

"Until something changed that."

"Yes, something changed that." He pulled off the main road into the parking area for the Abrams Falls Trail. "Someday I'll tell you about it, but like I said earlier, I'm trying to leave that part of my past behind me right now. Make a new beginning. I hope you can accept that. It's all I'm willing to give right now."

"Okay." She sighed. "But I'd like for you to think I'm a reliable person, who could be trusted with secrets and would keep them to herself."

"If I didn't believe that, I wouldn't have told you the things I did today." He pulled the Jeep into a parking space and turned off the motor. "I hope the things I shared with you today will stay with you, too."

"*Si, certo*—of course." She turned her eyes to him. "But surely you know my grandparents, my brother and his family, and my friends ask me a lot of questions about you, knowing I work at the store."

"Well, tell them to ask *me* those questions themselves if they want to know more about me."

"I may not pass on any information, but others will talk anyway." She shook her head at his naïveté. "You don't know much about our valley and the gossip chain, do you? Knowledge tends to travel. Eventually what you tell one person will travel around until everyone knows."

"I'm aware of the process. I told you I grew up in a small town." He turned to look at her. "That's why I'm sharing selectively only what I want people to know."

"People won't be content with that."

Walker frowned at her. "They won't have a choice."

"So you say." Juliette already knew people in the valley were curious about the new storeowner's past. Walker might be able to keep his secrets to himself for a time, but eventually they would get out. "If you don't share enough about yourself to satisfy people, eventually someone will dig something up and bandy it around behind your back."

"I'll deal with that if and when it happens. But for now I'd like to keep myself to myself. I gave up a lot to gain that liberty."

"Okay." She leaned over to give him a quick kiss, surprising him. "So let's go hike now, enjoy some fun and stop being so serious."

He laughed. "Sounds like a good idea to me."

Walker pulled his backpack from the seat behind them, tossed in their lunch bag and two bottles of water.

"Here, give me one of those waters to put in my waist pack. Water's heavy and I'll need it in my own pack if I want a drink along the way."

"Sure." He passed her the water and then locked up the Jeep.

Juliette glanced over to see him watching her as she propped a foot on the Jeep's bumper to tighten the laces on her hiking boots.

"What?" she asked, catching his eye.

"This is the first time I've seen you in shorts. You usually wear those long skirts."

She grinned. "Skirts are not a good choice for the hiking trail."

"Skirts look good on you. Shorts, too." His eyes skimmed up her legs.

"Well, you look cute in shorts yourself." She ran her eyes over his muscled, tan legs in return. "I haven't seen you in shorts before today either."

"A day of many firsts," he said, laughing and starting toward the trail.

Juliette glanced around the parking lot. "I don't think we'll have a crowd on the trail today. There aren't a large number of cars here."

"The traffic wasn't bad driving in either."

Passing the trail sign, they headed across a wooden bridge over Abrams Creek to begin their hike. Juliette pulled out her phone to snap a few photos of the trail sign, of Walker on the bridge, and then she passed him the camera to snap a shot of her.

"If you do Facebook or social media, *don't* post my photo," he said.

"Okay. People with secrets don't like Facebook." She changed the subject. "George always calls this a roller-coaster hike."

"Why's that?"

"The first half mile is flat, following alongside the creek, then the trail moves away from the creek, climbs up Arbutus Ridge and down. Then it rises to climb Stony Ridge and travels down again. After a few more ups and downs a side path drops to the base of the falls at two and a half miles."

"So the ups and downs make it feel like a roller-coaster ride."

"Yes." She flashed a smile at him. "And because the hike is basically short, only five miles roundtrip, many visitors underestimate its rises and falls and often have sore calf muscles the next day."

He grinned. "If you don't hike often, any trail can be physically taxing."

"That's the truth."

They chatted casually along their way, pointing out plants and ferns, stopping to hop big rocks in the stream to enjoy the cascades, trying to identify mushrooms tucked under the trees.

As they paused on one of the high ridges, leaning against a rock for a moment to drink some water, Walker said, "Tell me about your younger life and family. I told you about mine."

Juliette smiled. "My father, Wyatt Dalton Hollander, is a lieutenant commander in the naval school at Bethesda, Maryland. He directs the residency program of Bethesda's dental school, preparing officers to practice, teach, and conduct research in dentistry. Before my birth, he was an officer and dentist at the US naval base in Napoli, Italy, a pretty little coastal city about 145 miles from Rome. He met my mother at a local gathering he'd been invited to at the Lamon's home in nearby Casalnuovo, a small province or municipality outside of Naples. My mother, Lucia, was at the gathering with her parents, Lorenzo and Emiliana Ravetti, her two brothers Salvadore and Dino, and her sister Raimonda, who is married to one of the Lamon's sons, Gaspere. Italians are very big on family."

"I've never been to Italy."

"Italy is a wonderful country. It's beautiful there, especially around Naples. I haven't been back as often as I'd like."

They started down the trail again, Juliette continuing her story. "The Ravetti family owns a tailoring business that has been in the family for generations. My mother did exquisite needlework and embroidery and I learned those skills, as well as how to sew, from her and from my grandmother Ravetti."

"So your artistry and needlework skills come from your mother's family."

"Partially. My Gramma Newell also sews and makes beautiful handmade quilts, too."

"Like yours?"

"No, Gramma makes more traditional quilts from patterns— Dutch doll, flower garden, pinwheel, log cabin, fan block, and other patterns. I'll show you some of her work sometime."

"I'd like to see it."

Juliette moved around a couple with small children on the trail before she continued. "When Mother died when I was ten, killed in a train wreck, my father came back to the States and brought me to his mother's, as he had my brother George when George's mother died. Patsy died of complications of pneumonia."

"Your father has known heartache, losing two wives."

"Yes. It's sad—*è tragico*. He's a serious man by nature, and both Patsy and my mother brought laughter and joy into his life. He loved both very much."

"Why didn't you stay with your Italian family?"

"My father's time in Italy was ending. He moved back to the States a month after Mother died. Naturally he wanted me to live stateside so he could spend as much time with me as possible. I always went to stay with him on my holidays if he didn't come to the farm."

"Are you close to your father?"

"Yes, actually I am, despite the times we had to be apart. Like me, Dad didn't develop the strong ties to the farm his father hoped he would as the only son. It caused problems when Dad was younger, but fortunately, my brother George loves the farm. George lives and breathes farming and has never understood why his father didn't love it, too."

"So George and your father are not close?"

"No, and George's grandparents, the Rheas, didn't help that either."

"You told me before they resented your father marrying again."

"Yes, they did, and they are still hostile toward my father and toward me because of that. They also worked to damage my relationship with George's wife, Laura, and their two children, Robert and Kirsten, both young teens now."

"That's unfair."

"A lot of life is unfair." She kicked at a pine cone in the path as she said the words.

"You're right about that," he agreed.

Their conversation drifted off now as they started their climb down the steep side trail leading to the base of the falls. At the bottom of the trail, Juliette paused to enjoy the scene ahead where Abrams Creek spilled over a high ledge in a long cascade to drop into a wide green pool below.

"Pretty, isn't it?"

He shaded his eyes to study the falls. "It's a beauty."

She and Walker moved closer to the falls to explore, and Juliette snapped a few more photo memories to keep.

A group of children waded in the shallows near the falls, splashing each other and laughing, enjoying the day. Abrams Falls was seldom a spot you could have to yourself, and there were about a dozen or more visitors here today. Around the edge of the pool lay many large rock boulders, and Juliette led them to one of these, almost flat on the top.

"We can stop and eat our lunch here," she said, climbing up on the boulder.

"Nice spot." Walker climbed up behind her, pulled off his backpack and settled down on the rock. "Do you know how tall the falls is?"

"It drops twenty feet."

"Can you climb to the top of it?" He put a hand up to shade his eyes again, looking toward the rocks at the top.

"You can, but it's dangerous. A lot of people have fallen from the rocks to their death, and several drowned while swimming below the falls. There's an undertow people don't understand and they underestimate it."

"I can enjoy the falls well enough from here." Walker began to pull out their lunch from his backpack, passing out sandwiches, chips, and cookies.

The roar of the falls and the laughter and chatter of the hikers and tourists offered them a happy mix of background noise for their picnic.

Walker paused after wolfing down the first half of his sandwich. "Since it was two and a half miles to the falls from the parking lot at Cades Cove, how far would it be to hike to the falls from Abrams Campground?"

She glanced back up the trail, trying to remember. "It's about five miles from the campground. You first hike up the Cooper Road Trail, then across Little Bottoms Trail, which connects to the Abrams Falls Trail. The trail comes in near the last footbridge we crossed. It's twice as far hiking to the falls from Abrams Campground and the steep trail over Pine Mountain is a rough, narrow one. I've hiked it often enough but I like this route better, even if you do need to drive to Cades Cove to begin."

"I walked many of the trails out of the Abrams Campground with Marsh and others later with Jonas Rasnic. Jonas and I hiked over Pine Mountain on the Little Bottoms Trail but we forded the creek at the Hatcher Mountain Trail intersection and hiked the loop route around to Scott Gap and down Rabbit Creek Trail to the campground area again versus hiking to the falls."

"You forded that creek?" Juliette knew her mouth dropped open. "That's a dangerous crossing. Abrams Creek is swift and deep there."

He grinned. "We got a little wet, that's a fact."

"Well, I would suggest being very careful about fording that creek unless the water's really low. Grandpa has told me some frightening tales about people drowning or being seriously injured there."

"I can believe it. I've been back to that spot on days when I wouldn't have considered crossing at all."

They ate the rest of their lunch in quiet, enjoying the sunshine and the beauty of the waterfall.

"How did you get into serious quilting?" Walker asked after a time.

She considered how to answer. "I started developing my own style in high school and although my grandparents couldn't see a future in it, my father did. He paid for me to go to college at the Maryland Institute College of Art in Baltimore, not far from Bethesda, where he was stationed by that time at the naval medical center. It's only about an hour from Bethesda to Baltimore. Dad and I got really close in the years I stayed there."

"What did you study to become a quilter? Is there a major in that?"

She smiled. "Not really. Quilting programs for college credit are rare among colleges and universities, but many have a Bachelor of Fine Arts degree in textiles or fiber arts. The Maryland Institute is one of the schools that does. I studied basics like visual arts, drawing, painting, and art history and then moved on to learn fiber and textiles history, dyeing, sewing, weaving, and embroidery. It really enhanced and shaped my own skills."

"I'd imagine so." He finished off his sandwich. "What brought you back here after going away?"

"Believe it or not the mountains get into your blood and call you back." She gestured around her. "There is something highly inspirational to me about living near beauty like this. It's hard to explain."

"I felt that siren call, too, as soon as I began to visit around the Blue Ridge and Smoky Mountains. I can see what drew Horace Kephart here so many years ago and others after him."

She munched on a lemon cookie, enjoying the sound of the rushing falls and the cool breeze rising off the water.

"You create what you call crazy quilts. What exactly is the definition of a crazy quilt?" he asked.

"A traditional quilt is created around an organized pattern. A crazy quilt can follow any pattern, the patches and pieces of fabrics cut and arranged in any way the quilter desires. A crazy quilt usually doesn't have repeating motifs and is often heavily embroidered or embellished with additions like ribbons, beading, lace, or buttons— whatever the quilter wants to work into the pattern. So it becomes a very artistic and personal creation."

"I've seen that artistry in your work." He skipped some rocks across the water. "Some of the fabrics you use are unusual, too. A lot of your quilts look like the materials might have been recycled."

She laughed. "That's an understatement. I shop flea markets, thrift shops, and garage sales looking for interesting old fabrics. Sometimes I get lucky and find a whole bag of fabric scraps, trim, lace, or embroidery yarn. I might use silky fabric from an old prom dress or men's ties, too. Whatever gives me a new idea or inspiration can start me collecting similar fabrics and embellishments that suit."

"Do you ever draw your patterns?"

"Almost always." She stretched her legs out on the rock to catch the sun. "Even though a crazy quilt may look helter-skelter, each one usually takes careful planning to achieve a distinctive look. I plan my designs on paper first, playing with colors I might use with pencils or paints, pinning fabrics in place to try out a design idea or creating a small block to show me the way. It's fun. I've even done custom quilts for people using specialty items they've collected in my designs."

He stretched his neck and rubbed it. "I admire artistry but I don't have special talents in that area. My Aunt Jessie sewed and crafted and Vee always loved decorating and design. I remember she used to pore through old magazines and cut out ideas even as a girl."

"You're not without your own talents. You possess excellent business and organizational skills, are comfortable and diplomatic with people. You listen well and are genuinely interested in others' lives. That's an art form of its own."

"Thank you."

She studied his profile in the sunshine. "Was your cousin happy to take over the family store when you left?"

He frowned. "No, not at first, but he came around. Taking the leadership role proved good for Stewart. He finally got up the courage to propose to the girl he's loved since elementary school, too."

"Oh? That sounds like a romantic story—*romantico*."

He laughed. "Actually, it's not. Stewart kept his feelings so close to himself that Kathy married someone else, never even knowing he cared. When her husband cheated on her and she divorced him, Kathy came back home and Stewart got a second chance."

"Awww. A happy ending."

"It has been."

She stretched. "I guess we should start back."

"Yes." He glanced at his watch and then started packing up the remains of their lunch.

Juliette stood and put her waist pack back on. "Do you need to be back to close the store tonight?"

"No. Eldon will do it after Quillen comes in. He's very capable."

"If you'd like, we could drive to Gatlinburg, walk around and play tourist, check out some of the crafts shops, maybe eat dinner at one of the restaurants there." She watched him consider it.

"We could do that." He smiled. "Does this mean you're asking me out on a date now?"

"Perhaps." She swatted at him playfully. "But I still plan to let you buy dinner."

They drove over the scenic roads from Cades Cove to Gatlinburg and parked on the River Road. Then they walked up and down the streets of Gatlinburg, exploring the shops and riding the tram up the mountain, as well. It was fun. Juliette hadn't seen Walker laugh so much since she met him. It made her wonder what he'd been like before problems put him on the run. They ate at Bennett's Pit Bar-B-Que on the River Road, not feeling dressed up enough for some of the nicer restaurants on the Parkway.

On the way home to Happy Valley, Juliette almost fell asleep after their long day on the trail and afternoon in Gatlinburg.

"I'm going to drop you off at your house," Walker said as they drove into the valley. "It's dark and I don't want you walking home by yourself." He smiled at her. "Besides, you're worn out."

She yawned, despite herself. "We did have a big day."

"It's been a great day." He hesitated. "I've been on my own a lot these last years. It felt nice to share a whole day with someone."

"I had a good time, too," she said. "*Grazie.*"

As Walker headed his Jeep into the driveway leading into the Hollander farm, Juliette pointed ahead. "Pull off by that big oak tree. I'll walk on to the house. It's only around the corner."

"I gather you still don't want your grandparents to know you've been fraternizing with the boss."

She wrinkled her nose. "Grandpa or Gramma will probably be watching for me because it's late. If they see a car, they'll come out. Then I'll have to invite you in and …"

He pulled into the spot she'd pointed out by the tree. "I do want to meet your grandparents, Juliette." He turned off the motor and leaned closer to her. "I think we'll be seeing more of each other and I don't like the idea that someone else will tell them we're dating before we do."

She bit her lip. "I know. I'll talk to them, I promise, but not tonight. This has been such a nice day. I don't want to risk something spoiling it."

"All right." He leaned in closer. "Let's end the day like this instead." He brushed his lips over hers softly and then gathered her into his arms for a deeper kiss.

"Ummm," Juliette murmured. "This is even sweeter than the last of those lemon cookies we ate in the car. And distinctly better."

"Much better." He pulled her closer.

On a sigh, Juliette wrapped her arms around his neck.

Walker had just pulled her almost onto his lap, when a thud against the Jeep shocked them apart. When another thud shook the vehicle, Juliette realized someone was kicking the car.

"I've got a gun if I need it," a voice called out. A face leaned over to look in the car. "Juliette?" her brother said, his eyes popping wide. "What the heck are you doing in there and who is that?"

"That's my brother," she told Walker before opening the door.

George stepped back, scowling now.

"Would you put that gun down, George? *Sei pazzo*—are you crazy?" She pushed at the gun barrel. "And what are you doing out here running around in the dark with a gun? Shouldn't you be home?"

He dropped the rifle to his side, the butt toward the ground. "Gramma heard someone prowling around near the barn and called me to come over and have a look around. She didn't want to wake Grandpa or get him stirred up. He'd fallen asleep with the TV on. With all the thievery going on in the valley, she was scared."

She looked around in alarm. "Have you seen anyone?"

"Only a raccoon in the barn, but Gramma got upset earlier today when she learned someone broke into the Hearons' place on the Happy Valley Loop behind our farm. It's sad to think about the thieves targeting the Hearons. The family doesn't have much and the thieves stole a cigar box full of money that Whitey Hearon kept in the house. They took the family's TV, some electronics, and two new bikes Whitey bought the boys for Christmas this year.

Whitey and Nelle saved a long time for those bikes, and the kids are heartsick."

"How mean." Juliette crossed her arms.

George frowned and looked into the car again. "Who the heck is that man, Juliette?"

Glancing at Walker and accepting the inevitable, she made the introductions. "Walker Logan, this is my brother, George Hollander. George, this is Walker Logan ..."

"Your boss?" George interrupted. "You're out here necking in the driveway with your new boss?" His voice rose.

"Would you quiet down," she snapped in warning. "You'll have Gramma and Grandpa out here next."

"Well, maybe they oughta be out here." He made a fist, glaring at Walker. "I don't much like finding you out here taking advantage of my sister. Even more so because you're her boss. It isn't right."

Walker pushed open the door of the Jeep and climbed out, coming around to the other side of the vehicle to help Juliette out.

"You may be right, George," he said. "If you'd like we can walk down to the house to talk to your grandparents right now."

"No!" Juliette said. She turned to George. "Walker and I have only recently started seeing each other. I planned to talk to Gramma and Grandpa about it, but I haven't yet. You know how they can be about quizzing anyone I'm seeing."

George scowled. "Last I knew you were seeing Dade Claiborne, and to hear him tell it the two of you are practically engaged."

"That is not true." Juliette moved closer to George, annoyed. "I have told Dade Claiborne repeatedly I do not want to be more than friends with him. He simply isn't listening."

Irritated, George snapped back. "I suppose that's why you went out with him the other week. Because you're just friends?"

She ran a hand through her hair. "You, Dade, and my grandparents manipulated me into accepting that dinner invitation with him. I accepted in part, too, so I could sit down with Dade privately and make it clear to him I didn't want our relationship moving to another level."

George sent her another angry look. "Perhaps Walker Logan here doesn't know you've been dating Dade Claiborne for years or that both the Claiborne and Hollander families have expected you two to get married for some time."

"I do *not* want to marry Dade Claiborne." Juliette stomped her foot. "How often do I need to say that before you believe me."

Walker cleared his throat. "Maybe I ought to head on home so you two can talk about this more on your own."

"I think that would be a real good idea." George glared at him.

Juliette turned to Walker. "I'm sorry about this."

"So am I." He turned to George. "I'll be over to meet Juliette's grandparents soon. You're correct that it's not right for us to be sneaking around, seeing each other like two teenagers. Since Juliette and I are invited to the Rasnics for dinner on Saturday, I'll pick her up at her house in the proper way before we go and meet her grandparents then."

Juliette rolled her eyes.

Walker reached into the truck to get her waist pack and handed it to her. "Let me know when you find a chance to talk to your grandparents. I can come over sooner if they prefer."

"Saturday will be soon enough. You can come a little early to pick me up. There's no chance I can keep our relationship quiet now that George has stuck his nose into it."

"You act like I was out here spying on you," George complained with an edge to his voice. "I told you why I was here."

"So you did."

George tucked his rifle under his arm. "If Dade gets wind of this, he isn't going to like it."

Juliette put her hands on her hips. "I better not find out you're the one who tells him about it."

George's face reddened. "Dade and Ronnie Claiborne are my good friends. I've known them all my life." He glanced at Walker. "I don't even know your boss. Who are his people anyway? Where did he come from? Hardly anyone around here knows anything about him. You ought to be dating people you know and not strangers."

Juliette closed her eyes. "George, I'm twenty-eight years old. I think I ought to be able to make my own decisions about who I date, don't you?"

"To be real honest, Juliette, I've never been able to figure you out, and about half the decisions you make don't seem sensible to me. You *are* my sister, though, and I think I have a right to protect you when I find you sneaking around and necking with your boss—especially when nobody even knew the two of you were seeing each other." His eyes moved to Walker's again. "Once again, that isn't right at all, and I don't mind saying it in front of Mr. Logan or you, Juliette."

A few moments of silence fell.

Then Walker put out his hand to George. "It was good to meet you, George, and I wish it had been under better circumstances. You're kind to be concerned about your sister. I'd have been upset if I found my sister in a similar situation." He walked toward the driver's side of the Jeep and climbed in. "I'll head on home now. Juliette, I'll see you at the store tomorrow. Thanks for the nice day today."

With that he started the Jeep and drove back down the farm road.

Juliette put a fist to her mouth and started to cry. "You ruined a perfectly nice day for me, George. Believe it or not, Walker Logan is a really good and kind man. We went hiking to Abrams Falls and then over to Gatlinburg. We had such fun until now."

George gave her an awkward pat. "Well, I'm sorry you're upset, but when I saw the car parked here in the dark under the tree, I thought it might be those thieves getting ready to sneak into Gramma and Grandpa's place once night fell. How was I to know it was you getting it on with your new boss?"

She pushed at him. "Oh, you make it sound awful every time you say it. We were only kissing good night."

"Humph. Looked to me like you were half in his lap."

She lifted her chin. "It's hard to kiss proper in a car."

George grinned. "Seems like I can remember finding a lot of ways to be resourceful in a car when Laura and I dated."

Juliette sighed. "I'm going up to the house," she said, starting down the driveway.

George stepped into stride beside her. "I need to walk to the house with you so I can go in and reassure Gramma that nothing but a raccoon in the barn made those noises she heard."

"All right, but let me tell them about Walker in my own time and my own way and *not* tonight."

"Sure."

They walked down the winding lane to the old farmhouse.

George caught her arm before she started up the steps. "Are you starting to care about that man?"

"Maybe."

"Well, it would be good to learn more about him before you let yourself get further involved. I said nearly the same thing to my girl Kirsten the other day about a boy she's getting sweet on in the 4-H."

Seeing the obvious concern in his face, she forced a smile. "Thanks for caring," she said begrudgingly before the two of them headed into the house.

CHAPTER 9

The busy days of August and late summer slid away, and September arrived, bringing quieter days to the store. Today Walker worked with Eldon Johnson, who alternated days with Juliette and was growing more and more valuable to Walker as a helper.

"Hard to believe the month of September is almost over," Eldon said from behind the counter where he cleaned up from the earlier lunch traffic. "I saw a few trees already changing color as I drove over today, a red sassafras, a yellow birch, a few maple trees dressing up in orange and gold."

"I need to plan another hike soon to enjoy the fall color," Walker said, pausing in his work at his laptop. He sat perched on a stool at the lunch counter, checking emails. "Maybe Juliette will go with me."

Eldon raised an eyebrow. "Seems to me things have grown a bit strained between you and Juliette these last weeks."

Walker frowned over the comment and then waited. When Eldon had something to say, he usually worked his way into it gradually.

The older man cleaned the counter a little more, putting a few items into the refrigerator. He'd turned sixty recently, but age suited him well. His dark hair was graying, with a few spots thinning on the crown, his weight a little chunkier than ideal. But he was still a good-looking man, sturdy and strong in build, capable with his hands, wise, kind, and very astute in sizing up people and situations. Not much got past Eldon Johnson, and his observations were usually accurate.

"What happened to make things awkward between you two?" he asked at last. "Seems to me back in August I saw a real affection building. You acted easier with each other then."

"Is that right?" Walker asked evasively.

Eldon grinned. "Don't you want things to be better?"

Walker rubbed his neck. "It's complicated."

"Life generally is."

"And there have been some problems."

Eldon sat down on the stool behind the counter. "I'd say I could guess some. Juliette's grandparents aren't too excited about her getting more involved with an outsider like you they don't know much about."

"There is that."

"And Dade Claiborne has kicked up a stink since he learned you and Juliette went on a few dates together."

Walker glanced across at Eldon. "Juliette told me her brother, George, let that news slip to his grandmother Hettie Rhea and then Hettie made sure Dade learned about it, taking pleasure in stirring up trouble for Juliette." He paused. "Hettie Rhea has been in the store a few times—a nasty, critical woman, don't you think? Wonder what makes her like that? She seems to enjoy picking on people, making others unhappy."

"Usually something unhappy deep inside causes that, some old bitterness allowed to fester and grow. I've seen a lot of that in the ministry. Sometimes people can get help. I've had the privilege of being used by the Lord to lend a hand with problems like that now and again, but I doubt Hettie Rhea would be comfortable having a black man help her in any area of faith."

Walker took a long drink from the cola sitting beside his computer. "You often make me think of my Uncle Gene. He was a minister, too."

"Of a particular church?"

"First Congregational."

"We don't have many of those around here. Was that where you churched when you lived out west?"

Walker nodded.

"Tell me something about that faith. I'm not too familiar with it."

Walker stopped to think. "The church beliefs trace back to New England Puritans. It's an old denomination, more ruled by the congregation than a hierarchy but it's pretty typical otherwise in its Christian faith tenets." He pointed toward a sign over the door of the store. "That's the church's motto: In essentials unity, in nonessentials diversity, in all things charity."

"Those are good words."

"The three core values of the church were faith, freedom, and fellowship. One thing I especially remember Uncle Gene preaching about was that each person should always be on a personal and persistent search for God, to find his or her own authentic relationship with the Lord. In that journey you find your life purpose and direction as well as growing in faith."

"I've always thought each Christian faith holds some special nuggets of wisdom and revelation in their individual beliefs." Eldon scratched his chin, thinking the idea over. "It's not so much which church you go to but who you are in the Lord. That's what a person needs to be most sure of—that relationship and being wrapped in the love of God and the purpose of God."

A few customers came in the store, and they both got busy working for an hour or so, but when the store grew quiet later, Eldon picked up the thread of his conversation again. "I've noticed you're not attending church now, but I know you visited both the churches in the valley. You went to the big Homecoming at the Missionary Baptist Church a few weeks back."

"That's Juliette's family's church."

"Have a good time?"

"Yes, I did. The people were welcoming, the music good, and the food bountiful. They held an incredible outdoor picnic lunch after the service. My plate was full before I got halfway down the line of food."

Eldon patted his stomach. "Churches have always been good for food and fellowship, as well as building faith."

Walker laughed.

Eldon put a hand on his arm then. "Walker, you've run for a long time from something, but it's time for you to rest in the Lord about it now, to give your cares and concerns to Him, your hurts and disappointments, and to let Him heal you and direct you."

Walker dropped his eyes. "I've been trying to do that, Eldon."

"Well, maybe you have, but you still keep a lot of yourself to yourself. That's a hindrance in moving your relationship forward with Juliette. It's likely to hold you back in other areas, too."

"Sometimes the things you do are to protect other people."

"That's true, but my Lula snapped at me the other day and said, 'Don't you try to protect me so much, old man; it makes me feel you don't trust me or think I'm strong.' Often others are stronger than we give them credit for."

Walker couldn't help smiling. "I wish the answers were easy."

Eldon studied him. "In my spirit, I think you're moving in the right direction. Settling down at last, getting to know people, letting others get a little closer than you have for a long time. I've watched you change and get more easy with life since you came here."

"You, Quillen, and your whole family have been good friends to me."

"And you to us. Quillen sure is proud of his new truck. That was good of you to help with it."

"You and Quillen have been a help to me, too. I don't know what I'd have done those first months without all the help you gave me cleaning up my house and property and then working here at the store."

The older man's eyes twinkled. "You did pay us, Walker. Don't make it sound too fine."

"I know, but you've always gone beyond."

Eldon turned to put a few clean glasses on the shelf. "I've enjoyed finding a new way to be useful since moving out of the ministry full-time. I like working here at the store. I live in a houseful of women mostly, so it's been a good change from all that girl talk."

He paused. "I find the Lord has used me here some as well to help folks, to ease their burdens a little now and then."

"I've watched that."

"See that wooden cattle yoke hanging on the wall there?" Eldon pointed to an old oxen yoke that added to the store's country character. "That's the way God means our relationship with Him to be, Him always helping, yoked with us, pulling most of the load, smoothing the way and easing the journey. Jesus said 'take my yoke, it's easy; the burden's light.' If you'll let God in a little more—and good people, too—you'll find that's true. Your journey will grow easier."

"Maybe I simply want people to know me as I am, not colored by anything of my past."

"Well, it's obvious your past has sent some hurts and disappointments your way, sent you running. But you're settling down again now. That's good. Maybe trust will come forward in time."

"Maybe. We'll see how things go."

In the late afternoon, the store always grew busier. Mothers picking up their kids from school or teenagers carpooling from the high school who stopped in to enjoy an ice cream cone, buy a small bag of candy from the barrels, or get a cola. They took their treats out on the front porch or sat clustered around one of the café tables on the side porch, chattering, laughing, and texting on their phones. Even in this small valley with few high-income families, every teen still seemed to have a phone tucked into their back pocket or purse.

As the day lengthened, people who lived in the valley stopped by the store to pick up small needs—a loaf of bread, a carton of milk, a can of soup, chips, or doughnuts left from the morning breakfast rush. People knew Walker now, and many chatted when they stopped by, sharing local news, passing along pleasantries, laughing or grumbling over the events of their day.

The life of a store was comfortable to Walker. He felt more at home than he had during the years on the road. He was still an outsider, but he was becoming a more accepted member of the community now.

Since Quillen had a school club meeting today, Walker clipped the leash on Marsh and walked him around the mile-long path that wove from the store through the field, behind Stone House and into the woods, and then back down the other side of his property in a loop before returning to the store again.

After returning, he sent Eldon on home and started cleaning the store to get ready for close. Hearing a noise on the porch, he glanced out the window to see Vernon and Harley skulking their way toward the door.

"We was waiting till everyone left to stop by," Harley said, letting himself and his brother inside. "It's been dangerous around here lately."

"Because of the helicopters flying through the valley again?"

Seeing Harley's eyes widen, Walker added, "One of the men in the Whitehead family who stopped by the store earlier said property assessors have been taking aerial shots over the last month or two. That's why we've seen so many helicopters lately."

"I suppose that's what *them* would say for flying down low spying on people's homes." He leaned closer. "But we know that ain't the real reason."

Vernon eyed the counter area. "Got any of them hot dogs left?"

Walker smiled. The brothers had discovered late drop-ins at the store often yielded free leftover food.

"Sure, and there's some slaw and chili, too. I'll fix you a plate." He went behind the counter while the two brothers perched on stools to wait.

"You wanted us to let you know if we saw anything suspicious," Harley said. "There was a van cruising up and down the roads around here one day, slowed down near the drive to your place."

Walker tensed.

"But it was a realtor showing people some property," Harley added. "We saw them get out after a while to walk around and look at that lot for sale on the other side of the road. We got close enough to read the sign on the side of their van, one of those realtor signs."

Vernon piped in. "Those signs ain't always reliable, though. *Them* are cagey, you know. That's why you have to be careful." He bit into the hot dog Walker set before him.

"Thank you for watching," Walker said, relieved over their words about the van.

"We didn't like it that two of those thieveries occurred right near our place, the last one on the road starting toward the Foothills Parkway," Harley said. "It weren't but a mile from our place, and the theft at the Hearons' place was even closer."

Walker fixed two sodas for the brothers, knowing what they liked by now, and snagged them both a bag of chips.

Vernon chuckled at a thought. "That Barney Fife deputy came snooping around our place after the Hearon theft, but the tree over the road kept him from driving in too close."

Walker turned to hide a smirk. Juliette had told him the brothers felled a tree over the gravel and dirt driveway to their old cabin in the woods just to keep people out. They'd created a rough side route through the woods they used to get to their place instead, the entry to it blocked with brush and logs they moved every time they came and went.

Today instead of their usual camouflage clothes, Harley wore an old plaid shirt and blue jeans rolled up above the top of his boots—and his trademark brown fedora. Vernon, too, wore jeans and a faded striped T-shirt, although he seldom wore a hat.

"The deputy came by here, too," Walker told them. "I think the sheriff's office is trying harder to get to the bottom of the thefts."

"So are we," Harley said. "We scouted around Whitey Hearon's place after they got hit. We know Whitey. There was tracks going in and out from the back of his place toward the woods and truck tracks in the soft dirt in the drive. It's queer, that. Whitey said it looked like they might have come and gone two ways."

Walker thought about their words. "If there's a group involved, some of them may hike or walk in to case things out first and then contact the others to bring the truck when they're ready to load."

Harley's eyes widened. "You think there's a whole ring of 'em, maybe? We saw what looked like about four sets of prints. If you know how to look smart, you can see when tracks are different. Our daddy taught us to track when we were only kids."

Marsh came over to greet the brothers, and they talked to the big dog with affection, having gotten used to him now.

"He sure is a purty dog," Vernon said. "We used to have us an old coon dog but he died. I'd like to get another."

"Go over to Pearl and Earline Walker's place. They have two or three dogs that need homes right now," Walker said.

"We'll think on it." Harley finished off his hot dog and chips and began to peel the wrapper off the candy bar Walker had put beside his plate. Harley always liked a plain Hershey bar, and he'd break it into neat pieces and eat each piece separately. Vernon's favorite was a Baby Ruth, which he generally wolfed down in three or four bites.

Vernon ran a hand through his stubbly beard. "I heard someone gave those Walker sisters a new truck to tote their animals around in, a brand-new computer and money for what they do."

"Whitey said it was some charity that believes in works that rescue animals and such like those two sisters do," Harley added. "He said they heard about Pearl and Earline getting robbed somehow and contacted them to help."

"That sounds like a good thing," Walker said.

"Yeah, but it's queer. Whitey said someone delivered two bikes to his house for his kids, too. His kids' bikes got stolen, you know. Whitey bought the family a new TV set to replace the one that got stole but he didn't have enough to buy bikes." Harley drummed his fingers on the counter. "Seems like there's been a rash of that sort of do-gooding going on around here."

Walker grinned. "You got something against doing good for folks?"

"No." Harley scowled at him. "It's only that I wonder when people suddenly seem to know a lot about others' business, good or bad. It don't happen like that much around here."

"It's like Santy Claus." Vernon grinned that silly grin of his. "Remember when we were kids how Santy Claus used to come around the valley and bring toys. He'd come right up to the house and leave the toys and presents so we could find 'em. Maybe it's Santy Claus doing good again."

Harley frowned. "It ain't Christmas, Vernon, and besides, everybody knows it was one of them Boring brothers that played Santa Claus in the valley back when we were kids."

"Well, it was a nice thing," Vernon argued. "And you know how happy Whitey's boys were to get those bikes no matter who brought them." He wadded up his candy bar wrapper and tossed it neatly across the counter into the trash. "Maybe it's Dade Claiborne helping out. He sells trucks at his dealership, and he's got a lot of money."

"Naw, I don't think it's him. Probably outsiders behind all this do-gooding." Harley snorted. "If you remember, it was Dade Claiborne that sicced that Barney Fife deputy on us."

"Yeah," Vernon said. "We never have liked him anyway."

Harley turned to Walker. "I hear Dade sent that deputy to check you out, too. You'd better watch out for him. He's got a mean streak most people don't see underneath all that smarm and charm."

"A deputy did stop by and asked me some questions," admitted Walker. "He also said he received a complaint about my dog, so I knew Dade sent the deputy over. Dade threatened to cause trouble about Marsh. One day in the store Dade acted aggressive toward Juliette, and Marsh didn't like it."

Vernon cackled. "I'd like to have seen that."

Walker tried to hold back a grin. "It's rare that Marsh is aggressive toward anyone, but he is protective."

"See?" Vernon nudged Harley. "That's why we need to get us another dog to watch our place."

Harley overlooked his comment. "We saw Dade Claiborne grab Juliette out in their side yard the other day. We'd been over at Whitey's. Me and Vernon almost started to head in to help. But then we saw she handled it herself pretty well, kicked him right in the shin. Always was a plucky girl."

Vernon added, "We saw her granddaddy coming along, too, so we slunk on off."

Walker banked down his temper. "I'm glad you're looking out for Juliette," he said after a few minutes.

Vernon licked the last of the chocolate from his candy bar off his fingers. "We like Juliette. We always watch out for her when she's home."

As the Vernon and Harley got ready to leave, Walker asked, "Do you boys need anything?"

"What do you mean?" Harley gave him a suspicious look.

"I own a store. You help me. I thought you might need something here."

Vernon's eyes moved to a guitar on a high shelf. "Harley's old guitar got broke. I sure miss it."

Harley glared at him. "That ain't a need, Vernon."

"Do you play the guitar?" Walker asked.

"A mite."

And that was how the last of Walker's day ended with Harley Ledford entertaining him with picking and singing for nearly an hour. The man had an incredible talent, all self-taught.

"Life's a wonder, isn't it?" Walker said to Marsh with a smile as they closed the store later. And, of course, Walker sent the guitar home with Harley and Vernon as a gift.

CHAPTER 10

Since fall had arrived, Juliette found herself wishing, on many days, that she was back in North Carolina. She sat on the stool behind the Happy Valley Store register today venting to her friend Sharon Bard on her cell phone.

"I wish I was back working with you at The Full Moon. There are always problems when I come to the valley, but this time even more than usual."

"Is Hettie Rhea causing difficulties for you?"

Juliette sighed. "She always does. I have never done a single thing to annoy that woman except for being alive, either."

"I seem to remember a few instances when you worked in a jab or two of your own toward her." Sharon laughed. "Unless you exaggerated."

Juliette drummed her fingers on the counter. "Well, perhaps there were a few times when I spoke a piece of my mind—trying to defend myself or to get Hettie to see things more rationally. Not that it did any good."

"Some people are born difficult. You've met my brother. I think he's one of those."

"Your brother Carlson is a close second to Hettie, I admit."

"Your own brother wasn't exactly a peach to tell Hettie about catching you smooching with the boss."

"That made me so mad. Even George should have known better than to drop gossip like that in Hettie's lap, for all our family's sake, if not for mine alone. Whatever was he thinking to let that slip?"

"You always said George could never see any fault in Hettie."

"That's for sure." Juliette got up to walk to the refrigerator to get a bottle of water. "But it's certainly made things difficult for me with Dade."

"Maybe that's a good thing. You've tried for years to convince Dade you don't care for him seriously. However, whenever you're home, you never date anyone else, so that hardly helps get the message across to him."

"Well, he still hasn't gotten the message regardless of what I've said or done." Juliette ran a hand through her hair in irritation. "He's become more aggressive since I started seeing Walker, coming by the store when he knows I'm working alone, pushing for dates, stopping by the house more often. The other day he found me out in the side yard alone reading on an old quilt and got rather physical. He tried to get me in a vise grip to kiss me, his hands moving like octopus arms. I had to resort to kicking him in the shin to get away. I thought I'd have to knee him, but fortunately, he saw Grandpa coming across the field and turned nice."

"Has that happened before?"

"Not lately, but I've experienced my share of wrestling matches in the past with Dade. It's one of the reasons I backed away from him. It's also one of the reasons I always hate coming back to the valley." She took a long drink from the bottle of water she'd pulled from the refrigerator. "Dade has a long string of girls chasing after him. I keep hoping he'll link up with one of them and get married or something."

"He sounds like the type who always wants what he can't have."

"The big question is why he's so interested in me."

Sharon laughed. "That's obvious to anyone but you, Juliette. You are pretty, charming, and talented. You should know that."

"These days I mostly feel harassed and pressured. The other night George, Laura, and the kids invited me over to dinner, and they all pushed on me to 'make up' with Dade. My niece, Kirsten, thinks Dade is so good-looking and even my nephew, Robert, offered reasons for why Dade would be a good match for me. Can you believe it? That's my entire family, counting my grandparents, pressuring me to marry someone I don't even like, much less love."

"What do they think about Walker?"

"They're uncomfortable with Walker. They don't really know him and he seems a threat to what they've set their hopes on."

"But you're still seeing Walker, aren't you?"

"At the store, of course, but less outside of work since all this trouble started. Hettie and Dade spread rumors and unpleasant gossip about Walker as well as stories about me. I'm sure Walker picked up on it, and I heard that a few of Hettie's friends made very pointed remarks to Walker when in the store."

The friends paused in their conversation while Sharon answered a question for RuthAnn, one of Sharon's employees at The Full Moon.

"Do you need to go?" Juliette asked.

"No. I'm working in the back office, but RuthAnn stuck her head in the door to ask me where I'd stored something. She doesn't know the store as well as you. I wish you could come back today, Juliette. I miss you, not only in the store but as a friend."

"Thanks. I miss you, too. I hope you haven't rented out that basement apartment in your house."

"No. You're the only decent renter I've had since I moved to Murphy. I'm keeping that apartment open in hopes that you'll come back when your grandfather is better."

"He is better, but he's stubborn and that's another problem." Juliette curled her legs under the stool, trying to get more comfortable. "He doesn't like the diet the doctors put him on. And Gramma isn't helping with that as much as she should either. She tends to cater to what Grandpa wants rather than insisting he stay true to the diet. She clings to her own stubborn ideas about what good nutrition is and she's very set in her ways of cooking, so Grandpa is eating too many fried and greasy foods, and sweets. Laura and I try to push for change, but it's difficult."

"It's hard to change ways that have become long-established habits."

"That's true. Grandpa doesn't rest enough either. He thinks hard work is healthy. He's been stubborn about that, too, and he often does things around the farm he shouldn't—lifting heavy bales of hay, working too long out in the fields in the heat. I caught him on a ladder the other day, getting ready to climb on the barn to nail down a loose shingle."

Sharon laughed. "I'm sorry to laugh, but I can easily visualize that. I've met both your grandparents, and you know I love them."

"So do I. But it's hard being here right now."

"It's not easy living in their home after being on your own for so long or having to play the parent role with them, driving them places, policing their diet and activities. I'm sure it makes them feel old."

"My gramma has said as much. She and Grandpa even snapped at George and Laura the other day—that's a first. It's a difficult situation. I'll be glad when Grandpa is back to normal."

"Juliette, you need to accept the fact that both your grandparents are growing older. Your dad is only sixty years old now, but your grandparents are in their eighties."

"You're right and no matter how cross I get at them sometimes, I love them so much."

"They know it, too." Sharon changed the subject. "What are you working on with your quilting now?"

"A new crazy quilt with flower shapes and cute crocheted buttons. Gramma was making decorative buttons for a pillow and taught me how to do them. They're fun and whimsical to tuck into the quilt pattern, especially as flower centers."

"It sounds pretty. Take a photo and text it to me."

"I will. I'll also send you a photo of the yo-yo monkeys we're working on. Gramma taught me how to make those, too. She had an old pattern in one of her boxes and I fell in love with it. We're having a good time making the monkeys together. I think they'll sell great on my Etsy site, at your store, or at the store here in the valley."

"Walker's been good to let you sell your quilts and craft items at the Happy Valley Store."

"Maybe," she conceded. "But the quilt and craft sales have been good for his business, too."

"You've liked working for Walker." Sharon shifted the subject.

"Yes, but it hasn't changed the fact that I plan to come back after Christmas as soon as Grandpa is better. I have classes scheduled at the folk school this spring and I miss my life there."

Even as she said the words, Juliette knew she felt torn about going back. She was developing feelings for Walker Logan despite their differences. It would be hard to leave when it was time.

"Keep an open mind," Sharon said, as if reading her thoughts. "I'm trying to do that, too."

Juliette caught her last words. "What? Are you finally getting serious about Evan?"

"The change is more in Evan. It's as if he suddenly discovered I'm a woman as well as a colleague at the college."

"No kidding?" Juliette laughed. "Well, good for Evan. Goes to show that even professors can wise up." She glanced at the clock. "I will definitely want a full report on this the next time we talk, but the lunch crowd will be coming soon. I need to get ready to feed some of the locals who usually stop in."

"Still only hot dogs?"

"Actually, no. We are now officially serving barbecue sandwiches, with slaw or plain, as an addition to the menu. Eldon bought a smoker and he and Lula make the barbecue. All I have to do is put the pans of barbecue in a warmer oven Walker bought and then make the sandwiches up as ordered. It's been a hit, I can tell you."

She heard Marsh barking and knew Walker would soon head in through the back door of the store to help with lunch.

"I'll talk to you again soon, Sharon," she said.

"Morning, Juliette," Walker called out, unleashing Marsh inside the door. The big dog bounded over for a greeting and then began his usual prowl around the store, covering what he considered his territory and sniffing for other potential dog smells.

She studied Walker while he ambled toward her, feeling that lift in her heart at the sight of him.

"I need to talk to you for a minute before the lunch crowd starts to come in." He sat down on a stool at the counter across from her.

"Is anything wrong?"

He cocked his head. "No, except I don't see you often enough anymore."

She glanced away.

"Maybe we can talk about that later, perhaps when we go on another hike together. Would you go?"

"Yes, I'd like that, and I'm sorry about all the trouble with Dade, my family, and Hettie Rhea and her friends," Juliette said in a rush. "I didn't mean to bring more problems into your life."

He reached across the counter to put a hand on her cheek. "You are what Eldon would call one of the blessings in my life since I've been here, Juliette. I hope you might say the same of me, despite all the difficulties."

She put a hand over his. "Yes, I can. Please know that. And I want you to know I have no vested feelings or any commitments toward Dade Claiborne no matter what you might have heard."

"What I heard is that he's been acting aggressive toward you. That's what I wanted to talk to you about. Is that true?"

She felt a blush climb up her neck. "Who told you that?"

"Harley and Vernon. They told me they saw Dade practically attack you in your side yard one day. They were ready to move in but said you countered pretty well and then your grandpa ambled on the scene, putting a halt to anything more Dade had in mind."

She shook her head. "Those two snoopy men. They sure seem to know a lot about what happens in this valley."

"Do you want me to talk with Dade?" Walker asked.

"With your fists?"

He grinned. "I'll try words first. I can talk to your grandparents, too, if you want—and to your brother. None of them would want Dade manhandling you. That's inappropriate, Juliette, and dangerous."

She crossed her arms. "I kept hoping he would finally get the message that I am not interested."

"He seems slow to arrive at that message."

"I know. I haven't wanted to worry the family with it. It would upset Grandpa and …"

"Your grandpa would be much more upset if some serious harm came to you. Surely you know that."

She tapped her fingers on the counter, looking away from him again. "I know."

"Will you promise me that you will talk to your family? You can tell them there are witnesses if you need to. Besides Harley and Vernon as witnesses, Quillen saw Dade acting aggressively toward you in the store one day, too. This has to stop, Juliette."

"Yes," she said, knowing it was true. "We're having a family dinner tonight for Kirsten's fourteenth birthday. I'll talk to everyone then."

"They may favor Dade for you as a potential husband, but they won't be happy to hear about him threatening you with his behavior. I can assure you of that."

She sighed. "Thanks. I probably needed you to push me to take some action about this." She grinned at him. "I guess I owe you."

"Good. I'll collect on that debt by asking you to help me with a dinner party I want to give at Stone House."

She knew her mouth dropped open. "You want to entertain?"

He wrinkled his nose at her. "Don't look so surprised. I'm really a sociable guy. Surely you've seen that by now."

She avoided comment.

"I know I've been somewhat secretive and reclusive in my private life, but I think I'm ready to make some changes about that. Eldon had a talk with me and encouraged me to let people in more."

"Well, good for Eldon," she couldn't help but add.

He swatted at her playfully. "Besides, I owe the Rasnics dinner for having me over to their house so many times. I'd like to invite Cameron and his latest girlfriend—Letitia, I think her name is—and I'd like to invite your friends Keith and Amy if you think they'd come."

"How nice. I think Keith and Amy would love to come, and it

would be good for them to have a night out together."

"I've had a few talks with Keith when he's stopped by the store. He's a fine man. I agree with you that the community center should be renovated, and Keith thinks so, too. I know some funding sources that may be interested in the project, and as you suggested, Keith is very interested in the idea of managing the center if we can get it renovated and improved. He likes the idea of having a daycare and after-school care program on-site, too, and of utilizing the building for other community activities and groups. The center was deeded to the community back in 1980, and Keith and I had a meeting last week with several of the community leaders involved with it. All are in favor of improving the building and increasing ways that the community center can benefit the valley. Other groups already using the building will gain from the renovation, too."

"Amy hasn't mentioned any of this to me."

"Keith said he wanted to wait to talk to her about it until the funding was more certain. I think that's in place now."

She studied him. "A lot of unexpected funding has been showing up around here lately. Do you know anything more about that?"

His eyes didn't quite meet hers. "That longtime friend of mine I talked to you about—Burton—is an attorney out west and linked to a number of philanthropic charities. Several of them like to support projects related to good causes in rural communities with need."

"I see." She decided not to push him on this. "Well, whatever you've had to do with causing this to happen for Keith and Amy makes me very happy, Walker. Thank you. They are deserving of some good coming their way." She leaned over the counter to kiss him.

He glanced toward the door before putting a hand behind her neck to pull her closer for another kiss.

"Remember I'm your employee," she said, teasing him.

"Yes, and it was a happy day for me when you asked for a job here." He drew back, hearing sounds on the porch.

Two couples came in, chatting happily and telling Walker and

Juliette they'd been hearing about the new barbecue sandwiches on the menu.

"We're heading down to Abrams Campground to take a hike and thought we'd pick up sandwiches to eat at one of the picnic tables by the creek," one of the women said. "After we eat, enjoy the stream and a rest, we plan to take a little hike up the Cooper Road Trail."

"We love that trail," one of the men added. "We live in Maryville and try to get over here to Abrams to hike whenever we can."

The conversation moved on to a discussion about favorite trails and hikes as Walker and Juliette made lunch for four. After the hikers left, a flurry of other local customers began to arrive, most opting to take their lunches out onto the café screened porch to eat, a few staying at the counter.

It wasn't until later in the day that Juliette and Walker had time to talk again about the dinner Walker wanted to plan.

"When do you hope to host this special event at your house?" she asked when the store finally grew quiet again.

He glanced at the calendar on his phone. "Would this Saturday be too soon? Today is Monday so that would give us all week to make plans."

"Sounds good to me. Call the couples involved to see if they're free. If not, ask if the next weekend would work. I can do either."

He typed some notes into his phone and then looked across at her. "I know you need to attend your family party tonight but maybe we could get together and talk about this more later on."

"Sure."

Walker stroked his chin like he often did when he was thinking. "Could you come up to the house for dinner tomorrow night? I can grill something and we could make plans then." He squared his shoulders. "I'd like to come by your house and pick you up in the proper way, too, say my hellos to your grandparents, and bring you home after. I know your grandparents wouldn't want you walking back by yourself after dark."

"All right," she said, knowing it was the best thing to do.

"Would five be too early?" he asked. "You've said your grandmother serves dinner around six. I wouldn't want to interrupt their meal."

"That's thoughtful and five is perfect." She paused in wiping down the counter. "What are you planning to grill?"

"Steak, if that's okay with you," he answered. "I can pop some potatoes in the oven to bake, make a salad."

"I'll make the salad and help with the preparations when I get there, and I'll bring dessert, too. I make a fine homemade apple pie." She grinned at him.

He laughed, and she liked the sound of it. Walker didn't laugh often enough to her way of thinking.

"I'll pick up a bottle of wine, if that would be all right," he added. "And maybe some ice cream to spoon over that pie."

"It sounds like a nice evening."

"I think we're due a nice evening," he said, before another group of customers came in, signaling the busy hours of the late afternoon.

CHAPTER 11

Walker took off work early the next day to make a trip to the chain grocery in Maryville where he did his major shopping every week, and to tidy up the house before picking up Juliette. With time to spare, he headed upstairs to his office, located in the bonus room like Cameron had suggested. He settled at his desk, and punched in a familiar number on his cell phone.

"Hey, Burton, how are you?" he asked when his friend answered. "I know you're probably at the office but I hoped you'd have a minute to talk."

Burton Franklin's deep voice rolled back. "I can spare a few minutes before my next appointment comes in. What's up?"

"I wanted to check on the funding plans for the renovation of the community center. Do you have all that worked out yet?"

"Yes. Your builder friend Cooper Garrison sent his estimates in for the renovations. He's given you an excellent price since it's for a good cause. I gather the two of you have talked about a time frame, and the money is ready to be released through one of those charities we organized. The major corporate foundation we set up, Goodman Brothers, has chosen RHC, Rural Help Connection, as one of its grant recipients after learning of their need to renovate a historic building in a bucolic mountain community."

"Sweet." Walker chuckled over the professional wording.

"That's the way you can talk it up, too, to keep secret the fact that you are the funding source behind both groups."

"Do you disapprove, Burton?"

"Of course not. Money needs to move. And money needs to be donated philanthropically to provide a tax break." He hesitated. "Besides, I like the idea of you getting back into the real world again. It's good to see. When you run into other small needs like the sisters' animal rescue operation or a family in need like the Hearons, we can funnel money again from the REA, the Rural Economic Aid group, that we created. Hopefully, we won't need to set up any others. It might begin to draw attention if I am handling too many."

"I'll keep that in mind."

"When are you going to take a trip out west to see your friends? Stewart and I could both get away one weekend, if you can, for a guys' hangout at our cabin. Do some fishing. Hike and relax. Catch up."

"I'd like that. Hopefully, we can find a way."

"We did before. It only takes a little planning on all our parts to be careful. Let's do it before winter hits in the mountains here in the Denver area. I don't want us getting caught at that cabin in five feet of snow like on one of our visits."

Walker laughed. "I remember that trip and I agree."

"Hey, my client is here, so I've gotta jet, brother. Call Stewart."

"Anything wrong?" Walker tensed.

"No. Sometimes there's good news and it's his to share. Just call."

Walker punched in Stewart's number at the store in Greeley, a phone number he knew as well as his school multiplication tables.

"Marshall's General Store, this is Stewart."

"Hey, this is your worst enemy."

He heard Stewart laugh. "Hold on."

Walker listened to Stewart make excuses to leave the front of the store so he could move to his private office in the back.

"It's good to hear your voice," Stewart said a few minutes later.

"Back at you," Walker said, listening to the familiar creak of the old leather chair as Stewart settled into it—once his chair at Marshall's. He closed his eyes for a moment over the memory, seeing the battered rolltop desk piled high with ledgers and papers;

its cubby holes stuffed with stamps, paper clips and notes; the tan file cabinets crammed in the corner; the framed prints of Greeley landmarks hanging, usually crooked, on the walls.

"Is everything okay?" Stewart asked.

"Everything's fine. I was talking to Burton earlier and got you on my mind. How's life with you?"

"Good." Stewart paused, then with excitement in his voice announced, "Kathy and I are going to have a baby. How about that?"

Walker smiled. "I'm happy for you."

He listened to Stewart rattle on about baby news, when the baby was due, how Kathy felt, how they planned to fix up the spare bedroom into a nursery. Sometimes Stewart could talk more than most women Walker knew. Even though his cousin had always been shy and awkward in general—especially with women or people he didn't know well—he could really talk a blue streak with his friends.

"I think early March will be a great time for a baby to arrive. Maybe you can come out then." Stewart's voice grew hopeful.

"We'll see. You know I'd like that."

As they talked more, Stewart caught him up on life in Greeley, at Marshall's, and shared updates about their friends and family. It was always bittersweet to hear, although of course Walker wanted to know about everyone. It was a world he'd left behind, but it still held a big piece of his heart.

Walker glanced at his watch. "Hey, Stewart, I hate to cut you off, but I have a date with Juliette and need to go pick her up."

"That's great. I'm glad you're making a good life there, that you built the store and met someone." A touch of anxiety threaded his voice. "You haven't had any problems there, have you?"

"No. So far all is good."

He heard Stewart sigh. "I'm real glad to hear that. Call again soon."

"I will. Tell Kathy I sent my best."

Walker disconnected and then gazed out the window in silence for a time. These last years had proved hard, but life was getting better now. Life did move on, and the passing of time changed things. Even the way Walker felt and how he'd personally changed. He wasn't the same man who'd left Greeley—running, angry, scared for those he loved. Travel had altered him from the innocent, idealistic small-town boy he'd been before.

Glancing at his watch, he headed toward the door. The regret he'd felt while talking to Stewart lifted as he started the car to head for Juliette's, and he whistled as he drove the short distance to her house.

The winding fence-lined drive into the Hollander farm passed under old maple trees shading the narrow road and wandered by well-kept red barns and outbuildings. To either side of the road lay green fields, dotted with hay bales. A shallow creek wandered through the property and cattle grazed under a spreading oak or stood cooling their feet in the water. Walker knew, from past visits, that the farm was a large one and that on the backside of the property, facing the Happy Valley Loop road, another winding drive led to Juliette's brother George's home. George and his family handled the bulk of the farming operation now with a few occasional part-time workers.

Walker had met George's family when they dropped by the store. His wife Laura, dressed in farm jeans and boots, or in her neat nurse's uniform, seemed a friendly no-nonsense, hard working woman. Their children took after Laura and George in looks and personality—Robert, sixteen, a clean-cut, serious boy, always full of talk about the farm or some 4-H or FFA project and very proud to be driving now. The younger Kirsten seemed equally happy to be a Hollander Farm descendant. Walker knew she was fond of animals and had racked up some impressive 4-H awards for her sheep and chickens. He liked all the family—good, wholesome easy-natured people—despite his earlier problems with George.

As Walker had gotten to know Juliette's family, including her grandparents, he could see why she seemed like a black sheep among them. First, she looked different from all of them, with her mother's Italian genetics winning out in her appearance. Second, her main interests were creative ones, especially her quilting, with excellent marketing and business skills mixed in. He knew it was Juliette's love for family that kept drawing her back, versus a desire to be a part of the busy, ongoing farm life that formed the central world for the other Hollanders.

He wished they appreciated her gifts more and saw the incredible talent she possessed. Walker had seen many of Juliette's lavish, rich quilts now, her beautiful handmade bags, clothing items, and other design projects. She had a unique style in her work—every piece pure artistry. He liked showcasing it in the store, and the sales for her work proved their appeal. Walker had sent a few pieces of Juliette's work to his sister, Victoria, along with links to Juliette's website and Etsy site. Vee and Chandler had now already ordered items to use in several of their decorating projects. It only confirmed to Walker that Juliette possessed a talent that would take her far professionally in time, but her family didn't seem to see that.

He pulled up in front of the big Hollander farmhouse, tucked between deep shade trees and a cluster of flowering shrubs. It was a typical farmhouse in appearance—white, two-storied with a broad front porch, gray shutters and roof. George's home looked similar, although newer in construction, with a red roof and shutters and a colorful array of rose bushes around the house, revealing a favorite hobby of Laura's. Most of the Hollander land was flat, weaving its way through a low area wedged between Happy Valley Road and the Happy Valley Loop. Shallow Bell Branch Creek wound through the property and a green hillside rose toward the mountains at one end of the farmland. George and his son, Robert, had planted a Christmas tree farm in that upper area over the last years, another way to bring in extra money in the winter when farm income dropped.

George, despite his narrow-minded attitudes in many areas, seemed industrious and smart. Juliette worried that Dade had begun pressuring George about repayment of money he'd loaned him. Walker meant to talk to George about that soon. Dade had grown somewhat threatening and antagonistic toward the Hollanders since Juliette pulled back from his advances, and he'd begun to use the idea of a marriage as a condition for not pushing for heavier payments than George could afford. Walker didn't like that tactic.

As he walked up on the Hollander's shady porch, Juliette's grandfather Dalton Hollander opened the door to him. He was dressed in his usual farm overalls with a faded plaid shirt underneath, his hair solid white now and thinning on the top with a short white beard curling around his jaw, his face weathered from age and outdoor life. Despite his years, and the heart attack that had slowed his pace, he was strong, good-hearted, and land-wise, if a little gruff at times.

"Mr. Hollander." Walker put out his hand.

A firm grip met his. "Come on in. The wife's in the kitchen working at dinner and I'm sure Juliette will be downstairs in a minute, having heard your car pull up."

Gramma Newell walked into the big living room from the kitchen as Walker settled into the chair Grandpa Dalton gestured to. She carried two jars of pretty red jelly. "Here's you some jelly made from those Jonathan apples from your place. I've been meaning to send it over to you."

"Thank you, Mrs. Hollander." Walker took the jelly, placing it on the coffee table in front of him.

"Just call me Gramma Newell like everyone else does around here. And I thank you for letting Juliette get fruit for me from your orchard. There's some fine old trees on your place that yield well."

"You're welcome to get apples or fruit anytime, and I thank you for the jelly you sent earlier from the Pippin apples and for that nice pie, too."

She beamed a little with pleasure. "I like to putter about the kitchen."

Walker cleared his throat. "Since you're both here, I'd like to say a word to you for a moment, if it's okay."

Grandpa Dalton lifted an eyebrow to Walker in question while Gramma Newell sat down near him in a side chair.

"Perhaps you don't know that I met Juliette—somewhat informally—picking apples on the day I first looked at the Stone House property." He could tell by the expressions passed between them that Juliette had not shared this story with them. "When she came by the store this summer, I was pleased to hire her to work part-time for me. I needed help at the store, but I will admit to you I also hired Juliette because she had stayed in my thoughts over the year. There's a decided attraction between the two of us. My uncle, a minister back in my old hometown, made the comment to me recently that it was probably of the Lord's orchestration bringing me here, linking me to Juliette and to this place."

He could tell from a nod Gramma Newell passed to her husband that the two liked those last words.

"I know I'm not a local man, but I come from a strong, good Christian family. My grandfather started a store in my hometown out west, my father inherited it, and then me. My cousin, who worked with us in the family business, runs it now. So I'm following in my heritage with my store here in Happy Valley, sort of like how your family follows their heritage with Hollander Farm."

Grandpa nodded and Gramma even smiled at him then.

"A situation developed in my life that caused me to leave my original store, nothing wrong that I did. In fact, I chose to leave because of problems threatening my family—related to me. I know that sounds vague but since the situation is still under investigation, I'm not at liberty to share more right now. I know, loving your own family as you do, that you would do a lot to protect them from harm, even giving up something you love for them. That's what I did."

Walker could see both of them considering these words.

"Because I'm developing strong feelings for Juliette and seeing her now, I felt I should offer you some explanation for the secrecy behind my past life. If I was too forthcoming at this time, it might bring that trouble here to Happy Valley. I don't want that, either for the friends I have made here or for my family members where they are, safer now that my whereabouts are unknown to most."

Grandpa Dalton scratched his chin. "Juliette told us you don't have a criminal past and aren't running from wrongdoing."

"Yes, and she said she thought you'd been through some disappointments and hard times," Juliette's grandmother added.

"I have known some hard times but not financial ones. Disappointments with people can be equally difficult—especially when criminal intent is involved."

Grandpa leaned forward. "Have you been personally threatened, son?"

"I have, and please know I tell you this in confidence since I'm seeing your granddaughter. However, of more concern to me when I left were the threats against my family."

"Who or what lay behind these threats? Can you say?"

Walker could feel Grandpa Dalton's eyes on him as he asked the questions. He hesitated. "Money," he said at last. "I came into some money. That's all I can say for now."

"The Good Book says money is the root of all evil, at least when folks covet after it," Gramma Newell said, laying her hand on a worn black Bible on the table by her chair.

"I've unfortunately seen that to be true."

Grandpa Dalton gave him a considering look then. "Money can also be a blessing and a way to bless and help folks in need. There's been a lot of that around here lately. You know anything about that, son?"

Juliette walked into the room. "If Walker does, that can be a story for another day. I think he's shared enough of his private affairs for now."

"How long you been listening, girl?" Grandpa frowned at her.

"Long enough," she replied with a toss of her hair. "And it was good of Walker to try to reassure you both about his past so that you'd quit being so edgy around him."

"He was doing better before you put your oar in with these saucy comments." Grandpa frowned at her. "Did you know all this?"

She swallowed and looked away.

He chuckled. "Well, that's what you're all het up about then, that he shared with us afore you." He turned to Walker. "You might need to soothe on her this evening to work your way back into her good graces."

Walker frowned. "I can see that, but I intended to tell Juliette the same things I told you a little later. In fact, if she'd been downstairs when I arrived, I'd have shared with her at the same time."

Gramma Newell stood. "Well, I need to get back in the kitchen to tend to my dinner. Walker, it was good of you to share with us as you did. You come on to church Sunday and then back home with us for Sunday dinner if you like. Our grandson George, Laura, and the kids are coming and probably a few more folks from the church. We're setting up a picnic on tables in the side yard under the trees since the weather's still nice. You come join us if you can."

"That's kind of you to ask, but all the Johnsons are attending a special event at their church this Sunday, so I'll need to open and work the store." Walker stood, picking up his jars of jelly as he did.

"Maybe Juliette will bring you over a plate," Grandpa put in, pushing himself to his feet from his own chair. "Son, I appreciate you sharing with us as you did. Newell and I will hold your confidences until you feel you can open up and share with folks around the valley. You might be surprised to find most would feel right protective and respectful of what you've done."

"Not everyone," Juliette added.

Her grandfather scowled at her but then shook his head in grudging agreement. "You're right about that. There's some that's not particularly happy with you or Juliette right now. Guess the less known the better for a time."

Walker said his good-byes while Juliette went to the kitchen to get the pie she'd made for dinner, and then they both left. He held the door of the Jeep for her, helped her in, and they drove all the way to Walker's place without a word spoken.

He stopped the car in his driveway and turned to look at her. "You going to stay mad at me all night?"

"I might," she said. "It's not flattering for you to share with my grandparents what you wouldn't share with me."

"As I said, I'd made up my mind to share a little with them and with you tonight." He leaned toward her, running a hand down her cheek. "I'm falling in love with you, Juliette Lucia Hollander. It makes me willing to take some risks I wasn't willing to take before."

Tears trickled down her face then. "I really wanted to stay mad at you for a while."

"But now?" he said, moving nearer to trace his fingers from her cheek to her neck, feeling the tension heighten in the air between them.

She sighed. "Now I just want you to kiss me. Surely you know that."

Leaning closer, Walker did exactly that, losing a few more inhibitions in the process, letting his heart slide into the kiss.

"Do you really think you're falling in love with me?" she asked softly after a while.

"I do. I think you cast a spell on me the first day you fell out of that apple tree into my arms."

She laughed. "You make that sound very romantic, when actually we both tumbled in a heap to the ground after I fell."

"Yes. With you on top of me. That was a perk to my way of thinking." He kissed her again. "I never have thanked Marsh for helping that to happen a second time either."

She giggled and threaded her fingers through his hair, looking into his eyes. "I think I'm falling in love with you, too, Walker Owen Logan."

"I'm glad," he said, kissing her again. "But we'd better go inside. Marsh is barking. He's heard the car."

They busied themselves starting dinner after that, Juliette working on the salad while Walker took Marsh on a stroll around the yard and started the charcoal in the grill. Over their meal, they kept their conversation casual, talking about mundane things and the upcoming social event at Walker's.

As they finished dinner and settled in to a dessert of apple pie and coffee, Juliette leaned toward him. "Was it really money that started the problems for you back home?"

He nodded, taking another bite of pie.

"This is great pie," he said. "I think you inherited your grandmother's cooking genes whether you want to acknowledge it or not."

"You're avoiding the subject," she said.

"I am." He took a sip of coffee, thinking what he wanted to say. "I will tell you more as I can, Juliette. Right now I still need to be careful."

She bit her lip. "Even with me?"

"Yes. I shared more than I felt wise to reassure your grandparents about me, so they'd ease off pressuring you into a relationship with Dade Claiborne you don't want and pressuring you away from a relationship with me."

She looked out the window to where dark was falling gradually. "My grandparents aren't very happy with Dade right now after I shared with them last night about his aggressive behavior. George tried to make excuses for Dade, saying he felt frustrated over my dangling him, but Grandpa and Gramma intervened for me, even Laura." She smiled over the name. "Laura said there was never an excuse for a man to try to force himself on a woman. She cautioned Kirsten to watch out for Dade, too, saying a man who would act that way with one woman would act the same with another. She said she'd heard stories like that all too often working at the hospital."

"Good for Laura."

"It helped, but you need to remember George grew up playing with Dade and Ronnie Claiborne. It's hard for George to see fault in Dade, remembering him as the cute little kid who tagged along behind him. Those memories make it difficult for my grandparents to see problems with Dade, too. Thankfully, Laura sees more clearly, not having grown up in the valley. As she said, people do change."

"So your grandparents aren't pushing you to marry Dade Claiborne anymore?"

"Oh, they still think Dade is a good match for me, but they aren't happy with his behavior recently."

"How do they feel about me?"

"I'd say you went up a few notches in their admiration tonight. My grandpa appreciates an upfront manner and he likes a man who declares his intentions. You'll notice, too, that my gramma invited you to Sunday dinner with the family. That's a stamp of approval from her."

He smiled. "I wish I could have said yes, but it's my Sunday to work. In the winter I may start closing the store on Sundays, but right now I would lose a lot of revenue to do so. Quillen and I have been alternating Sundays, as you know. We get locals, the traffic driving to and from church, and Sunday tourists. I need the revenue."

She met his eyes. "But you could do without it."

He gazed back at her. "Even if traffic fell off, I'd never have to close the store unless I wanted to. Is that what you wanted to know?"

"Yes." She got up to pour herself another cup of coffee and sat back down. "Are you behind the philanthropic efforts going on around the valley, like my grandpa suggested?"

"I think you had that figured out on your own. I'm linked to a couple of charitable organizations and a foundation."

"Your foundation?"

"Pretty much." He got up to clear their dishes off the table. "Would you like to go sit on the screened porch? It's a nice night. We can take another cup of coffee outside with us or I could pour us a glass of wine."

"I think a glass of wine would be nice," she said.

They settled on the porch a few minutes later, Marsh padding out to join them, the big dog enjoying the smells and sounds of the night.

"Walker, I'm glad to know more about you. Will you tell me everything one day?"

"I will when I can." He scooted closer to her on the rattan sofa and draped an arm around her shoulders. "I promise I will when

I can."

"Good." She let out a little sigh. "It keeps me from really letting go with all my feelings when there are secrets. I need full candor in a relationship and full trust before…." Her words drifted off.

"I understand. I won't ask you for anything more, for any kind of commitment until I can share more."

"Okay." She smiled at him and then changed the subject. "Since everybody agreed to come to the party this Saturday, let's get our plans finalized about that. I'll come early to help you set up, and I'll help with some of the food. I can make hors d'oeuvres for snacks before dinner and I want to make a homemade apple cake for dessert. It's a shame not to capitalize on all the great apples on your trees right now. Fresh apple cake is heavenly, especially with thick, homemade whipped cream on top."

Walker felt the tension ease out of his shoulders as she rattled on with plans. He'd taken a big step sharing more about his life with Juliette's grandparents, and with Juliette, and he was glad both had received his words well and not grown angry when he wouldn't share more. He felt grateful, too, that Juliette's grandfather understood the need for keeping his confidences. Gossip traveled quickly in a small area like Happy Valley, and for now, Walker needed to continue to protect his identity.

CHAPTER 12

Over the next week, Juliette felt happy that she and Walker had moved to a new level in their relationship. Sort of. She hated adding those two words to the mix, but there were aspects about her life that seemed to keep her feeling restless and edgy.

She'd tried talking with Amy about her feelings, but Amy was so caught up with excitement about the renovations starting at the community center, the new position opening for Keith, and the plans for her expanded daycare center that she didn't seem to pick up on Juliette's unrest. Juliette could hardly talk to her gramma, either. There were enough problems going on already with Grandpa pushing the boundaries set up about his eating and work activities. Juliette hated to trouble her gramma with anything else.

When the phone rang with an invitation from Amy's mother, Lenora, to stop by for coffee, Juliette jumped at the opportunity.

"I've meant to invite you over," Lenora said. "Today I don't need to be at the college until after lunch, and I think Amy said you didn't work until later today, too. Can you come?"

"I'd love to," Juliette said, and meant it. She was overdue a visit with Lenora anyway, and it would be good to have another woman to talk to.

Lenora's rustic log home was only a short walk or drive from Juliette's grandparents' house and built on a piece of property that had once belonged to Boone descendants in the valley. Juliette knew Lenora and her husband, Caleb, had delighted in planning and building this home in their early marriage. Lenora was already teaching at Maryville College in the Appalachian Studies program then, and Caleb was on the staff at Tremont Environmental Institute. It still saddened Juliette to remember Lenora lost Caleb only a few years after they'd moved into the house.

"I love your place and how you've let the late flowers riot and grow wild all over the grounds, not mowing them down," Juliette told Lenora when she answered the door.

The older woman, blond and attractive in slacks and a loose woven shirt, glanced toward her yard and laughed. "Honey, the more natural I can keep the property, the less maintenance I have with it." She gestured Juliette inside. "Go on back to the kitchen. I have coffee ready and a loaf of banana bread I picked up at the bakery yesterday."

Juliette knew the house well and found her way easily to the kitchen. The home, with its split-log walls and deep windows, had an open, inviting living, dining, and kitchen area, spread around a big rock fireplace. Juliette knew two bedrooms and a bath opened off the hallway on the main floor of the house. A third bedroom— that used to be Amy's—snuggled under the eaves upstairs, along with a second bath and a neat office where Lenora worked at home when she wasn't at the college. The décor throughout was rustic and simple, with most of the colors neutral except for bright touches in the rag rugs, art, and quilts—many of the latter Juliette's.

"It's about time you came by to see me," Lenora said, pouring both of them coffee and putting the banana bread on the table.

Juliette settled into a chair at the table, glancing out the picture window as she did. The kitchen looked out on a woodsy backyard with a creek threading through it, the foothills of the mountains beyond.

Over coffee and banana bread, the women chatted and caught up on their lives and news, enjoying being together again. Juliette, soon feeling better from time in Lenora's good company, decided not to dump any of her trivial problems at this visit. After a pause in their conversation, though, Lenora leaned forward across the table, a hand under her chin, and asked, "And how is Juliette deep inside where no one sees?"

It was an old familiar line of Lenora's and brought tears to Juliette's eyes to hear it.

"Talk to me," Lenora said. "You're unhappy. I can feel it."

"Well, I feel guilty to be unhappy. There's nothing wrong with my life. Sharon graciously let me leave The Full Moon to come home to help Gramma and Grandpa, and another woman took the quilting class I'd scheduled at the folk school this fall. Grandpa is getting better, even if cantankerous and difficult some days. I found a nice part-time job at the store to keep me from going crazy while at the farm." She dropped her eyes. "And Walker Logan is developing feelings for me."

"And you for him?"

She nodded. "Yes, and I'd hoped for that, so there's no reason I should feel edgy, restless, and discontent."

"But you do."

"I do." She shook her head. "I shouldn't either. I don't know what in the world is wrong with me."

Lenora smiled. "Sometimes it takes a while to sort ourselves out in life, to know who we are *within* ourselves."

"You think that's it?" Juliette asked. "Gramma said you need to be right in your faith to be right in yourself."

"She's correct in that advice, of course. That's a part of learning who you are, too, who you're intended to be, the path you need to take in life."

Juliette wrinkled her nose. "Do you think I'm still figuring that out?"

"Maybe." Lenora finished a last bite of banana bread, thinking. "Tell me your worries. Everyone has them."

Juliette pushed her silverware around on the table restlessly, deciding what to say. Then she blurted out. "I guess I worry most, like everyone says, that I don't have a real, steady job with retirement and benefits or a sound future. Only my art I'm hoping to develop. I worry that maybe when I'm old someday I'll have to move back in with George and Laura at the farm, when my grandparents and Daddy are gone, and that everyone will tsk-tsk about how I wasted my life doodling after my art."

Lenora waited, sipping her coffee.

"I love my art and my quilting business, but it doesn't bring in enough income on its own to take care of me. Being an artist is difficult in this world today. It's not as though we have patrons like in the Renaissance period. Few people make enough money with art—in quilting, painting, writing, or any other artistic field today—to work in that alone. But during the times when I try to be more sensible and work a full-time job, I'm left with precious little time for my art." She sighed. "I always feel so torn. Like I can't figure out who I am or what I should be."

Lenora sat quietly for a time and then said, "Forging an identity takes hard work and involves some struggle and searching for most people. For women especially, raised eager to please, we hope for an affirmation from others that we're on the right course, pursuing the right thing, becoming what we should become. But frankly, Juliette, the courage to be who you are and to pursue your own dreams must come from within. You have to decide personally that your goals are worth pursuing, your talents valuable, your contributions and service good—despite what others may say or think. You need to be willing to pay the price to follow your heart and your destiny, so to speak."

She smiled at Juliette. "You are an artist, and a gifted one. I see that, many others see that, but you must see that. And you must want to pursue that, to perfect the art that cries inside you for expression, that drives you to yearn to create again and again, that makes you hungry to return to it when you try to leave it behind or put it down to pursue other things. There is a rich creativity inside you, a gift placed there—yes, put there by God—that yearns to find its place in the world. It would be wrong to suppress it. Why would you want to do that?"

"I don't know. It's only that..." Her words drifted off.

"It's only that you wish those that you loved affirmed your gift more."

Juliette dropped her eyes.

"Listen. When I began to pursue my interests and studies in Appalachian culture, I didn't get much support from my parents, family, and friends. They didn't understand my interest in past cultures, in Appalachian people—their lives, customs, religion, and music. They didn't think the study practical, thought I was overly obsessed with the past. They didn't understand me taking courses in Appalachian Studies at college and didn't like me taking trips into mountain regions, talking to strangers and taking notes. My parents even had trouble relating to my first college major in sociology, not seeing it as leading to anything practical. Mother suggested studying nursing, where I might meet a nice doctor."

Juliette laughed. "Gosh, that sounds like my family. They thought Daddy crazy to encourage me to study and major in textiles or to fan my interests in quilting and art as a career."

Lenora laughed with her. "When I went on to pursue my master's and my doctorate in my field area later, my parents still didn't approve. Of course, by that time, I'd won assistantships and scholarships, and worked at the colleges where I studied, so there was little they could do about it. But they pushed on me subtly whenever I came home, trying to fix me up with a nice boy, hinting I needed to find a husband before I got too old, suggesting a lot of men wouldn't want to marry a woman who was too smart or had more education than they did."

"They really said that?" Juliette knew her mouth dropped open.

Lenora shook her head. "Do you think you're the only woman who has needed to battle the disapproval of her family to become who she was intended to be? My parents didn't even approve of Caleb. When we met, he was working on a graduate Appalachian research project and then took a job at the Tremont Environmental Institute as a special programs coordinator. You can imagine how that went over with my parents. They thought he would encourage what they saw as my oddities." A soft smile touched her mouth. "But to my great joy, Caleb thought I was wonderful, brilliant, and perfect the way I was. Such a gift. He was so proud of my work at the college, so thrilled at every promotion, at every paper I wrote of merit, of every student I influenced and helped to grow."

"You still miss him."

"I do. And it's nice to receive approval." She leaned toward Juliette. "But I don't need to have it. I know who I am. I know who Dr. Lenora Abbott Boone, coordinator of the Appalachian Studies program and professor, is. I love what I do and I know it has value. It makes me."

She put her hand over Juliette's. "You have value, too. Deep down inside you know who you are—an artist, a creator, a quilter. And you are a fine businesswoman, too. You are strong enough and smart enough to make your dreams happen, to pay the price of people's disapproval if necessary to be who you really are. I want you to start affirming and celebrating yourself more, to doggedly believe in your talent and your ability. You are the only person who can make your dreams come true."

Juliette bit her lip. "If that's all true, then why am I so confused?"

"Because you're not focused, because you're not accepting and celebrating who you are. And, quite frankly, because you're too fragmented, trying to do this and trying to do that and forgetting to develop and do the main thing. I don't mean to hurt your feelings in saying that."

"What should I do?"

"Think out and find the way to make quilting your life. Give your all to it." Lenora crossed her arms. "Maybe open a shop where you can work with it full-time. Maybe teach and quilt. You could return to school to get some graduate credentials to teach college. Perhaps write a book, quilt and lecture." She laughed. "I see you frowning. That means you're rejecting some of these ideas. Good. Knowing what you don't want helps to show you what you do want."

Juliette scratched her neck, thinking. "I teach some now at the folk school, I work some in Sharon's shop, I sell some of my products on my Etsy site, and I sell quilt products at several other places...."

Lenora interrupted. "Did you hear all the 'somes' you mentioned? You're fragmented. Right now even more, trying to help out on the farm and working part-time at Walker's store."

"But I need to be here now!" Juliette almost shouted the words.

Lenora sighed. "Of course you do. But what about when this time is over? What then? More bouncing around?"

Juliette dropped her head into her hands. "I think you've made me feel worse, and I came here hoping you'd make me feel better."

"I have made you feel better. You just don't see it yet. I've told you who you are—an artist, a quilter of worth and value. That's who you are. Quit wondering about it. Quit caring what others think about it. Pursue it. Perfect it. Give it your heart." She smiled then. "At least most of it. I think there is a man right now who believes in you, too. Don't discount the importance of that. Love enhances talent and ability. Getting that aspect of intimacy settled in one's life along with self-identity opens the door for a less confused and lonely life. It stops all those searching, wondering aspects. You'll see that as time moves on."

"Fine, so why don't I feel better?"

Lenora got up to take their coffee cups to the sink. "Because you haven't decided to feel better yet. The only hindrance to your happiness and contentment is yourself."

Juliette tried to keep an open mind rather than letting Lenora's words hurt her feelings. "A quote that I stitched on a purse I created last week said 'Happiness comes from within.'"

Lenora smiled. "You keep that purse and carry it around with you. It's the truth."

She came back to sit down again. "Life is never easy, Juliette. But you can be easy in yourself and you can gift yourself with believing in yourself and your gifts—and in using them with all that is within you. But only you can do that. Wishing and hoping and dreaming won't do it. You know much of that wisdom already. Look around my house at all the beautiful quilts, pillows, and wall hangings of yours I own. I didn't buy those because you're Amy's friend. I bought them because they're exquisite."

"Thank you. I know you're trying to encourage and help me."

"Search your heart and get a vision, Juliette. Then you can pursue it. I think you need more in life than to sit in a room quilting all day, too. You're an extrovert. Your vision will need to be broader. That's why you keep staying fragmented, needing to connect with people and your artistry both."

"That's true, Lenora," she admitted, having never really thought about it before. "In the seasons when I was holed up during snows in the mountains in North Carolina, when the store closed, when I could quilt all I wanted for weeks, I started to go nuts."

She laughed and Lenora joined in. "You'll find your way. Just don't think your right way is a direction others suggest for you, especially when you know that way feels wrong."

Juliette walked over to the window to look out on the creek. "I do feel better for talking everything out with you. Thanks. I've been bottling this up until I felt like a shaken-up cola ready to explode."

"Anytime, darling." Lenora came over to stand beside her. "You think carefully about allowing love a chance, too. Don't think about Walker as a part of the problem. He *may* be a part of the solution. Remember what I shared with you about Caleb."

Juliette smiled, thinking about Walker. "I will. I promise." She glanced at her watch. "And speaking of Walker, I need to head to the store to work."

A short time later, Juliette opened the door to the Happy Valley Store, wiggling her fingers in a wave to Walker. "Sorry I'm a few minutes late. I was visiting Lenora."

"That's nice," Walker said, looking up from his computer. "Did you have a good time?"

"Yes, I did." She sat down on the stool at the counter across from where Walker sat working on his laptop. "Lenora gave me some needed advice."

He lifted his eyebrows in question.

"She said I needed to be prouder of my art and abilities, more sure of who I am in that area. Not always questioning my art and caring so much about what others think about it."

"Sounds like good advice to me. Why would you doubt yourself when you're so gifted? Don't you listen to all the compliments when the tourists stop in at the store? It ought to give you a big head. You should hear my sister talk about how beautiful your quilts are." He paused. "That reminds me, she sent a custom order for you if you want it."

"Really?" Juliette leaned forward. "What does she want?"

"Let me find the email." He popped over to his email server on his computer. "It's here somewhere," he said, scrolling through emails. "Ah, here it is." He turned the computer toward her after glancing at it.

Juliette read it. "She wants two whimsical twin quilts for a little girl's room, white in background with lots of colorful hearts and a fanciful design. She says she can send extra fabric for me to incorporate from the curtains and a valance she's working on, plus additional fabric she wants to use to upholster a love seat in a window and throw pillows."

She stopped to read more. "She can send me paint chips, maybe even pictures of the room if it would help." Juliette looked up. "She's very thorough."

"Totally anal." Walker grinned.

"Maybe, but she really wants me to use my artistic liberty with the quilts, to make them the focal points of the room. She says she can create other facets of the room's décor after she receives the quilts." She read further. "A family she and Chandler are working with are building a new home and Pendleton Interiors is decorating the whole house. The twin quilts are for the family's youngest daughter, who is six."

"That shouldn't be any problem for you," Walker put in.

"No." Juliette knew her mouth dropped open as she finished the email. "Oh, my. She's offering me a lot of money for these quilts."

Walker glanced at the computer to the amount. "Nice."

She frowned at him. "You don't have anything to do with padding this price or anything, do you?"

"No." He stood up, obviously annoyed. "My sister, Victoria, and her husband decorate for very well-to-do families. I'm always stunned when she tells me the prices that they are willing to pay for things."

"Okay." She smiled at him. "I'm sorry. It just seemed impossible that someone would pay that amount for two twin quilts."

"You don't have to do them."

"Are you kidding? This is a great opportunity. She says she might have more custom jobs for me if I want them in the future." She scanned through the last of the email. "She's very complimentary about my work."

Walker grinned. "One more affirmation of your talents."

"It does make me feel good." Juliette glanced over the email again. "She asked me to call her."

The door of the store opened to let several customers in.

"Scribble down her number and go out on the back porch and call her. I'll take care of the store."

Juliette went out on the back porch with the number and called. When she came back, she slipped behind the counter to help Walker. The lunch crowd was starting to arrive.

"She's nice," Juliette whispered to Walker as they worked to make plates of barbecue and a couple of Valley Dogs. "She's sending me a package to the store and she's already talking about another lavish jewel-toned quilt she'd like me to create for a master bedroom in another job they're doing."

"Starting to feel like a professional?" He kidded her.

"I am, and thanks for recommending me."

He rang up the finished lunch plates and started working on two banana splits.

"Here, let me help with those." Juliette began to scoop out ice cream to put over sliced bananas in the two glass dishes.

"Kimmie thinks she knows some people who may be interested in your work in Atlanta, too," Walker said later when the store quieted after the busy lunch hours. "Remember, she mentioned it at the party at my house."

Juliette looked up from the display she sat rearranging near the front door. "I thought she was simply being nice."

"I doubt it. Kimmie has built a huge network with her fabric design business. She and Jonas are in Atlanta on business right now. They took the boys by her mother's. I wouldn't be surprised if she came back with some more opportunities for you."

"It's funny how at the moment when you're feeling the most uncertain about yourself, a bunch of doors open to boost your ego."

"You shouldn't need anyone to boost your ego, Juliette. What's really concerning you?"

She paused. "Art is so unstable. Sometimes I get a lot of orders, other times none. Some months I'm comfortable financially; other months I struggle to make ends meet and I wonder if I'm being foolish to keep chasing after this dream of being an artist."

"Do you wish you didn't have to work at the store here or for Sharon in Murphy? Does it take too much time away from your art?" Walker took a fresh bowl of water to Marsh and stopped to pet the dog while they talked.

"Sometimes." She considered his question. "But like Lenora said, I'm an extroverted person and I wouldn't want to spend all my time sitting alone in a room quilting every day."

"I guess you need to think through how you could combine the best of both worlds in one."

"Lenora had some ideas about that."

"Any of them feel right?"

"Not really." She made a face. "One of the things I talked about with Sharon in Murphy was wishing we had a room off the store where I could quilt and teach others to quilt. Quilting in the past was a shared social activity for women."

A group of kids came in for ice cream, interrupting their talk. Juliette fixed their cones and talked to their mother at the counter.

Walker strolled around the store, checking stock and straightening things, Marsh padding behind him.

In a quiet moment later, he came over to lean on the counter. "Is the back porch big enough?"

"Big enough for what?"

"To teach quilting classes. Isn't that what we were talking about?"

He glanced toward the back of the store. "We rarely use that porch for the purpose Vee intended. There's a table there, some chairs. You could add more. Whatever you need. I don't care if you use the space. It might draw new people to the store, too."

She knew her mouth dropped open. "You'd really let me do that?"

"Sure." He glanced toward the door before leaning over to give her a quick kiss. "Maybe you'll decide to stay around longer if you start your own business here. Do quilt demonstrations. Teach. Whatever you want. Set up a little office in the back of the room if you like. The room has heat and air. You know we're not that busy here most of the time that I couldn't do without you. Or you could do the quilting business earlier, before your work hours."

Juliette couldn't think what to say. "I can't believe you would offer this," she said finally.

He shrugged. "It's a big porch room, hardly ever used. Why not put it to good use?" He snagged a bottle of glass cleaner from under the counter and a roll of paper towels and headed toward the front of the store. "You think about it as another of those possible ideas. You're a quilter and an artist. Lenora's right. You just need to make up your mind to it."

"Make up my mind to it." She repeated the words.

Walker turned to grin at her after spritzing one of the front windows. "Most things come down to simply making up your mind about them." He laughed. "Daddy used to have a sign in the store that said: '*Make up your mind before somebody else does it for you.*' He liked to make jokes about it, but there's a lot of truth in those words."

Juliette thought about that throughout the rest of the busy afternoon.

CHAPTER 13

Except for Dade Claiborne stopping by the store and acting surly, the rest of the day moved by without incident until it was almost time to lock up. Quillen now swept the store before close while Juliette cleaned the tables on the café porch, humming a little tune as she did. Walker smiled to hear it as he wiped down the counters behind the soda fountain a last time.

Although they each carried cell phones, Walker had put in a landline phone at the store, too, for business calls. It rang now, and he picked it up, tossing the towel he held over one shoulder.

"Happy Valley Store," he said.

"It's George. Grandpa's having another heart attack," Walker heard him say in a rush. "We're on our way to the hospital. Laura is with us, thank goodness. Juliette will want to come. Is she still at the store?"

"Yes. I'll bring her. Drive carefully."

The next hours were anxious ones. Walker left Quillen to close the store, and he and Juliette headed straight to Blount Memorial Hospital in Maryville. They found George, Laura, and Gramma Newell gathered in one of the waiting areas.

Juliette moved quickly to her grandmother. "What happened?"

Laura answered, her voice touched with sarcasm. "Your grandfather decided he needed to dig postholes for a back fence he and George wanted to repair."

"Don't be too hard on him," George put in. "Those two Clevenger boys were supposed to come do it. I thought Grandpa could supervise their work while I cleaned out the garden and dug up potatoes. I needed to climb on the barn roof to make some repairs, too, and I thought keeping an eye on the fence repair job would keep Dad from getting overheated in the garden or trying to get up on the roof with me. You know how he can be."

George slumped into a chair beside Juliette. "The Clevenger boys didn't show up. Grandpa got mad and tired of waiting for them, so he started doing the job himself."

Her grandmother entered the conversation then. "The boys called the house after a while to say their truck broke down. They kept trying to fix it but couldn't get it running. They apologized for the problem and said they would try to get over tomorrow to dig the postholes." She sighed. "I walked out to tell Dalton, knowing he'd be waitin' on them. I saw him pushing that posthole digger into the ground and then watched him grab his chest and fall."

"It was a blessing she found him," Laura put in. "When he slumped over, she took off running to find me at the house, knowing I was home. It probably saved Dalton's life that she came out to give him that message when she did and ran to get me."

"I sure was scared," Gramma said, tears filling her eyes. "You don't think we'll lose him, do you, Laura?"

"We got him here quickly and I did what I could until the ambulance came. Now we'll wait and see." Her eyes moved to Juliette's. "He's in surgery now."

Walker sat down in a seat by Juliette across from George and Laura. He looked at Laura. "What surgery are they doing?"

"The doctor hasn't come out to talk with us since they started, but I can tell you that Dalton's had an acute coronary thrombosis, a more major heart attack than the last episode. He experienced pain and strangling in the chest. That pain, or angina, meant there is obstruction in the coronary arteries. His blood pressure was also highly elevated, probably from getting overexerted. When blood pressure elevates, the heart must expend greater energy to circulate the blood. If that load gets sustained over too long a period of time, the heart can't meet the demands placed on it and heart failure ensues." She paused. "My guess is they'll put a stent in if they can, maybe more than one if needed."

Juliette gripped Walker's hand. "Will he be okay?"

"The doctor promised to come talk with us as soon as they know something," George said.

Juliette's grandmother pulled a floral cotton handkerchief out of her purse to wipe her eyes. "That old man, he won't make himself slow down even when he needs to."

"Maybe this will wake him up," Laura said. "If he doesn't slow down, Gramma Newell, he may shorten his life."

George dropped his head in his hands. "I shouldn't have left him behind the barn by himself until those Clevenger boys showed up."

"Now don't go blaming yourself." Laura frowned at him. "You expected your grandpa to sit sensibly on that old bench and wait until those boys showed up, not to try taking on a strenuous job like that on his own. He knew better, George. It's not your fault he acted foolishly like he did."

"He got mad," Gramma Newell put in. "When the old man wants to see something get done and plans don't go his way, he always tends to get mad. I've seen it before. When someone don't show up to do a job, he'll just set in to do it himself, stubborn-like and impatient, whether he ought to do it or not." She wiped her eyes again. "That old fool."

"It must have scared you to see him falling over like you did," Juliette said, putting an arm around her.

"It about took a year off my life, I can tell you." She shook her head.

Laura smiled at her. "I didn't know you could run that fast, Gramma. I was working out in the front yard with my roses, and I saw you holding up your skirts and running like the devil was after you."

Gramma chuckled a little, as Laura had intended. "Fear can set your feet to running faster than they think they can run, even old feet."

They all smiled over the humor, lessening some of the tension in the room for a minute.

"What's a stent, exactly?" Juliette asked Laura. "I don't understand medical things enough to know what this surgery is they're doing on Grandpa."

"After a heart attack with a blocked artery like your grandpa's, the cardiologist first does an angioplasty procedure to reopen the artery," Laura explained. "A thin tube called a catheter is threaded, usually from the groin, to the artery and then manipulated to restore the blood flow. Then a metal mesh tube called a stent is placed at the site of the former blockage to prop the artery open."

Gramma looked surprised. "Oh, I thought they might cut open his chest."

"No, although they do sometimes with surgery for a heart attack."

"How long does all this take?" George asked, his eyes moving to the clock again.

"The surgery can take an hour to several hours, not counting the time for prep and recovery. It depends on the number of stents needed and the complexity of the procedure and other factors."

"Looks like we're in for a wait, then," George said, sighing.

"You don't have to stay," Juliette said to Walker. "It will probably be a long evening."

"I'd like to wait." He slipped a hand into hers.

The time crept by afterward, with them all watching the clock and the door, waiting for word. George alternately paced and sat, and once Walker joined him in walking down to the cafeteria to get some coffee and drinks.

When they returned, the door to the waiting room opened to let in George and Laura's children, Kirsten and Robert, along with their other grandparents, Stanley and Hettie Rhea.

"Mercy, we just heard the bad news," Hettie said, coming in to hug Gramma Newell, George, and then Laura. "We're so sorry."

Walker noticed that even in this time of tragedy, Hettie ignored Juliette completely, as did Stanley.

Stanley thumped George on the back in sympathy. "We brought

Kirsten and Robert over for a bit. They were getting anxious at home waiting. I hope you don't mind."

"No. I'm sure they're upset and worried, too," he replied. "I called them as we headed to the hospital. They were still at a 4-H meeting after school."

The teens clustered around their grandmother and parents in sympathy, asking the same questions Walker and Juliette had asked earlier.

Juliette got up and went to the window to look outside as they talked, and Walker followed her.

"She really does exclude you," Walker said quietly to her. "Even at a time like this."

"Yes," Juliette answered.

He glanced back at the family group and saw Stanley Rhea's eyes shift toward them with a quick look of guilt, while Hettie took Juliette's chair without another glance her way.

Walker let Juliette lean her back against him at the window, and he purposed in that moment he would find a way to resolve this issue with the Rheas for her.

After a short space of time, Onalee and her son Ronnie Claiborne arrived as well, but not Dade. Juliette told Walker that Onalee Claiborne was one of Gramma Newell's best friends, so it didn't surprise him to see her. The minister of their church and his wife—another good friend of Newell Hollander's—was with them. The gathering reminded Walker of times back in Colorado when tragedy struck. Friends came quickly to be a help and support.

Ronnie and his mother walked over to join them at the window after speaking to Gramma and the rest of the family. "We were so sorry to hear about your grandfather," Ronnie said to Juliette. Ronnie was a tall, lanky man, his dark looks resembled those of his mother, a lean, wiry woman who looked like she carried Cherokee heritage.

"Dade couldn't be here," Onalee said to Juliette. "He's out of town on a buying trip. Left this afternoon."

Juliette nodded. "It was good of you to come." She accepted

Onalee's hug along with Ronnie's pats on her back gracefully.

Noticing Walker, Mrs. Claiborne put out a hand to him. "I'm Onalee Claiborne. I think I've missed meeting you the times I've stopped by your store. It sure is a fine one and we're happy to see a store again in the valley."

"Thank you." Walker shook her hand, liking her forthright manner and honest eyes.

They chatted a few minutes and then Onalee said, "I think I'll find a seat and visit with Newell a bit now." She smiled. "You young ones can stand on your feet if you like, but I've had a long day on my feet already with the canning I've been doing."

She walked back over to take a seat on the other side of Newell, reaching over to hug her and offering talk and friendship.

Ronnie leaned against the wall. "My wife, Dottie, sends her best, Juliette. She had to stay at home and get the kids to bed—it's getting late."

Juliette smiled at him. "Your Hillary is getting prettier every day and I saw her flying across the field on her horse the other day. She's eight now, isn't she?"

Ronnie grinned. "Yes and she sure loves to ride."

Juliette's eyes moved to Walker's. "The Claibornes have always kept horses. George and I used to ride there as kids, and Ronnie's daughter is horse crazy right now. She can really ride on that pinto of hers."

"Little Scott's already crying to get up on that horse with her," Ronnie said. "Even with him only two and barely walking."

Juliette chuckled over the word picture he painted, turning to Walker. "My brother, George, and Ronnie grew up best friends," she explained. "They're only a year apart in age. Dade, six years younger than Ronnie, ran along behind them whenever he could and sometimes I tried to tag along, too. Onalee kept me often when I was little and she taught me to ride."

"Our families have always been close," Ronnie said. He shifted then with discomfort, looking back toward his mother. "George told me about some of the ways Dade has been acting, Juliette.

I'm real sorry about that. I don't know what's gotten into him. Somehow he hasn't acted the same since Daddy died. He was always a little cocksure, but he's gotten worse. Spends money like it's going out of style. I guess he's done really well with Daddy's car business, but it seems extravagant to us."

Ronnie glanced back toward his mother again. "I wanted you to know Ma and I don't hold any grudges toward you because you're not sweet on Dade anymore and don't want to go out with him." He grinned. "Seems to me you've tried to let him know subtly for the last few years your feelings changed. But Dade's always wanted what he can't have."

"Thanks, Ronnie," Juliette said.

He looked at Walker. "Ma and I don't hold any hard feelings toward you for seeing Juliette now, either. This may not be the best time to say these things, but I haven't found the opportunity before."

Walker nodded. "Thank you. I know Juliette appreciates any kindness on a day like this."

The minister and his wife came to speak to them then, a sweet older couple, and Ronnie moved over to talk with George and Laura.

Somehow the time passed until the doctor appeared in the door, bringing the news that Dalton came through the surgery well. The doctor said they put two stents in and anticipated Dalton would be in the hospital for two to three days, because of his age, before he could go home. He said close family members could go in to see Dalton after he came out of recovery, but he encouraged Gramma Newell to head home afterward and not stay the night. He also suggested other friends and family members should plan to come back another day for a visit.

After that, people trickled out—the minister and his wife, Onalee and Ronnie, then Stanley and Hettie Rhea, who offered to take Robert and Kirsten back home again. With everyone gone at last, Juliette went over to wrap her arms around her grandmother, and the two wept in gratitude that Dalton had come through his surgery and not died.

"I would sure have hated to lose that old man," Gramma Newell said, wiping away tears. "I'm purposed to see he behaves after this, too. I know he'll need to rest and take it easy whether he likes it or not."

"He'll need to modify his diet more, as well," Laura put in. "He can't keep eating big breakfasts of salt ham, gravy and biscuits anymore, Gramma. He'll need to reduce salt, salt products, heavy meals, sweets and pastries and to eat more healthy vegetables, fruits, and lean meats, despite what he tells you he wants to eat. Habits are hard to break, but you and Grandpa will need to work together to make some changes. You'll get the same talk from his doctor and more."

Gramma lifted her chin. "Well then, we'll just have to do it, like it or not. I'm not too old to be a-changing, if I have to, and neither is the old man."

"I'll help you, Gramma," Juliette offered. "We'll pick up some of those heart-healthy recipe books and find some good new recipes to try."

The family members still at the hospital visited Juliette's grandfather in shifts when Dalton came out of recovery, and afterward George suggested to Walker that he take Juliette and their grandmother home.

"Laura and I will stay on for a time," he said to Walker on the side. "But I believe Gramma should go home and get some rest. We think she'll do better if Juliette is with her, and she hasn't even eaten supper. Juliette can fix something for both of them, and see that Gramma goes on to bed. I know she'll want to come back to sit with Grandpa tomorrow, and Laura says we don't want her getting run-down and sick, too."

"I'll see to it they both get home, get something to eat, and I'll stay with them for a while, too," Walker said.

George offered him a lopsided grin. "I'm starting to like you despite my earlier reservations."

At the house after Juliette heated up leftovers for a late dinner and settled her grandmother into bed with a book, she suggested they sit on the front porch for a few minutes before Walker headed home. She brought out two glasses of raspberry tea and a plate of peanut butter cookies before sitting down beside him on the old metal glider, which was a little rusted with time and wear.

"Good cookies," Walker said after sampling one.

"I actually made those myself." She smiled. "I *can* cook, although Gramma's skills far excel mine."

He let a small silence settle and heard her sigh. "How are you doing? It's been a long day."

She leaned her head back against the rocker. "I am worn out from all the stress and waiting. Hospitals, for all the healing that goes on within them, are not restful places. Too many emotions swim in the air, I think." She opened her eyes to look at him. "You were kind to take me to the hospital and stay with me. You didn't have to."

"No, but I wanted to be with you." He reached over to touch her face and watched tears well in her eyes.

"I was so scared Grandpa would die. I know he hasn't been taking care of himself like he should. This morning he wolfed down biscuits, gravy, country ham, and eggs. No matter how often Laura or I talk to him and Gramma, they just kept on eating the way they're used to —Grandpa pooh-poohing me anytime I fuss and try to get him to be more careful. Even Gramma kept telling me good, healthy food never hurt anyone." She wiped at her eyes. "I tried to get them to change, and I tried to get Grandpa to be more careful. I knew he pushed too hard many days."

"It's not your fault, any more than it was George's."

She closed her eyes. "But I felt so guilty at the hospital. I came home to the farm to try to help out, to see that Grandpa rested enough, ate better, and changed his lifestyle so he would get better."

"You can't make people change, Juliette. You can encourage them to change, but you can't make it happen. People have to *want* to change. Maybe this situation will finally convince your grandpa and your gramma to make the adjustments needed."

"I hope so. I really do." She sipped at her tea, thinking. "Laura said she would get the doctor to sit down and be really clear to them about the changes they need to make in their diet and lifestyle. She thought the cardiologist too gentle in his suggestions when Grandpa had his first minor attack, not wanting to overly alarm them. She believes this time the doctor will use tough love and be more direct with them. Grandpa is eighty-five now, but Laura said if he would make some changes, eat right, not overdo, take his medications, and be more cautious, he might live to be a hundred. The Hollanders are hardy people."

She sat her tea glass on the small table in front of the glider. "I may need to miss some days of work while Grandpa is in the hospital."

"That's no problem. Take off any days you need now—and later when he comes home. Eldon, Quillen, and I will manage fine."

"Thanks." She leaned over to give him a quick kiss. "I'll come over whenever I can—if only because I'll miss seeing you otherwise."

"Well, that's sweet to hear." Walker curled his arm around her and kissed her back, settling her head on his shoulder.

She sighed. "It was nice of Ronnie to let me know he and Onalee didn't hold hard feelings toward me because I wasn't seeing Dade anymore."

"Yeah, and I really liked both him and his mother. Dade seems very different from them. Is he more like his father?"

"He's somewhat like his father, especially in looks. But I think his father had more strength of character than Dade. Mr. Claiborne loved the car dealership, like Dade does, but he was kinder, more prudent in his dealings, less extravagant. Dade has always been sort of a braggart, always wanting to let people know how important he is, how much money he has." She made a face. "He took me to see the house he's building on the mountain behind Happy Valley that time we went out together. It's lavish. Some guys he knows through work are staying in the old family cabin in the woods below his house, to work on Dade's place all the time. He's spending a lot on it, and he bragged about his plans for furnishing it. I think

I heard him say 'Nothing but the best, sugar' at least thirty times, like that should really impress me."

"I'm sure he was trying to impress you. He hoped you'd marry him and make your home there with him."

She winced at the words. "Oh, probably so. But Dade and I wouldn't suit even if I carried feelings for him, which I don't. Dade is too restless and driven, too much of a party guy and a show-off. I'm not comfortable with his friends either, and those guys working for Dade on the house gave me the creeps." She hesitated. "Actually, come to think of it, I never liked any of Dade's friends. Even in high school."

"I wouldn't worry about it. I'm sure Dade will meet someone else soon." He changed the subject. "I'm more concerned right now about how Hettie and Stanley act around you. Hettie totally snubbed you at the hospital, and most everyone seemed to accept it without comment."

She shrugged. "Everyone's used to it. Hettie has acted like that around me since I was little, sort of pretending like I'm not even really there."

"It's wrong and it's rude." He scowled.

"Maybe, but I don't know what to do about it. I've tried every sensible thing I can think of to resolve the situation. Nothing works."

Walker pushed the glider into motion with one foot. "Tell me about Patsy, their daughter."

Juliette smiled at his question. "Patsy was actually a very nice person. Daddy told me all about her, and I've seen pictures of her and heard stories from other people. From what I heard, Patsy was loving, warmhearted, and gracious."

"Doesn't sound like her mother."

"No." She laughed. "Even Daddy found Hettie a somewhat difficult woman, even before all the trouble after Patsy's death."

She stopped for a minute, thinking back. "You know, I was telling Amy the other day how Patsy actually started the valley's first daycare program right in the old community center. She babysat kids after school while in high school, created games for them, tutored them with their homework—and all for free. In the summers she ran a sort of free daycare several days a week, too, like a day camp. It started as a project she did for a scout troop she belonged to, but then she continued it afterward because she enjoyed it. Patsy was a genuinely caring person. Gramma told me Patsy's nature softened both Hettie and Stanley's hard edges. Hettie never made friends easily, but Patsy did and that drew friendships to Hettie and Stanley. They hated seeing Daddy carry Patsy off with him into the military life. They wanted Daddy to stay in the valley, like his parents. It's probably another reason Hettie grew so bitter toward Daddy. He took her only daughter away, and then Patsy died away from home—and away from them—in Hawaii."

Walker considered this. "And when your father remarried, that old anger flared up again. In an odd, twisted way, Hettie felt he should have kept Patsy's memory enshrined and never married."

"Yes. That's it, and she is worse than Stanley about it. A few times I've felt Stanley soften, and sometimes he'll talk to me when I run into him without Hettie around. I think he sees that whatever happened, it isn't *my* fault. But Hettie can't see that at all and doesn't want to see it. I'm her way to stay angry over Patsy's death and for Daddy daring to remarry."

He shook his head. "People sure get some irrational ideas about things somehow."

"Tell me about it." She looked at her watch. "It's late. Marsh will be looking for you, and we both need to get some sleep. I'm sure Gramma will want to head to the hospital after an early breakfast, and you'll need to open the store."

"You're right." He stood, pulling her up from the glider to draw her against him for another long kiss before he left. He loved the feel of her against him, how she molded into all the angles of his body like a glove, and how the sweet scent of her drifted over him and stayed, lingering on his clothes after he told her good-night. Holding her tight against him, he wondered—not for the first time—what it might be like to spend his life with her, sleep with her every night, wake up with her curled against him every morning, her warmth and scent always close. But he knew, with his life as unsettled as it was, that he could never consider the idea seriously. Today, everything was good, but tomorrow....Who knew? As before, his world could implode, and he might need to run again.

CHAPTER 14

The weeks flew by after Grandpa's heart attack. He returned home and gradually regained his strength. With counseling from his doctor and from Laura, both Gramma and Grandpa began to work to make needed changes in their lives and daily routine. Of course, Grandpa often grumbled about it, and sometimes Gramma did, too, but things were better. Juliette felt relieved she didn't have to hold angry arguments with the two of them any longer. She spent more time in the kitchen with her gramma now, helping her learn to modify old recipes to make them more heart friendly.

"I'm becoming a rather good cook," she told Kimmie with pride one afternoon at her house. They were in the Rasnics' kitchen fixing dinner for Jonas, Walker, and Kimmie's boys, Brevan and Bryan, who'd gone hiking on this fine October day.

"The potato salad you're making right now looks fantastic," Kimmie said, looking up from a baked beans dish she was adding finishing touches to. "We picked up a honey-baked ham when shopping, the beans are ready to stick in the oven, and I fixed slaw earlier." She turned to smile at Juliette. "Plus, you brought that sinful-looking dessert and stuck it in the freezer earlier. What was that?"

"It's called Ice Cream Sandwich Delight and it is *not* a heart-healthy recipe." She covered the bowl of potato salad with plastic wrap and put it in the refrigerator. "I made it with the boys in mind. It's basically layers of ice cream sandwiches smothered in whipped cream, crushed candy bars, and toasted pecans, drizzled over with chocolate syrup. I thought something cold would be good after the boys had been on the trail all day."

Kimmie laughed. "I'm drooling simply thinking about it."

"I admit it is good."

"Don't even tell me the calorie count." She spread foil over the beans, stuck them in the oven, and then glanced at the clock. "Do you want to go sit on the screened porch to visit while the beans bake? I'll cut the oven off when they're done. If the guys are late, we can heat them back up. Everything else is ready."

"A break sounds wonderful."

"I'll grab a couple of bottles of water from the fridge," Kimmie said, walking over to the big refrigerator. "Do you want Perrier or San Pellegrino?"

Juliette grinned at the gourmet choices. "Either would be a treat. I'm used to generic labels or whatever comes out of the tap."

Kimmie wrinkled her nose. "Special moments with special friends call for special drinks."

"That's nice," Juliette said, following her to the big screened porch under the trees with its views across the mountain ridges. "You're sweet to think of me as a special friend."

"You're my treasure," Kimmie said with sincerity. "I was so lonely here until we started hanging out. I had Jonas, the boys, and my work, of course, but literally no women friends. It was simply dismal." She settled into a deep chair and put her feet up on a matching ottoman.

Juliette curled up on the small sofa next to her, dropping her shoes and tucking her legs under her. She studied Kimmie, with her dark hair and brown eyes.

Kimmie grinned. "Thinking about what that woman said at the store today? That we look like sisters?"

"Do you think we do?"

"A little. People see two tall women with black hair, brown eyes, olive skin, a similar build and a touch of European ancestry and assume we're sisters. They don't see all the small differences."

"I guess there is more of a similarity than I realized. What was your name before you married?"

"Markos. My people are from Greece originally. In Greece, the Markos family run restaurants, and here in America my parents run restaurants, too. My grandparents started the first Markos Restaurant when they came to the US. They worked hard, prospered, and now the family owns three restaurants in the Atlanta area. I was raised with more affluence than my parents, Dimitri and Eleni Markos, ever knew. I've been blessed. My brothers, Leon and Nicholas, love the restaurant business and help my parents with it. I got the artistic bent of my great-grandmother, a well-known artist in Greece in the past. Fortunately, my parents were simply thrilled with every artistic effort I ever made from the time I was three, scribbling on napkins at the restaurant. They called me 'the little artist' with pride from the time I could skip rope."

"You're lucky in that."

"I've heard you talk enough to know you weren't lucky in that way, but it doesn't change who you are or the talent you have."

Juliette looked out into the trees thoughtfully. "I've felt stronger about my work these last months with the commissions from Victoria's decorating firm and the orders from the specialty shops where you sell your design items in Atlanta. Thanks for introducing me to that market."

"It's only the beginning for you." Kimmie crossed her legs on the ottoman. "You have a great talent and a strong artistic eye."

"Thanks. So do you. I love the fabric designs you create, vivid with color, almost rhythmic and lyrical in composition, and full of so many exuberant florals."

Kimmie giggled. "Great words. I need to get you to write those down for some of my advertisements." She glanced across at Juliette, her brows drawing together in a little frown. "You don't feel bad that I talked you out of going hiking with the boys today, do you? They planned a rather ambitious hike and I loved the idea better of spending the day with you. We went to that fabulous quilt show in Townsend and then into Maryville to those thrift stores to look for fabric."

"You weren't bored?"

Kimmie blinked in astonishment. "Did I look bored or act bored? I imagine my enthusiasm might have become wearying. I got so many glorious ideas for new designs looking at all those quilts and poking through those marvelous cluttered shops. I can't wait to get to my desk tomorrow to start sketching and painting."

Juliette laughed. "I didn't realize until we got acquainted that you paint your ideas first for your fabric designs. Your lavish floral paintings all over the walls of your house are almost as wonderful as Jonas's dramatic outdoor scenes."

"Oh, pooh, there is no comparison. My work is fun and entertaining, perhaps charming, but Jonas's work is definitive. Striking, awe-inspiring, memorable. His are the kinds of paintings that will live on, leave a legacy."

"That doesn't bother you to consider that?"

She looked shocked. "Of course not. We each carry our own gifts and talents. The main thing is to find a way to use them to our best ability—as any artist should."

Kimmie shifted the subject. "What are you planning to make with all those rich satiny fabrics you bought today? Some were old prom dresses, and I know you said you plan to cut them up. Tell me."

Juliette thought again how wonderful it was she'd connected with Kimmie and her positive enthusiasm for art and life. She was such a joy to spend time with, so interested in Juliette's work, so eager to share of her own work and efforts. Juliette had forgotten life could be so much fun until she'd found Kimmie.

"The other day when I was helping Gramma clean out some drawers," Juliette answered, "we found an old painted accordion fan, a pretty memento my dad had sent my grandmother from abroad one Christmas. I kept studying its rich colors and started to envision a fan design for a quilt, with each fan's panels in different colors embellished with rich embroidery. So I'm going to make a fan quilt with the satins. I think I might add whimsical half-moons, stars, and maybe butterflies to the design to make it more playful.

I'll work with the ideas now that I have the fabrics and begin to plan the design and colors."

Kimmie closed her eyes. "I can so envision that, rich and elegant, with that shiny gold fabric you bought mixed in and possibly gold thread for some of the embroidery and trim."

"I had that idea, too, when I bought that bolt of gold fabric; I already have gold embroidery thread. I'm thinking of using a black background to make all the colors jump out and to give the quilt a richer look. What do you think?"

"Ooh, that sounds wonderful. I'm playing with a design of flowers on black right now myself. I think black brings that rich, fabulous Victorian look to things."

They chatted on like this, talking about art, sharing ideas, until Kimmie heard the timer go off in the kitchen. She glanced at her watch. "That's the timer. Let me go turn off the oven. The boys should be back soon unless they got held up. Jonas's last text said they were nearly home and all hungry." She laughed.

Juliette glanced outside to the forest views beyond as Kimmie headed to the kitchen. The Rasnics lived in a sprawling log home high on a hillside above Abrams Creek Road. A long drive wound up to it, twining around the ridgelines to the home site. Porches and gables jutted out all around the big house, and long, deep windows opened to the mountain views. Inside the house, the rooms were open and spacious with high ceilings and decorated with Kimmie and Jonas's fabulous artwork spotlighted among warm, comfortable furnishings. Kimmie's flair for fashion caused all to blend in beautiful harmony.

Picking up the empty water bottles to take to the kitchen, Juliette heard the sound of Jonas's big SUV heading up the hillside.

"Here come the boys," Kimmie called. "Get ready to hear about hiking trails, salamanders, lizards, and snakes for the rest of the night."

"Mom," Brevan hollered a few minutes later, racing into the kitchen. "Guess what we saw? This huge, big rattlesnake!"

"You see?" Kimmie mouthed to Juliette before she turned

toward the door. "All four of you, dump all that hiking gear in the mudroom and take off those filthy boots. They're covered with dirt. I don't want the Smoky Mountains tracked all through my kitchen and house."

Gear and shoes were dumped, and soon the house filled with the sounds of a happy group, ready to enjoy dinner and an evening together.

"Did you have a good time with Kimmie?" Walker asked later as he drove Juliette home.

"Yes. You were right—Kimmie and I have a lot in common. I'm so glad we met. I love spending time with her and talking shop." She glanced across at him. "I gather from the boys' enthusiastic accounts you enjoyed the hike today, too."

"We did. The boys loved the views off the Appalachian Trail and hiking out to Charlies Bunion. They're hardy boys to walk that eight-mile roundtrip hike without complaining. It has some steep climbs and the trail is often rough and narrow in spots." He chuckled. "We ran into through-hikers doing the entire Appalachian Trail at the Icewater Spring Shelter and the boys got excited after talking with them and decided they want to hike the AT one day."

"Perhaps they will. A lot of people take on that challenge now." She glanced out the window as they passed the familiar shadow of the store, closed and quiet for the night. "I read a book about Grandma Gatewood, the sixty-seven-year-old grandmother who was the first woman to hike the Appalachian Trail, in 1955. Her story was incredible."

"I liked Horace Kephart's writings. They inspired me to camp near Bryson City, North Carolina, where he once lived."

She smiled at him. "John Muir wrote the words 'The mountains are calling and I must go.' A lot of people are called to the mountains."

"I can see why. The fall colors were beautiful on the Appalachian Trail and at Charlies Bunion, but I thought them almost as pretty on our hike on the Cooper Road Trail near the campground last week."

"We do live in a pretty place."

Walker drove under the arch into the Hollander farm and up the quiet drive cloaked in darkness now that the days had grown longer.

As he stopped the car, he said, "I need to talk to you about something."

"Okay." She studied him with some wariness in the dark, trying to read his expression. "Is anything wrong?"

He scratched his neck, seeming to look for the right words. "You know it troubles me the way Hettie and Stanley Rhea act around you."

She interrupted, annoyed at the subject. "It troubles me, too, but honestly, Walker, there's nothing I can do to change Hettie Rhea. We've talked about this before."

Walker cleared his throat. "Well, *I* decided there might be something I could do and that's what I wanted to talk to you about."

Juliette tried to read his face. "Is this idea something you're thinking about doing or something you've already done?"

He shifted again. "It's something I've already done."

She rolled her eyes. "Well, you'd better tell me about it."

"I kept remembering the little story you told me about Patsy Rhea and her work at the community center, and I began to ask other people who'd lived in the valley all their lives to tell me what they remembered about her—the minister at your church, Pearl and Earline Walker, Keith and his father. One of the older women, whose grandmother taught school at the Happy Valley School that once used the community center, proved to be a fount of knowledge. She'd kept a box of old clippings and photos from events at the center. In it were actually a couple of brief news articles that mentioned the volunteer work Patsy and others did for the valley children at the center. I learned even more from Esther Boone. She goes to the Red Top Church where the Rheas attend and she and Patsy not only went to church together but were best friends growing up."

"I didn't know that about Esther, although I knew the Boones went to the same church with the Rheas."

"Esther had a photo that I really loved and she let me borrow it to make a copy for you." He reached across her to the glove compartment to pull out a manila envelope and took the photo out. "It's of Patsy and your dad when they were courting. Esther took it and kept it all these years."

"Ahhh, look at that." Juliette studied the old photo. "Daddy and Patsy leaning against each other in overalls and smiling. So young and happy."

She leaned across to give him a quick kiss. "Thanks for getting this for me. I know George will love it. Maybe we can make him a copy. Could you do that?"

"Sure." He cleared his throat.

Juliette saw him shift in his seat, uncomfortable. "Spit it out, Walker. There's obviously more on your mind about this."

"I talked to Keith about the idea of making a dedication wall to Patsy in the community center, something in glass with old photos, a plaque underneath it. He and Amy really liked the idea."

"So you think that would bother me since my relationship with Hettie is so poor? It doesn't, Walker."

"No, it's the fact that I shared a sit-down visit with Hettie and Stanley at their home that might bother you."

She lifted an eyebrow, waiting.

"Hettie came in the store last week and said, right in front of a lot of locals at the lunch hour, that she wanted me to know most everyone had figured out I was behind the recent spree of philanthropies in the valley. She claimed she might have complimented me for my actions if I wasn't involved with you."

Juliette rolled her eyes. "She truly is the rudest woman."

"I agree. She also added that she hoped I came to my senses before our relationship progressed any further." He rubbed his neck again. "She talked loudly the entire time, making sure everyone in the store could hear her. Hettie also said pointedly she hoped I would dump you, like Dade Claiborne did, so you would leave the valley again and this time stay gone."

"Dade dumped me?" Juliette repeated the words slowly. "Where did that crazy idea come from?"

"Evidently Dade has spread a little story around that he only dated you because of old ties with your family. He claimed he was trying to do the neighborly thing, thinking an alignment with you might help your family with the farm. He also spread it around he had to loan George money."

"That creep!"

"I talked with George and your grandfather after Hettie came to the store, and I loaned George the money myself to pay Dade off in full. We've kept the loan agreement quiet, but we made it a point to spread the word around that George paid his debt to Dade. We made up a little tale that Laura inherited some money. A relative of Laura's *did* die recently and left her some money, so it wasn't a lie to say she inherited some money."

"That was her Aunt Ruby."

He nodded.

Juliette closed her eyes, feeling suddenly weary. "It was nice of you to do this for my family."

"It wasn't totally guileless. Hettie also announced that Dade had been looking into my background. She claimed she wouldn't be surprised to learn I had secrets to hide myself, stressing that folks who couldn't be more forthright about their background usually did." He paused and sighed. "Hettie seems to actually enjoy causing trouble. She said Dade mentioned to a newspaper friend of his that there might be a good story about me for someone who cared to snoop a little. She added with a smirk that one of her friends worked for the newspaper and that she might give her a little call."

"And this worried you?" She studied his face.

"Yes." He rubbed his neck again. "I'd rather not have reporters looking into my life or leaking stories to a local newspaper someone might discover with a little internet searching. It could jeopardize my family."

"Is that why you went to see Hettie and Stanley?" She reached over to put a hand on his leg, realizing he was upset.

"Only in small part." He took a breath. "I told Hettie and Stanley they were right in saying my ties to some strong philanthropies had helped families in the valley. I also admitted my own finances partially backed the renovations to the community center. I briefly explained to them, as I had to your grandparents, why I needed to leave my home. I asked Hettie not to encourage reporters to look into my life, that it could threaten my family."

"How did she act? Was she nice?"

"No, she wasn't nice but Stanley was." He shook his head. "Hettie asked me point-blank why they should want to do anything for me."

"I told you that woman was a piece of work. You probably wasted your time going over there."

"No." A small smile curled his lips then. "There was a little more to the visit than that."

Juliette watched him. "I'm listening."

"I suggested there might be something I could do for her in return. Then I told her about the stories you shared with me about Patsy, the work I later discovered Patsy had done at the community center as a young girl, and how it interested me. I explained how I began to do research after first hearing about it and I shared the things I learned. I also disclosed that Keith and I had been talking about creating a memorial to Patsy in the new community center."

Juliette's mouth dropped open. "That's news to me. What did Hettie say?"

"Despite herself, she was touched. She almost started crying when I brought out clippings and photos of Patsy that I'd already collected."

"She and Stanley really did love Patsy."

"Stanley actually spoke up then and said that they would be honored if I did this memorial for their daughter. He asked what they could do to help."

"What did you say?"

He crossed his arms. "I reminded them that I never would have known about their daughter's work at the center if it hadn't been for you. Then I told them point-blank I would only create and fund the memorial if they resolved their differences with you. I let them know clearly how I felt about the way they'd treated you through the years and how objectionable I found it. I told them that since I'd grown to love you and your family that I simply couldn't give honor to their family if they couldn't find a way to let their bitterness go toward you."

"Oh my goodness." Juliette knew her mouth was hanging open now.

"I showed them pictures at that point of what the memorial would look like that would be placed on the wall inside the community center, and I showed them a photo of a plaque and a stone monument that would be placed in a garden area in front of the center when it's finished. I also let them understand that we would give verbal honor to Patsy at the dedication ceremony for the center, which would include a covered dish supper, music, and a big gathering of everyone in the valley, including many families who once lived here. I added that I hoped to ask Patsy's friend Esther Boone to prepare a speech to give."

Juliette leaned forward. "What did Hettie say?"

"She cried. She got mad. She said I was trying to bribe them."

Juliette looked at him, tight-lipped. "That sounds like her."

He held up a finger. "However, Stanley stayed calm. He said he'd felt for years they should have stopped harboring bitterness toward you simply because your father chose to remarry and because you were the child of your father's second wife. He reminded Hettie that their minister even came to talk to them about the very same thing more than once. Stanley actually admitted to Hettie that he'd felt guilty about their behavior toward you for a long time."

Juliette willed herself not to start to cry. "I told you he often acted nice to me when Hettie wasn't around. What happened next?"

"Since Hettie was still upset, Stanley suggested I give them time to talk over my offer and that they would get back to me."

"Did they?" She leaned forward.

"Yes. Stanley came into the store two days later—yesterday,

when you were off—to say they'd agreed to lay aside their feelings about you and your father, to bring this honor to their daughter. He brought a scrapbook and a box of photos for me to look through to help with more information, and he sat at the counter between customers and told me stories about Patsy working with the kids at the center after school and in the summer camp project she initiated. It was sweet to listen to him. He obviously loved her a lot."

"I simply don't know what to say about all this, Walker Logan." She shook her head in disbelief. "Should I now expect Hettie and Stanley to suddenly start acting sweet to me?"

A faint smile played on his lips. "Stanley and I discussed the best way to handle things. I told him I would keep our conversations private, but I suggested he and Hettie pay a visit to your family in the near future to talk about these issues and to apologize for treating you with such disrespect. Stanley agreed to that idea. I made it clear to him that from now on I expected both of them to be cordial to you at any encounter or meeting, and that if they reneged on their agreement after the ceremony, the memorial would be dismantled and the reason given."

"Oh, my gosh. I can't believe you said all that." Juliette put her hands to her face, trying to take it all in.

Walker turned to look at her fully. "I had to tell you so you would be prepared. You may also want to talk to your family. My guess is that Stanley will be making a call to your grandparents this week to schedule a time to come over to meet with them and with you."

She gave a disgusted snort. "I'm trying to envision what this new and improved Hettie Rhea might act like."

He frowned at her. "You'll need to work on your attitude in order to make this work, Juliette. If she is willing to forgive, even under pressure, you'll need to be gracious enough to forgive, too."

Juliette sat still, looking out into the darkness for a minute. "Why did you do this, Walker?"

"I told you. Because I'm in love with you and I didn't like seeing how Hettie and Stanley Rhea behaved toward you. It was like an old feud that made no sense, and no one seemed able to bring it to an end. I noticed people around the valley, even your own family, seemed to have grown accustomed to Hettie and Stanley's actions, as though the fact that it had continued for so long made it right. And it wasn't."

The tears started now. Juliette couldn't help them. "This has hurt me for so many years. I can't believe it might finally be at an end." She dug in her purse for a tissue. "Do you really think Hettie will act differently toward me?"

His jaw tightened. "She'd better or the deal's off."

"I'm not sure all this is honorable, but I do know in my heart, deep down, that Hettie and Stanley hated the fact that Patsy died so young and they always yearned in a twisted way for her memory to live on. For her not to be forgotten."

"So now she'll be remembered in an honorable way. I think your family will be pleased about this, don't you?"

"Oh, yes, especially George and my grandparents. They loved Patsy. It was tragic to them that she died so young."

He grinned at her. "I hope you'll let me know how the visit turns out."

Juliette nodded and then sat quietly again, looking out across the farmyard into the darkness. "I'm so overwhelmed by all this. It's almost too much to take in." She felt the tears welling up again. "All this time no one has ever gone to bat for me about this, even my own family. They just made excuses for Hettie and Stanley. Called it simply the way they were. Accepted it. Didn't seem to notice how much it hurt me. It's one of the reasons I always dreaded coming back home to visit after I left for college."

"I sensed that." Walker pulled her into his arms. "Selfishly, I want you to be happy here so you might consider staying. I can't honorably offer you what I want to right now, not with the problems in my life that still exist, but I keep hoping something might change in time." His voice softened. "That we might have a future together."

Juliette wasn't sure what to say to that idea, but the words sounded sweet. She pulled Walker closer, settling her lips over his, wanting to show him how grateful she was to him for caring so much about her and for loving her so selflessly.

CHAPTER 15

A few days later, Walker was working in the store in the late afternoon with Juliette, when Vernon and Harley came in the door, both sauntering and smirking.

"We done you a little favor, storekeeper, for some of the favors you've done for us," Harley said with a grin.

"What kind of favor?" Walker asked, setting down the box of canned goods he'd just brought from the storage room to unpack.

Vernon angled his way over toward the soda fountain. "We ate lunch late, but I sure would like to try one of them big banana splits in that picture up there." He pointed.

Juliette, behind the counter working, smiled at him. "I'd say Walker might give you a banana split for the favor you've done for him, if it's a good favor."

"Oh, it's a good 'un, all right." Vernon laughed.

She glanced at Harley. "You want one, too?"

He studied the picture on the wall menu. "Yeah, it looks right good."

Walker studied the brothers as he walked behind the counter. They wore camouflage pants and faded brown T-shirts today, and Harley wore his trademark brown fedora.

"You guys look like you have on your work gear today." Juliette peeled and sliced bananas to lay them in two long glass dishes.

Vernon looked around as if to be sure no one else was in the store before answering. "The right clothes are good for times when you don't want *them* to see you."

Walker saw Juliette hide a smirk.

He went to the refrigerator to get out two bottles of water for the brothers while Juliette spooned ice cream on the bananas.

Harley caught his eye as he turned around and lowered his voice. "There were folks in the valley looking for you, Walker Logan."

Walker tensed at the words, pushing the waters across the counter to the brothers before sitting down on a stool behind the register across from them. He felt his hands knot into fists and tucked them out of sight.

Juliette, hearing Harley's words, turned to ask, "Who was looking for Walker?"

"Two guys." Harley leaned forward. "We were over here near the store about closing time yesterday when we saw them looking around, peeking in the windows. We'd stopped by to see if you were here, but that other man was working instead."

"That was Eldon Johnson," Juliette put in.

Harley shrugged. "We sort of sneaked up toward the door. We could hear through the screen they was asking about you. The man told 'em you'd be back in the morning."

"Me and Vernon didn't like the way they was taking little notes when they come out, how they was talking about looking for your house."

"So we sent 'em off on a fine wild-goose chase." Vernon cackled and slapped his leg. "I don't think they'll be back anytime soon."

"What did you do?" Juliette said, putting their banana splits on the counter in front of them and perching on the other stool beside Walker.

Harley grinned. "We sashayed up and told them we knew where you lived, that we could give them directions."

Walker frowned.

"Don't worry, storekeeper. We didn't send 'em to your house. We made up a place. Sent 'em off up to that old Shackleford cabin, the old deserted place at the end of Razar Road." Harley laughed. "That old road's beat-up and washed out for sure. It crosses through a creek and winds up a steep narrow hill around Ledford

Ridge, not far from our place."

Vernon waved his spoon between two bites of his banana split. "That road ain't fit for a horse to ride up anymore, much less a fancy car like them boys had."

Harley crossed his arms with a smug smile. "We followed them at a distance and after they crossed the creek we put a few obstacles in their path for when they come back down. Felled a tree over the road so they couldn't get back out except by walking. Left an old snake in a cardboard box over at the side of the road beyond it. Figured their curiosity would cause them to open it and look inside."

Vernon laughed, punching Harley's arm as he did. "We hung out in the woods to watch the fun. They was a-cussin' and carrying on something awful when they hit the tree. They tried using them fancy phones but couldn't get no internet signal up on the mountain. Then they started walking out and had to cross that creek in their city shoes. And when they opened that box by the roadside they scared old Jack-snake something awful, both squalling and a-hollering. So Mr. Snake started hissing and showing a little attitude for being disturbed."

Juliette gasped. "You boys could have caused those men to get bit and killed putting a rattlesnake in a box for them to find!"

"Aw." Harley waved a hand. "It was only old Jack bull snake. He's got a lot of attitude and hisses and looks like a rattlesnake, but he's harmless. He just weren't happy to be shut up in that box."

Vernon arched his hand in a snake pose, wiggling it toward Juliette.

"Those men ran off hollering down that old road like the devil himself were after them."

"Well, I feel sorry for them," Juliette said. "What did they do to deserve that?"

Harley lifted his chin. "They was snooping, sent in by that Dade Claiborne—we heard them say so—and they was set on trying to find out stuff about Walker. We didn't like that."

"They weren't driving a black van, were they?" Walker asked.

"Nah. They drove a fine city sedan-type car. A blue Lincoln with fancy wheels." Harley paused, leaning forward again. "We went up to look in their car later after they left. Papers in it said they worked for the newspaper. We don't want no snoopy newspaper folks in our valley. I don't think they'll be coming back anytime soon after the day they had yesterday."

Vernon cackled again. "Some other boys came up today to move the felled tree off the road, but they had to call a tow truck to get the car out. Seems the tires had gone flat somehow overnight."

Both the brothers laughed then, and even Juliette couldn't help giggling.

Harley shifted his eyes toward Walker. "We heard you got some secrets and that you're not wanting it known where you are. We did what we could so *them* wouldn't find you."

"Thank you," Walker said. "It's still best if some of my past stays where it is for now. It could be a danger to my family if media did a lot of meddling, connected my past and my present and publicized it."

"A man's got a right to his privacy."

Juliette drummed her fingers on the table while the Ledford brothers finished off the banana splits she'd made them.

"I'm real sorry, Walker," she said at last, "that Dade stirred up trouble for you. I know it's because of me."

Harley lifted an eyebrow. "Our daddy always said a jealous man can be a real devilish problem, but we've watched Dade Claiborne become a mean 'un right along. Likes to bully. Throw his weight around. He's got good people, but he's not much a credit to them these days." He paused. "I wouldn't like to think about you spending much time with him, Julie-girl."

"Don't worry. I don't expect to," she answered.

Vernon cleaned out the last bite of his banana split and rubbed his stomach with a grin. "That sure was good, Juliette. Thank you."

"You can thank Walker," she said. "It's his store."

Vernon got down from the stool and gave a little whistle to Marsh so he could visit with the big dog before the boys left.

"You need to get him a dog," Walker said to Harley, watching them.

"I'm thinking on it," Harley said. He turned to Juliette. "Your grandpa doing better?"

"Yes, thank you."

"We seen him out working on the farm here and there, so we figured he was okay now. I'm glad. He and your gramma have always been good to us. Sometimes she gives us food and things she's put up."

"Stop by and I'm sure she'll send you home with some canned beans, corn, and some of her homemade jelly," Juliette said. "She was saying the other day you hadn't been by for a while."

Harley tipped his hat. "We'll drop by on our way home. See if there's a little work around she needs us to do. We like an odd job every now and then."

"You both do good carpentry work when you take a mind to," Juliette said. She turned to Walker. "Remember Harley and Vernon if you have repair work around your house that needs doing."

"I'll do that," he said, and then they waved the boys off as a sweep of customers came in, giving he and Juliette little time to talk.

About an hour later, Juliette's brother, George, stopped by to pick up milk and a couple of other small items.

"There's been another theft," he told them as he checked out at the register. "They hit Ben and Irma Lee Whitehead's home on the road leading to the Boone Cemetery. You know the place," he said to Juliette. "Pretty white farmhouse with a red roof and lots of flowers in the yard."

"Oh, I hate to hear that. They're such a sweet couple. Are they okay? Were they at home when it happened?"

"No, they'd gone over to Asheville to spend the weekend with their daughter. Got home this afternoon and found their place ransacked. The thieves took electronics, their television and computer, jewelry, cash they kept in a box under the bed, tools from Ben's shop, two old rifles Ben kept in a gun rack, even clothes. Gramma said it really upset Ben and Irma to come home and find their house torn up and so many of their things taken." George propped an elbow on the counter. "The minister has been over talking with them, and a group of the women at the church are getting food together to take over. I've got some things from Gramma and Laura in the truck I'm dropping off before I head back to the house."

"If I get together a box of store goods, will you take it with you, too?" Walker asked George.

"Sure. That would be good of you."

Walker headed to the back of the store to get a box.

Juliette visited with George and rang up sales while Walker went around the store, filling up the box.

When George left, Juliette said, "I hate that happened to Irma Lee and Ben. They are such nice people. They live on social security, too, and it will be hard for them to replace all those stolen items. Maybe they carry a little homeowners insurance that will help."

"Let me know what you find out about that," Walker said, going back to start unpacking the box of canned goods he'd brought out earlier.

"I will. Maybe the charity that likes to help rural Appalachian families will hear about the Whiteheads, like they did about other families who've been hit by the thieves or had problems." She grinned at him.

"Maybe they will," Walker said, beginning to stack cans on the shelf.

A short time later during a lull in business at the store, Walker came over to lean on the counter by the register. "I think my sister and her family, and my Aunt Jessie, may come for Thanksgiving. I'd like for you to meet them." He pushed a stray piece of hair back. "I know you have your own family to be with on a holiday like that, but I wondered if we had our Thanksgiving meal at dinner instead of lunch if you could come."

She smiled. "I'd like that, and I look forward to meeting your family."

He scowled. "I'm hoping everything works out so they get to come. We need to plan things carefully, but I think it will be okay."

"I hope so." Juliette didn't press for more details, and Walker felt glad of it. He hated all the careful subterfuge he had to go through to get together with any of his family or friends now.

She changed the topic. "Halloween is coming up. It might be fun if we decorated the store a little."

They talked about decorating ideas then as they prepared to shut the store for the day.

Near closing, four men trooped in, wearing work clothes. Walker had seen them in the store before. They snagged chips, colas, and a package or two of cookies, before heading to the register.

"You got any of that barbecue from lunch left over?" the taller of the four men said.

Juliette looked in the warmer. "Enough for sandwiches for all of you and maybe a few extra."

"Make what you can," he said.

Marsh growled, surprising Walker.

The tall man glanced toward the big dog. "We got a dog out on the porch. Your dog probably smells him."

One of the other men laughed. "Glad we didn't bring him in," he said. "They might have gone at it."

"You guys live around here?" Walker asked.

"We're builders, constructing a house on the mountain. Staying nearby while we work on it."

Juliette turned from making the sandwiches. "I thought I recognized you. You're the guys working on Dade Claiborne's house."

One of the men, propped against a stool at the counter, ran his eyes over her. "And you're that girl Dade Claiborne was dating?"

"*Was* is the correct term," she said.

The man laughed. "Dade is a rich man. You'd do well to stay hooked up to him."

"No, thanks." She wrapped the sandwiches, bagged them, and passed them over the counter. "You guys want anything else?"

"Nothing for sale," the man said, letting his eyes slide over Juliette.

Walker sent him a warning look. "Ring up their sales, Juliette. We need to close the store."

The tall man paid and they left. Walker followed them to the door to lock up. He noticed Marsh had padded across the store to offer another low growl.

"They had a big black-and-white dog with them. Rough looking," he said to Juliette, glancing out the window at their truck heading out of the parking lot.

"They're a rough-looking bunch, too. I had the pleasure, if you'd call it that, of meeting them when Dade took me up to see his house." She offered the last comment with obvious sarcasm. "I guess they do good work, but I don't much care for them. Dade is letting them stay at the old Claiborne cabin below his property on the mountain. He said they could get more construction work done and put in longer hours if they lived close and didn't have to drive in every day. He probably has a point. It's a long trip into town."

"I think I remember Quillen telling me the land on the mountain where developers are building new homes was once Claiborne land."

"Some of it, but not all of it." She began to clean up the counter area so they could close. "Dade asked to keep a piece of the land that bordered between the end of the development and the Claiborne farm. It's a prime spot for a house, with incredible views and privacy since it's at the end of the road."

She turned to toss her paper towels into the trash. "George thought it nice that Dade kept that piece of land. The original Claiborne cabin is in the woods up there, too. Old graves are in a family cemetery behind the cabin, but most of the rest of the Claibornes are buried in the church cemetery. Access to that old cabin—except from Dade's new place—is only by a rutted-out trail, not easy to get to."

"The cabin must be livable for those guys to stay in it."

"Yes. The Claibornes have always kept it up, but it's not the ritz. Most people wouldn't want to stay in it for long." She shrugged. "The men probably hang out a lot at the house Dade is building."

Walker moved behind the counter to close out the register.

As she leaned over to get her purse in the cabinet underneath, Walker smoothed a hand through her hair. "I love your hair."

"Do you?" She stood up, moving closer to him. "I like yours, too." She let her soft hands skim the sides of it behind his ears.

Pulling her into him, Walker let his lips close over hers, his blood heating and his heartbeat escalating as he deepened the kiss and felt her hands slide behind his head to his neck and then down his back to draw him closer. Walker let his hands trace down her arms and then slide around her back, loving the way she felt pressed against him, dreaming of more.

"I do love the job perks here," she said in a soft voice.

Walker kissed her forehead as he released her, wishing with everything in him he could offer her more. Wanting more, too.

"Hey, I want to ask you something," she said, moving away to lean against the counter nearby.

"What?" he said, letting his eyes skim over her plaid shirt and slim-fitting black pants and then back to her sunny face he saw so often now in his dreams.

She fidgeted. "You said it might be all right if I use the back porch for something to do with my quilting." She hesitated.

"And?" he prompted.

"Lenora has an ongoing class in Appalachian Studies that would love to see a quilting demonstration, maybe learn the art a little. She proposed bringing her students down for a couple of their classes when I told her you'd offered the space. I thought I might also hold a workshop on the porch for the Knoxville quilting association I belong to. I've considered starting a Maryville/Townsend branch. The association's goal is to encourage and promote quilt making as a craft and to get women together to quilt and share." She twisted a strand of her hair as she talked.

"Sounds fine to me. People coming in for your classes and

workshops will also discover the store. Maybe come back." He grinned.

She relaxed a little then. "Since I'll be fixing up the porch, I thought I might start a valley quilting group, too. We could work on a memory quilt for the community center together, create squares for it representing significant places, people, or events in the valley. It might be special."

"It *would* be special."

Juliette smiled at his encouragement. "The Maryville College class meets on Tuesday mornings. I think the valley group would like a morning time, too—maybe Thursdays. And the monthly Quilting Association group would need to meet on a Saturday, since a lot of the women work at other jobs during the week."

"Those times sound fine to me. You'll be in the back on the porch. It won't interfere with business up front." He didn't ask her if these activities would continue in the spring, when she planned to return to North Carolina for her classes and her job at the shop. Maybe she would love this new work and not want to go.

"Try whatever you'd like," he said.

"Thanks," she said, her eyes sparkling. "I think it might be fun."

CHAPTER 16

November arrived, and the valley roads lay dressed in their full autumn splendor. It was hard to drive across the Foothills Parkway without wanting to get out to enjoy the stupendous views of the mountainsides in their rich fall colors.

Walker was talking to his cousin Stewart this morning during a lull at the store.

"I'm glad your family is coming to see you for Thanksgiving," Stewart said. "I wish all of you could be here with us like old times." He hesitated. "Have any more reporters from the local paper been around?"

"No." Walker chuckled. "I guess the Ledford brothers scared them off."

Stewart laughed. "You've met some real characters in that valley."

"Yes, but a lot of good people, too."

Stewart shifted the subject. "Have you talked to Burton lately?"

"No, why?" Walker asked, hearing a change in Stewart's voice.

"A murder occurred here last week. A crazy man went berserk and killed old Bill Copeland."

Walker felt a prickle up his arm. "Bill served with my father in the war. I knew him."

"Yes, and a witness saw a black van with tinted windows leaving the scene."

Walker blew out a breath. "So the man's still in the area and he's surfaced again. Do the police and Burton think this murder is linked to the threats I received?"

"Yes to both questions. Bill's family said several of them received odd, threatening messages in the weeks before the murder happened. A man's muffled voice saying he wanted money. Saying he deserved it. Just like with you. A couple of times Bill's son Raymond said that his dad told him he thought someone was following him, that a van tried to run him off the road one day out by the old cliffs."

"Could the link to all this be the war, since my father and Bill both served together?"

"Burton thinks it's probable. It's the only link he can see between you and Bill Copeland, except that Bill has a lot of money. He said the police are now looking more closely at the veterans association that came after you pushing for money earlier. You remember?"

Walker searched his memory. "Yes, but they weren't much more aggressive than other groups or charities that contacted me, or stopped by the store, laying out reasons for wanting donations, getting a little pushy."

"Well, I called to complain about how those volunteers acted in our store," Stewart reminded him. "It's bad enough people came in the store during business hours all the time to hit you up for money, but they could have been nice about it."

Walker got up to pace with his phone, thinking back. "One of the executives in that organization actually called to apologize for the way I'd been approached by their group, too. He said they didn't mean to sound threatening. He told me a lot of their volunteers sometimes got overly zealous about their work. He talked about PTSD and emotional stuff like that being a big factor with some of their veteran volunteers."

"Well, the police are looking at any military groups that approached you, following up any possible connections with Bill Copeland. It seems obvious this is the same man—or group—as before." Stewart paused. "Only this time it's murder. Burton says they're taking the investigation much more seriously now."

Walker rubbed his neck. "I hate that this happened."

"Bill Copeland's family is real worried now, as you might imagine.

They're afraid this person—or group—might cause more trouble. Bill's property, all the rentals he owned, and his construction business went to his two sons. Burton says it's a lot of money."

"I certainly know how they feel."

Stewart cleared his throat. "I feel bad about something, too. I gave you a hard time for running and leaving, even suggested it was somewhat cowardly, but maybe I was wrong. You saw the reality of how dangerous the threats you received were better than I did."

"Thanks," Walker said. "It wasn't an easy decision."

When he hung up from talking to Stewart a few minutes later, he called Burton. "Hey, I just talked to Stewart. Is there anything I need to do in this?"

"No. My gut feeling has always been that the guy who threatened you and your family was a wacko. He's evidently targeting his mental instability in another direction without you around anymore."

"Should I feel guilty about the Copelands?"

"No, you shouldn't. Angry, mentally unstable types find trouble. They get things twisted in their minds. Greed is a nasty motivator, too. Be assured that if there is a military link between the Copeland family and your family, the police will uncover it. This man—and I personally think it's more likely an individual than a group now—has brought serious attention to himself since he's moved from petty harassments and fear tactics to murder."

"Do you think he'll go after my family again, now that he's surfaced once more?"

"No. You disappeared. He probably searched for you for a time, then found a new focus. As long as you stay invisible, he'll stay diverted. He may continue to harass the Copelands, focusing on a new target, or go underground for a while with the murder investigation at large."

"I hope the police catch him."

"So do I."

"Listen, Stewart apologized to me for giving me a hard time for leaving two years ago," Walker added.

"He hasn't seen as many crazies in action as I have. I knew the danger was real." Burton's voice grew more serious. "Don't get some misguided idea in your head to call the Copeland boys or to reach out to their family."

"Will the police need to talk to me?"

"No. They have all your statements from before. They can talk to Stewart if they need to ask further questions. Also, I told Stewart if they contacted him to call me. I'll get involved if I need to, but I think the police will be working with fresh evidence in this now."

"I'll always be grateful for your help through all of this."

Burton chuckled. "That's what friends are for, buddy. I'm keeping a tally."

Walker wished he could laugh heartily with his friend, but the tension coiling inside him would hardly let him loosen up that much. "I see customers coming in," he said, hearing voices out on the porch.

"And I need to head to court. We'll be in touch."

Walker felt grateful for a busy day after his phone calls. It was Juliette's day off, and Eldon had called in sick earlier, battling a stomach bug, leaving him to handle the store on his own. The lunch traffic and the steady stream of customers throughout the day kept Walker from thinking too much about the situation in Colorado.

Near the end of the day he was surprised to see Juliette's grandfather head into the store.

"It's good to see you, Dalton," Walker said.

The old man looked around. "I guess I haven't been here often to see how fine things look in your store, but everybody's real glad for this place you built." He gave Walker a crooked smile. "I admit that I thought you a mite touched to build a store like this in the valley. Glad to say I was wrong about that."

"Thank you. The store is doing well."

Walker studied the older man in his brown farm overalls and faded plaid shirt. As usual, he wore work boots and an old ball cap with a farm product logo across it.

"Can I get you something?" Walker asked, seeing the old man

looking at the menu board above the soda fountain.

"Maybe something cool to drink. Got any orange soda?"

"I do. I keep some bottled orange and grape Nehis in the cooler. I'll get you one and fix you a glass of ice for it." He walked to the cooler in the back and then returned to fill a glass with ice.

Dalton drank his soda while another customer checked out. When the store fell empty again, he cleared his throat. "I've come to say thank you for a couple of things."

He scratched his short beard. "I know from Juliette you had a talk with Hettie and Stanley Rhea. It was probably something the wife or I should have done long ago. Hettie never acted kind to Juliette, from the time she first came to us. We sort of made allowances for it at the time, but we ought not to have kept overlooking it. I tried talking to Stanley once but Hettie isn't an easy woman to persuade about anything."

"There is that," Walker admitted with a twitch of a smile.

"Hettie's come around now—as best as can be expected for her—and Stanley more." He scratched his beard again. "It was good of you to set up that memorial for Patsy. Our son, Wyatt, loved her a lot and Patsy was a fine, fine girl. The wife and I felt touched to see her honored at the opening of the renovated community center."

He looked at Walker more directly now. "You've been good to folks in the valley, been a credit. Helped families in need, showed kindness. Made yourself a part of the community. I wanted to offer you a thank-you for it."

"I appreciate that, sir."

"You can just call me Grandpa Dalton like everyone else, boy."

Walker nodded.

Another customer popped in to pick up a few store items, but Grandpa stayed until they left again.

"You've been marking a lot of time with my granddaughter," he said then. "Are your intentions honorable?"

Walker sighed. "They are. I'd offer marriage to Juliette today if my situation was different."

"Nothing's changed with that?" The old man's eyes grew soft

over the question, touching Walker.

Walker dropped onto the stool behind the counter across from him. "Today I learned a man was killed in my hometown this week, possibly by the same man who threatened me and my family three years ago. It's thought he could be mentally deranged and that there could be links between my family and his. I knew the man who was murdered. He and my father served in the war together. Many facts between the threats to his family and mine are similar."

The old man considered this. "I'd say that's disturbed you a mite."

"Yes. It's been weighing on my mind all day." Walker threaded a hand through his hair. "It made me realize how wise I'd been to leave in order to protect those I love. It reminded me, too, that I still need to be careful."

"You told Juliette this?"

"No. She didn't work today."

He nodded. "I'd find me a time, son. I've learned women don't like a man to keep things from them. It seems sensible to me for a man to keep himself to himself sometimes, but women don't see things quite the same way about that. The wife can get herself real het up at me if I don't tell her about every little thing."

Walker smiled. "I think Eldon Johnson gave me some similar advice to that one day."

"A young man could do well sometimes to listen to his elders. Save him some grief." He grinned at Walker.

"I'll keep that in mind."

A group of after-school kids banged in through the front door then, heading for the candy barrels to ogle the sweets and then pointing out what they planned to order on the menu board above the fountain.

Grandpa Dalton smiled at them, speaking to each one, asking about their families and calling most by name. He turned to Walker as he got up, retrieving his walking stick from beside the door. "I'll be heading on out. The old woman said for you to come for Sunday lunch after church this week if you're not working."

"I'll do that if I can."

As Dalton left, Walker turned to start filling ice cream orders for the kids.

Later that day, near closing, Juliette gave him a call at the store.

"Hi, Walker," she said. "Gramma and I made lasagna for supper and Grandpa suggested I bring half over to share with you. Do you have any dinner plans yet? I can bring bread, salad, and dessert, too. Gramma and I made peanut butter pies with fat-free dairy products and reduced-fat peanut butter. We made two pies. Grandpa said he'd part with one for you."

"That sounds like a noble sacrifice," Walker replied, smirking over Grandpa's obvious efforts to get him together with Juliette. "Pack it up and head my way. I'm closing now and I should be at the house in fifteen minutes."

"It may take me a little longer," she said. "I need to throw a salad together. You'll have time to walk Marsh, too, before I get there."

She wafted into his house thirty minutes later, greeting Marsh with affection after Walker opened the door, the soft, familiar smell of her lingering in the air behind her, as she made her way to the kitchen. She put a cardboard box filled with dishes on a low stool by the kitchen counter and then pulled off a hoodie to drape it over the back of a chair.

"The nights are getting chilly now," she said, leaning over to start pulling items out of the box she'd brought.

Walker tried hard not to stare at her rounded bottom in the tight blue jeans she wore. His mind never seemed to stay in sensible places these days whenever Juliette came around. As she turned to smile at him, his traitorous eyes drifted from her mouth to her breasts, tucked snugly into a pink stretchy top.

He turned toward the kitchen to alter his focus. "I'll get some dishes down. Do you need to heat anything up?"

"Nope. The lasagna and bread are straight from the oven." She put the food on the table, adding plates and silverware, while Walker pulled stick butter and bottles of salad dressing from the refrigerator, poured them both glasses of tea, and started some coffee for later.

They soon settled down to eat at Walker's big kitchen table, chatting over their dinner together and catching up on their day. After finishing dinner, they took their pie and coffee into the big den to sit around the crackling fire Walker had made.

"I wish this could be our life every day," Walker said, leaning his head back against the couch.

"You're upset about something. I've sensed it much of the evening. Can you talk to me about it?"

He told her then about talking to Stewart and then Burton.

"I see," she said, propping her feet on an ottoman and considering his words. "This criminal could be the same demented person you've been running from. In both cases, he pressured and threatened for money. I've read stories about sick people like that, who even kidnapped children for money. Like with the Lindbergh family."

His eyes popped wide and he stiffened, her words bringing back unpleasant memories.

"You're thinking of your little nieces." She picked up on his reaction. "Did that man try to kidnap your nieces?"

Walker sighed. "He threatened to. He called describing their school in Virginia, where they lived, saying he could easily see they disappeared one day if I wouldn't cooperate, give him the money he wanted."

"You didn't, did you?"

"No. Burton and the police said that wouldn't be the best answer, that he'd only come back for more, feel more emboldened the next time." Walker blew out a long breath. "He threw a firebomb into the window of my uncle's house, too. It didn't burn down the house, but it caused damage and scared them. There was a string of other ugly events, too."

"And all of this for money." She shook her head. "Has your family always been wealthy, like the Lindberghs? Has this sort of thing happened before? No wonder you said to me that money wasn't always a blessing."

Walker didn't answer, staring into the fire.

She rattled on for a little while longer and then realized he'd stopped responding. "You're not answering any of my questions." She paused to stare at him. "Something triggered all this and you're still not wanting to talk about it. You've gone all quiet."

He reached down to pet the dog at his feet and then looked up to see tears in her eyes.

"It hurts me when you shut me out like this," she said, wiping at her cheeks. "Am I still not someone you can trust?"

Walker fidgeted.

"Something in your life instigated all this with that crazy man, didn't it?"

He didn't answer.

She stomped to her feet and paced over to look out the window. "I hate it when you won't talk to me. Do you hear me, I hate it!" She headed toward the kitchen.

Walker got up to follow her. "I told you I would tell what I felt I could when I can. You said you understood."

"Well, that doesn't mean I have to like it." She snatched up her hoodie and jerked it on. "I'm going home and I'm going to let you clean up the kitchen. Bring the dishes back to the store tomorrow."

He reached out to catch her arm. "My whole life changed three years ago and spiraled out of control," he tried to explain. "I'm sharing with you what I can."

She turned flashing eyes toward his. "My whole life changed when I started working for you this summer. So welcome to the club. You've kept me confused and at arm's length ever since. You say you love me. You talk about wishing we could be together all the time. Then you shut me out when I ask you questions. I don't like secrets and I don't like this game where you get to tell me only what you want and only when you want to tell it. How do you think that makes me feel?"

He tried to think what to say.

"Maybe one of these days you'll decide to try to trust me." She headed for the door and then turned back to look at him with more tears in her eyes. "Trust and love go together. Think about that, Walker."

He sat staring into the fire for a long time after she left.

Marsh, seeming to sense he was upset, moved over to sit by his feet, looking up at him.

"Grandpa Dalton didn't mention that when you confide in a woman about some things she thinks she has a right to know every other detail of your life, too," he said to the dog.

He got up and poked at the fire viciously. "I'm not ready to share everything yet. Especially what started all this trouble for me, changed everything, and ruined my life."

He paced over to stare out the window at the full moon on the horizon, Marsh leaning up against his leg.

"If things get really bad, we can always go on the road again, pal. I didn't sell the Sportsmobile." He leaned down to pet the big dog. "She says I don't trust her. But I wish she would trust me to tell her everything when I think the time is right. Is that too much to ask?"

CHAPTER 17

Juliette stayed angry at Walker for several days, but she hated the strain of keeping it up. She was peaceable and forgiving by nature.

Weary from the disharmony, she felt glad to see Amy come by the store early one morning to pick up some items for the daycare center. Amy chatted away happily about the new center, the after-school program, and how well things were working out, cheering Juliette up.

"Keith and I hired Dora Walker, Eldridge and Ada Blanche's youngest girl, to work with us at the center," she said. "She's nineteen and taking classes over at Pellissippi State Community College near Friendsville. Dora is studying education and really likes kids. She's good with the little ones and has great ideas to keep the older ones entertained after school, too. She and I are trading around hours and it's giving me a lot more free time."

"That's great, Amy. I like Dora."

Walker came in the door after taking Marsh on a short walk, said hello to Amy while putting Marsh's leash away, and reminded Juliette to put new gift cards in the racks when she had some time.

After he walked toward the back of the store with the dog, Amy turned to Juliette. "Did you and Walker have a fight?" she asked in a whispered tone. "The air sure felt frosty between you two."

Juliette crossed her arms, glancing back to where Walker worked in the back of the store now. "Walker still won't be candid with me about his past life. We had words about it earlier this week."

Amy leaned on the counter beside the register, where she'd piled her store items. "Keith said he thinks Walker passed through some real painful times. He knows how that can feel and he hasn't pushed on Walker to talk about things he doesn't want to share yet."

She glanced back toward Walker to be sure he couldn't hear them. "When I had my counseling meetings after Keith got hurt, they advised me to give Keith time to open up as he felt led to. I remember a quote from Henry Wadsworth Longfellow printed on the front of the workbook they gave me. It said: 'Every man has his secret sorrows which the world knows not; and often times we call a man cold when he is only sad.'" She gave Juliette one of those sweet smiles of hers. "You need to be patient and loving and give Walker time, not get mad at him."

"You're probably right." Juliette rang up Amy's store items and then bagged them.

Amy leaned toward her again. "Besides, it's fun to make up when you've had a little spat."

After Amy left, Juliette's eyes followed Walker as he worked straightening shelf items in the back of the store.

When she headed back toward the storeroom a few minutes later for gift cards to replenish the card rack, she stopped beside him. "Let's not be mad at each other anymore."

He studied her face. "I think it's you who has been mad at me."

"I felt hurt, but I don't want to be mad anymore."

"Okay." He put a hand to her face and smiled at her. "What brought on this change of heart?"

"Two things. First, I hate discord and I have never liked to hold a grudge." She twisted her hands. "Second, Amy suggested I should be more patient and loving with you, that your secret sorrows make it hard for you to share."

He tried not to laugh. "She said that?"

Juliette grinned. "Well, actually, she quoted Wordsworth."

"The poet?"

Juliette nodded. "The line Amy recited said something about every man having his secret sorrows, but that a person ought not to view a man as cold when he is only sad."

"I'm sorry if I've seemed cold and that I hurt you." Walker leaned over to kiss her. "Sometimes I simply hate to remember and talk about all the detestable, disappointing things of the past. Also, Burton urged me to keep my counsel about some things for now. There is reason."

Juliette kissed him back, glad to put the weight of their disagreement behind them. "How do people stay mad for years and years over something, like Hettie did toward me? I felt miserable trying to stay mad at you for only a few days."

He laughed and hugged her to him. "You are such a joy and a blessing to me. I do love you and I'm sorry when I hurt you."

"Making up is nice." She pulled his face down to kiss him again.

Laughter and footsteps on the porch reminded them where they were. Walker let her go just before the door opened to let in Lenora Boone followed by her Appalachian Studies class.

"Are you ready for our visit?" Lenora asked.

"Yes, and looking forward to it," Juliette said, not mentioning her preoccupation with Walker almost made her forget the first class meeting today.

She glanced over the group of fifteen students in Lenora's class. "Come on back to the Quilt Room."

"Who made the cute sign?" Lenora pointed to the rustic sign over the door to the back porch with the words "Quilt Room" on it.

Walker answered her. "I asked Boyce Hart, an artist friend of mine in Townsend, to make it. I thought it would add a nice touch." He smiled at Lenora and the group. "I put a cooler of ice and bottled drinks in the Quilt Room earlier—plus a bowl of assorted candies from the store barrels. Help yourself to those as you settle in."

He headed back toward the register as Juliette led her class into the big porch room. A spacious work table that Eldon and Quillen built for her from unfinished doors now sat in the middle of the porch. Around it sat a mix of wooden chairs Juliette found at thrift stores in Maryville. She'd hung quilts on the walls for decoration, tucked low cabinets underneath for storage, and set up a quilting frame and sewing area in a back corner. The long room proved the perfect size for a workshop or group meeting, allowing space for everyone to work, with good lighting from the long windows.

As the students settled in, Juliette moved to stand at a simple wood lectern she'd placed near one end of the room, providing her a teaching area where she could put her laptop and notes.

As a certified professional teacher through the National Quilting Association, and used to teaching classes at the Campbell Folk School, Juliette wasn't nervous about sharing the history and art of quilting with Lenora's students. She fell quickly into the initial discussion she usually offered in beginner classes.

The time sped by, and as usual, the young students who came in looking somewhat bored and indifferent soon began asking questions and getting excited about the colorful history and stories Juliette shared.

"Today as a quilting example, we're going to start a signature quilt," she told them after her discussion. "You've seen many examples of quilts already from the actual quilts I brought today, the samples on the wall, and the photos I showed you on the computer. Perhaps all of you will look at quilts in a new way from now on."

"What's a signature quilt?" one of the girls asked.

"A basic signature quilt has blocks, each one made individually by the different people in a group. In the past signature quilts were created as friendship quilts, wedding gifts, or used as fundraisers. Some quilts are very simple and some highly elaborate, with each block a small artistic masterpiece representing the artisan who created it."

One of the boys groaned. "I don't even know how to thread a needle."

Everyone laughed.

"You'll learn," Juliette told him. "It isn't hard, and later at the dorm if you lose a button off your shirt, you'll be able to sew it back on."

She turned the computer around to show them a picture of a quilt. "This is a quilted wall hanging that a group of my students made in a workshop I did for beginning quilters. Like all of you, many of them had never made any part of a quilt before and few had good sewing skills."

"Oh, that's pretty," Lenora said.

"It's basically a small twenty-square block quilt with sewn-on tabs so the quilt can be hung on the wall," Juliette explained. "Each of you will make a signature block and we'll put solid squares between. For now, pick a solid-colored square of fabric from this box that you think is a good color to represent yourself. All are relatively light colors so our black signature thread will show well on each."

Interest picked up as the students searched through the squares for favorite colors. Next Juliette had them write their first names across the square lightly with a pencil, going over it with a black fabric pen.

"The color from this pen won't run if the hanging later needs to be washed." She walked around, making sure they all wrote their signatures in large, legible script, centered in the squares. Then she showed them how to hook their squares over an embroidery hoop and outline the signatures with black embroidery floss.

She enjoyed the giggles and comments while the students centered and tightened their fabric properly inside their embroidery hoops.

"Now, after threading the needle, you simply start underneath the square and outline the signature with thread." She demonstrated with her own sample.

After the students gathered around her to watch the process for a few minutes, she got one of the boys to try the running stitch, with her guidance, to give him and the others confidence.

Around laughter, talking, and occasional knotted threads and mistakes to be pulled out, the students finished their squares. Juliette then showed them how to turn back the sides of their squares a quarter of an inch to get them ready to piece together.

As they finished, she said, "At the next class, I'll have all these squares already pinned, and basted onto backing on a small quilting frame, and you'll learn how to finish the piece out."

Juliette gave a homework assignment for them to complete before the next class, answered questions, and then let Lenora take over. She sent the students out to explore the store for a few minutes before they needed to board the van to head back to campus.

Lenora beamed at Juliette as the last student made her way out of the room. "You're a natural, darling. You had them eating out of the palm of your hand with interest, even the boys."

"Thank you," Juliette said as she cleared off fabric scraps from the table and picked up empty soda bottles.

"I hope bringing students from my class can become a regular part of this course in the future." Lenora picked up her purse, laptop, and papers. "Are we still good to come back for the next two weeks as planned?"

"Sure, if you think the experience is valuable to them."

"Absolutely." She headed out the door to say good-bye to Walker and to round up her students.

After cleaning the room, Juliette headed back into the store. "Anything I need to do to get ready for the lunch crowd?" she asked.

"No, I'm ready to go and there's less traffic during the week now since the fall colors started fading in the Smokies. The days are growing colder, too."

"Sometimes we get a first snow around Thanksgiving, but most of the time we won't see the white stuff until Christmas or after." Juliette tucked her purse under the counter and put on one of the colorful aprons she'd made with the words "Happy Valley Store" embroidered across the front.

"You look cute in that red apron."

"Want me to make you one?"

He grinned. "No, but they're charming on you."

She smoothed down the apron. "I kept spilling chili and mustard on my good clothes. The apron is for protection."

"How did the class go?"

"Good, I think."

"Lenora said you were fantastic, and the college kids chatting around the store sounded positive about the experience. What was the quilt you had them trying out?"

"A signature quilt." She explained what it was. "It's a good initial activity. People like choosing their own fabric color for the squares and decorating it with their own name. Fans their ego."

"I'm continually impressed by your talents."

"Well, aren't you sweet?" She glanced toward the door before giving him a quick kiss on the cheek.

Hearing a car pull up outside, Walker didn't follow up with more, moving behind the counter to get ready for the lunch crowd.

"Your Valley Quilters group meets on Thursday this week, too, doesn't it?" he asked as Juliette came around to join him.

"Yes, and they loved the idea of making a commemorative quilt to put in the community center. Everybody is bringing ideas to the meeting this week." She got out a stack of the paper plates they used for lunch.

Walker waved to a couple of locals coming in the door. "Your new Blount County Quilters Group meets Saturday, too, doesn't it? The one you created as a new branch of the National Quilting Association?"

"Yes." She turned to look at him. "I put everything on your calendar. Are you having second thoughts about those groups meeting in the Quilt Room in the back of the store?"

"No." He shifted from one foot to another and then cleared his throat. "I was only thinking how much these folks will miss you when you go back to North Carolina this spring."

Her eyes met his. "I have two classes scheduled at the Campbell Folk School, Walker. Sharon hasn't rented out the apartment in her house. I'm expected back." She started fixing Valley Dogs, already knowing what the men at the counter, Wheeler Finch and Reese Atley, wanted. They fished together over at the lake every Tuesday afternoon and always came over for lunch before heading out on the water in their boat.

Juliette heard Walker sigh. "Perhaps I was thinking about how much I will miss you," he said only loud enough for her to hear.

She didn't answer, not sure what to say. He picked the oddest times to say serious things, with the minister and his wife heading in the door now. They loved Eldon's barbecue and stopped by occasionally to enjoy it after they'd been to Maryville shopping.

What does he expect? Juliette thought as she worked at the counter, fixing barbecue sandwiches. *That I'd stay?* It wasn't as if she'd received a proposal of marriage from him or anything. She wouldn't accept one if he offered it, either, with all the secrets still between them. No, she'd go back to North Carolina as planned. Perhaps while she was away, Walker could get things worked out in his life. Decide he could share with her and trust her. She needed that from him if they were to go beyond this dating stage.

Dade came into the store then, not adding anything positive to her day.

"Hey, sugar," he said to her as if there weren't a stack of negative feelings between them a mile high.

However, with the two fishermen and the minister and his wife all eating at the counter, it wasn't likely Dade would misbehave. Besides, the two Walker sisters, Pearl and Earline, had just ambled into the store, as well, to pick up some needed grocery items. Dade usually put on the charm when others were around.

Juliette nodded to him when he came over to the counter to lean on it. "What will you have, Dade?"

"A couple of cherry colas to go, please. Mama likes them and I thought I'd take her one since I'm going by the farm."

"Okay." She turned to start making them.

"I sure like that fancy new boat you bought, Dade," Reese said, glancing his way. "It can flat-out fly up the water."

"It's a Tahoe," Dade said. "Powerglide, 4.5-liter MPI, two hundred horsepower. It's got fore and aft fishing-seat positions, and a ten-gallon aerated aft livewell."

"Man, I bet you can reel in a whopper bass with that one," Wheeler added with a grin. "I hear tell boats like that cost more than thirty grand, too. You sure got yourself a fine boat."

Juliette heard the minister mumble something about extravagant spending to his wife, but she didn't think Dade heard.

"The days are still warm enough for a spin down the lake," Dade said to Juliette. "I'll take you out one day if you like. We can cruise down to the dam, leave our worries in the wake."

"No, thanks," she said, spritzing cherry into the colas. "But I appreciate the thought. I'll bet George, Laura, and the kids would love you to invite them out on the lake one day."

She saw him frown out of the corner of her eye. If no one had been in the store, she'd have confronted him about all the tales he'd spread about only dating her to help out her family and the farm. She was still annoyed about that.

"I hear tell there's been another of those thefts in the valley," Reese said, addressing the group at large.

The minister shook his head. "They broke into Cora Beth Myers's place down near the Red Top Church."

"Is that the Baptist church on the hill near the lake?" Reese asked.

"Yes," he replied. "And Cora Beth only recently lost her husband, Wade. She'd gone to Atlanta to see her grandkids. The thieves broke in while she was gone. Stole money, electronics and valuables and killed her little rat terrier, Dixie. That tore her up more than anything."

"They killed her dog?" Dade sounded shocked.

Wheeler slapped a hand on the counter, annoyed. "Well, that's downright mean, even for thieves."

"You got that right," Reese added.

"That little dog was real protective about the house," the minister explained. "I'm sure little Dixie kicked up a fuss when someone broke in."

"Poor thing." Juliette put a hand to her heart. "And poor Cora." She felt like crying to think of Cora coming home to find her house ransacked and her little dog dead.

Pearl walked over to the counter to bring her grocery items for Juliette to ring up. "However do these thieves always know when people around our valley will be away from home? And what sort of creep would break into a recent widow's house, take her things, and kill her little dog and companion. It makes me sick to think about it."

"When Cora's heart heals some, maybe Pearl and I can find a new dog for her," Earline added, coming over to join Pearl.

"That would be nice," Juliette said, bagging their groceries so they could leave. "I know you and Pearl know exactly how Cora feels."

Pearl nodded. "We'll stop over to see her."

As the women left, Wheeler asked Dade, "Any of your family been broken into yet?"

"No, and I hope that doesn't happen," he snapped, still scowling. "I bet it's those Ledford brothers behind all this. They're always creeping around the neighborhood, showing up where they shouldn't."

"You take that back," Juliette demanded, stamping her foot in annoyance. "Vernon and Harley may be odd, but they don't steal. And I'll tell you right now those two would never kill a dog someone loved and that's a fact."

She saw Walker grin at her from across the store, where he stood. He'd put Marsh out on the Quilt Porch when he saw Dade come in the door, and he was obviously staying near the porch area in case Marsh started to bark or growl. The dog still didn't like Dade one bit.

"I don't know why you're taking up for those two weirdos." Dade frowned at her. "They live in a ratty old shack up in the woods. They'd be the types you'd suspect to sneak around the valley, thieving."

"You're wrong. I know Vernon and Harley and they wouldn't do anything to hurt the people in the valley." Juliette glared at Dade as she passed him the colas.

He shot an angry look back at her, paid for the colas, and left in a huff.

"Do you think we upset him, asking if his family had experienced any thefts?" Wheeler said, watching Dade push out of the store, obviously mad.

The minister's wife shook her head. "No, I think he got upset when we were talking about poor Cora's little dog. It would upset anyone to hear about that."

Juliette doubted either was the case, but she felt glad Dade didn't stay longer today. She thankfully hadn't experienced any trouble lately from Dade, and he'd finally stopped dropping by the Hollander house to visit her. She couldn't say she was sorry.

CHAPTER 18

Almost a month had passed and Walker sat in the kitchen of his house enjoying the lively talk and laughter of his family, visiting for the Thanksgiving weekend. Somehow they'd worked out a way for all of them to come. This was the first holiday he'd shared with his sister and her family or his Aunt Jessie since all the problems started.

"Isn't it good to be together like this again?" his Aunt Jessie said, as if echoing his thoughts.

"I was just thinking the same thing," Victoria said, looking around the table with a smile.

While they chatted about mundane things over a late breakfast, Walker let his eyes travel over the familiar faces. His brother-in-law, Chandler Pendleton, was a tall, white-haired man, ten years older than his sister, Victoria. He had a long, angular distinguished face and intelligent gray eyes. Victoria met him doing an internship at Pendleton's after graduating from design school, and despite their age differences, they fell head over heels in love.

Victoria, his older sister by three years, tall with red hair, looked enough like their mother, Alberta, to keep her memory ever near the surface. Walker resembled more their dark-haired father.

"I wish your father Ed and your mother Alberta were here," Aunt Jessie said, her thoughts seeming to follow Walker's again. "Sometimes it's hard for me to remember they're both gone."

Vee patted her hand, which lay on the table. "Dad, Walker, and I were lucky you agreed to come and stay with us when Mom died."

Walker grinned at his sister. "We might have starved to death otherwise. Dad couldn't boil water, much less cook, and, Vee, you were too young to do much in the kitchen at eleven."

Aunt Jessie chuckled. "I didn't intend to stay when I came," she said. "But I felt needed with you children so young. Since my own Robert had died a few years before, I was at loose ends. I knew Robert's store manager, Jared, could easily run the print business that Robert started, so I decided to stay for a spell and rented out my house in Virginia."

"You taught me to cook and to sew," Vee said. "You also taught Walker to cook."

Aunt Jessie lifted her chin. "I believe boys need to learn to cook as well as women and to keep house. I've never sanctioned those defined gender roles. They're too restrictive. Basic life skills, like cooking, are good for both men and women to know, not just one or the other."

Walker smiled at her words. "Those skills you taught me came in handy after you headed home and left Dad and me on our own when Vee started college."

She waved a hand dismissively. "I knew you and your father could get along without me by that time, and I wanted to go back to my home in Blacksburg again."

"By you going back, I was able to live with you and go to design school at Virginia Tech in Blacksburg, too," Victoria said. "I'm so grateful for that. There weren't any good design schools near our home in Greeley."

"I'm grateful for that, too." Chandler grinned.

Walker knew that had been the main reason his Aunt Jessie Sheridan went back to Virginia when she did.

"It was a bit of a challenge taking care of things around the house, working in the store with Dad, and trying to finish high school," Walker added, remembering that time when he'd missed Jessie and Victoria. "Our old house felt too quiet suddenly with only me and Dad rambling around in it."

"You did fine," Aunt Jessie assured him. "I arranged for my

friend Barbara Jean Baker to come in and clean for you and Ed once a week, too. She kept me in touch with how you two were doing."

Walker grinned, remembering there was little Barbara Jean didn't know about anyone's business in Greeley, including theirs. She had continued cleaning for him after his dad died and had been a comfort to him in that time as well.

He studied Aunt Jessie as she talked and shared old family stories now. She wore her short blond hair, now sprinkled with gray, much as he remembered. Although she was their father's only sister, there was little resemblance between the two except around the eyes. Aunt Jessie, like Victoria, had gone east to college—to the same school where Vee went—and met her husband Robert Sheridan there. Robert had owned a small printing company in Blacksburg. Old memories made it hard for Aunt Jessie to work there right after he died, but when she returned later, she worked at the company again with her usual efficiency and grew and expanded it.

Aunt Jessie, like a second mother to them, always joined in family holidays. Before all the problems, they always spent Thanksgiving together at Walker's in Colorado and Christmas in Virginia at Jessie's or at Chandler and Victoria's place. Walker felt touched they'd followed the old tradition and all made the trip to be with him at his new home this Thanksgiving. It meant a lot to him.

The nine-year-old twins giggled about something then, drawing Walker's attention their way. Like Chandler and Vee, they were tall and slim in build, with laughing brown eyes and short curly dark hair, sprinkled with red highlights—and nearly identical in looks. Outsiders found it hard to tell them apart, but Walker never had a problem knowing which was which. Emma was quieter, her smile sweeter, with a small beauty mark near her left ear, while Kaycie was more exuberant, animated by nature and more talkative.

"We're finished with breakfast," Kaycie said, noticing Walker watching her. "Can we take Marsh out for a walk? We'll walk him around the loop to the store and back, like you showed us yesterday."

Hearing his name and the word "walk," the big dog got up from his spot in the sun near the window to pad over toward the girls, his tail waving.

"See? Marsh wants to go, don't you, Marsh?" said Emma, reaching down to snuggle him.

Walker glanced toward Chandler and Victoria to get their thoughts.

"I'll go with them," Chandler said.

Walker nodded, feeling better knowing Chandler would walk with the girls. If Marsh saw a rabbit or an unexpected stranger, Chandler would be able to keep him in check.

Walker found Marsh's leash, saw them out the back door, and then came back to butter another of the fresh blueberry muffins Aunt Jessie had made.

"What time will Juliette be here today?" Victoria asked. "I can't wait to meet her."

"Around five," he answered.

His family had arrived yesterday, on Wednesday, for the Thanksgiving weekend. Today, Aunt Jessie and Victoria would spend the day in the kitchen preparing a lavish Thanksgiving supper for them all. The Hollander family celebrated their Thanksgiving dinner at lunch, allowing Juliette the chance to celebrate with Walker's family for dinner.

To keep the girls busy today, Chandler and Walker planned to take Kaycie and Emma to nearby Fort Loudoun State Historic Park on the Tellico Lake in Vonore. He knew the girls would enjoy exploring the old fort—as would Chandler, a history buff. With the sun shining bright today and the temperatures unseasonably warm, they'd only need light jackets and could share a picnic lunch after visiting the fort and then walk the Meadow Loop Trail along the banks of the river. Most places were closed for Thanksgiving Day, like Walker's store, but the park would be open, except for the visitor center.

As Walker's mind wandered to the day ahead at the park, Aunt Jessie and Victoria began looking over a checklist, planning their afternoon cooking. The women had hit the food market in town after arriving on the plane yesterday, hauling home bags of groceries.

"I'll get the turkey and dressing started while you make the pies, Vee," Aunt Jessie said.

"Pumpkin and pecan?" Walker asked, finishing the last bite of his muffin.

"Yes, pumpkin for the girls and pecan for you and Chandler." Vee smiled at him. "Plus all the standard dishes—Aunt Jessie's sweet potato casserole with brown sugar and pecans, green bean casserole, cranberry-orange salad, a raw vegetable plate with my sour cream–dill dip, and yeast rolls." She paused. "Do we need anything else?"

"Juliette said to tell you she was bringing corn casserole, a jar of her Gramma Newell's pickled beets, and some kind of brownies."

"She didn't need to bring anything," Aunt Jessie said.

"Here in the valley, you never go anywhere for a shared meal without taking a dish or two. It wouldn't be right." He grinned. "There was no point in suggesting to her not to bring anything. I told her the dishes you usually fixed and she told me what she'd bring to add to it."

Vee propped her elbows on the table and leaned toward him. "Tell us what Juliette knows, so we won't mess up and say more than we should."

Walker filled them in.

Aunt Jessie looked surprised as he finished. "That's all you've told the child? I thought Victoria said the two of you were getting serious, that you admitted you'd fallen in love with this girl."

Walker frowned at her. "Burton asked me to be sparing in what I share—with that demented man, or deranged group, still on the loose. He said it's hard for people to keep secrets, to not share sensational stories, and that the fewer people who know about the events of my life, the better."

Victoria shook her head. "I realize Burton has your best interests and our safety at heart, but this is the woman you're considering proposing marriage to."

Aunt Jessie crossed her arms and shook her head. "I can't believe you haven't told that girl more than this about yourself. Personally, I'd be purely hurt if a man claimed to love me but refused to share every aspect of his life with me. I certainly wouldn't have married Robert if there had been secrets lingering all around him."

"I doubt Juliette has answered yes to a proposal, with Walker holding back so much information." Vee lifted her eyes to his. "Am I right?"

Walker got up to pace toward the window to look out on the lawn. "I don't have the right to propose until I can share more."

Victoria snorted. "I can imagine Juliette made it perfectly clear that you'd better *not* ask until you feel you can share more."

He turned to snap at her. "I thought you'd both understand and be on my side with this."

"So there *are* sides." She gave him a smug look.

"You need to think carefully about this," Aunt Jessie advised. "Not trusting someone makes them very wary of commitment. Juliette may begin to feel that if you won't share this aspect of your life with her, you might withhold other important things from her later. The precedent for the way a couple will live begins long before a marriage."

He stomped over to the kitchen with annoyance to pour himself another cup of coffee.

"We've upset you and I'm sorry," Victoria said, watching him. "But I'm already fond of Juliette from talking with her and from working with her these last months. I like her. I know it would hurt me if you shut me out of your life as you've been shutting her out."

He came to slump into his seat again. "Juliette might change in how she feels about me if she knew everything. Everyone else did."

Victoria's mouth dropped open. "Not everyone. That's not true, Walker. You exaggerate."

He glared at her. "Most everyone, and I hated it."

Aunt Jessie reached across the table to take his hand. "Honey, I don't think Juliette will change in how she feels about you when you share with her. At some point you're going to need to talk to her."

"When you love, you have to take a risk," Vee offered. "I think it's time for you to take that risk and let Juliette all the way in."

They heard the girls and Chandler coming in the back door then, sparing Walker from more discussion on this topic. Relieved, he got up to greet them and to put Marsh's leash away.

He found Chandler only a little more understanding later in the day. He'd asked a similar question of Walker as they sat at a picnic table while the girls explored by the lake.

"People can be disappointing, but not all people are the same," Chandler said. "I haven't met Juliette, but Victoria's and your good opinion of her probably tells you that she is someone your heart can trust in." He grinned. "That's an expression I picked up watching all these girly movies with Vee and the twins. I hope they'll let us catch a little of one of the NFL games this afternoon when we get back."

Walker grinned. "It's our turn. The girls hogged the television and watched the Macy's parade early this morning."

"You need more than one television."

Walker shrugged, packing up the remains of their picnic. "I haven't needed more than one with only myself in the house. I don't watch much with the store hours I keep, either."

Chandler stood up and called for the girls. "You know you don't have to work that many hours either."

"You're one to talk." Walker punched at his arm. "I well know how many hours you put in at Pendleton's. I learned while traveling that I missed the meaning of being involved in work. It's fulfilling, makes you feel like you're making a difference, serving and contributing to something. I like the way the store has helped the people of Happy Valley, too, not only giving them a place to get grocery needs but providing a place to congregate and to visit—a place to stop in for a milkshake and to share news. A general store serves a purpose in a small community. I like being a part of that."

Chandler started toward Walker's car. "It's probably in your blood from growing up in the store in Greeley like you did. A good work ethic brings a happiness and satisfaction to life that a lot of people don't understand. Many can't wait to retire, sit around, watch television, and basically do nothing. I could never stand that."

"Me neither. We have that in common."

"Fortunately, Victoria loves her work and the business, too. I doubt she'll be pushing on me to sit around either."

Back at the house later, he and Chandler got to watch a little football while the women finished getting dinner ready. Kaycie and Emma sat in the kitchen with Victoria and Aunt Jessie, coloring pictures in an elaborate coloring book Vee bought them for the trip, each picture an intricate, detailed design with an under-the-sea theme.

"How can those mermaids swim with all that long hair trailing after them, weighed down with sea flowers and shells?" Walker asked, looking over their shoulders.

"It's fantasy, Uncle Walker," Kaycie explained in her matter-of-fact way, filling in a starfish with a yellow pen.

"And it's pretty." Emma sent him a sweet smile. "*Pretty* doesn't have to be practical."

"You have smart girls," he told Chandler as he headed back into the den with two colas.

Chandler rolled his eyes. "Tell me about it. And their mother is the same. I'm surrounded by female mind power and female hormones."

The doorbell rang before Walker could settle back into his chair again. The girls ran to the door, letting Juliette in. As he headed out to greet her, she waved him toward the den again, where she could hear the sound of the ballgame. "I came early to help with dinner," she explained, shifting a box with food items in her arms. "And to visit with Victoria and your aunt. I know you're watching football. So are George, Robert, and Grandpa over at our house, except that Grandpa was asleep in his chair the last time I looked."

He took the box from her. "Let me at least introduce you to everyone."

Walker watched her out of the corner of his eye as they walked back to the kitchen. She wore a long turquoise cardigan over a white top with a pair of sleek black slacks. She'd pulled her wavy hair back today and braided it in some way on the sides.

"Do I pass inspection?" She teased him.

"You look beautiful, as always."

"I made an effort." She gave him a saucy smile. "At home, I had on faded jeans and a ratty sweater with food spots on it from cooking with Gramma most of the day."

Walker introduced Juliette around as they entered the sunny kitchen area. Chandler had left the game for a moment to come meet her. She hugged all of them. That was Juliette's way, making them comfortable right away and breaking any iciness or formality that might have been present.

"I am so pleased to meet you all at last," she said with her usual joyous ease and enthusiasm. "Walker has told me so much about you."

She took a casserole dish out of her box. "This is a corn casserole. You can leave it out on the counter if you're getting close to dinner. We can zap it into the microwave to heat it up later if we need to." She took out several jars then. "These are Gramma Newell's pickled beets for our meal and a jar of her blackberry preserves and another of strawberry jam I thought you might like for breakfast tomorrow. I did help to make the jellies, but I won't take much credit for either. My gramma is the fabulous cook in the family."

Pulling out a colorful tin, she pulled off its lid to display the brownies inside. "These I did make myself—sinfully rich peanut butter and cookie-batter brownies with a layer of Reese's Peanut Butter Cups right in the middle. I thought the girls would like them."

Kaycie's eyes popped open with interest. "Can we try one right now, Mom? Please?"

"Just one little one won't spoil our dinner," Emma added.

"All right," Victoria agreed. "But only one, and only if I can have one, too." She giggled, reaching into the tin for a brownie.

"Then Walker and I also get one," Chandler insisted.

"Fine, but then head back to the football game, so we can finish getting dinner ready," Aunt Jessie said. "I'll get Juliette to cut celery and carrots into strips while we get acquainted."

Walker left Juliette with his sister, aunt, and nieces to head back to the den. It felt so comfortable and normal, being with family again, falling into the familiar routines of the holiday. How he wished life could be like this every day again, easy and natural without an element of fear lurking outside the door. Funny how he'd taken normalcy for granted until it was gone.

Shaking off his thoughts, Walker settled down to watch the NFL game again and was soon caught up in the action. Now and then, he could hear the women's laughter float out to them, letting him know all was well with Juliette and his family and that she was having a good time.

"I enjoyed my time with your family," Juliette told him later when he walked her out to her car around eight.

"You could stay longer," he offered.

"No, I've had a long day. I'll head back to help Gramma clean up from their dinner, and then I'll be ready to pile up in bed with a good book."

"My family is crazy about you," he said. "The girls are already begging for you to come back again before they leave. Victoria and Aunt Jessie want to see your quilting room at the store and some of your quilts, too."

"I know. I promised I'd give them a little tour after you get back from your trip to Gatlinburg and the mountains tomorrow."

"Do you want to come? I know they'd like that."

"No, I think you should have that day as a family." Her eyes dropped. "Without me along everyone won't need to tiptoe around past subjects or catch themselves up when they start to discuss something that I don't know about."

Walker wasn't sure what to say. He'd noticed a few times when someone got excited about an old memory and then realized it related to times they weren't supposed to mention. He'd hoped Juliette hadn't noticed the hesitations and quick subject changes.

He reached for her then, hoping to kiss her. Wanting to erase any bad memory.

She pulled back from his embrace. "Thanks for inviting me to meet your family," she said. "They're wonderful."

Should he apologize, he wondered? But what would he say?

She got into the car, shutting the door, and gave him a little wave as she drove away. He felt suddenly chilly, watching her leave.

CHAPTER 19

As December began, the weather turned cold, a match to Juliette's feelings these days. She'd felt different about Walker ever since his family came to visit. Being with them made her feel more left out than before. It reminded her of the times when, as a little girl new to the valley, the school children left her out of their play.

She finished her fall classes for Lenora but continued working with the quilting group in the valley. Around her schedule at the store, Juliette traveled to teach a workshop on quilting, took her quilts to a Christmas craft fair in the area, and began helping her grandmother prepare for the holidays.

George cut down a tree from the Hollanders' tree farm and brought it to the house to set up for his grandparents, and Juliette dragged down the ornaments and lights to decorate it. She and her gramma made wreaths for the front windows and door, hung garlands on the stairs, and put the Christmas nativity scene and her gramma's angel collection in their traditional places. They started their Christmas shopping, Juliette taking her grandmother to the mall in Maryville and to favorite shops where she liked to find gifts. Juliette's father, Wyatt, would fly in for Christmas, and they all looked forward to seeing him.

At the store today she worked twining holiday lights around the store windows and adding a few more ornaments to the Christmas tree Walker had set up inside the store. With the flavor of Christmas in the air and everyone cheerful who dropped by, Juliette hated that she felt so depressed and downcast. Taking a break, she fixed herself a cup of Christmas tea, a holiday specialty the store was offering, and called Sharon.

"Are you busy?" she asked, hearing Sharon's voice.

"No, it's early, bitterly cold and spitting snow here. It was sunny and nice yesterday, but the weather turned the corner last night. I doubt the store will do much business today. Is it cold there?"

"It's a little cold now, but it's supposed to be sunny and mild tomorrow. The weather flip-flops a lot this time of year."

"It sure does. How are you?"

"Okay."

"Just okay?"

"Yes, and I think I may head back to North Carolina after Christmas and not wait until spring. Grandpa is better, and Laura said it would be okay if I left. I talked to her about it. She said she, George, and the kids can see to Gramma and Grandpa now, that I don't need to stay on unless I want to."

"I gather you don't want to."

"Don't you want me to come back?" Juliette asked.

"Don't be ridiculous," Sharon said. "You know what I mean."

Juliette sighed. "Why delay things? I don't feel the same about Walker since his family came to visit. He's still shutting me out, and I don't see what can come of a relationship where I keep hoping for something he might never be able to offer me."

"Have you talked to him about it?"

"There's no point. He clams up about so many issues, sidesteps questions I ask. He hangs up the phone quickly when I find him talking with one of his family, or with his friend Burton or his cousin Stewart back in Colorado. I tolerated it all for a season, thinking things would change, but now I don't think they will."

"And you're unhappy. I can hear it in your voice."

"I may be a little less cheerful when I come back to North Carolina, but I'll get past it. Will RuthAnn be upset if I come back to work and take her job?"

"No. She's leaving at the end of this week anyway to take a full-time job at the Good Thymes Herb and Coffee Shop around the corner. I'm working full-time again over the Christmas holiday, which is okay while classes are out at the college, but I'll need someone when I go back to teach in January. Your timing couldn't be better."

"It must be a sign." Juliette sighed.

They talked a little longer, sharing about art projects they were working on and catching up.

"I'm going home to meet Evan's family over the holidays," Sharon told her.

"I'm glad your relationship with Evan is growing. I've always liked him."

A group of women headed into the store then, talking and laughing loudly.

"Sounds like customers," Sharon said, hearing their voices in the background. "I need to go, too. The UPS man is here with a delivery."

Juliette waited on the women, and then began arranging the Christmas gift items she and Walker had ordered in prominent spots around the store. She felt glad that she could settle back in at The Full Moon so easily without taking another employee's place. The store here would be quieter in the winter, and in the spring Walker could easily find another part-time employee if he needed one.

In her heart Juliette knew that the longer she stayed here, the more her heart would break when she left. It would be bad enough as it was. She knew Walker would linger in her mind and haunt her sleep. Her love for him had grown to the point where she craved him in a physical way, too, a dangerous road for her to go down. Foolish though it seemed to many, she wanted that intimacy to be with a husband.

As the late morning arrived, Walker and Marsh headed in the front door, letting in a burst of cold air behind them. "The Christmas lights and decorations look great," he said, unleashing the dog so Marsh could head to Juliette in greeting. "You've been busy."

"Yes, and a lot of customers have been buying the holiday items we've put out. I'll try to get the rest unboxed and put on display before I leave today." Her eyes followed him as he moved toward the back of the store to hang up his coat on the rack inside the Quilt Room.

He paused by the Christmas tree on his way back. "You did a great job decorating the tree." Walker turned to grin at her. "Last night at my house I put lights on the tree that I picked up from George. I started decorating it but I didn't finish. It could probably use your artistic touch."

Juliette watched him with a catch in her throat. He hadn't seemed to notice the change in her feelings these last weeks.

He came over to prop an arm on the counter. "I was watching the news and weather this morning. Tomorrow is supposed to be sunny and warmer, but with a cold front moving in afterward and maybe even snow. I thought we might go hiking one more time while we have a good day for it. We're both off tomorrow."

"I heard the weather tomorrow might be nice, too."

"If you don't mind a climb, I thought we could hike up Rabbit Creek Trail. It's two miles from Abrams Creek to the top of Pine Mountain, another half mile to the junction with the Hannah Mountain Trail, and then a mile on along that stretch of trail to Campsite No.15—about three and half miles total, seven miles roundtrip. I hear the trail is pretty steep in sections, so a hike to the campsite may be all we'll want to tackle, but we can continue to Coon Butt if you want. The hikers I've talked with said there are fine views on the Rabbit Creek Trail, especially in winter with the trees bare."

"Hmmm." Juliette considered the offer. She wouldn't have many more days with Walker or many more days in the mountains. It would be nice to make another good memory.

"Is 'hmmm' a yes?" Walker grinned at her.

"I suppose, and it's a good thing we've hiked a lot this fall and are in good shape. That trail is a steep one." She hesitated. "Be sure to wear waterproof boots for this one, too. There is a creek crossing near the campsite that is a wide one. Since it's been dry over the last weeks, we can probably navigate over the rocks, but if the creek is up, the water can be well over your boots." She turned to catch his eye. "I'll tell you right now that if that creek is really high tomorrow I will not be going over it."

"Okay." He pulled a hiking guidebook, *The Afternoon Hiker*, off a nearby shelf to open to the trail description. "The authors of this book warn that Rabbit Creek is a difficult hike, but I wanted to do it because several of the locals told me early settlers drove wagons, and even cars, over this road to get to the Richwoods area eighty-five years or so ago."

Juliette sat down on the bench by the door to start putting Christmas cards into a display. "Most people don't even know there was an old settlement community called the Richwoods between Happy Valley and Cades Cove. After the Richwoods area was absorbed into the parkland purchase, it went back to the wild. You'd need to really know the area to even locate where the old homes, a school, and other buildings once stood. I've been down some of the unmarked trails with Grandpa in the past, but I wouldn't want to try to find them now."

"Me neither. It's wise to stay on the maintained park trails unless a keen guide is with you to take you elsewhere. People get lost, run into bears, snakes, and other problems by getting off the main trails."

"Well, I guess I'm game for another hike, assuming the weather is still good tomorrow. Sharon said it was snowing in North Carolina."

"How is Sharon?" Walker said, changing the subject.

"She's fine."

They talked randomly while Juliette finished stocking the cards into the rack, and then both got busy with the lunch crowd. As the day ended, the Ledford brothers came into the store stomping mad.

"That Dade Claiborne's been spreading stories it's me and Vernon causing all the thieving around the valley," Harley said. "We done some work down at the Allens' place a few weeks back. They own that little gray vacation cabin on the creek. The Allens came up to the cabin this weekend and found someone had ransacked the house and took all kinds of stuff. Dade's been telling folks we scoped out the job and then went in later to steal their stuff."

The brothers walked over to settle onto their favorite stools at the counter.

"We didn't do it," Vernon said, obviously upset. "We work a lot doing odd jobs at Dick and Connie Allen's place. Both are too fat to do much fer themselves, but they're nice folks. Cora lives near them and she recommended us to them after we helped her out."

Harley interrupted, shaking a fist. "Dade spread it around we probably robbed Cora's place, too, and killed her little dog."

Vernon shook his head sadly, his voice softening. "You know we wouldn't ever kill no dog."

"Of course you wouldn't," Juliette soothed, moving around behind the counter to start fixing them both a Valley Dog.

"I'm so mad I could spit nails over this," Harley said, scowling. "Dade even called the police and told them what he thought and they sent another of those deputies to talk with us."

"Did you talk with the deputy this time?" Walker asked.

"Only 'cause he found us where we was working over at Whitey's, helping him fix fences," Vernon answered. "Someone told him we were there this week."

"That little deputy threatened us." Harley said the words with menace.

"How?" Juliette asked.

"Suggested he'd be watching us, that we'd better be careful."

"That was a warning, not a threat," Walker clarified.

Harley leaned toward Walker with a frown. "If he'd come into your store here, giving you a *warning* like that, suggesting you done something you didn't do and talking down to you like he did to us, you'd have seen it as a threat, too."

Walker sighed. "I probably would have."

"Well, I'll tell you right now we're going to be doubling up on our efforts of searching and watching to find out who's doing these thievings around our valley. Vernon and I don't like folks talking about us like we're criminals or paying so much attention to us either. Makes us wonder if Dade is one of *them*." He glanced around as if someone might be listening. "He could be, you know. He goes out of the valley a lot, talks to police."

Juliette turned to the counter to hide a smirk.

"No one likes to be falsely accused," Walker said, pushing colas he'd made for them across the counter.

"What did the thieves take from the Allens?" Juliette asked.

"All the usual stuff—electrical things, televisions, their riding mower from out of the shed, tools, valuables from in their house, even paintings from right off the wall by some artist around the area."

"The Allens collected Boyce Hart's and Jim Gray's art," Juliette said, remembering the few times she visited at their place. "Dick is a dentist in Maryville. He makes a lot of money and likes to collect art."

"Well, they took all he had at the vacation house," Harley said.

"Those paintings were worth a lot of money. That's a shame."

"We're real mad at Dade Claiborne," Vernon said, shifting the subject, his usual humor absent today.

"Well, don't do anything silly or vengeful about Dade," Juliette warned. "It would only make matters worse."

"Whitey told us that, too," Harley said. "But it would make me feel better to see Dade gets some of his own."

"Dade may be disagreeable, but he knows people in high places through his car business," Walker advised. "Juliette's right that you shouldn't try to pull any tricks on Dade to get even."

The brothers ate their hot dogs, continuing to grumble.

"I really hate these thefts are still going on," Juliette said to Walker after the brothers left. "Robberies have occurred for over a year now. One of Amy and Keith's friends in the Tallassee area said they got hit by the thieves recently. And Keith said he heard some people in the Top of the World Community reported break-ins."

Walker flipped off the main lights to begin locking up the store.

"It seems like the police should have been able to track down the people behind these thefts by now, but as I've seen myself, sometimes catching criminals isn't easy. And petty, small crimes and threats don't get the attention murders and other major crimes do."

Juliette heard the change in his voice over the last words. "Have the police back in your hometown caught the man who committed the murder you told me about?"

"No." He scowled, not adding more.

She waited, hoping he might talk to her, but he walked to the back of the store instead to lock up, a frown on his face. Acting sullen and moody.

Juliette finished cleaning the counter in silence, wishing she knew what to say to make him want to open up to her.

Glancing at the clock, she felt glad it was time to leave and head back to the farm. "I'll see you tomorrow, ten o'clock, at your place," she said, retrieving her coat and purse.

He lifted a hand, without answering her in words, lost in his own thoughts.

Juliette left with a sigh, knowing it would be useless to probe further.

CHAPTER 20

Walker heard Juliette's car pull up shortly before ten the next day. Marsh headed toward the door to greet her, his tail wagging like a flag. The dog knew the sound of Juliette's car now.

"You're right on time," he said, opening the door to her.

"I thought we should head out early as planned. Grandpa says there was a ring around the moon last night and that bad weather might be heading in later, maybe even a little snow by tomorrow."

"It's sunny out now." Walker looked toward the sky.

"But cold. I wore my long underwear." She headed back toward the kitchen, unbuttoning her heavy coat as she walked. "If you don't have yours on, you should add some under your clothes. We'll warm up as we hike, of course, but layers help you stay warmer."

"I layered, too," he said. "I also picked up a couple of rain ponchos to take with us in case we get an unexpected shower later. You get colder in the winter if you're wet."

He studied her, dressed in jeans, a long thick sweater, sturdy hiking boots that rose high above her ankles, and a thick, lined parka. He was dressed similarly, ready for a day out of doors.

Entering the kitchen, Juliette spotted the waist packs he'd tossed on the kitchen table earlier. She picked one up, her eyes shining. "Oh, I love these new Knockabout waist packs. You can wear them around your waist or as a shoulder sling bag." She demonstrated the latter by draping one over her shoulder. "There are two here. Is one for me?"

"Yes. You said you liked them when they arrived at the store a few weeks ago so I snagged two for our hike today. There's ample room in each for everything we'll need—water bottles, lunch snacks, first aid kit, knife, map, compass, and more."

"I'm claiming this cranberry waist pack," she said, still admiring it. "You can have the tan one."

"I planned to argue for the tan one versus that girly color, you can be sure." He grinned.

She began to unload items from the smaller pack she'd brought with her, transferring them to the new one.

Walker went over to the kitchen counter and returned with their lunch items to add. "I made sandwiches on hot dog buns today, thought they'd fit easier in the packs."

"Oh, good idea." Her eyes brightened. "What kind did you make?"

"Turkey and provolone. I bought packs of peanuts, raisins, and some trail bars, too."

"Sounds like plenty to me. We won't want to sit in the cold for long to eat our lunch today." She sighed. "I miss warm weather already, and the winter is only just beginning."

He leaned over to kiss her. "Be glad you're not out in the Rockies or up in Montana or Wisconsin. Winter is mild here in comparison to many areas I traveled through."

She lifted a hand toward heaven with a giggle. "I thank God often I'm a Southern girl. Winters can be cold here but nothing like the winters in Baltimore, where I went to college, or in places farther north or out west."

They tucked their lunches and water into their waist packs, as well as their rain ponchos, and stuffed gloves and hats into their coat pockets while they talked. Walker took Marsh outdoors a last time, and then they piled into his Jeep to drive from his place down the winding Abrams Creek Road to the parking lot and trailhead near the ranger station.

"There's our trailhead sign." Juliette pointed, spotting the rustic sign near the parking lot.

Walker had hiked many of the trails out of the Abrams

Campground area, but he had only hiked Rabbit Creek Trail as far as the Hannah Mountain intersection on his explorations. The path began by winding through a wooded area and then came to a long footbridge across Abrams Creek at about a quarter of a mile. Sturdier than some rough-hewn bridges he'd crossed in the Smoky Mountains, this one had a long handrail on one side to hold on to.

"This old bridge washes out a lot," Juliette told him, following him across it. "But when it does there's a spot to ford a little ways up stream."

"You have a lot of memories about this area, growing up here as you did." He stopped at the end of the bridge to give her a hand down.

"I do. All this flat section of the trail we're walking through now used to belong to the Boring and Hearon families. Their descendants still live in the Happy Valley area. In the spring you'll see a lot of daffodils along this trail, planted by the families that lived here before the park came."

The trail meandered through the open forest and then began to climb uphill. Juliette hiked along behind Walker cheerfully, humming under her breath and pointing out nature sites along the way. They gained elevation quickly as the trail rose up the side of Pine Mountain.

"I'd forgotten what a steep trail this is, really different from the Cooper Road Trail winding over to Cades Cove from the campground," Juliette said.

"Harley told me his daddy used to call this the Gourley Trail because Gourley families once lived at both ends of it."

"I heard that, too, and Indians used this trail to travel across the mountains to their villages along the Little Tennessee River. We often forget they were the first to explore and create pathways through the area. Later settlers drove their wagons over this trail and, like you heard from Harley, even Model T cars used to drive up to the old settlements on this path." She laughed. "I bet they had a bumpy ride."

"No kidding." Walker stepped over a pile of rocks in the narrow trail, trying to imagine it.

They climbed on, winding around the ridgelines, enjoying the day even in the cold. The uphill march soon helped to warm them up, although Walker could see his breath on the cold air when he breathed out deeply.

After an hour, they reached the top of Pine Mountain, where the trail flattened out for a short space.

"Three seconds to catch our breath." Juliette grinned at him as they paused for a minute to get a drink of water. She pulled her toboggan down over her ears more tightly. "I think it's getting colder."

"The sun is behind the clouds now. It makes a difference."

"Look at that huge tulip tree on the left there." Juliette pointed. "I don't think I could even reach my arms around it."

"I read it was about thirteen feet in circumference in one of my hiking guidebooks. There's supposed to be a huge pine a little farther up the trail."

"There it is." She pointed ahead as they hiked on. "And it's huge, too." Juliette walked over to try to wrap her arms around its trunk before they moved on.

Walker studied the big tree towering up into the forest. "I think it's as wide as the poplar. With all the logging that went on in this part of the mountains, virgin trees like these are few and far between."

"Yes, and they're especially beautiful in the spring or fall. Everything looks a little barren and grim right now with all the leaves gone from the trees, but in springtime there will be wildflowers on this trail. It's pretty then."

The trail began to march downhill now, an easier walk, although Walker knew it would be a steep uphill climb coming back. Beyond the gap the trail narrowed, too, growing rougher and rockier, the forest thicker, with rhododendrons sometimes thick along the sides of the path.

"Yuck. I'd forgotten how rocky this part of the trail is. It's a good thing we wore hiking boots," Juliette said. "Look." She stopped to lean over to pick up a white rock. "Here's a quartz chunk."

"Nice." Walker turned to look at it. "That's a keeper. I've seen a lot of quartz in this area."

"You're not supposed to take anything out of the park, but I don't think this one small rock will be missed much." She tucked it into her pocket. "I'll take it to Amy to add to the rock collection she's started for the kids at the daycare."

The trail broadened as they came to Scott Gap, where the Hannah Mountain Trail crossed Rabbit Creek Trail in an intersection.

"The sun is still hiding and it's getting colder, don't you think?" Juliette shivered.

"We've gained elevation. It's always colder as you climb higher into the mountains." Walker glanced at the sky as he said it, noticing more layers of dark clouds now gathering. "We can eat our lunch here if you want and turn around and head back."

"No, I'm good." She shifted her waist pack, draped over her shoulder. "It's only another mile to the campsite. There are old logs there we can sit on to eat our lunch by the creek, but I think we should turn back then. It's bitter out today, much colder than when we started out."

They hiked on, Walker remembering to ask Juliette about an idea he had with Christmas coming. "Do you remember Vernon telling us about the local man who used to play Santa Claus in Happy Valley, delivering toys to the kids?"

"Yes. I've heard my grandparents talk about that, too. It was one of the Boring men, I think, who used to play Santa Claus. I don't know if he bought the gifts or if someone else did. But the kids looked forward to his visits. He would usually leave the gifts on the porch, but I think sometimes he went in the houses if the kids were watching for him."

"I'd like to do that," Walker told her.

"You would?" She sounded surprised.

"Yeah."

"Only for the kids that might be in need?" she asked.

"No, I'd like to do it for all the kids in the valley, for fun."

"Hmmm, that's a lot of gifts, but it does sound like it would be fun."

"You want to help me?" He glanced back at her.

"How?" She flashed him a smile. "Dress up like an elf or Mrs. Santa?"

"Either one you'd like. After going around the valley with Jonas and his boys for Halloween trick-or-treating, and seeing the kids at the community center when we've helped with events, I don't think it would take that long to make the rounds. Maybe a few hours. A lot of the kids are in the same families. You and Amy could help to get names, and we could buy extra generic gifts in case we came across more kids along the way."

They slowed to work their way around another rocky spot in the trail.

"Walker, if there are one hundred kids in the valley—taking a quick guess—and you spent ten dollars on a gift for each, plus money for a stocking, candy, and small toys to add in, you might be looking at two thousand dollars."

He paused to turn and look at her. "I'm not worried about the money. I simply thought it might be fun to do some gift giving at the holiday, a way to say thanks to all the people in the valley for supporting the store."

"Well, I think it's a sweet idea and if you decide to do it, I would love to help you buy gifts, wrap, and deliver them. I know Gramma would help us stuff stockings and possibly make homemade candies we can add to each. I think Kimmie would help, too, if we asked her." She gave him a saucy smile when he looked back at her. "I rather like the idea of dressing up like Mrs. Santa. I could sew Santa clothes for us if we can't find any."

"You probably won't need to. Many companies sell costumes. My dad used to dress up like Santa at the store and he played Santa at the church every year."

She laughed. "So it runs in the family."

"Maybe." He grinned at the idea.

"I think we're nearly to the creek crossing before the camp," she said. "And I am so glad. My feet and my face are freezing cold. I don't like the look of that darkening sky either. I think we might get that predicted snow flurry tonight."

"You could be right," Walker said, feeling a little shift in the air.

When they got to the creek, they were able to cross over the rocks, only needing to wade in a few spots. After the crossing, the trail headed uphill and soon arrived at the rustic backcountry campsite nestled under a group of tall hemlocks.

Around a former firepit, Walker and Juliette found logs to sit on to eat their lunch and also found a private place in the woods to go to the bathroom.

Before they sat down to eat, Juliette showed him an old survey marker near the campsite. "Look at this date," she said, running her fingers over the metal marker embedded in a large stone. "This was placed here by the U.S. Geological Survey in 1928. It's incredible that it's still here."

They both shivered in the cold as they settled down on the logs a few minutes later to eat their sandwiches.

Walker pulled out his phone to check it. "No service," he said.

She shrugged. "You know by now it does little good to carry a phone on the trail. Wi-Fi service is usually nonexistent in the mountains and poor even in the valley without a satellite."

He tucked the phone back in his pack. "I thought I might get lucky up higher like this and pick up a signal."

"Your phone is probably frozen, like I am." Juliette laughed. "Notice I am eating lunch with my gloves on. It is freezing today."

"We'll warm up when we start walking back again."

They sat in the quiet, eating their lunch.

"Have you noticed how silent it is, Walker?" she asked as they finished. "That's a bad omen. I can't hear any birds singing or insects buzzing or anything. That's a sign of snow. My grandpa taught me that. And the clouds are hanging lower in the sky now and darker than before."

"You're right." He glanced toward the sky and felt a moist chill in the air he hadn't noticed before. "We'd better head back. We're at a higher elevation here on the mountain. Bad weather might come earlier at this altitude."

As if in reply to his words, white flakes began to drift down from the sky.

"Uh-oh," Juliette said.

"We'd definitely better start back," Walker said, stuffing the remains of his lunch back into his pack and helping Juliette to her feet.

By the time they crossed the creek again, the snow was falling more steadily and had begun to lie on the ground.

"It's pretty," Juliette said, lifting her face to the white flakes.

"Yes," he said, but he felt worried. He'd camped enough in the wilderness and trekked enough miles in the backwoods to know snow piling up on the trail made for hazardous walking.

"Maybe we ought to put those ponchos on," Juliette suggested. "This is a damp, wet snow."

"It is." They stopped to get out their ponchos, then unfolded and draped them over their coats.

Walker glanced at the snow coming down more heavily now. "I'd like to set a little faster pace if it's okay with you."

"You don't need to encourage me in that direction. I like snow when I can look out the window at it, but I'm not too crazy about being caught out in it." She pulled her toboggan down lower over her ears. "I know this isn't a good situation, Walker. Getting caught in a snowstorm can be dangerous."

It was eerily quiet as they trudged on, snow falling thick and wet around them. Guilt nagged at Walker's conscience that he hadn't checked the weather reports more carefully before they set out or paid more attention to the sky darkening and the air growing colder. He should have been more protective of Juliette.

By the time they reached Scott Gap a mile later, snow was an inch deep on the ground and still falling fast.

"I guess we didn't choose the best day to go hiking," Juliette said, trying to stay cheerful as they picked their way along the wet trail thick with snow, trying not to trip over rocks and roots increasingly difficult to see.

As they crested the top of Pine Mountain to start the two-mile downhill climb, Walker grew even more worried. Snow fell now in a heavy white blanket, and they had a long way yet to go.

"How much more snow do you think will fall?" Juliette asked, an anxious edge to her voice.

"I don't know," he told her, trying to see the sky through the trees. "The weather report didn't even predict snow today. They only suggested possible flurries tonight after the temperature dropped."

She snorted. "Well, obviously they were wrong."

"Yeah, that's a fact."

With nearly two inches of snow on the ground now, the trail ahead was almost obliterated. Juliette stumbled over a rock and fell, catching herself on one knee. "Ouch."

Walker turned to help her back up and to wipe snow off her jeans and coat.

"Are you okay? Am I walking too fast?"

"No, I simply can't see the ground to know where to walk safely." She brushed the snow off her gloves. "There are a lot of rocks and roots in this section of the trail. Maybe it will be better farther along."

As they started to walk again, Walker could see she was limping.

"You hurt yourself."

"Not much, but I think I hit my knee on a rock underneath all that snow. I'll be okay. Thankfully, I didn't turn my ankle or anything."

He dropped back to walk beside her, putting an arm around her, but she pulled away from him.

"You'll only hinder us both trying to walk with me," she said. "We need to get on down this trail and back to the house. You keep walking ahead of me and try to warn me of rocks and roots in the trail whenever you can. I'll follow close behind you and try to walk in your tracks now. I can hardly see the trail at all."

He leaned over to kiss her before he turned back. "I feel so guilty for bringing you out in this."

She wrinkled her nose. "You didn't plan to take me hiking in the snow. Stop feeling guilty. Neither of us realized this might happen. Weather in the mountains is unpredictable, especially in the winter."

"I know you're right," he said. "But I still feel guilty."

"Keep moving, Walker Logan," she said, pushing him.

They trudged on down the mountain path, staying away from the edges of the trail, where the ground often dropped off treacherously. Neither wanted to take any more risks than they had to. Both stumbled and fell several times, not being able to see roots across the pathway or even rocks as the snow piled up.

Spotting a pile of limbs sticking out of the snow to one side of the path, Walker pulled two long, sturdy sticks out of the pile, breaking them off to serve as hiking sticks. "Maybe these will help." He handed one to Juliette.

"Thanks. That's a good idea. Having something to hold on to will keep me from being so scared, too." Her voice grew soft. "I really am scared, Walker. Can we pray?"

He sighed. "I've certainly been doing a lot of that already."

"I mean out loud together," she said. "It would make me feel better."

"All right," he answered, wanting to ease her anxiety in any way he could. He thought for a minute how to begin as he walked on. "Lord, we thank You for Your presence with us always, in good times and bad. We remember the Psalm that tells us that even though we walk through difficulty and danger You will be with us, that You will guide and help us. We pray You will be with us to lead and direct us off this mountain and back to safety." He paused. "I ask You to forgive me if I missed signs I should have seen to know this storm might have been coming—the sky darkening, the temperature dropping, Marsh acting restless and edgy this morning. Help me get Juliette back home safely to her family. We thank You for Your peace and love with us always. Our trust is ever in You. In Jesus name we pray, Amen."

"Thanks." Juliette caught up to him in the snow to hug him. "That was nice. It knocked the fear out of me to pray."

Touched by her words, he brushed snow off her face with the back of his glove. "I love you, Juliette Hollander."

"I love you, too, even in a snowstorm." She gave him a pained little smile. "I only wish …" Her words drifted off, swirling away in the snowy air.

A tree branch broke off near them with a crack, weighed down from the snow, making them both jump.

"We'd better get moving," she said, looking around. "It's not getting any better out here."

For the next hour they trudged at a snail's pace down the steep snow-covered trail, with more snow continuing to fall on them as they walked. Gratefully, the wind had not picked up with the incoming snowstorm, but the temperature continued to fall and the cold was numbing. Walker's mind, around the ongoing anxiety of trying to discern the path on the steep hillside, kept thinking of Juliette's unfinished words … *I only wish*.

He knew she'd distanced her emotions from him since his family visited at Thanksgiving, and he knew she felt more left out than before, knowing they knew all about his past but that he still hadn't shared with her. Walker had thought often, since Thanksgiving, about the counsel his sister, Vee, and his Aunt Jessie offered him about sharing more freely with Juliette, but he still felt torn about what to do.

"I think the cold and damp has crept into my bones," Juliette said, interrupting his thoughts. She stumbled again as she said the words, but caught herself with her walking stick before she fell.

"How's your knee?" He turned back to be sure she was okay.

"Too frozen to even consider aching." She made an effort to smile. "How's your hand? Still bleeding?"

"I think the blood froze solid a few minutes after I fell." He made an effort at humor, too. He'd slipped and fallen hard one time, catching himself on his hand and jabbing it on a sharp rock or stick underneath the snow, bloodying it even through his glove.

He slowed to study the trail ahead, trying to see to gauge where they were.

"The trail is widening and getting less steep," Juliette said, slowing with him to peer ahead. "That means we're closer to the old settlement area. Praise God." She heaved a deep sigh.

Walker looked at his watch. "It's almost five o'clock," he told her. "We started up the trail this morning at ten thirty and it took us about two hours to hike in, but it's taken nearly twice as long to hike out."

"At least we'll get out of the mountains before dark." He heard her shudder. "Can you imagine how scary it would be trying to hike out in the dark in all this mess or to get trapped on the mountain in it? I've read stories about hikers getting caught in the snow in the Smokies and seen news clips about storm survivors on television. I'll certainly carry a new sympathy for them after this."

He headed down the trail again. "If the storm had turned into a blizzard with blowing winds and heavier snowfall, we might have been in real trouble."

"I thought we might see less snow as we dropped down off the mountain, but there's as much here as higher up," Juliette observed. "It looks like the snow is at least three inches deep in some places now and getting crunchy and icy underfoot."

"I hope we can get the Jeep out of the parking lot and up the hill to the house."

"I hadn't thought about that," she said. "That road is steep, with drop-offs along the side. It might be safer to walk back to your place. If we've come this far, we can hike up the road to your house if we need to. Believe me, I am highly motivated to get to that big fireplace in your den. I hope you have a lot of firewood. With things icing up, we might lose power, too. It happens a lot in the valley."

"I have generators at the house and the store." Walker dropped back to walk with Juliette now so they could help each other through the drifts piling up in the woods.

She paused to look around. "It's beautiful, isn't it, this white wonderland? If I wasn't so cold, tired, and a little bit scared, I might be able to appreciate it more."

"Yeah," he agreed, helping her pick her way through an area where it was hard to discern where the path even lay.

"Look, there's the bridge up ahead," she said a little later.

Like everything else around them, the long log bridge over Abrams Creek had several inches of snow piled on it.

"We'll need to be really careful going across that thing," Walker said, studying it. "But the stream is too deep and swift to wade. We'd get soaked to try. If we go slow and hold the rail, I think we'll be okay." He climbed the rock steps to the beginning of the bridge. "I'll try to kick off some of the snow ahead of us as we walk. You walk close behind me, hold on to me and to the rail. That will help to steady you and it will probably make me feel psychologically safer, too." He laughed. "Ready?"

"I guess." Her voice trembled a little on the words.

Walker moved carefully across the long bridge, trying not to look down and trying not to slip.

Behind him Juliette paraphrased random Scriptures as they walked. "God strengthens us and helps us so we can do all things. No evil will befall us. He gives his angels charge over us to keep us. Nothing is impossible with God."

Walker almost grinned listening to her, despite the difficulty of navigating the slippery log.

Juliette fell into his arms on the other side. "That was the worst experience of the whole day," she said, letting out a big sigh. "I kept trying not to envision falling into that icy water."

He kissed her on the forehead. "Let's go check out the car and see how bad the road is."

Walker's big Jeep Grand Cherokee was, not surprisingly, the only vehicle in the whole parking lot. The snow had piled up several inches deep in the lot and on the road, but with the snow still fresh, it wasn't as icy underneath on the road as it would be later. He tucked Juliette into the Jeep, turned on the heater, and then got out to scrape all the snow he could from the vehicle, especially from the windshields.

"Do you think we can make it up the hill to your driveway?" she asked when he climbed back into the car with her. "There's a lot of snow on the road."

"I think so. This vehicle is made for harsh road conditions like this and it's less than a mile up the road to the driveway and only a little farther to the house. We'll be okay. I've driven on a lot of snowy roads these last years, many worse than this." He reached into the back of the car to snag an old blanket and wrapped it around her.

"What can I do to help?" she asked.

"Just keep those prayers going." Under his breath, he added a few of his own that they could get back to the house in safety.

CHAPTER 21

Juliette let out a huge breath of relief as Walker's house finally came into view. "What a beautiful sight. I admit I felt scared a few times when the tires spun on that gravel road and your Jeep almost slid off into the ditch."

"But we made it," Walker said, maneuvering with care up the driveway. "Old Stone House is pretty sitting on the hill in the snow, isn't she?"

"Yes." Juliette looked ahead at the welcome sight of his house nestled in the thick snow, with more still falling. "It looks like a Currier & Ives Christmas card."

"It does, doesn't it?" Walker smiled across at her.

They heard Marsh barking as they pulled up to the garage door.

"I bet Marsh will be glad to see us."

Walker frowned. "I should have known when he acted restless and edgy this morning that bad weather was on the way. Animals sense threatening weather before people do."

"Well, we're back safe now." She glanced toward the carport beside the garage. "I'm glad I pulled my little car into your carport this morning. She'd be piled high with snow if I hadn't."

"After that adventure getting up my driveway, I have no intention of risking your safety further by letting you drive home or in attempting to drive you home in all this." He pushed the remote to open the garage door. "You can stay over at the house tonight until the storm passes and the roads improve. I'll call your grandfather when I get inside."

She didn't comment but wondered how her grandparents would like the idea of her spending the night with Walker, emergency or not.

Once inside the garage and out of the car, Walker and Juliette greeted Marsh and then pulled off their wet boots, ponchos, coats, hats, and gloves, and draped them all over a rack to dry out.

They padded into the kitchen, glad to be inside and out of the cold.

"Gosh, it's great to be home and safe," Juliette said before she thought. She saw Walker's brows lift at the word "*home*."

Marsh fanned around the kitchen with excitement, glad to see them back, nuzzling up against their legs. Walker had let him out to frisk around in the snow for a few minutes while they took off their wet clothes and shoes in the garage.

"You're a sweet thing," Juliette said, sitting down in a kitchen chair to rub the big dog's back with affection. She glanced at Walker. "I doubt Quillen came up to walk Marsh after school. The county probably let school out early today when the snow started, and I'm sure Eldon closed the store before the roads got bad."

Walker pulled his cell phone out of his waist pack to check his messages. They could pick up reception again with Walker's big satellite dish outside. "Eldon said he closed the store not long after lunch when the snow started to lay on the roads. He said he hoped we got back all right."

"Just barely." She grinned at him.

She watched him scroll through his other messages. "Your grandparents called and your brother," he told her. "I'd better call them to let them know we're back and safe. Then I'll call Eldon, too."

"I can call Gramma if you like," she said.

"Maybe with the situation as it is I'd better talk to your grandpa. I want to let him know I don't think it's safe for you to try to get home. You're already cold and wet and you don't need to try to get out and risk the roads." He walked over to the window. "It's still snowing, too."

He started punching in a number on the phone.

"I'm going to start some coffee," she said. "I'll rummage around in your refrigerator and cabinets and see what I can find for dinner."

She listened to Walker talk sensibly and calmly to her grandfather while she dug around in his cabinets. It didn't sound like Grandpa was offering too much argument.

"I understand, sir. You have nothing to worry about," she heard Walker say. She rolled her eyes, imagining what kinds of cautions her grandfather offered to bring that comment on.

"Your grandfather said he'd call George," Walker said, coming in to the kitchen. "He also asked you to call your grandmother later when you're warm and dry and have had a chance to eat something."

"I'll do that. She'll want to hear my voice. I know they've been worried."

Walker rang Eldon next.

When he hung up, Juliette said, "I discovered one of those vegetable beef soup mixes in your pantry, plus ground beef and some packages of frozen vegetables in your freezer. I can whip up a pot of vegetable soup with that. I found a box of cornbread mix, too. How does hot soup and cornbread sound for supper?"

"Terrific. I'll help, but first I want us to shed these damp clothes and get a hot shower to warm up." He looked her over. "I think Vee left a few clothes behind in her dresser when she stayed here last. Not much, but there might be something you can wear. You can check. I'll give you one of my flannel shirts, too, and some socks."

"I can make do."

"Here, follow me," he said. He led her up the stairs to the bedroom Victoria used when she stayed at the house. "Rummage around in the drawers to see what you can find. The bathroom is through that door off the bedroom." He pointed. "Towels and sundries are already there. I'll put one of my shirts and some socks on the bed. Bring all your damp clothes downstairs when you finish and we'll dump them in the washer and dryer."

"I'll be fine," she assured him.

A short time later, Juliette stood under the shower in the guest bath, luxuriating in the glory of hot water and steam. She sighed in pleasure, turning to let the shower jets pelt water on her tired back.

After her shower, she found a pair of navy knit pajamas in the dresser drawer that would serve well for the moment. She pulled on the plaid flannel shirt Walker laid out over the pajamas, rolling up the sleeves, and then tugged on the socks he'd left her, deciding that they would have to do, even if too large.

Downstairs she found Walker working in the kitchen, thawing out the hamburger meat in the microwave. He turned to run his eyes over her, trying to hide a smirk.

She glanced down at herself. "The shirt and socks are a little big, but I did find a pair of knit pajamas Vee left behind to wear underneath."

"The main thing is that you are warm and dry. Maybe even a little cute with my shirt hanging down to your knees." He took the pile of damp clothes from her and headed to the laundry room with them.

Moving to the counter where he'd been working, Juliette began to gather the other ingredients they would need for soup.

Later after finishing their meal, Juliette and Walker sat in front of a roaring fire in the den, watching the snow continue to fall outside the window.

"There must be a foot of snow out there now," Juliette said, feeling drowsy after such a stressful day.

Walker had put on some soft classical CDs, and the music wafted gently around them, making Juliette even sleepier.

"Did you share a nice talk with your gramma?"

"I did. She and Grandpa were really worried." Juliette leaned her head back against the sofa. "She said they prayed for us."

"Good to hear." He started telling her about talking to Vee and Chandler and about predictions of snow for Virginia, but she didn't hear the rest.

Later, she woke up, disoriented at first, to find herself snuggled across Walker's lap, his arm around her. Blinking her eyes, she looked up to find him looking down at her with soft eyes.

"I guess I fell asleep."

"Yes, you did." He smiled at her.

She started to get up, but he slipped his arms around her instead, pulling her against him and kissing her with a depth of feeling Juliette wasn't used to. Her breathing quickened, and with a soft noise she let herself fall into the kiss, wrapping her arms around him, pressing against his warmth.

"You are so beautiful," he whispered against her neck, as he slid his lips down her throat across her shoulders, and then trailed them back to her lips again.

Passion exploded like the crackling of the logs in the big fireplace, and Juliette was soon lost in the feelings, reveling in Walker's kisses and his touch, the beat of their hearts, and the roar of emotions rising between them.

"I love you so much," she heard him murmur as he pulled her on top of him, drawing her even closer. His hands roamed down her back now as he kissed her with deeper passion. She gave back, her senses swimming, threading her hands in his hair, pressing against him. It felt so good to be close to him, to have him kissing her like this. Then his hands began exploring more intimate areas.

Juliette tensed, not sure she wanted things to go further, no matter how wonderful everything felt. She made an effort to shift his hands, to little avail, and then with resignation, she struggled out of his arms to sit up.

He sat watching her for a few moments, settling his breathing and trying to get a grip on his emotions. Then he closed his eyes, leaning his head back against the sofa. "Your grandfather was right," he said eventually.

She pulled the big flannel shirt across her breasts, feeling suddenly self-conscious she wore so little clothing underneath it. "Right about what?" she asked.

He opened his eyes to glance her way. "He said it was dangerous for a young man and a young woman to spend the night alone with only a foot of snow and a big fire for chaperone, said it set the scene for wanting more. He was right." Walker offered her a wry smile. "He also said when a young man and a young woman yielded to such feelings, they bore a glow the next day showing clearly, to those with eyes to see, where they'd journeyed. He said he'd be watching for that and if he saw it, he hoped I'd keep in mind that he'd expect a wedding to follow by month's end. Your grandpa ended with the words, 'You do understand what I'm saying, boy?'"

"Oh, my gosh." Juliette knew her mouth fell open. "I can't believe my grandpa said that to you."

"Your grandpa is a wise man. I told him there was nothing for him to worry about, but I was wrong." His grin widened. "I'd have let my passions roar ahead like a car without brakes if you hadn't given me a check. Ready to push for more even then, your grandfather's words came back to me. A good thing."

She felt a slow flush spread up her face.

"I've never wanted a woman like I want you, Juliette." He reached over to trace a hand down her cheek. "Some days it's agony for me at the store being around you so closely, feeling you brush up against me, glancing down your shirt like a voyeur when you lean over, watching your swaying little walk from behind as you move around the store."

"I think you're embarrassing me." She dropped her eyes, not sure what to say to him.

"No, I'm complimenting you. Even on the trail today, cold and worried about getting you back to safety, I wanted you. Felt fearful something might happen to you and that I might lose you. Don't let me lose you, Juliette."

She looked out the window toward the snow, still falling. Her voice soft, she said, "I do plan to go back to North Carolina after Christmas, Walker. I've been meaning to tell you. I share a lot of the same strong feelings you do but I can't go on the way things are."

He didn't say anything in response.

To fill up the awful silence, she added, "It won't be hard for you to find someone else to fill in at the store part-time, and later if things change for you, you'll know where I am and ..."

"No!" He got up and paced to the window, causing Marsh to lift his head from sleep. "I don't want you to go. Please don't go."

"Walker, I can't stay with all these unspoken things and issues between us. I simply can't. It hurts me inside too much. I'm sorry."

"No, I'm sorry." He took a deep breath. "There have been too many secrets, but I was afraid I would lose you if you learned more about my past. If you knew more ..."

"What could be so terrible?"

He turned to look at her from the window, obviously struggling over how to answer. "I'm not even who you think I am." He threw out the words in agony. "I'm not even really Walker Logan."

"What?" She knew her mouth gaped open at the words.

A long silence ensued. "My real name is Owen Walker Marshall," he said at last. "When I left Colorado I had to get Burton to legally change my name so the threats wouldn't continue to follow me, so no one could find me to make more threats or to ask for more money not to carry them out. You can do that legally when your family is endangered, when your life is threatened. I thought if I left, disappeared, all the problems would stop." He paused. "And they basically did."

Juliette couldn't think what to say.

He walked over to slump into the chair across from her. "We know now it was probably only one man behind the threats, rather than a group or organization, although we're still not sure about that, even since the murder in Greeley happened. I know, too, that the man continued to look for me for a long time. Left notes in different places and with different people saying he was looking for me, that he would find me. We spread it around I'd gone out of the country. I did leave the mainland at first. Went to Hawaii, then to Alaska." He laughed. "That's when I got the idea of traveling the US. I read a book about someone traveling to all the states and I thought, 'Hey, I could do that.' I was getting bored doing nothing by then. I'm used to being busy, used to working, and I couldn't do that anymore. So I decided to have an adventure. I researched, bought a Sportsmobile to travel in and a little motorcycle for side trips, and off I went. Along the way I found Marsh and that gave me a little company." He reached down to pet the big dog at his feet.

Juliette felt stunned at his words. "You once said your family's store was named after your family," she said at last. "I remember wondering about that."

"That was a slip. I've always wanted to open up to you. From the first, I've shared more with you than with anyone before. But I've been afraid to share everything." He ran his hands through his hair. "If that man tracked me here, if he found me, I'd need to run again. He doesn't only seek to hurt me, he threatens to hurt those I love."

She tried to think. "When and why did this start, Walker? Was it because of money? Were you always wealthy or did becoming wealthy in some way trigger all of this?" She leaned across the gap between them to put a hand on his knee. "Talk to me, Walker. Let me in."

He leaned his head back, a muscle in his jaw bunching, obviously struggling about what to do.

She went over and got on her knees on the floor in front of him. "I love you, Walker Owen or Owen Walker. The name doesn't matter, and nothing else does either. Nothing you can tell me will change that. I want you to share with me. Loving is trusting and risking your heart, risking your secrets with someone else. Being real."

He shook his head. "There is so much you don't know."

She gave him a little smile. "Well, as it happens, we have all night here, snowed in as we are. It's a good time for sharing."

He gave her a slow, lopsided grin. "You may regret walking deeper into my life."

"I don't think so." She looped her arms around his neck and pulled him down to kiss her.

He groaned. "I think I could use some coffee for this ordeal."

"Excellent idea." Her eyes searched his face. "I'll go get some and maybe heat some of that apple pie I saw in your freezer."

"Sounds like a plan." He spoke the words with a tight nod. "I have some things upstairs I want to bring down to show you. I'll go get them while you get us some coffee and pie." He got up and pulled her to her feet.

She kissed him again, wrapping her arms around him.

He groaned. "No more of that. Remember your grandpa will be looking for that glow tomorrow. I don't want to get on his bad side. As on outsider, it's taken me a long time to win your grandparents over."

Feeling a little lighter in her heart, Juliette headed to the kitchen. No matter what he told her now, it was better than being shut out.

"I brought three scrapbooks," he said, coming back to join her a little later in the den. "A family scrapbook, a travel book, and one other. Let's start with the family book while we eat our pie."

He sat down next to her on the couch, laying the big scrapbook across their knees. "My sister, Victoria, made me this scrapbook when I started my travels in the Sportsmobile, gave it to me for Christmas. I bought a metal lockbox and carried it around with me. Got it out for comfort sometimes. I'm really a home guy, and I missed my family. Missed Greeley. Missed the store. Missed Stewart, who was my assistant manager at the store and best friend to hang out with."

He opened the scrapbook, showing her photos of his mom and dad, of himself and Vee as kids, and of the big white two-storied home he'd grown up in. He pointed out pictures of Burton, his cousin Stewart, and himself as boys; shots of the family store in downtown Greeley; and more—pictures of Aunt Jessie when younger, of Vee's and his graduations from high school and college, photos of Chandler and Vee's wedding, of their twins at different ages.

Walker eyed her warily. "Your Gramma Newell got out her family scrapbooks and showed me photos of you growing up, pictures of George when a little boy, of your dad as a young man, others of

Patsy and your mother. Now you've seen some of my life, too, and you can connect the memories to what I've told you. As I said to you before, I grew up in a small town, in Greeley, Colorado, lived in the same house from the time I was born, worked in the family store, seldom traveled. My life was small and simple."

She looked through the pages again while he finished his pie. "Your hair looks different in these last pictures. You wore glasses, and you weren't as fit as you are now. You dressed differently, too." She ran her finger over the photo of him, obviously taken in the family store.

"I needed to change my appearance. I let my hair grow out a little, got contacts, changed the way I dressed, developed new interests. I needed to reinvent myself."

He studied the scrapbook on their lap and the photo of himself behind the counter in the family store. "That was Owen, sort of a nerdy guy. The kind of guy active in scouts, who made the honor society but not the football team, just a regular sort of everyday guy. He had friends but he wasn't particularly popular by school standards." He shrugged. "You know what I mean. But Owen was a happy guy. Loved life, loved his family. Biked and fished with his buddies. Worked hard. Always knew exactly who he was from a young age, the Marshall kid who lived in the house on Hensley Street near the park. His family owned a general store downtown, his uncle pastored the Congregational church. His cousin Stewart and his neighbor Burton Franklin were his best friends."

"You talk about yourself in the past tense."

"I do." He ran his hand over the photo she'd been looking at. "I had to leave that man behind, and even if everything resolved itself tomorrow, I still wouldn't ever be that man again if I went back. Too much has happened. I could never really feel at home in Greeley again after all that occurred, either."

"Because of that man?" She considered his words. "If he was found, wouldn't that change everything?"

"No. Other things happened, too, to change how I feel about Greeley, and helped push me to decide to leave."

Juliette waited, thumbing through the photo book as she did and occasionally asking a few questions. There was obviously more to Walker's story, and it seemed likely he was leading into that part of the story now.

He finished his last bite of pie, drank a little more coffee, and then laid the first scrapbook aside to open another.

"Victoria made me this second scrapbook, too. She's artistic like you." He ran his hand over the cover. "She said one day I'd want to remember this time in my life, that I'd want to share it with my children." He shook his head as though the idea was still absurd. Then he opened the book.

On the first page was a photocopy of a news article with Walker's face plastered in the middle of it. He didn't say anything; he just let her read it.

She glanced at the headlines and then read them out loud. "Small-Town Boy in Greeley, Colorado, Wins the Big Powerball Jackpot." She looked at the figure, at nearly a billion, below the picture and knew her mouth dropped open.

"Those Powerball jackpots really build up sometimes."

Shocked, she put a hand to her chest. "Walker, this is unbelievable. I can't even imagine this kind of money." She scanned through the article, reading the media details. Then she turned the page to find more newspaper and magazine articles and more photos, one of Walker and Stewart grinning in the store, another of a copy of the winning ticket.

Walker looked over her shoulder. "Stewart talked me into buying a lottery ticket for my birthday. He was always buying them, thinking how great it would be to win a lot of money. He bought a bunch of tickets for himself the same day I bought only one." He shook his head. "Ironic, isn't it?"

She flipped the pages, looking at more of the photos and news articles. "You don't look happy in many of these photos."

"I wasn't. I hated all that publicity. I felt shocked when I realized I won." He looked out toward the snow, still falling outside. "Of course, I felt excited at first, thought about some of the good things I could do with a windfall like that, ways to fix up the store, make a difference around the town. I thought of being able to send Vee's girls through college, to pay off Vee's and my house notes, to make Aunt Jessie more secure after all she'd done for us."

"I'm sure you had some more personal pleasures in mind, too."

He nodded. "I did. I got a new truck and a used boat. Went in with Burton on a little cabin in the mountains where Burton, Stewart, and I could go fish and hunt—get away as guys. I did some big renovations at the store like I'd dreamed of doing for a long time."

She waited. "And?"

"And Burton helped me invest the rest. You remember he's an attorney in Denver and a good one. I thought things would pretty much go on as before after that." He frowned. "But they didn't."

"What happened?"

"Everyone in town started treating me differently. Hitting me up for money, asking me for money for one thing or the other." He rolled his eyes. "Girls I'd never met, who never noticed me before, starting hanging around the store trying to flirt with me, asking me to go places with them. Stuffy people in the town who'd always treated me like a storekeeper's kid—which is exactly what I was—started pushing on me to be different, to act different, to join groups I wasn't interested in, to do my civic duty and such."

"Surely that faded away after a time."

"No, it didn't." He snapped the words, his eyes flashing in remembrance. "It got worse. People grew more aggressive in their demands and they were always jabbing at me: 'If I had that kind of money I wouldn't be working every day anymore and I wouldn't be driving a plain ole truck; I'd buy me a fine Mercedes-Benz or something.' Or another would say: 'If you don't want to buy a fancy car for yourself, I sure could use me a new car. We've been through some hard times and it would be a kindness as much business as I've done in your store.'"

He rubbed his arm in irritation. "That last request came from a guy who won't even work a job. Made his wife go to the factory every day and his kids do without. And he called that hard times."

She turned some of the pages in the book, looking at pictures Victoria placed there—of Walker giving checks to philanthropic organizations, standing with leaders of civic groups or the mayor in relation to one thing or the other, cutting a ribbon at an opening ceremony of a building he'd sponsored.

"It looks like you did some good things for the people of Greeley."

"I did, but it was never enough." His voice sounded angry. "Someone was always bitter, always saying something to make me feel guilty about being well-to-do. They complained when they bought things in the store about buying from a rich guy like me, helping me get richer. Stuff like that all the time. Women tried to push their daughters off on me, telling me how I needed to get married. A lot of girls practically offered themselves to me, sometimes right in the store around our customers. It embarrassed me. People invited me to events or to their homes for a social evening, not because they liked me but because they wanted to hit me up for money while there. Guys I'd known all my life started acting like they didn't like me anymore."

He got up to pace around the room. "I hated it. I didn't have any peace in my life. I never knew people could be so manipulative and contriving, and so phony. So enamored about money. Caring so dang much about material things." He stopped to stare out the window again. "Sure, I liked the idea at first that I wouldn't have money worries anymore. That I could buy a nice television if mine broke down or take a vacation without worrying if I could afford it. The old house I'd grown up in needed some updating and it was nice to be able to do that."

Walker seemed to check himself then, picking up his coffee to drink it, not adding more, lost in his own thoughts.

She flipped through the scrapbook. There were some happy pictures of Walker with his family at a beach resort, of him with his friends at a mountainside cabin. "You said once that having money wasn't all I imagined it could be."

He turned to look at her, his eyes sad. "You'd think it would be a blessing, but it isn't in so many ways. People often hate you and grow bitter toward you simply because you have money. I tried to be generous and help with worthwhile causes, but it never seemed to be enough. There was always someone with another dig, another poke, suggesting I ought to dress more fashionably, sell the store and not work, provide the money for their church's new building, send their kids to college or pay for their whole family to go to Disney World. You wouldn't believe some of the twisted reasoning and stories people brought to me trying to justify why I ought to give them money for one thing or another."

She offered him a small smile. "It reminds me of the Share the Wealth cards in the Life board game. Do you remember those? When someone drew one, they usually offered it to the player who'd accumulated the most money in the game. I used to hate it when someone drew one of those cards and presented it to me with a big smirk when I landed on a Collect space."

He came over to sit down beside her again. "That's exactly what it was like all the time, Juliette—someone always showing up with a Share the Wealth card. It went on for two years. Not only did my friends and the locals around Greeley push on me for money, but all sorts of philanthropies began to show up with Share the Wealth cards, too, wanting me to give them big donations for this or that. It never ended. It never stopped. And many of those groups who approached me were very pushy and aggressive. They often turned mean and belligerent when I said no or even said I wanted to think about it first. They felt I should write a big check right on the spot, not even check them out."

"That's sad."

He shook his head. "The first time I suggested to someone I would pray about the matter, they really came down on me, grew angry and offended I'd even consider for a moment that their organization wasn't worthy, that God wouldn't want to see their good works continue."

He dropped his head into his hands. "It got to the point where

I almost dreaded coming into the store to work every day. The jabs and pointed comments never quit. I kept thinking I'd get used to it, to the way people acted. Stewart kept saying people would eventually let me get back to normal after a time, that I was simply the new seven-day wonder. But things never changed. Then the crazy stuff started. I began to get anonymous threats from someone who wanted a lot of money and felt it his due from me to have it."

"That must have been scary."

"It was. I had to go to the police and that visit escalated the threats. I was followed sometimes by a black van. I got notes threatening my life if I wouldn't leave money at a certain place at a certain time. When I didn't comply, the threats grew nastier."

Juliette reached over to take his hand. "Then that person started threatening your family, didn't they? Threw a firebomb into your uncle's home, let you know he knew things about your nieces?"

"Yes." He shot her a look of fury.

"Is that when you left?'

"Shortly after." He stiffened. "I was in the store one day working with Stewart. I'd received another threatening note the day before, and then Mrs. Jenkins came in the store and started in on me about how she thought my mother, God bless her sainted memory, would be deeply disappointed that I didn't want to fund the building of the new wing for one of Greeley's branch libraries outside of town. She reminded me she knew my mother loved to read and told me she felt sure Mother would be real disappointed if I didn't want to support a worthwhile project like helping their library fund."

He winced at the memory. "I had only recently financed a full renovation of the downtown library in Greeley and attended the dedication ceremony. But, of course, she didn't mention that."

"That was mean of her, Walker, to throw your mother up to you."

"Yes, it was mean," he agreed. "Then Mrs. Jenkins further registered her offense that I'd stopped seeing her daughter Teresa Jean, saying I'd led her on."

"Did you?"

He shook his head. "I shared lunch with Teresa Jean one day to discuss a project we were both working on with the mayor's office."

Juliette tried not to laugh.

"After Mrs. Jenkins left, Stewart shook his head and said, 'Sometimes, I think if I were you, I'd totally disappear, leave town and never come back.'" Walker smiled at her then. "Stewart was joking of course, but I went home after work and started making plans to leave. I worked with Burton on how to do it, and before I left I gave the store to Stewart to run."

"Then you traveled around the US for two years."

"That's right, and then I saw Stone House when I was walking Marsh on the ridge above it and it somehow called to me. I don't know why. I kept thinking about it and I called the realtor to look at it. I was so tired of traveling by then, of having no place to call home." He leaned toward her and touched her face. "Then I met you that same day and kissed you for the first time, and it seemed like my life was looking up."

She felt tears start in her eyes. "Oh, Walker. I had no idea you'd been through all this."

"Can you see why I didn't want to tell anyone?"

She sighed. "Did you think people would act the same way here if they learned you were very rich and had won that big jackpot?"

He nodded.

She swallowed, a sudden lump in her throat. "Even me? Did you believe I would act differently?"

His dropped eyes gave her the answer.

"It doesn't change things," she said, feeling disappointed he thought it would. But even as she told him that, she knew it had changed her view about him somewhat.

Marsh woofed softly to go out, and Juliette took their pie dishes and coffee cups back to the kitchen while Walker let the big dog out briefly to attend to business.

"He wasn't eager to stay out long," Walker said, coming back into the den. "He zipped from the garage through the carport and back in a hurry."

"I'll bet." She petted the big dog. "His nose is cold. I'd say the temperature has continued to drop."

"It has." Walker added some logs to the fire and then settled back down on the sofa beside her.

He showed her his travel scrapbook then, two pages for every state he'd visited—and he'd been to every state, several more than once over the last two years.

It was late when they finished.

"We need to get some sleep," he said, seeing her yawn. "We had a rough day. I hope I didn't make it worse."

"No, you made it better," she assured him, leaning across to kiss him. "I'm sorry you experienced so many sorrows. Please know that all you shared with me tonight will stay confidential until you decide to share with others."

"Thanks." He stood up, giving her a hand. "You go on upstairs to bed now. You know where Vee's room is. I'll stay down here for a while, let Marsh out a last time. I'll come up later to my own room or sleep down here by the fire."

She made her way up the stairs, glad he hadn't asked again if she would stay on after Christmas. Her feelings were so mixed up right now, she wasn't sure how she'd answer. Walker was right. He wasn't who she thought he was. And his past and all that it involved, both then and now, were things she really needed to think about long and hard.

CHAPTER 22

The snow melted over the next days, and life moved on. Juliette's brother, George, tromped through the snow the next morning after she stayed overnight, arriving before they even finished breakfast, to walk her back to the farm. He'd brought snow boots, and he'd worn a scowl of disapproval, but he seemed to soften over a cup of coffee in Walker's kitchen.

"George, this was an emergency situation," Juliette told him in her matter-of-fact way. "Don't read more into it than needed." She'd been provoked that George showed up as he did, but she left with him.

Walker noticed she had acted a little too cheerful the next morning over breakfast after all his revelations, and he watched those changes in her continue over the next days. Not that she said anything. Just that he caught her watching him every now and again when she didn't think he noticed.

He imagined it was taking time for her to process all the information he shared with her. It would be a lot for anyone to think about. He said as much to Victoria on the phone as he talked to her, with the store quiet this morning.

"Should I speak to her, too?" Victoria asked. "Even though she is acting a little wary and standoffish, you did the right thing, Walker."

"Maybe, but now that she knows everything, I've watched her change. She realizes I can't move forward with everything as it is, with my problems still out there and unresolved."

"It's a lot for her to process that you have so much money, too," Victoria said in all honesty. "It took me a while to adjust to the idea, and I'm your sister."

Walker stood by the window, looking out on the beginnings of a clear, warm day as they talked. "I see a customer coming," he said, watching Dade Claiborne's truck pull into the parking lot. "Let me get back to you."

He walked to the back of the store quickly and put Marsh in the Quilt Room, not wanting more trouble with Dade. Turning back toward the front of the store, he saw Dade stride into the store, an angry look on his face.

His eyes shot around the store. "Where's Juliette?"

Walker looked at his watch. "She's due any minute." Walking behind the counter, he asked, "Would you like coffee or a doughnut?"

"No." He snapped out the word. "But I'd like to offer you a word of warning."

Dade moved closer to lean on the counter, scowling at him. "I know Juliette stayed over with you in that snowstorm. Things get around in a small place like this." He clenched a fist. "I don't like that. You've gotten her real confused, moving into this valley and taking up with her. You and all your secrets."

Walker poured himself a cup of coffee. There was no point in asking how Dade found out Juliette stayed over at his place. Someone probably saw George walking her home the next morning. It only took one person to start a little gossip running around the valley.

"Juliette was my girl before you showed up," Dade continued. "We were getting close before you came along. You know her folks would like her to marry a boy from the valley. They favored me until you started sucking up to them and flashing your money around." He leaned closer to Walker. "I want you to know I'm researching you. I've got people looking into your background. I'm following up a few leads, knowing you came from Colorado. I'll find out about you, and I'll be sure Juliette is the first to know when I do. And others after."

Walker considered telling Dade that Juliette already knew about his past, but he quickly thought better of the idea. He didn't want to give Dade any reason to pressure Juliette to reveal more information later.

"I'm only a small-town guy like you, Dade. I have a little money, but there's nothing illegal or scandalous to unearth. You're wasting your time looking."

"I'm looking all the same," Dade said, as Juliette opened the front door to let herself in. He shut his mouth then on whatever he'd planned to say next, and a small silence fell.

As Juliette came over to put her purse under the counter and started taking off her coat, she let her eyes move from Dade's face to Walker's. "I gather you two were having an interesting conservation before I came in the door. Since you've now both gone quiet and look uncomfortable, my guess is it was about me."

Dade recovered himself with a swagger and a grin. "There could only be sweet things I could say about you, sugar. I stopped in to say hello to you this morning on my way to visit Mama. Thought I might get her another cherry coke."

"I see." She rolled her eyes before heading back to hang up her coat.

"Leave your coat here for now," Walker said quickly, a few minutes before they all heard a welcoming bark from Marsh, who'd heard Juliette's voice.

Dade scowled. "I see you're still keeping that ill-tempered dog at your store. I warned you about that."

"Oh, hush." Juliette walked back to the front of the store and draped her coat over the end of the counter. "You're the only person that dog has ever had any trouble with. Walker puts him up whenever he sees you coming into the store to be polite. What more do you want?"

Dade's eyes moved with irritation toward the back of the store, but he wisely said nothing in reply.

Juliette slipped behind the counter and past Walker. "I'll fix your colas, Dade, so you can head on to your mother's with them. Do you want one or two?"

He held up two fingers and then asked, "You still going back to North Carolina after Christmas or staying here now?" He moved over to lean on the counter closer to where Juliette worked.

She didn't turn around. "I'm expected back at my job in January, and I have quilting classes scheduled at the folk school starting in early spring."

Dade lifted his eyebrows and gave Walker a smug look.

"Maybe I'll drive down there and pay you a visit one day." He pushed his cowboy hat up an inch on his brow. "I go down that way every now and then to pick up a car from a dealer friend of mine in the area."

She didn't reply, working on his colas.

He flirted a little more with her and then paid for his drinks and left.

"Are you still planning to go back to North Carolina in January after Christmas?" Walker asked quietly, hoping it wasn't true.

"Whatever I'm doing, it's none of Dade Claiborne's business to know it," she answered. She wiped off the counter and then snatched up her coat to take it to the back, letting Marsh out as she did. Walker watched her squat down to pet and talk to the big dog as Marsh greeted her with his usual doggy enthusiasm.

"Do you still want me to replenish the Christmas stock that's getting low around the store today?" she asked, putting on that cheerful front and starting back toward the front of the store again.

Annoyed, Walker moved from behind the counter to block her path. "I told you that if you knew more about me you'd change toward me."

Juliette's eyes lifted to his. "I don't like it that you and Dade were talking about me," she said, avoiding the unspoken question he'd brought up.

"I can't help what subjects Dade brings up when he drops by. Usually he brings you up as a subject. He still resents me for coming into your life and, as he put it, for changing your feelings toward him."

"That's ridiculous."

"He doesn't think so."

"Well, I'm not worried about his threats toward me."

"I am." He grabbed her arms at the words.

She stiffened. "What do you mean?"

"He warned me that he was researching my background, that he'd learned I came from Colorado." He dropped his hands from her arms. "Dade said he was determined to track down information about me."

Her eyes grew soft. "Would it be so bad if people knew?"

"I might need to run again if problems came here." He felt his jaw tighten.

"Surely that awful man wouldn't come here. Victoria said he was threatening another family out west now and had a new focus."

Walker rubbed his neck. "He might not keep that focus if he learns where I am now. He might come here."

She shook her head and sat down on the stool at the end of the counter. "Fear is a horrible thing. I hate that it pursues you like it does." She looked down at her fingers laced in her lap. "I'm trying to understand everything, Walker, but it's difficult."

He leaned against the wall, waiting for her to continue her thoughts.

"Maybe the man might come here," she said. "Maybe he might be a threat, like the thieves around our valley who are still causing trouble and haven't been caught yet. But nobody's moving away because of it. We know the police are trying to find these people, and everyone in the valley is trying to be watchful until they do."

"It's hardly the same thing."

She picked at a fingernail. "I'm aware of that. I'm only saying if people knew about your situation, they would help you be watchful. They would stand with you, be concerned for you. They'd want to see this man caught, for everything to be all right for you again. People have started to like and respect you here." She took a breath. "I don't think they would act like the people in Greeley if they learned you'd won a lot of money either. They already know you have money and that you do good things to help people around the valley. You haven't seen them make a fuss about it, have you? Or come and put pressure on you to give them money?"

"They don't know everything."

"I'm aware of that," she said with annoyance. "But sometimes you simply have to begin living, trusting, and risking again. What happened to you in Colorado was awful. But that was then and this is now. You deserve a real life again."

"Don't you think I want that?" He knew he snapped out the question.

Juliette crossed her arms. "I think you've decided that what happened before will automatically happen again. I don't think that's necessarily true. Granted, people were annoying to deal with in Greeley after you won that big jackpot. I'd have grown angry, too, at how everyone there acted. Like Stewart said, it might have died down after a time but you didn't get a chance to find out with the threats beginning. You were younger then, too, with your father and mother both gone, your sister far away. You had to stand up against all that by yourself."

She laid a hand on his arm. "You're stronger now, older and wiser. You have people who love you here. I don't think the same things would happen again, even though you're afraid they would."

"You can't know that." He felt his irritation spike.

"No, but I've prayed about it. And I know that whenever we let fear rule, faith can't rule as it should. The two are opposite forces."

He frowned. "You sound like Eldon now."

"You should talk to Eldon about this. He gives wise counsel and he lives close to God." She traced her fingers lightly up his arm. "He loves you, too, Walker, as I do. We don't want to see you trapped and tied to your past."

"It's complicated."

"Life usually is, but sometimes we build matters up in our minds to be bigger and more awful than they really are."

He moved his eyes to hers. "You think I've done that."

"A little." She hesitated. "Maybe more than a little." She twisted the necklace she wore around her neck. "Can I be honest with you?"

He nodded. It seemed a joke for her to ask this after what she'd already said.

"I thought a lot about you winning that money and how everyone acted." She drummed her fingers on the counter. "I tried to imagine how I'd feel if someone here in the valley won that much money, and I had to admit I might have felt a little envious. I know I shouldn't feel envious of anyone ever, but I felt forced to honestly admit to myself I probably would have. I even found myself thinking how blessed and wonderful it might feel to receive that kind of money, no matter how anyone acted toward me or what they said."

"But you don't know how they acted. I tried to tell you—"

"I remember what you told me," she interrupted. "But in your life in Greeley, where you'd always lived, you'd never dealt with the nastiness of people like that before, their ugliness, their greed, their bad manners. People are not always kind. They're often hateful and disappointing, but that still doesn't mean it wasn't a great blessing for you to win that money. Think of all the good you've been able to do. Even the adventures you've enjoyed seeing the United States like you did, buying Stone House simply because you liked it, building a store from scratch and not needing to worry about having the money to do it." She hesitated. "I don't think you've been grateful and thankful enough for the blessing God sent your way. You've only focused on the bad. Granted, there have been more problems than you ever could have expected, but there has been good, too."

Biting his tongue, Walker moved behind the counter to begin getting items out for the lunch hour. It was amazing no one had popped into the store since Dade left, even though the winter brought less traffic now.

"You're annoyed with me," she said from behind him. "I guess I can understand that. But I needed to tell you what I've been thinking. You know I told you that if you love someone you have to be real. You need to be honest."

"I'd say you've been honest," he bit out.

"Let me ask you something," she said. "If you could turn back the clock and be exactly as you were before you won the jackpot, go back to being Owen Walker Marshall running the store in Greeley, not having won even a penny, never having traveled around the USA, not ever coming to Happy Valley or buying your house here or building the store, not knowing anyone you've met since then, would you go back?"

He started to say yes, and then caught himself. "That's not a fair question."

She smiled at him. "Isn't it?"

He sat down on the stool beside her. "I hate the way you and Eldon make me think about things sometimes."

"When you bottle things up, you never get the opportunity to let other people offer you another perspective. Sometimes getting that other perspective can help."

He sent her an annoyed look. "So you think I ought to tell everyone here everything about me. Take my chances that my past won't come back looking for me. Take a chance that no one will get shot and killed here like that man in Greeley was shot and killed."

"There you go painting the worst scenario again." She shook her head. "And be assured, I am *not* telling you what to do. What I am advising, though, is that you rethink this situation, get more counsel about it—perhaps from Eldon—and pray about it, of course. God knows the best thing to do and the best way to resolve this issue. I am praying it will be resolved in some good way and you should be praying for that, too, if you aren't already."

"I have been praying, Juliette."

She lowered her voice. "Remember when you were helping me to work out things with Hettie Rhea? Remember you told me I had to be willing to forgive her. I didn't really want to, and I didn't really like you telling me that. But you were right. I needed to do that for my own peace and well-being. You need to forgive those people in

Greeley for being greedy and hateful, for making life difficult for you. For not being kind."

He looked away from her. "Even though I'm not liking all your candor today, I'm glad you're talking to me again."

She raised an eyebrow. "I've been here in the store every day talking to you."

"You know what I mean. There's been a distance."

"Okay, I admit that's true. I had to process everything. Pray and think." Her lips twitched. "There was a lot to process."

"Yes, there was. But you wanted to know it all."

"I did." She leaned over and kissed him then. "Walker, I'm not sure right now if I should stay on or go back to North Carolina after Christmas. If I do go back, it's not far for us to visit, only two hours. Maybe time apart will help clarify to both of us what we should do." She dropped her eyes. "To know if there's a future."

"You know I want a future."

"Yes, but we've both been honest enough to admit how hard it is to continue being together every day without wanting something more."

He stood and pulled her into his arms to kiss her with a sweep of the pent-up passion he'd been holding in. "That hasn't changed," he said after a few minutes. "Every time I see you my heart tap dances."

"That's sweet to hear." She patted his cheek. "But you'd better tap dance behind the counter now because I just heard a car pull up in the parking lot. This is the day those two fishermen, Reese and Wheeler, usually stop in for lunch. You know they fish rain or shine, cold or hot. I'm sure they'll want lunch before they head out on the lake. The minister and his wife might stop by, too, after their church calls."

He headed behind the counter to check the chili warming in the Crock-Pot. Despite all of Juliette's words, some that pricked and hurt a little, he felt glad they were talking again.

After Reese and Wheeler left, along with a stream of midday customers, Walker was surprised to see Keith and Amy come in the store together.

"This is a real treat," Juliette said, moving from the Christmas display she sat replenishing to hug them both. "How did you two escape the daycare center during the week?"

"Dora is taking care of things for a little while, so we could come over to talk to both of you," Amy answered.

"If you have any of Eldon's barbecue today, Amy and I would love some of it for lunch while we're here, too," Keith said, sitting down on one of the counter stools.

"Coming right up," Walker said, turning to fix the sandwiches.

"What did you want to talk about?" Juliette asked, coming over to join them. "It's quiet for a few minutes right now."

Keith pulled a sheet of paper from his back pocket and unfolded it to lay it on the counter. "Here's our list of all the kids in the valley you asked us to get together for your idea of delivering Christmas gifts." He cleared his throat. "It's a great idea. Generous, too. And Amy and I wondered if you two might consider dressing up as Santa and Mrs. Claus and bringing everything to the community center for a party instead of driving around the valley. It's hard for the kids to wait until Christmas. They get so excited, and this would make a great culminating activity for the center as school ends and the holidays move in. We could hold the party late next Friday, or on the following Friday, and invite all the kids who live in the valley to come, along with the ones we keep at the center."

Amy chimed in. "If you guys don't like this idea, it's okay. Honest. But we got to thinking how uncertain the weather is, and how hard it might be for you two to get around at Christmas to deliver gifts, especially if it snows again. A lot of people travel at the holidays, too. I know several families already who won't even be in the valley at Christmas."

"It was different in the old days," Keith added. "People in the valley lived more limited lives. They were all here at Christmas, but now so much is going on Christmas week—church gatherings, shopping, parties, holiday events."

"You do have a point." Juliette looked toward Walker. "But this was really Walker's plan."

He thought for a moment. "I simply wanted to find a way to give some gifts to the kids in the valley. I think your idea is a great one and probably a lot more practical than going house to house."

Amy's face lit up. "Oh, good. Keith and I both felt that helping with this would be a way of saying thank you, too, for all you've done for the center—and for us. The new programs are going so well. It's been a blessing to us and to everyone in the valley."

"It has," Keith agreed. "It's helping to bring new families to the valley, too. A family with kids bought a house this month because Cameron was able to tell them we had a daycare center with after-school pickup." Keith smiled over the words, and Walker felt happy to see that new contented smile. Keith was doing an excellent job managing the renovated center, and he and Amy had come up with many creative ideas to utilize the facility for other community events.

Juliette put their lunch plates and drinks in front of them and then sat down on the stool to visit while she could. "Kimmie and Jonas want to help with this. And they will love the idea of their twins getting to interact in an event with all the other valley children. They want them to make more local friends."

"The new family moving in has a boy about the age of theirs, according to Cameron," Keith added.

"This is going to be so much fun." Amy's eyes lit up.

The four then talked about which Friday to select for the children's Christmas party, deciding on the earlier date in December, and each proposed ways they could help.

"Kimmie offered to let us all come to their place this Saturday for a work session to wrap all the gifts we've bought and to fill up the stockings," Juliette said. "She said she'd provide dinner, too. The timing is good if we hope to have the children's party next week."

"Cameron and Letitia want to help, too," Walker put in. "With eight of us all working, we should finish everything on Saturday. Jonas has a big storage room under his house where he said we can stash everything until it's time for delivery."

They made plans for the upcoming party while Keith and Amy ate lunch, Walker stopping to help customers in between.

The afternoon proved a busy one for midweek, leaving no quiet time for Walker and Juliette to talk again. When Juliette put on her coat to leave and waved good-bye to Quillen, Walker followed her outside.

"Did I forget something?" she said, looking back.

He walked her out of sight of Quillen's view and then gathered her up to kiss her again. "Thanks for the talk earlier," he said, looking down into her face, letting his eyes rove over it, smoothing her hair back from where the December wind had caught and tossed it.

"You're not mad?" Her eyes looked into his in question.

Walker knew he'd been mad earlier and was still a little annoyed, but he didn't want to admit it. "You spoke honestly and I'm grateful," he said, knowing that, at least, was the truth. He could hardly expect her to understand all he'd walked through.

She turned to wave at him as she headed toward home a few minutes later, and Walker felt a wrench at his heart. Certainly no one wanted life to be normal again more than he did. He hated to think of Juliette leaving after Christmas, but he couldn't think of any way to make her stay. She was right that the passion between them was becoming a problem. Walker knew it kept him up at night, tossing and turning. But he doubted that Juliette being in North Carolina would make it stop. It would only make it worse.

CHAPTER 23

Christmas was usually Juliette's favorite time of year, but this year a tinge of sadness seemed to coat every aspect of the holiday season. Another snow hit the valley, and today was the first day Walker could open the store again after two days of bad roads. Snow still lay on the ground in many areas, but traffic was finally moving around in the valley again.

"I'm glad we held the Christmas party earlier this month like Keith and Amy proposed," Walker said as they worked together putting out stock and waiting on customers in between. "With snow hitting over the weekend, starting on Friday like it did, we'd have been forced to cancel and postpone everything."

"Everyone had a great time and you made a wonderful Santa." Her eyes moved to Quillen, working with them in the store this afternoon. "You made a cute Santa's elf, too, Quillen. Thanks again for helping."

He looked a little embarrassed but grinned at her words. "The kids really loved that party and getting all those gifts, stockings, and treats. Jaida had a blast. I wish we'd had parties like that when I was little." He glanced toward Walker. "Will you do it again next year?"

"I think so." He glanced toward her. "Maybe Juliette will come back from North Carolina to be Mrs. Claus again."

"Oh, man, I wish you wouldn't go back to North Carolina," Quillen complained. "It won't be the same around here without you. Dad and Walker and I will miss you. Marsh, too. Won't you, Marsh?" The dog gave a mournful roo-roo sound as if to agree with Quillen.

Walker's eyes turned to study Juliette's face, and she felt like crying. *What did he expect?* For her to stay on with no certain plans? For them to keep seeing each other and wanting each other like this day after day? She couldn't do it.

She turned back to the tree, afraid to look at Walker with her emotions rising to the surface and threatening to break through. She knew she would miss him so much. She'd been crying herself to sleep the last nights over the whole situation and then trying to feign cheerfulness during the day with everyone.

"Is your dad still coming this week?" Quillen asked, oblivious to the feelings swirling around in the room.

"Yes. He's flying in on Thursday and will stay through Christmas next week." She felt glad for a change of subject.

"I hope you'll bring him over to the store to meet us," Quillen said. He finished stocking a row of canned goods on the shelf and began to flatten the empty box they'd been packed in.

"I'll be sure to do that," Juliette said.

She hung a snowflake ornament on the Christmas tree and thought of the night Walker shared his past with her in the snow after Thanksgiving. She'd thought it would change everything, but it didn't.

"Are you still going to your sister's in Virginia for Christmas?" Quillen asked Walker.

He nodded. "I'm invited to Juliette's grandparents on Christmas Eve but then early on Christmas Day I'm flying to Virginia. We'll keep the store open on Christmas Eve, for last minute shoppers, but I'm closing it for Christmas Day and the day after. Your dad said that the two of you could handle things here the rest of the week so I can stay over in Virginia longer. I'll be back on the weekend on Sunday."

"We'll be fine and I'll take care of Marsh and stay up at the house with him." Quillen went over to talk to the big dog, who then followed him out back behind the store to dump a pile of empty boxes.

Juliette glanced at the clock. It was nearly time to close. They had opened the store around noon after the roads began to clear out, and a lot of people walked in to get milk, bread, juice, and other essentials they'd run out of.

She put away the box of Christmas ornaments, and then went to find the broom to start sweeping up.

As she worked near the front door, she saw Harley and Vernon coming across the porch, peeking into the windows to see if everyone had gone. She opened the door for them.

"We got *big news* today." Harley flashed her a big grin as he sauntered into the store.

"Boy howdy! We sure do," Vernon added, slapping his hand against Harley's in a high five.

"What's up?" Walker asked from behind the register, where he'd started to count out the money at the end of the day.

"We done helped the police catch those thieves today." Harley drew out every word and then grinned widely again.

This got their full attention in a hurry.

"No kidding?" Quillen's eyes grew wide as he headed from the back porch toward the soda fountain. "You guys want some hot dogs?"

At their nod, Quillen went behind the counter to start fixing them while the Ledford brothers settled onto their favorite stools.

"Let's hear this story while you wait," Juliette said, leaning her broom against the wall to come sit beside the brothers at the counter.

"It's a real good story." Vernon giggled his silly laugh while he took off his ratty coat to drape it over the stool beside him.

Harley shed his own jacket and then looked around to see that he had their full attention. "Ya'll know we had a pretty good snow this weekend. About six inches this time." He pushed back his old brown fedora. "We took us a walk in it this morning across Ledford Ridge, down by the Missionary Baptist Church and across the road to Daddy's grave spot in the old cemetery. We thought we saw somebody over at the community center as we walked by. While at the cemetery, we got to thinking that on a Sunday afternoon, with no schools open, and the roads bad, that there ought not to be anybody over there."

"So we went over there to look around a little afterward," Vernon added. "We've been keeping a watch and checking out anything we've seen that doesn't seem right fer a long time. And we didn't see no car parked nowhere when we got near the center."

"We knowed we'd seen somebody, so we sort of hung around and gradually moved in so we could look in the windows," Harley explained. "Check things out."

Vernon shook his head. "No one was there, but we could see what looked like a broke latch on the back door."

Juliette put a hand to her mouth. "Oh my, I hope the thieves didn't break into the community center. It has new computers, a new television, and a lot of other nice things added for the after-school program and the daycare center."

"Don't be a-trying to finish my story," Harley cautioned, frowning at her.

Quillen put two plates of hot dogs and chips in front of the brothers, along with two bottles of root beer. "Go on," he encouraged Harley, perching on an empty stool behind the counter.

"We started looking around outside the building then, to see what we might find," he continued.

Vernon butted in. "Harley said we couldn't go inside even with the latch broken. He said someone might see us and think we was up to no good. You know we've had a lot of talk about us since Dade Claiborne started all them bad rumors."

Harley picked up the story again. "We saw some tracks around the door behind the center. It looked like about four sets of prints as we got to checking closer, all heading toward the door in the snow and then away from it."

"And we saw sled tracks." Vernon jumped in. "Tracks from one of them old sleds with metal runners, like we had as kids. You know the kind; they leave lines in the snow when it's fresh."

Harley gave him a warning glance for continuing to interrupt, and Vernon sent a sheepish grin his way before picking up his hot dog to start wolfing it down.

"We thought it a little queer there were so many tracks around the back door," Harley continued. "Since it looked like someone might have broke into the center, we decided to follow the tracks. See where they went. Maybe learn who'd made them."

Harley paused to eat a couple of bites of his hot dog. "We followed them up through the woods, heading toward Razar Ridge and then over along Mill Creek. It was easy to follow with the snow fresh. There hadn't been no other tracks back in the woods except for tracks from a few rabbits and squirrels and maybe a deer or two. As the tracks started moving up the mountain higher we got even more curious. Ain't nobody lives up there that would have needed to be down at the community center in Happy Valley. The only thing up on that mountain below the parkway is them new rich houses spread out to catch the views."

Harley finished his hot dog and took a long drink of his root beer before continuing.

"I'm dying for you to finish this," Juliette said, urging him on.

"Well, the tracks stopped at the old Claiborne cabin—you know the one tucked up on the mountain above the Claiborne's farm property. We didn't think nobody lived there, so we were real surprised to see smoke coming out of the rock chimney and some trucks around the place, layered up in snow."

"Dade has let some men stay in that old place who are helping him with the house he's building," Juliette said.

"We learned that a little later on," Harley said with a smug grin.

Vernon couldn't resist adding to the story now. "We could see four men inside, and the old sled was leaned up against the porch, with wet snowy ropes still tied on it and a bunch of old black plastic garbage bags wadded up nearby, all wet and soggy, too."

"We stayed quiet watching them," Harley said. "We could see inside the cabin real good from behind the trees on the ridge without getting too close." He described the four men.

"That sounds like the same men who came in the store one day,"

Walker said. "They told me they were helping Dade build his house on the mountain."

Harley offered a toothy grin and laughed. "Well, they was a-helping him with a little more than his house. We watched them celebrating and looking at a couple of computers, a television, some of them laptop things and other stuff all piled on a big table and around the room. All drinking some beers and seeming real proud of themselves."

Juliette crossed her arms. "Just because you obviously saw they'd taken things from the community center up to Dade's family's old cabin doesn't mean Dade was involved, Harley."

"I didn't figure you'd be the one to take up for him." Harley glared at her. "Not after the way he's acted around you."

Vernon leaned toward her. "Besides, we saw Dade, too. He came down a path through the woods and they let him right in. Then he started looking over everything, too, joining in the good time."

"Gracious," Juliette said, trying to wrap her mind around the idea of Dade involved in criminal activity.

"What did you do then?" Walker asked.

"Well, we don't carry no phones around, so we high-tailed it across Razar Ridge to our place and we called Buddy Harmon that lives up at that Top of the World community. He lives next door to this police officer up there that got thieved and weren't none too happy about it. Buddy went over and got the man and then we talked to him about what we saw. His name was Marvin Garvey and he called the police office in Maryville and then we met Marvin, and more police they sent out, at the community center and walked them all up to make some arrests."

"Why didn't you call the police yourself?" Quillen asked.

Harley gave him a patient look. "Police sometimes don't take folks like us serious, Quillen. Buddy knew us and we knew he lived next to a police."

"Besides, we don't like to talk to police," Vernon added.

Walker hid a smirk, but Juliette felt more like crying. "Did they arrest them—all the men and Dade?"

"Sure did." Harley grinned with pride. "Found all kinds of evidence there and up at Dade Claiborne's big place on the hill that showed they'd been selling off the stuff they stole. Dade, he kept trying to deny he were a part of it all, but it didn't do him no good with the other guys getting mad at him and ratting him out. Marvin told Buddy they'd all be in some big-time trouble after getting caught red-handed like they did with all that evidence."

"What about the equipment they found from the center?" Walker asked.

"They'll get it all back after a bit. I heard them say they'd be calling Keith Butler about the break-in, and I think they planned to meet with him to check all that out. He'll probably call you, with you being friends and putting up money for the center, but we wanted to be the first to let you know. We just left the police at the community center and walked on over here afore we headed for home."

Vernon looked at his empty plate. "Besides, we hadn't had no lunch, busy like we were."

Walker laughed. "For catching those thieves, I'll take you both out for a steak dinner if you like."

Harley looked alarmed. "We don't go out of the valley much."

"How about a banana split then? I'm real proud of both of you for tracking those thieves and learning their identity." Walker reached across to shake both their hands.

"Me too," Quillen said, getting up. "And I'll make your banana splits. On the house." He turned to set to work.

"You're awfully quiet," Walker said, noticing Juliette hadn't joined in with their congratulations.

"I'm sorry," she said. "I'm thinking about how hard this will be for Dade's mother Onalee and his brother, Ronnie, and family. They're good people. This will really hurt them."

Walker reached across to take her hand. "Why don't you go home early to tell your grandparents about this? Maybe you and your grandmother can go over to sit with Onalee for a while."

Her eyes filled with tears. "Oh, that's a nice idea, Walker. We can take some dinner, too. Gramma Newell always keeps a couple of extra casseroles in the freezer and she made pies yesterday."

Juliette went to get her coat.

Before she left, she gave Harley and Vernon hugs, embarrassing them both. "Even though I'm sad for Onalee and her family, I am really proud of both of you. It's wonderful you were able to solve what the police haven't been able to resolve for more than a year."

She gave them all a little wave good-bye and then headed home.

Later that evening, as she was sitting by the fire after her grandmother and grandfather went to bed, the phone rang, startling her. She grabbed it quickly before it could wake them. "Hello?"

"Juliette, this is Eldon. Sorry to call late."

"It's all right. I'm sure Quillen told you everything that happened."

"He did." The older man hesitated. "Walker has had an emergency with his family. He's flown out to Colorado. Quillen went up to Walker's house to stay with the dog and look after things there. I was wondering if you could help us cover Walker's shifts at the store until he gets back."

"Of course." A streak of fear threaded through her. "Is anyone hurt?" She knew Walker still had family in Colorado.

"He didn't say so, but he's upset. We'll need to lift him up in our prayers along with Dade's family."

She chewed on a nail. "When will Walker be back? By Christmas Eve?"

"I don't know. But I promised we would take care of everything until he comes back. He said to tell you he tried to call you at the house and on your cell."

"We were all over at Onalee's and I didn't even take my phone."

"He'll probably call you when he can."

Walker did call the house the next day, after she'd left to go to the store early to help Eldon. He left a message with her grandfather that he hoped to be back by Christmas Eve but wasn't sure if he would make it or not. That was all. He didn't call her on her cell later or at the store, and as the week slipped by before Christmas, she didn't hear another word from him.

CHAPTER 24

With annoyance, Walker looked at his watch again. Bad weather and ice in Colorado had delayed his flight, but his plane was nearly ready to land at the airport now. The situation he'd dealt with had threatened to postpone his return for another week at least, but he and Burton managed to get it resolved earlier.

It was Christmas Eve now, and he wanted to get home to Juliette. He had so little time left to be with her and to make memories that might draw her back to him or cause her to want to stay. In reality, he wasn't sure of her heart anymore. He had disappointed her time and again. What did he expect?

An hour later he stopped his Jeep in front of the Hollander farmhouse. Night was beginning to fall in the valley, and the lights in the farmhouse window twinkled in the gathering darkness. Juliette said dinner would be at six, and he'd arrived just in time.

A man Walker didn't know answered the door. Of medium height and build, he had dark hair with a slightly receding hairline, a strong physique for his years, and intelligent eyes behind wire-rimmed glasses. The two stood looking at each other for a moment before the man said, "You must be Walker Logan. I'm Juliette's father, Wyatt Hollander. Come in." He held open the door.

"Thank you," Walker said, coming inside and draping his winter coat over the hall rack. "I'm pleased to meet you." He shook the man's hand, noting he had a firm grip.

"We wondered if you would make it. Juliette said you had to fly out to Colorado for an emergency. I hope all is well now."

"Yes, sir, it is," he replied, glad the man hadn't probed for more.

In the big living room, Grandpa Dalton stood to greet him, and then Gramma bustled into the room to hug him. "We're sure pleased to see you, boy. I was just telling Wyatt it looked like you wouldn't get here for our dinner."

"I'm sorry I didn't call to say I'd been delayed. It's been a hectic week. I hope I'm still welcome." Looking toward the doorway to the kitchen, he saw Juliette leaning there, her eyes wide, blinking back tears.

"Of course you're welcome." Gramma patted his cheek with fondness. "Juliette and I are finishing up dinner now, and George, Laura, and the kids are due any minute. We ought to be ready to eat right at six."

Juliette arranged her face into a welcoming smile and walked toward him then. "It's good to see you back safe. I hope you met my father."

"I did," he said, wishing with all his heart he could grab and hug her and erase that plastic smile.

"We noted the weather was bad out west," Juliette's father said.

"Yes, an ice storm delayed the earlier flight I hoped to take. I worried for a time I'd spend Christmas Eve in the airport."

Gramma straightened her apron. "Well, sit yourself down with the men while Juliette and I finish dinner."

She turned back toward the kitchen and Juliette followed.

As Walker settled into a chair, Grandpa said, "The kids, Robert and Kirsten, have been wishing for a white Christmas but I don't think we'll be getting one this year. I told them we'd had enough snow already since Thanksgiving to suit me. Snow makes for a lot of extra work on the farm."

They talked about random things then, Walker mostly listening in, his attention not really on their subjects. He was tired, too. He sat back in the old living room chair, glad to relax after the stress of the week. With pleasure, he glanced around the comfortable room. The house was festively decorated for Christmas. A thick cedar tree stood in the corner of the living room, loaded with heirloom ornaments, old-fashioned string lights, tinsel, and handcrafted quilted hearts. Gramma's collection of Christmas angels covered the mantel and nestled among evergreen clusters around the room. He'd passed a nativity scene on an entry table in the hallway and evergreen garlands draped the stairway. The smells of pine, Christmas candles, cinnamon, spices, and the heavenly odors of holiday baking filled the air.

"You seem tired, boy," Grandpa said, pausing in his conversation with Wyatt.

"Yes, sir. I'm sorry if I let my attention drift. It's been a difficult week, but it's a pleasure to be here. I'm enjoying the Christmas decorations and the tree. Everything looks nice."

"The women did all that. They like to make everything festive for the holidays." He paused. "You might want to keep it in mind that women don't take to it much when a man don't call them when he's away. You may find Juliette a mite testy until you straighten that out. She may be acting nice and cordial-like on the surface but she's put out. You can see it in her eyes if you look close."

"Yes, sir. I thought of calling again to speak with her after talking with you, but a lot was happening. It seemed the kind of thing to tell in person rather than over the phone."

"I hear you," Grandpa said. "But remember womenfolk don't see things like men do sometimes. You need to keep that in mind more often as you go along in this life."

Walker heard Wyatt chuckle. "Dad has always been direct in his speaking. But Juliette has been worried. She hasn't spoken of it to us, but we could all tell. It's obvious she's fond of you and I know from talks on the phone with her you've been seeing each other."

Walker rubbed his neck. "I'll work on trying to make amends with her a little later. There's a lot to explain."

George, Laura, and their teenagers, Robert and Kirsten, came in the door then carrying more dishes for Christmas Eve dinner and a stack of presents to put under the tree. The air filled with jovial greetings and anticipation of the dinner to come, changing the course of the conversation.

A short time later everyone settled around the large table in the Hollander dining room. With the leaf added, the table could seat ten—twelve in a squeeze. As at other Hollander occasions, Grandpa sat at the head of the table, Gramma at the foot, with George and his family on the right side of the table tonight, and Wyatt, Juliette, and Walker on the left. The table and sideboard groaned with food, and a big clove-studded ham sat in the middle of the table with sprigs of greenery and bits of colorful fruit around it.

After grace, everyone filled plates and passed dishes around the table, laughing and talking, all glad to be together. Walker, who had missed lunch, dug in to enjoy the bounty of good food. Out of the corner of his eye he watched Juliette, who as Grandpa had predicted, feigned a cordiality and cheerfulness that lacked her usual ease and joy. He hated to realize he'd caused that, dulled her enjoyment with her family.

"This sure is good," George said after a time, when everyone was almost stuffed from second helpings. "It's a less happy Christmas for the Claibornes, though. Gramma, it was good of you to take that basket of baked goods and sweets to Onalee yesterday. I stopped by today to take more things from us. Onalee said to tell you again how much she appreciated your visits and kindness. She and Ronnie's wife, Dottie, haven't felt much like baking this year."

"How is Onalee doing?" Juliette asked.

"Fair considering," George answered. "She has been going to the car dealership and working with Hershel Jenkins, the manager that her husband, R. D., trained and hired years ago. Hershel has been as shocked about this trouble as Onalee and the family. He's known Dade since he was only a kid."

"She gonna keep that dealership?" Grandpa asked.

"She's not sure," George answered. "Dade is looking at a long time in prison for all he got involved in."

"I remember him as a personable kid," Juliette's father said. "How did this mess get started for him?"

George shrugged. "Onalee told me Dade has always been overly hungry for things, wantin' to be rich, feeling money made a man important. She said she'd never been able to make him see character counted the most. It always worried her. She said as long as Dade's father, R. D., was alive, he kept Dade in check, but when he passed, temptations overtook Dade. He got into deeper and deeper debt for things he craved beyond his means—fancy cars, a big house, boat, expensive clothes, electronics, and more. He borrowed against the dealership and ran up debts, and when things got bad, the boys working on his house suggested a little thieving and fencing of goods would start to turn things around. They'd dabbled profitably in theft before. It started little by little after that, like all crime does, and grew easier as the money came."

Gramma shook her finger at her grandchildren over his words. "You mind those words. It only takes a little wrongdoing, and then justifying it to yourself, to start you down a wrong road with a bad end."

Kirsten and Robert rolled their eyes at one another.

George ignored her. "Onalee, Ronnie, and the family are in for a hard time until the trial and all the publicity settles down. People in the valley are being kind and supportive, for the most part, and the Claibornes don't intend to leave the valley. They'll see it through."

Walker saw Juliette shoot him a significant look.

Clearing his throat, Walker caught everyone's attention. "I understand the problems they're facing to some degree. You all know I had problems with a criminal in Colorado, threatening me and my family, and then others after I left. Even committing murder. I went to Colorado this week because the man made another attempt on a member of the Copeland family. He broke into one of the son's homes, threatened him with a gun, wanting money. They got into an altercation, and the man was shot in the struggle. After I got to Colorado, he died in the hospital."

"It's always sad when a man loses his life, even when doing wrong," Wyatt said, shaking his head.

"Does that settle the worries and problems you've been dealing with for so long?" Grandpa asked.

"Yes, it does. Although it still seems hard for me to believe."

"Well, there's one fine blessing we can all be grateful for this Christmas Eve." Gramma smiled at him. "We'll say some extra thanks to the good Lord while we have our dessert." She turned to Juliette. "Isn't that good news?"

Juliette put a fist to her mouth, burst into tears, and then pushed back her chair and ran out of the room.

"You'd better go after her, boy," Grandpa said. "She'll head to the red barn near the house and maybe even climb up in the loft. It's always been her place to go when she's tore up about something."

Walker stood. "I'll do that. Thank you."

Gramma got up, too. "I'll get her coat for you. She's run out the back door without it. You take it with you. It's cold out."

Walker headed to the front door, snagging his own coat from the hall rack, and taking Juliette's from Gramma.

"Talk sweet to her and be patient," she advised. "Juliette's been real upset this week about you being gone, afeared she wouldn't even get to see you again before she had to leave. Her heart's real engaged, boy, no matter how cool she's trying to act."

"Thank you. I hope you're right." Walker leaned over to plant a kiss on Gramma's cheek.

He cut down the driveway from the house, climbed over the fence, and headed into the big red barn. It was warmer inside the barn than he'd expected, shut away from the chill of the December breeze.

He saw footprints on the dusty rails of the ladder leading up to the loft and started climbing up. Getting to the top of the ladder, he saw Juliette huddled amid a pile of hay bales on a battered quilt in the corner of the loft.

She glanced up. "I don't want to talk to you right now."

"Guess we have a problem then," he said, pulling himself up from the ladder and walking across the loft. "Because I want to talk to you."

She turned her head away when he sat down on the quilt beside her.

"Did you make this quilt?" he asked, fingering the old quilt with its array of colorful patches.

She turned to glare at him. "I'm hardly in the mood to talk about quilts. And I'm too mad at you to even sit this close to you right now." She snapped out the words as she moved away from him.

"I'm not mad at you." He said the words softly, moving closer to her to drape her coat around her shoulders. "All I've wanted to do since I came in the door tonight is to be alone with you." He pulled her into his arms and began to thoroughly kiss her, despite her struggling against it.

She fought him at first and then yielded, weaving her hands into his hair, thrilling him with soft little moans. "I hate you for going off like you did and then not even calling me all week. Didn't you know I'd be worried?" Tears welled in her eyes and spilled over. "And then you dumped all that information on me at the table with my family sitting around us. That was wretched of you. Surely you realized it would tear me up to hear that."

He curled her against him and wiped off her tears. "I thought you'd be glad to hear it."

"Maybe from you, but not that way in front of the family after I was already so wound up from simply seeing you again."

"I like that you were wound up. You keep me wound up all the time. You drive me crazy wanting to be close to you, always thinking about you." He let kisses travel down her neck.

She pushed at him. "Stop trying to sweet talk your way out of this and tell me everything that happened."

"Okay." He leaned back against the hay bale, pulling her up against him. "Right after I closed the store on Sunday, I got a call from Burton. He said I needed to fly out to Greeley, that the man threatening me all this time had been apprehended. Burton said he'd fly in, too, and that the police would need to talk to us. He advised me they would possibly ask me to help identify the man as the same one who followed me numerous times, tried to run me off the road, and broke into my home once. He also said they would question me to see if they could confirm links between the attacks on our family and the Copeland family."

Walker took a deep breath. "Burton had already called to schedule me an immediate flight to Colorado and said Stewart planned to meet me if I could make it. I called Quillen to come stay with Marsh, asked Eldon to cover the store, threw my clothes in a duffel, and headed to the airport."

"Do they think it was the same man?"

"Yes."

"And he's dead now?"

Walker sighed. "He died in the hospital. He'd broken into Raymond Copeland's house, a son of the man, Bill Copeland, that he killed earlier. He wore a ski mask and threatened to kill Raymond or his family if he didn't give him money, a lot of money. In my case before, a neighbor came to the door, scaring the man off, but this time there were no interruptions. Raymond distracted him with talk, got to a gun, and shot him in a struggle between them. Raymond got shot in the arm, too, but he's recovering. The intruder wasn't so lucky. He died the next day. His name was Yancy Hughes."

She reached for his hand. "Did the police learn *why* he focused on your family and the Copelands with all his threats?"

"Yes, they did," he said, still finding it hard to believe this nightmare over. "Yancy was a veteran and mentally unstable. It's probable that he was unstable before he went into the military as well. At first the police thought the link between our families was the military, but that wasn't it. It was something else."

"What?" Juliette asked as he hesitated.

"Yancy's father, Willard Hughes, was an alcoholic and found it hard to keep a job," he continued. "Willard worked for my father at the store for a time. Dad had to fire him, and then Willard got a job with Raymond's father, Bill Copeland, at his construction business. Bill was also forced to fire him because of his continuing alcohol abuse and behavioral problems. Willard couldn't get another job then around the area with his reputation for alcohol abuse and anger issues, and the Hughes family consequently lost their farm outside Greeley. It had been in their family for several generations.

Yancy's father blamed my dad and Bill Copeland for the farm's loss and Yancy's father Willard Hughes later committed suicide right before the family had to move off the property." He shifted to get more comfortable before continuing. "Life went bad for the Hughes family after that. Yancy grew up angry and bitter, got into alcohol and trouble. Mental instability seemed to run in the family. Yancy's mother died while he served in the military and Yancy returned home to her shack of a place outside of town to live afterward. With all his mental problems and injuries from the war, he got on disability and became involved with one of the local veterans' associations. Through that group he learned about the lottery money I won. It whipped up all his old bitterness about his family's farm being lost. His mind got focused then on getting his share back from me that he felt due. He believed the Copeland family and our family caused all his family's problems, were responsible for his family's loss of the farm, and for his father's suicide. He decided I should pay for their suffering."

"How did you learn all this?"

"The police gained this story primarily through his sister, who lives in Wisconsin somewhere. She saw the family's problems more realistically, but she said Yancy always looked for someone else to blame their problems—and his own problems—on. She often tried to help him but she never could. A few guys through the veterans' association that knew Yancy confirmed more. They said he babbled a lot, especially when drunk. After I left town and he couldn't track me down, he focused on the Copeland family, since his dad worked for Bill Copeland after mine. Yancy basically followed the same pattern of threats and demands with both families."

"That's a sad story."

"It is." Walker leaned his head back and closed his eyes. "I'm sorry I didn't call to talk to you about it this week, but there was so much to tell, so much going on, and so many people to talk to. Burton and I had a lot of things to discuss, as well." He opened his eyes to look at her then. "This does change things for me."

She studied his face, putting a hand to his cheek. "You'll never have to run again. The threat is really gone for you."

He nodded. "I'm still getting used to the idea that I don't need to look over my shoulder all the time anymore. It seems unreal."

She smiled at him. "It's a nice Christmas gift for you."

"I suppose it is." He traced his hand down her cheek, watching her face framed in a drift of moonlight filtering through the window in the old loft. "I have a Christmas gift for you."

She wrinkled her nose at him. "I bought one for you, too. We'll swap them when we get back to the house. I remember you're flying to your sister's early in the morning on Christmas day."

"I'd like to give you mine now." He dug in the deep pocket of his jacket to pull out a small box tied up in a square of quilting fabric with a piece of twine for a ribbon.

She giggled. "Very creative wrapping paper."

"Marshall's General Store sells quilting fabric. It looked like some of the fabrics you use in your quilts."

She untied the twine and then opened the box. Inside was another box, a smaller velvet one. He watched her eyes widen as she opened it.

"Oh, Walker." She put a hand to her heart again. Even in the glow of the moonlight, the diamond on the ring twinkled.

He shifted to his knees in the hay. "Will you marry me, Juliette Hollander? I can finally ask you now like I've wanted to for so long."

She put a hand to her heart, the tears gathering in her eyes again.

"You asked me once if I would go back to my old life if I could," he said, wiping away one of her tears. "I've thought about that question since, and the answer is no. If I hadn't passed through what I did, I wouldn't have come here and I wouldn't have met you. My life is richer and better because of you, Juliette. I love you and want to spend all my days with you. I want to grow old with you, share every day with you. I love you with all my heart. I hope you still love me after all that's happened."

"I do, Walker, and I want the same sweet things. It hurt my heart so much to think of leaving you."

He pulled her close to kiss her again, feeling happier and lighter than he had in years. "I suppose I should have waited for a more romantic time and location to propose." He looked around the loft with a smile.

"No, it's a perfect place for you to propose. This has been my special spot to dream of love and the future since I was a little girl." She kissed him again and then reached to retrieve the ring box she'd dropped on the quilt. "Let me try my ring on," she said, taking it out and slipping it on her finger. "Oh, look. It's a perfect fit." She held it out, admiring it, a square solitaire on a simple gold band.

"I asked Amy your ring size once, told her I might like to get you a ring for a special occasion."

"This is definitely a special occasion." A small frown crossed her brow then. "You can change your name back now if you want. Will you?"

"I'd like to if you wouldn't mind."

"So you'll be Owen Walker Marshall again, not Walker Owen Logan."

He nodded.

"Would I need to call you Owen instead of Walker?"

He grinned. "No. I've gotten used to Walker now, and I really still feel like Owen was a guy I knew before."

She gave him a mischievous grin. "Maybe we could name a little boy Logan one day, if we have one. The name would have a great story behind it."

"You're killing me with that kind of talk." He groaned. "When can we plan this wedding?"

She thought about it. "I'd like to get married here in the valley at the Missionary Baptist Church where I grew up, but it's not very large. We could probably only invite close friends and family. Would that be all right with you?"

"Anything is all right with me."

"That's sweet of you." She tapped her mouth, thinking. "The

church doesn't have a place for a reception though."

"We could rent a place in town. Anything you'd like."

She smiled at him. "Fortunately for you, you've chosen a very low-maintenance bride. I think a simple reception after the wedding at your house would be perfect, maybe a buffet dinner for everyone. I'd say Victoria could come up with some lovely ideas for making it perfect."

He laughed. "I'd say she could. It would be fun to have our reception at Stone House, too. The big rooms downstairs open into each other in a nice way. I think Vee could work with that, and I'm sure you'll have some ideas, too."

He kissed her once more, gathering her closer for more intimacy.

After a time, Walker pulled back to look into Juliette's brown eyes, so full of love and so beautiful. "I want you to know that if you'd like to go to North Carolina to teach your quilt classes, you can. I don't want you to think our marriage will restrict you or put demands on you that you aren't comfortable with."

Her eyes widened. "You wouldn't mind if I went to North Carolina to teach classes every now and then? I might need to stay during the week. My courses are usually weeklong ones."

"That would be okay. Your talents may take you traveling to other places in time to speak or give workshops. I'll come with you on occasions when I can. We can take the Sportsmobile."

She sighed wistfully. "I'm envious of all those trips you've taken in the Sportsmobile."

He grinned at her, a new thought hitting his mind. "We can take our honeymoon and travel south in the Sportsmobile, away from the winter cold, if you'd like. Eldon and Quillen can take care of the store. Eldon's wife, Lula, has been hinting that she wouldn't mind working with Eldon some at the store, too. I think we could get away for a few weeks and let you see some of the USA."

She sat up with excitement. "Oh, that would be so much fun. Can we really do that?"

"Sure. As soon as we're old married folks."

"Then let's get married soon," she said, her eyes shining. "We could travel until late March, when my quilting classes start. Maybe later on we could travel to some other places you've visited for vacations."

"We're going to have a great life, Juliette," he said.

She hugged him with enthusiasm, the old familiar sparkle back in her eyes again. "Let's go tell everyone," she said. "Besides, we didn't get any dessert."

They scrambled down from the loft, their future bright and full of promise.

A Reading Group Guide

HAPPY VALLEY

Lin Stepp

About This Guide

The questions on the following pages are included
to enhance your group's reading of
Lin Stepp's *Happy Valley*

DISCUSSION QUESTIONS

1. Walker Logan has been on the road—and on the run—for two years. What reasons does he give his sister, Victoria, for suddenly deciding to look at a house and property? Where is this property and what drew Walker to it? What does Victoria think about the idea, and where does she suggest Walker might settle down instead? Resigned to Walker's choice, what does Victoria offer to do to help with the house? Have you ever been to Happy Valley—a small rural community between Maryville and Townsend—or to Abrams Creek Campground nearby, where Walker is staying?

2. Area realtor Cameron Johnson, with his younger brother, Quillen, comes to show Walker the home and property. What does Cameron think about the real estate Walker is considering? What is the house like, and what is its history? Although the property is very run down, Walker sees past its current condition. What does he envision building on the property along the main road? How do Cameron and Quillen react to the idea of a store in Happy Valley? Have past stores in the valley been successful? When Quillen gets excited about Walker's idea and asks if he can work for him, how does this request begin a friendship for Walker with the Johnson family?

3. Walker encounters a young woman while walking around the mountain property after Cameron and Quillen leave. How do the two meet? What is Juliette doing on the Old Stone House property? Although Juliette never gives her name to Walker at this meeting, what does she tell him about herself and where she is staying? What does Walker think of Juliette? What small event sweetens their meeting in Happy Valley, leaving both with a memory that lingers?

4. After Walker and Juliette's meeting, the story picks up a year later when Juliette comes back to the family farm in Happy Valley again. Why did she come back? What has happened to her grandfather? What do you learn about Juliette's background and early life as the story moves forward? Where does she live and work when not visiting with her grandparents? What does her brother, George, tell her about Old Stone House and the property across the main road from their farm that surprises her? What do most people think about Walker Logan building a general store in Happy Valley?

5. Dade Claiborne stops by to visit at the Hollander farm the morning after Juliette returns. Who is Dade, and what kind of relationship does Juliette have with him? What does Dade do for a living, and where does he live? What do you learn about Dade's family and his character at this meeting? As you later meet Dade's mother, Onalee, and his brother, Ronnie, how do you see that they are different from Dade? Why does Juliette agree to go out with Dade when she doesn't like him much? What problems does Dade cause for Juliette and for Walker as the story progresses?

6. Juliette's grandmother encourages Juliette to walk over to the Old Stone House property to see if she can pick some apples for her again. Curious to see the new store, Juliette agrees. Who does Juliette unexpectedly meet there? What is the store like? Have you seen rural general stores like the one Walker created? What persuasive reasons does Juliette give Walker when she asks him to hire her to work at the Happy Valley Store? Who else has Walker hired to work at the store? What duties does Walker want Juliette to handle, and why does he worry about hiring her? After their meeting at the store, when Juliette goes to get apples for her grandmother, how does Walker's dog, Marsh, instigate a scene much like the one when Juliette and Walker first met?

7. Juliette is a quilter and specializes in a type of quilt called a "crazy quilt." What is a crazy quilt? Have you ever seen a crazy quilt? As the book progresses, what types of items besides quilts do you learn that Juliette makes? How did Juliette's mother and her grandmother influence her skill in quilting? Juliette sells her quilts and art at The Full Moon in Murphy, where she lives, and at a shop at the John C. Campbell Folk School nearby, where she teaches quilting. Have you ever visited Murphy or the folk school in Brasstown? Why has Juliette struggled so much with her identify as a quilter, and why has she often felt somewhat like a "black sheep" in her own family? How is the rest of her family in Happy Valley different from her—her grandparents; brother, George; his wife, Laura; and their children, Robert and Kirsten?

8. Moves and changes can often be difficult. Does Juliette tell Walker it's easy or hard to be a newcomer in a small tightly knit community like Happy Valley? What problems does she tell him she's experienced since coming to the valley when her mother died in Italy? Juliette and George have different mothers, who both died young. George's mother was Patsy Rhea Hollander, a valley girl. Why does Patsy's mother, Hettie Rhea, hold bitterness toward Juliette and her father even after all these years? How has this made life hard for Juliette? As you met Hettie in scenes in the book, what did you think about her? How did Walker, later in the story, help to bring about a partial truce to Juliette's problems with Hettie?

9. Happy Valley is full of rich and interesting people but none quite as unusual as Vernon and Harley Ledford. How does Walker first meet the Ledford brothers? What is different about them, and what did you think about the brothers? Have you ever known any survivalists like the Ledfords? How does Walker relate to and form an unexpected friendship with Vernon and Harley? How

does that friendship grow through the book, and how do the Ledfords help Walker as the book progresses?

10. Friendships greatly enrich our lives. Who are Walker's two best friends in Colorado he still keeps in touch with, and what does each do for a living? In Happy Valley, Walker builds friendships with Quillen, Cameron, and Eldon Johnson. How is Quillen a help to Walker, and how is Walker a help to Quillen in return? Walker also makes friends with Jonas Rasnic, who lives nearby. How did Walker and Jonas meet? What do Jonas and his wife, Kimmie, do? Kimmie later becomes a friend to Juliette, too. How is Kimmie a help to Juliette as the book progresses? Juliette's other close friends are Sharon Bard in Murphy and Amy Boone Butler in Happy Valley. How did Juliette and Amy meet? What problems have Amy and her husband, Keith, faced? Where do they live now, and what do both do? Juliette is also very close to Amy's mother, Lenora. How has Lenora Boone been a help to Juliette, and how does she encourage and wisely counsel her later in the book?

11. Hikes and time out of doors are pleasures both Juliette and Walker enjoy. Early in the book they hike to Abrams Falls in Cades Cove. Have you ever hiked this trail or visited Cades Cove in the Smoky Mountains? What makes Walker nervous as they drive over to the cove? When Juliette quizzes him about this, what does she learn about Walker? How does Walker's reluctance to share about his past with Juliette impact their relationship? What are Walker's reasons for keeping his identity secret? Do you think they are good ones?

12. Juliette doesn't want her family to know about her relationship with Walker, beyond the fact that she works for him. Why? What scene with her brother, George, causes this secrecy to backfire? Why is George upset about Juliette dating Walker? How does

Dade Claiborne react when he learns about Walker and Juliette dating? How do Juliette's grandparents' feelings for Walker change when he goes to talk with them? What other later understandings help Juliette's grandparents to like and trust Walker more as the book progresses? How is Walker a solid help when Juliette's grandfather has a heart attack?

13. Eldon Johnson, who works part-time in the store with Quillen, has been a minister all his life. How does he give Walker good advice about the problems with his relationship with Juliette? How does he use an old oxen yoke, hanging in the store, as a way to encourage Walker to grow closer to God and deepen his faith? Eldon said: "I've always thought each Christian faith holds some special nuggets of wisdom and revelation in their individual beliefs … It's not so much which church you go to but who you are in the Lord. That's what a person needs to be most sure of—that relationship and being wrapped in the love of God and the purpose of God." Do you agree with these thoughts?

14. When do you first learn of the thieves in the valley? Who have the thieves targeted? What answers have the police found as they investigated? Juliette confides in Walker about the hurt and sorrow the thefts have caused for many in the valley. How does Walker begin to respond to some of the problems he learns about? How does Walker's friend and attorney, Barton, help with his philanthropy? Who later tries to get the people in Happy Valley to finger Harley and Vernon for the ongoing thefts? How do they respond to this?

15. Over time Walker finds more and more ways to help the people in Happy Valley through corporate foundations Burton sets up for him, like the Goodman Brothers and the RHC— Rural Help Connection. How does Walker help to renovate the community center? How does this also benefit Keith and Amy

Butler? How does Walker help Juliette's brother, George, get free of debt to Dade? What are some other ways he provides help to people the thieves stole money and property from, and how does Walker later get the idea of playing Santa Claus in the valley?

16. Most people imagine a sudden unexpected windfall of wealth, as Walker experiences, can only be a wonderful blessing. How has wealth impacted Walker's life both positively and negatively? How did he get his unexpected windfall? How did the people in Greeley, Colorado, change toward Walker after he became wealthy? What events caused Walker to change his identity and leave his home, and what did he do with his house and family store in Greeley? Where has Walker traveled over the last two years? How did he find his dog, Marsh, who becomes his traveling companion? What kind of dog is Marsh, and what are some interesting things you remember about him?

17. Juliette likes working in her friend Sharon Bard's craft shop and also loves teaching quilting at the nearby John C. Campbell Folk School. However, from the first of the book, you see that Juliette feels torn between her love for her family in Happy Valley and her life and work in North Carolina. Why is this? Missing her work, how does she begin to find a way to teach quilting while staying in Happy Valley? What part does Lenora Boone play in initiating these classes? How does Lenora encourage Juliette in her art and in her personal life? In what ways does Walker also encourage her art and teaching? Do you agree with Lenora that happiness comes from within? What other wise counsel did she offer?

18. As Christmas grows closer, Juliette decides it will be best to return to Murphy, North Carolina, in January, since Walker simply won't trust his secrets to her. How does meeting Walker's family make Juliette feel even more left out of his life than she

already does? What happens unexpectedly on a winter hike that Juliette and Walker take? What does this show about the risk of hiking in the mountains in inclement weather? How do Juliette and Walker draw on their faith in this situation? The danger on this hike escalates Walker's feelings for Juliette and causes him to break down and share more of his past with her when they return. Who does he tell her he really is, and what does he tell her about why he left Colorado? How does Juliette feel about these revelations? What thoughts does she share with him the next day about his situation and about letting fear rule his life? What is Walker's response?

19. Toward the end of the book, two ongoing situations finally get resolved: the identity of the thieves in Happy Valley and the identity of the man who has caused so much trouble for Walker. Who do you learn is behind the thieving in the valley? Who helps the police to catch the thieves? How had the thieves been stealing from the people in the valley? Are people shocked to learn who is behind the valley's thefts? Not long after this revelation, Juliette learns from Eldon Johnson that Walker has flown to Colorado unexpectedly for an emergency. In the days to come she hears nothing from him, upsetting her. When he returns at Christmas to Juliette's home, what does he reveal to them all? How does Juliette respond when she learns Walker's problems are finally over and resolved and that the man stalking and threatening him is dead? Where does Walker find Juliette when he goes after her? What does he give her, and how does the book end?

About the Author

Lin Stepp

Dr. Lin Stepp is a *New York Times*, *USA Today*, and *Publishers Weekly* Best-Selling international author. A native Tenessean, she has also worked as a businesswoman and educator. A previous faculty member at Tusculum College, Stepp taught research and a variety of psychology and counseling courses for almost twenty years. Her business background includes over twenty-five years in marketing, sales, production art, and regional publishing.

CKatie Riley

Stepp writes engaging, heart-warming contemporary Southern fiction with a strong sense of place and has sixteen published novels set in different locations around the Smoky Mountains and the South Carolina coast. Her coastal novels in the Edisto Trilogy are *Return to Edisto* (2020) and *Claire at Edisto* (2019). The latest Tennessee and North Carolina mountain novels are *Happy Valley* (2020), *The Interlude* (2019), *Lost Inheritance* (2018) and *Daddy's Girl* (2017), with previous novels including *Welcome Back* (2016), *Saving Laurel Springs* (2015), *Makin' Miracles* (2015), *Down by the River* (2014) and a novella *A Smoky Mountain Gift* in the Christmas anthology *When The Snow Falls* (2014) published by Kensington of New York. Other earlier titles include: *Second Hand Rose* (2013), *Delia's Place* (2012), *For Six Good Reasons* (2011), *Tell Me About Orchard Hollow* (2010), and *The Foster Girls* (2009). In addition Stepp and her husband J.L. Stepp have co-authored a Smoky Mountains hiking guidebook titled *The Afternoon Hiker* (2014) and a Tennessee state parks guidebook *Discovering Tennessee State Parks* (2018).

For more about Stepp's work and to keep up with her monthly blog, newsletter, and ongoing appearances and signing events, see: *www.linstepp.com*.